Synod

A Novel

Dan C. Gunderman

3/10/18

Synod

A Novel

Dan C. Gunderman

Dan C. Gulem

ZIMBELL HOUSE
PUBLISHING
UNION LAKE, MICHIGAN

For permission requests, write to the publisher at the address below:
"Attention: Permissions Coordinator"
Zimbell House Publishing, LLC
PO Box 1172
Union Lake, Michigan 48387
mail to: info@zimbellhousepublishing.com

© 2018 Dan C. Gunderman

Published in the United States by Zimbell House Publishing
http://www.ZimbellHousePublishing.com
All Rights Reserved

Print ISBN: 978-1-947210-04-2
Kindle ISBN: 978-1-947210-05-9
Digital ISBN: 978-1-947210-06-6
Library of Congress Control Number: 2017960709

First Edition: January 2018

10 9 8 7 6 5 4 3 2 1

ZIMBELL HOUSE PUBLISHING
UNION LAKE

Acknowledgments

This book is dedicated to the brave souls that journeyed along the Underground Railroad for decades as the nation grappled with its own identity.

I'd like to recognize my grandma, Eileen, for all of her encouragement over the years, and my girlfriend, Rachel, for her kindness, patience and business acumen. I would also like to thank my MFA professors who helped breathe life into this novel from the outset. This includes Michael White and Da Chen.

A special thanks to my editor at Zimbell House, Tim Mies, for providing sound editorial advice and numerous suggestions.

Table of Contents

"Do the obligations of justice change with the color of the skin?"
                    –Senator Theodore Frelinghuysen, 1830

Foreword

This is a work of fiction. The village of Synod—which comes into its own during the Second Great Awakening—is loosely based on a nearly self-sustainable iron operation in northern New Jersey, circa the 1700s and 1800s. While the limits of the village were stretched, exaggerated, and utterly re-imagined, it provided visual inspiration for a novel. In fact, the remote setting is so alive and vibrant that I couldn't help but also make it a stop on the Underground Railroad. This is not a historical truth.

There are characters throughout who actually lived during this turbulent century, including the village's Founders: Lyman Beecher, Richard Allen, and Peter Cartwright. Their "synod" in the mountains is not a historical truth. What's more, Governor Peter Dumont Vroom and Catharine Beecher were real figures as well, though their arcs have been altered for storytelling purposes. Senator Theodore Frelinghuysen was entirely real as well, and was known to have opposed Andrew Jackson's Indian Removal and slavery. His other abilities, as depicted throughout the novel, are of course a part of the fiction.

What this novel aims to encapsulate is the *zeitgeist* of the early nineteenth century—a time of renewed spiritual revivalism and a rising awareness of the barbarity of slavery.

Chapter One

Minus Ten

Goldfinch crept through the tall but moribund brush with Solomon in tow. The latter was not used to the hunt or the rush it provided—the way the body clenched for that fleeting moment when the bullet fled the muzzle.

Solomon's heels, bound tightly by stiff, mid-calf leather lace-up boots, crunched into the dried leaves that had already fallen. This layer of shaken foliage padded the hard autumn ground, but it could give a man away with one careless swipe of his foot.

Goldfinch turned back to his companion, pressing his forefinger to his lips. He could see Solomon respond, moving lightly and more mindfully through the dense forest. Solomon was a stocky man with a wide, defined face, dark skin, and a fullness in his eyes. He had broad shoulders that seemed to take up two of Goldfinch. His clothes were weathered—but Goldfinch imagined his dress was only improved upon since his days plucking cotton on an Alabama plantation. As Solomon had said, it was "the heat in 'em 'Bama fields got to yer head."

Goldfinch's wide, black planter's hat opposed the vertical pattern of much of the underbrush they slunk through. The hollowed stems of crabgrass tickled the dangling fabric of his frock coat. Goldfinch was of average height, bordering middle age, with a slender frame that was neatly tucked away. He boasted placid features—a sort of buttoned-up persona that accentuated his dark, draping attire. Whiskers seemed to draw out or elongate his pointed features, leaving him with a permanent look of curiosity.

Leaves still clung to most of the branches. It was late October, and thus, just past peak foliage time in this dense grove within the Ramapough Mountain range.

"I think I dun see 'im, Mista Goldfinch," Solomon whispered as they continued to press into a meadow whose untamed grasses were patted down by animals and rainfall.

"*Shh!*" Goldfinch urged, placing his forefinger back to his lips.

"I jus' don' understand what we's doin' all the way out here. You coulda found you one much closer to th' gate."

As he spoke, Goldfinch imagined that this was the first time Solomon was on *this* side of the hunt. An escapee, he came to Goldfinch's village behind Reverend Richard Allen in April of 1825. Before that, he navigated the system up to "'delphia," as he had coined it. He'd been in the Reverend's service ever since. Now, that was no conventional sort of 'service'—tidying up, sweeping up Allen's AME church. He was an 'active participant.' Reverend Allen had told Goldfinch once, some years back, that Solomon may have been the best asset he'd ever had in running slaves up north.

"Hush up, Solomon," Goldfinch whispered. "And don't you go wearing your finest attire when we must kill." He was now prostrated, his Pennsylvania Long Rifle strapped to his back, his hat pressing against wiry, yellowed grass. Solomon stared blankly back at him.

"Why don't you press ahead?" Goldfinch urged. "Right through here." Goldfinch extended his arm outward and separated a clump of grass, opening up their cover to the expansive sunlight that had been permeating the day, above them and above the larger canopy.

Goldfinch saw the sun rays overwhelm Solomon's eyes, as though they were only accustomed to the cloak of darkness and blackened wagons pounding rough terrain in secrecy. On this day, Solomon was used to their earthen crawl, his skin contrasting with the lightness of the grass and the intense sunshine that seemed to refract after meeting the sweat on his forehead.

Goldfinch stretched back to tap Solomon's shoulder. With the contact, Solomon snapped out of the apparent gaze he held. Goldfinch grabbed hold of his Long Rifle and used the barrel to press the grasses aside.

Solomon continued his belly crawl through the thick, straw-like weeds. Goldfinch felt autumn's colors penetrating, ensconcing themselves further into the landscape. The colors—especially the apples and pumpkins up in Harriet's orchard—injected life into the mountains and then glistened in ruby red and marmalade-like orange on their plates as they consumed the fruits of their labor. When Solomon made it about fifteen feet ahead, he froze and looked back toward Goldfinch.

Goldfinch watched Solomon closely as he lay exposed in this meadow. The October chill was upon them, but still, Solomon continued to visibly sweat, the perspiration staining even the sliver of white shirt visible above the collar of his frock coat.

Solomon relayed in a loud, raspy whisper, but paused to clear his throat. At last, he was able to say, "Mista Goldfinch, think I see 'im."

Goldfinch responded by moving swiftly through the grasses, ruffling a particularly long section of feathered reed grass. The motion was familiar to him, though it had been some time since he'd been forced to put it into practice.

He approached Solomon in a low crouch. By the time he pressed his boots onto the same small plain of matted foxtail and barnyard grass, he already had his weapon out. He took aim but refrained from tightening his finger on the trigger. The beast was ahead of them, fifty paces or so off. It twitched with the rattling of the branches, hyper-aware of its surroundings, carefully attuned to the stampeding sounds of an intruder.

Solomon scrunched his face, wanting to release an impassioned yell. Clenching his fingers, he said, "Mista Goldfinch. That m' kill." He sought to abandon this forced whisper he could only coax out of himself.

A smile formed at the corners of Goldfinch's chapped lips. He pointed to the flintlock pan just above the trigger. "There's no powder on the pan," he whispered.

Solomon studied Goldfinch extensively. "Didn' have to use nothin' like dis with the Rev'rend. Just a sharp blade's all. Never once drew me that knife, neither."

Goldfinch exhaled in sync with the whisper of a passing wind, closed his eyes, and said, "Dammit, man, quiet." He used his weapon to point ahead. He turned to look across the meadow, near a tree-line where the land began to bulge and press upward. "I see him."

Solomon continued to stare at Goldfinch. Then he swallowed and grabbed at the powder horn hooked by a thread to his belt. He shook his head and clutched the barrel, peeling an inch or two of the ramrod out from its slot. Then he returned it, bit his lip, sighed, and looked at Goldfinch.

"Loaded already," Goldfinch whispered, his face reddening from frustration. "Pull the trigger."

Solomon nervously shook his head, as if the specifics of Goldfinch's earlier lesson on the rifle specs were too hard to absorb, something beyond his lowly station; something once considered a white burden. "Gimme a knife," he said, preparing to take aim. "All that whittlin' n' things I done on the plantation—"

Goldfinch was ready to explode with rage, a vein in his forehead showing, pulsating. Solomon must have recognized the indignation and hushed up. Although enraged, Goldfinch said in the faintest, but the sternest manner, "Quit your blathering, or you will *not* eat for a week. Beast'll croak from infirmity at this point."

Solomon awkwardly reached into a pack strapped to his side and retrieved a small, pointed wooden object. It was splintery and elemental—no glossy finish or sanded edges. It was a trinket. He rubbed the center of the object with his thumb. Then Solomon looked back up to Goldfinch, meeting his stare. He whispered, "It's th' North Star, ya see? Help all us some way or 'nother. Made it in my earlier days." Goldfinch nodded but turned toward their target, tilting the brim of his hat to expand his field of vision.

The runaway-turned-confidant of Goldfinch exhaled heavily and inspected his gun one last time. There was a sort of equilibrium he appeared to want to preserve. But nonetheless, his balance was steady, and he lifted the gun to his eye level, using the front sight to place his target evenly before him.

"The heart," Goldfinch whispered. "Fire." He watched Solomon's eyes.

"'Ere it goes," Solomon uttered. He prepared to squeeze the trigger but closed his eyes for a split second. He fired just as they reopened, and the gun kicked back and startled him.

Goldfinch turned from his friend's careful hunting stance and looked at the target. The animal stood still for a moment, then he took flight. "Can't miss a buck like that. Not this time of year," he said to Solomon.

Although the gunshot had spooked the buck, at least a ten-pointer in Goldfinch's opinion, the two men spotted a doe no farther than sixty yards away. She too was left motionless from the shot, attuned to nature's dynamism, but her flat tail twitched ever so slightly out behind an elm tree. Goldfinch recognized the fluttering and directed his eyes and his weapon to her locale. It took Solomon a moment to catch on, but as Goldfinch started creeping through the flora, so did the ex-slave.

From one trunk to another they moved, stealthily tapping their toes against the layer of wrinkled noisemakers. Solomon made the most noise, but Goldfinch monitored the animal upon each of his steps, each fluid motion of his limbs. The doe remained, presumably feasting on a cache of acorns that had fallen from a nearby oak.

He was soon within shooting distance. Solomon trailed behind, but he couldn't wait for the man each step of the way. The doe poked its head out from the side of the elm's trunk. Her eyes were fixed on Goldfinch's location, but she seemed to look even farther, miles farther, right through him.

He refused to hesitate any longer. In one motion, he clutched the rifle and brought it to his eye level. He placed the deer just above his front sight and squeezed the trigger. The ensuing blast sent a thick, opaque cloud of smoke into the air just off to his right, which fused with the chilling expanse.

Goldfinch turned back to Solomon, who was breathing heavily from the movement and the suppression of fatigue. His eyes widened with excitement. At last, Goldfinch turned toward his target. She had fallen—the shot struck her directly in the heart. *There was no suffering,* Goldfinch told himself.

This was the first time Goldfinch led Solomon on a guided hunt, though the freeman *had* gripped the rifles in Goldfinch's presence before. Still, the Leader did not have the audacity to test his luck with the chattering ex-slave by shouldering him out past the protective fence, toward the shelterbelt, and through the groves, until today. But witnessing this evolution had an emotional payoff, too, for the slave-at-large had begun to shed the chains that bound him. He had stepped closer toward a sort of spatial acuity.

The elation was short-lived. Goldfinch's mind scudded off, tugging him back even further than 1812, with its cacophony of death and despair. It had been fourteen years since the war ended, but the memories had become a bastion in his mind. Now though, they slipped past him and tugged at his shirtsleeves until finally, he landed in his childhood. It was the first hunt he could remember.

It was a cold morning on a homestead in the Hudson Valley. His father, a stern but affable veteran of the fight for independence, had brandished his weapon with gusto. He hauled another musket over his shoulder and scurried through the waist-high, bristly flora. A nine-year-old Goldfinch, then "Samuel," scampered close behind.

When finally they spotted a robust, young buck, Goldfinch's father pressed the side of his calloused hand across his son's chest, effectively barricading him, preventing any further motion. "Shh," he said, *"we've found one, Samuel." Goldfinch remembered looking skyward, toward the thorny facial hair of his father's chin. The burly man, with pointed leather boots, a stiff frock coat, and a well-starched white collar, smirked and looked down at him as he primed the weapon. "Watch closely, son. And don't you move too fast now. The animal, you see, contributes to the calm of this wood. You thin the herd for no good reason, and you alter His plan. Keep it in mind." Parts of the memory were foggy, but he could recall his father handing him the weapon, the gunshot, the ensuing plume of smoke, and the wobbly-legged animal bending and contorting toward the earth. But the sharpest, most memorable part was his father shaking his head slightly, almost grimacing. "You'll have to finish him off, son. Can't prolong something like that." He handed his son a blade. "Right 'cross the throat, and quick." Then he could remember the droplets of blood landing on his cheek, for he'd stepped too close to the bloody deed. The warm blood seeped down his cheek, leaving a trail down his face and into his subconscious.*

As he came to, he looked for his protégé, a man whose spirit he had bolstered over the past few years at the behest of Reverend Richard Allen. Solomon stood, staring back, inquiring, just a few feet away. But he shrugged his shoulders and turned from Goldfinch, moving rhythmically—in celebration of the kill. He was triumphant, though he hadn't done a thing. He seemed boastful, though he'd missed the buck horribly. It made no matter, for they would settle for the feeble doe. Meat was meat. Solomon shut his eyes and pranced up the slight incline toward the doe. He was jubilant, as though he had already eaten the warm, hearty meal.

"Looks like we gawn have er-selves some suppa to*night*," Solomon exclaimed. "We gawn tell folks it was me killed the an'mal?"

"I suppose Harriet will take one look at you and know it wasn't you, Solomon," Goldfinch responded, smiling and rising to a full-bodied, upright stance. Solomon followed his lead, and the two approached the doe, plodding through the slightly pitched meadow with long strides.

They hovered over the animal, a mature doe, and took a moment to inspect it. There *was* some blood that stained the amber-colored leaves in its vicinity, but altogether, the shot was clean. Goldfinch turned toward his partner, "Now for the third act," he said, smirking. Solomon looked unprepared but stepped closer.

"You'll field strip her," Goldfinch demanded, pointing to the carcass. He handed Solomon a blade he had tethered to his ankle. It was the same rite of passage he'd done at nine years old.

Goldfinch guided Solomon through the gutting process. He cut along the rear toward the abdomen. He watched Solomon closely as the man carefully applied pressure then cut right up to the sternum. He used hand gestures to illustrate pulling apart the last rib on each side, and Solomon put them to the test. From there, he had to reach up the chest cavity with the knife, toward the heart and lungs, then past them toward the windpipe and other blood vessels. Then from the pelvis, Solomon had to pull out the rear and sex organs, careful not to spill what lingered in the bladder. From there, the rest of the offal could be separated. As it was, the guts steamed as they met the October air. With bloodied hands, Solomon stepped away from the carcass and used his forearm to wipe his strained eyes. Goldfinch stepped in, flipped the deer over, spread its legs, and let the blood spill from the body.

Moments later, Goldfinch turned to a transfixed Solomon, who had absentmindedly nodded and repeated *"Mm-hmm,"* and said, "She's ready to haul." As he said this, he reached to the ground to collect the offal in a sack made of hide. These remnants would be used in various ways—for consumption, dyes, and medicinal purposes.

"Now, you grab a hold. Right at the base of her skull. You sling that animal over your shoulder. She's lighter now. Your left hand grasps at her belly beneath her front legs. The other stays firm up top."

Solomon made a few preparatory hand gestures. Then he obliged, peeling the animal off the ground from the spot it had fallen as the shot echoed through the forest. Goldfinch watched as his friend tossed her over his shoulder, almost afraid of streaking parts of his frock coat and undershirt with blood.

Goldfinch leaned backward, stretching. As he did so, the cravat fixed stiffly at the base of his neck loosened only slightly. Coming back to his natural stance, he fixed the cravat and his hat and wiped the dirt from his black trousers. He did the same to his draping black frock coat, and then his palms, blowing the dirt and clusters of leaves from his hands.

Solomon let out a sigh as he fought against the weight of the animal. He steadied himself and began to take the same path back.

"Suppose it's on back to Synod now," Goldfinch said, keeping pace just behind the persistent Solomon. Goldfinch, now considering Solomon a hunter, as his own father had done with him, took the slow return back to the village as an opportunity to talk about the thrill of the chase. He'd exaggerate their capabilities and reimagine the forests outside Synod as a paradise laden with sinewy young bucks.

"You see, Solomon, that there rifle, it's a peacemaker."

Solomon nodded, though even that seemed strenuous.

"A rifle we used back in 1812. It's had its time on the lines. A beauty, though," Goldfinch added.

"You say so," Solomon said, the air storming from his lungs.

"You know lead's the preferable bullet. Sure, it'll cut through a man. I've *seen* it."

"Bet you done seen a lot a that," Solomon said, lowering the animal back onto the ground to catch his breath. Goldfinch did not let up with his haranguing.

"But here, we don't have the luxury of lead. No imports, none of that. You see, what we do have is ore. It's wedged deep in these mountains." Goldfinch pointed upward, toward the tall peak of the mountain that lurked over Long Pond in the distance. "So, we make do with iron bullets. Can forge 'em right on the fire. You know about the forge Elizabeth and William labor at. We have them, we have fire, we keep bringing in small loads of ore—well, we'll melt it right into iron. And that's the material we'll have to jam down the barrels to protect this place."

Solomon kneaded his back with his fist and moved side to side. He then brushed the sweat off his forehead with one fluid swipe. Goldfinch carried Solomon's weapon and his knapsack, but still, Solomon looked to be carrying extra weight, a lifetime of it.

"Now, once you have you some iron, well, the Long Rifle, she can adapt," Goldfinch continued. "It takes anything from forty to forty-eight caliber. You plugged a forty cal in there earlier, remember?"

At this point, Solomon failed to respond. But that did not stop Goldfinch. "You'll need to know these sorts of details. You go out on these Jersey roads by your lonesome."

"Mista Goldfinch, I'm tryna take in all these diff'rent numbas you been tossin' my way. I am. But, I got to make sure this animal gets back, feeds us."

"But there'll come a time when those numbers will save your life, Solomon." He took on a more serious visage and continued. "You get in a scuffle, you use that barrel in anything hand-to-hand. It has a far reach, you see? Heavy, but it'll do."

"An' carryin' this here animal a real *scuffle* now," Solomon said, lifting the deer back around his shoulders.

By the time Goldfinch looked ahead, studying their path, he realized they were approaching the village's front gate.

"Synod's before us, friend," he said. "And we've brought supper."

"Now, anybody ask, I'ma say I done killed it," Solomon added.

"If you must," Goldfinch conceded, looking around the premises. He saw the far-reaching fence in the distance—it wrapped around an oddly formed meadow that dipped toward the middle.

As they got nearer, Goldfinch paused before a full, towering hackberry tree, delayed in its turn to the bare side of the season. Goldfinch looked up at its smooth bark and its long, prickly fingers that dipped down almost to ground level. He smiled, noticing a large wooden relic pinned up on the tree's trunk.

It was no time to study the looming object, though, with Solomon lugging the beast. He'd have to unhinge and grab hold of the cart in the shed beside the paddock. Along the way, someone would ask questions. He would have to quell *her* interrogation.

Once near the entrance, Goldfinch propped his forearm and his body weight against Solomon's wobbly gait. Together, the two approached their home, the safe haven in the woods. Victory, although it was a small dose, came in the form of Solomon's mastery of, or progress with, the rifle. It was a prerequisite for venturing alone. Soon, Goldfinch knew, Solomon would partake in the village's first rendezvous with the runaway system. It was a long time coming. Goldfinch felt

Reverend Allen must have been waiting for them in the city with open arms.

Chapter Two

These Crusades

It had been an hour or so since Goldfinch saw Solomon off into the heart of the village, assuring no wanderer, derelict of his or her chores, asked Solomon about the encounter or about the weapon strapped to his back. The former slave had never once pulled a trigger. Minister Mulvane, though, never saw the difference between a firearm and the blade Solomon seemed so comfortable with—and even flaunted on occasion.

Goldfinch stood encircled by the ever-thinning trees and the brisk ground. Yet the crumbling leaves, which broke into pieces like glass shards under Goldfinch's feet, tended to irk him. For it was hard to retain a degree of stealth. And before his initial sojourn to Reverend Allen's church, he had made a career of reconnaissance.

When the thought of this past life took hold of him and usurped his other, more tranquil thoughts, he felt he'd leap back to wartime in some way or another. He lost his bearings. He closed his eyes and tightened his lids.

He was lost in some nameless, labyrinthine forest pockmarked with loose soil atop fresh graves. An early morning mist swirled and careened through a row of tree trunks moist with dew. He was lost in one of his anonymous journeys of the mind. He walked farther, over a ridge, the sound of his advance echoing in his mind. Now, all he heard was gunfire—the reverberating, ear-piercing blasts that seemed so natural and close to home. But there was no one before him.

He looked down at his hands. Instead of his hunting knife, he found a '95 Springfield Musket. He knew it was not his, but that of a fellow soldier dismembered by a cannonball, a soldier he could not see, but knew was bleeding out back beyond the ridge. Goldfinch had picked up the musket, his eyes focused on the horizon, hoping the British would not penetrate their lines. He nearly tripped on a raised earthwork. A hidden soldier, his face muddied, looked up toward Goldfinch and protested the man's clumsiness. The soldier crouched back down, covering his ears.

Goldfinch's horizon shifted and transformed into a more visceral, penetrable setting with shrieks, bloodletting, and the sound of wounded, febrile men. It was later in the day. He heard someone, something, howl back in the direction he'd just come.

He hoped the musket was loaded and primed. He could not find his target but knew the enemy lingered, recouped, behind the trees. He checked the powder, reaching his hand out toward the pan near the frizzen. While he inspected his gun, he blinked harshly, the resulting effect keeping a streak of bright light before his mind's eye.

He opened his eyes, his temples pounding. There was no musket, no cannon fire. The earthworks and warfare's craters were gone. There was only the rise and fall of the autumnal earth, stretching as far as the eye could see. The bright colors spoke to him, just as the artillery once had.

His hand trembled. He had revisited 1812, his war days. Or some amended version of them. The visions were infrequent now, but he was certainly prone. *Where is this trip to?* He could not say for sure. *The scuffle at Queenston Heights? It had a cool, crisp Ontarian air about it.*

Goldfinch reached down and retrieved a long, jagged knife sheathed at his ankle. He let the blade just hardly graze the skin at his left forefinger—a final cue he knew would ground him in the present, in 1829. He had entered the perilous throes of war. Why couldn't it be an effusive, misty journey through the coppiced timber near *his* village?

Perhaps an hour later, his mind attempted to forsake this thick, gossamer-like web that had clouded his vision. At least now odd shapes of light seeped through. He kept a rocklike grip on the splintery cart he used to carry the remnants of the deer carcass. He had already skinned the animal and filleted the healthy chunks of meat beneath the ribs. He stashed away the innards and held onto the lengthier bones of the legs and rib cage. Now he was rolling out to the sequestered community dump, a spot frequently visited of late. It was no farther than a hundred yards from the entryway.

As he moved back over the unsteady terrain, there was only a muted idleness, a certain indolence. At last, his eyesight—in its entirety—returned to him. The silky web that had clogged his vision dissipated and crawled back to his animalistic subconscious.

Moments later, the entrails disposed of, he found himself at a tight corner of the village property near a gate. He smelled blood, an odor lifting from the stained knife sheathed at his side. He continued on with his splintery cart, hustling through the gate, the wheels leaving behind a mostly visible trail. His boots sunk into a few inches of mud. The gate creaked open, and he found his people, about fifteen of them, hard at work, balancing chores with conversation—and tea breaks, from leaves Reverend Allen insisted Goldfinch stow away for the winter.

Now alert, Goldfinch found his people staring blankly at him. He noticed Adam, the assistant farmer, first. "I assume the harvest reaps itself?" Goldfinch called out to him.

"Ah, don't mind me, Goldfinch. Been pressing the corn into the barrels, been mixing some more of it with the flour and water," Adam responded, fumbling with the sleeves of his coat. He was a young man, in his late twenties, with stark, raven-black hair and a narrow, fragile frame. He wore no hat, but his sepia-brown frock coat was spotless.

"We'll need the corn cakes tonight for venison. We have at least that doe to roast," Goldfinch said. Adam then waved his hand up toward Goldfinch, who tipped his hat and continued onward.

He noticed Solomon studying his movements too. He had emerged from his hut as Goldfinch sauntered through the village. Solomon was probably envisioning himself completing these routine tasks. *He came so close today.* Goldfinch bent over to wipe his dirtied hands on a patch of grass beneath his feet. With the butchering complete, he could relax for a moment. When he gazed around the place, which retained a certain golden sheen, at least to him, he found that most folks had returned to their duties or their huts. Solomon stood close behind, whittling some other rough piece of wood. Goldfinch was satisfied seeing all of the tasks his people had completed, for it was something he had grown accustomed to as the groundskeeper for Reverend Allen in Philadelphia.

He slipped his hands into his coat pockets and walked to the edge of the village, back through the gate. He returned to the tree that held the large, wooden creation. It was normally easy to decipher, but the sun pierced his vision, falling down on him with a vengeance. He knew this was the spot, the hackberry. Nailed to the trunk was a bulky cross held together at the perpendicular intersection by only five or six nails. Yet it had withstood some fierce winds since their arrival in April.

Looking skyward, he tried to study it, but the ominous, fiery glare did not let up its barrage. He turned his gaze back to the village sprawled before him. A tall, five-foot fence meticulously carved from oak wood bordered the property. The whole setup was only about eighty yards long, maybe fifty wide.

The village was made up of small, single-room shanties. Smoke whisked through the chimneys of some. A handful of outbuildings and other wooden structures dotted the small but dense land. They were corn cribs, a toolshed, storage space, and animal paddocks. Each villager had a mount, and there was a splintery wagon beside the cart Goldfinch used for odd jobs. One hut, a bit larger than the others, had a ten-foot steeple and a small attached nave. At the center of the trafficked property was a large, community fire pit. Each wooden building was constructed with pine logs and housed one villager with room enough for a guest, perhaps two.

The villagers were astir, returning with pails of water from the Long Pond River. Others moved to and from the corn cribs, or out the rear gate toward Harriet's furrowed fields. At this time of day, late morning, the air, the activity, made Synod resplendent. Goldfinch listened closely to the chatter of two women—Matilda, a dully dressed woman of about thirty, and Sophie, a wider-hipped woman of about thirty-five—who carried the pails. "Way that water's moving," Matilda said, "this is going to be a strong winter." Sophie chuckled and smiled. They both reached a larger basin near the paddock and placed the pails down. "Way a snowstorm rolls in can't be predicted from the current of this creek, Matilda," Sophie added. She looked over and smiled at Goldfinch. He did not acknowledge her but continued to listen from afar, from some twenty feet off. He smirked and then let the earthlier noises resume their gentle tapping and pattering in his ears.

The houses were set in a circle within the larger, imposing fence. The border was finely chiseled and sanded by Goldfinch—former Philadelphia groundskeeper—and enveloped the huts and also a thin shelterbelt that buffered the place from any encroachment. People could feasibly climb this fence, but not before reaching small but sharp wooden pickets that rested atop it. Every few feet, driven into the horizontal rail, was a sharpened picket—a word Goldfinch insisted on using. There was a certain craftsmanship associated with it.

Goldfinch sauntered over to his toolshed. It resembled the workstation of a butcher who had just taken an interest in botany. On his workbench, he found the intricately sliced venison. In its reddened stillness, the meat called out to Goldfinch. He could feel the salt tickling his taste buds. He grabbed hold of the meat, but was thrown off after hearing a riled, echoing voice in the distance.

"Don't you go and say you can't fire that weapon, Solomon. Comes down to it, best be mind over matter. Otherwise, we'll send Shepherd along."

Goldfinch knew it was Harriet, a mesmerizing brunette, finely curved, about thirty-five. She had a soft, mouse-like face and her complexion was pristine. When she frowned, a few furrowed rows appeared on her forehead. She tended to be outspoken, but also nurturing and affable. Even still, her personality was volatile. She'd once went from perfectly content and reserved to pointing the menacing side of a pitchfork at Goldfinch for calling off her harvest early—with a half hour of daylight left. "You'll respect my work, Mr. Goldfinch. Respect it," she had said. Goldfinch could remember the contradictory feelings this had charged in him and the way he sought to feel it again.

Goldfinch walked toward the ruckus. As he came around the corner of Harriet's small log home, he spotted her and Solomon. The ex-slave stood in his high-standing white-collar shirt now caked with blood, muddied boots, and cotton trousers. He looked even taller, burlier than before. He was holding his coat and a neatly folded indigo vest over the crook of his elbow, his hand in a fist out across his chest. He seemed embarrassed at being scorned by Harriet.

She was wearing a white skirt with a light floral pattern. The skirt had a high waistline, and beneath it, several layers of petticoats. She sported a dark brown bodice and an unbuttoned, navy-blue frock coat. She also wore a bonnet. Her hair poured out the sides of the bonnet, silky and appetizing. But he tried to act like the executive he had become. The first priority in accordance with that: upholding his strict abstinence decree.

"There'll be high time for romance, and intrigue, if that is what you desire from a spiritual community," Goldfinch had once said. "But only when we're past the solstice, when the light of the spring sun lies anxiously waiting to stream down. In the meantime, we'll keep the fence standing, our bellies filled. Gentlemen, ladies, there is work to be done."

Solomon turned toward her. "Missus, I don't wanna hurt nobody. I'm just headin' to 'delphia to set up the first pick-up. The Rev'rend, see, he told us that he'd take care of all the 'cifics. But I done told you, I *can* use it. Just used one tuh-day."

"Reverend Allen, you think he's watching our backs like he was? We're on our own now, friend. I'm telling you, muzzle-load it," she said, pointing at the rifle strapped to Solomon's back. Although he'd just had some practice with it, it still appeared so foreign. As a matter of fact, he looked torn just holding it. "You'll need it. If you're not ready, I'm going to put a round in your kneecap, set you down to convalesce, send Shepherd. You hear?"

Solomon slumped forward, staring at the ground. Goldfinch took the opportunity to intervene. "Love of God, for a small woman you've got a large mouth on you. What, pray, gives you the right?"

He paused for a moment, letting the comment sink in. She did not respond. Goldfinch turned to his hunting friend. "I've understood you to be a man of peace. But this is no peaceful endeavor. You've seen it today, at the meadow. Synod *will* be a refuge for runaways. This means we'll shelter fugitives, come across the law, and stare down one barrel or another."

"I understand, Mista Goldfinch. If ya call for it, I'll go back, fire a few shots out yonda."

"Now, what's the point in that? Spooking off all our game?" Harriet said, her face reddening. "Leading President Jackson right to our doorstep?"

Solomon feigned a smile, looking at Harriet and then back at Goldfinch. He chuckled but lowered his head again. Ignoring Harriet, he said, "S'pose you right, Mista Goldfinch. I'll see to most my chores."

As the man lifted his head back up to stare Goldfinch in the eyes, the latter patted his friend's shoulder, using a friendly nudge to send him off. Solomon gradually corrected his posture and ventured to his home, the door closing gently behind him.

Harriet licked the sides of her lips, sucked her teeth, and pressed a finger to her bonnet, fixing its thin strap. "Synod needs his efforts right now, Goldfinch," she said, staring off toward Solomon's hut.

"What this community needs are more guns, and enough faith to keep those bounty hunters away. We *will* snatch a few folks from the plantation, Harriet." He looked off into the distance, toward the northern side of the village, past a group of pines and a grassy foothill. There, three shanties, smaller than those in the Synod village, sat on a slice of earth pitching upwards ever so slightly, a compass toward the mountain range.

Goldfinch knew the hideaway was one of Synod's assets. All of his people knew of its existence. A few folks had even trekked out in early spring to help build it. As Goldfinch remembered, most of those men were Lyman Beecher's. Reverend Richard Allen's men stayed back on site, helping buttress the church. Peter Cartwright's congregants helped with the fences and with Goldfinch's construction of the huts and the meager forge. The forge had sprung up in just weeks. The masonry work was impressive—considering they were forced to work with materials packaged and thrown in some saddlebag. They had peeled rounded rocks from the mountainside and laid them in mortar. Steadily, the structure took form, leveled evenly at the back into the slope of the hill, which allowed for easy ore access atop the flames. The pig iron would then hit molds near the bottom. This contraption, though, was hidden in the woods. It was a deliberate act of suffusing the clouds of smoke with the harsh eddies of wind near the mountains.

The Founders—Allen, Beecher, and Cartwright—were gone now, returned to their zealous evangelism. These remaining folks were isolated, but not forsaken. It had been the plan all along. The three Founders would contribute their brainpower and then leave—some west, some east. And so, they did. Now Goldfinch held executive power.

Goldfinch gave Harriet a sideways glance but approached her and put a hand lightly on the fabric of her navy frock coat. She recoiled after his fingers brushed a few inches of it. She swiped at the hand, holding eye contact with him throughout. She quickly patted her coat, ridding herself of the nonexistent dirt. She made noises of disgust, but a smirk formed on her lips, and the eye contact failed to break. Goldfinch wasn't sure whether the smirk was intentional or not, but he returned his hand to his coat pocket.

"I assume you've lingered here to … have your way with me?" she roared, the sound carrying. She fixed her bangs which sunk beneath the bonnet's fabric. Goldfinch looked around for the nearest villagers. Most were still huddled around the core of the place, seemingly ignorant of anything more than fifty feet off. Adam was reading near the base of a tree, while Matilda leaned against the paddock and stroked her horse's coat.

"Like I said," Goldfinch replied. "Simply fascinating, the audacity."

She sarcastically curtsied and rushed off toward her hut. Goldfinch watched her the whole way, and he knew she felt his gaze. He watched her curves press tightly against the skirt, her hips oscillating. As she climbed the single step to her hut, she tossed a final, neutral look at Goldfinch, who still stood transfixed. Again, she curtsied. He assumed she would warm herself by her small hearth and prepare her supper. Of course, the meat would have to be coupled with leftover—and salted—cuts being preserved in the shed, inside crocks sealed with cheesecloth.

Before Goldfinch moved on with his day, he figured he would drop in on Solomon to make sure he was still comfortable with the rifle, or recovered from Harriet's onslaught. He walked up to the man's hut and knocked. Solomon opened up brandishing a forced smile. Before Goldfinch could say anything to him, he spoke up. "I'm ready,

Mista Goldfinch. Put me in the middle of a Comanche tribe, I'd fend 'em off."

Goldfinch noticed that Solomon's rifle was propped up against the modest wooden headboard of his hay mattress. The weapon looked majestic, reflecting the sunrays that seeped through the room's only window, its stock glistening. He looked at his companion and said, "You best be easy with that, Solomon. You keep that rifle safe out back. You pick it up when you need it. Strap it to your back. Utilize it if some bounty has you in his sights. Now, get some food in you—ready yourself for tomorrow's ride."

Solomon looked nervous and preoccupied. He said, "When I get to Reverend Allen's, I 'spect you'll want me to find his men, find his stop. Find the Founding Mother?"

"And you won't hesitate. Just imagine you're still working for the Reverend back in the city," Goldfinch confirmed. "You see, the Reverend preached it time and again—spread the news, be of service to *everyone*. You get to Philadelphia's African Methodist Episcopal, remember, it's just AME, and you find our Founder and his wife, and you coordinate the first pickup. If they return with you, it's subtle. It's at night if you must. It's following desolate trails right up to north Jersey."

"Well Mista Goldfinch, you prepped me real good for this. Trouble believin' we been here all these months already. And three without them Founders," Solomon responded, astounded. He narrowed his eyelids as if he were about to convey some edifying statement. "I's get them slaves, them *people*, back here, Goldfinch. From Synod to Ithaca and the AME there. We gonna do a marv'lous thing."

"Quit that sentimental blabbering now, Solomon," Goldfinch answered. "First you best be comfortable on that

Pennsylvania Rifle. You have items to pack, people to visit. Then we'll see you off."

"You a good man, Mista Goldfinch. A real good man. I mean before I made it north to 'delphia and the grace o' the Reverend's church I was in them fields and—" Solomon seemed to lose his train of thought, for Goldfinch stood smirking, shaking his head.

"I know your story, Solomon. It's hackneyed on these ears," Goldfinch said, amused. "I was the groundskeeper at your church for God knows how long. Now, fill your belly and say your farewells."

Solomon nodded and turned from Goldfinch. He began stuffing his saddlebag with canteens, silver coins, and some prepared goods that were nestled in a smaller cloth sack. He propped his rifle round his back, testing the motion. The weapon jutted out, the extended barrel looking awkward, even against Solomon's girth.

Goldfinch knew Solomon would have to devise a way to carry that weapon on him through the city. He *could* say he was a hunter passing right through, for as faulty a cover as that would be.

It had been a while since Solomon was around strangers, and white ones at that. Yet Goldfinch thought the gun might bolster the man's spirits. Still, what use would confidence be against a magistrate confirming the guilty verdict of some fallacious charge? They could ship Solomon back down south.

***

As night fell, and after enjoying a venison stew he had helped Shepherd cook in a cauldron smelted from Synod iron, Goldfinch began to settle down. He removed his clothing, put on a night robe, and set out to begin a fire at his small hearth.

After fueling the hearth with kindling and a leaf of paper, Goldfinch could hear the fire crackling, the wind biting at it atop the short chimney. He was drifting in and out of consciousness when he heard a knock at the door. He grabbed his coat, threw it across his body and peeked through his only window. It was the Elder, One. Had he come to discuss politics? Had he come to warn Goldfinch not to send Solomon off into the abyss? One had grown comfortable with his nuanced habits—his new way of life. Would it be so easy for him to see Solomon go? Goldfinch wrestled with these questions.

A few more knocks sounded at the door, each one increasing in ferocity. "You best open up, Goldfinch," One called. "I know you haven't drifted off yet, you hardly sleep. Open up."

Goldfinch watched for a few moments but still did not answer the door. He listened to One breathing heavily, scolding the door with his bare fist. Then he called out to the community's elder. "Can I help you, fella?" He was delaying One's entry.

"I've come to prepare for the send-off," One said. He was a stern old man, in his sixties, a trimmed white beard enveloping his face. He wore no top hat, except for the odd occasion when being fashionable and genteel trumped the more fundamental needs of the place. To him, it seemed, Synod was a means to channel a life's worth of energy. He would not squander his rank—third in charge—at the expense of simply looking sharp. So, he took to the more scholarly work of the place, writing accounts. He seemed to author and easily relay the psyche of the village. A few times, beside the fire, he'd read his drafts aloud—everything from their journey to the unforgiving summer heat.

At last, Goldfinch opened his home to One. He wore a low-cut, checkered vest beneath a frock coat and a black cravat above that. He adjusted the lapel area of his coat as Goldfinch quizzed him on his reasons for being there.

"I've decided to support the decision, a formality of sorts," One said. "As you know, I hold a type of veto power here."

Goldfinch rubbed his eyes, yawned, and said, "Glad to hear you have a say."

"You know quite well I do. That's the way the Reverend wanted it," One replied. "And Beecher—even Cartwright, that mad, baptizing genius."

"Since winter, we've lived as neighbors, as like-minded friends. Let it continue that way," Goldfinch advised, brushing off most of One's words. "Don't trouble me with a political argument."

"What do you suppose lies in wait in the illusory world now, Goldfinch? What wrath have we avoided, hiking to these mountains?" One asked. He presented his calm, stern visage.

"Why these questions now?" Goldfinch wondered, looking out around the place.

"I reckon plenty of places like this have sprung up before. But I am not quite sure so close to civilization," One added.

Goldfinch held eye contact with One for a moment, but then looked away. "You feel threatened?"

"Of course not."

"We thrive here, as an artery. You see, it is dependent on the slaves rushing through like warm blood. Without them, we don't exist, and vice versa. And *this* is where they travel, north, off to Canada."

Goldfinch unclenched a bit, stretching his stiff legs. He knew One's banter was aimless. He wished he could slip off to dream of the sprawling Ramapough Mountains and their burgeoning seasonal colors. He walked back to his mattress and sat down.

One looked puzzled, twitching his lips as though pondering some larger ideal. "Suppose so," he agreed.

"You don't like it, you can go back to that *illusory* world, become *Erskine* again," Goldfinch concluded, making reference to the elder's illusory name. It was a different time, before the Synod names were issued.

"Well then, Mr. Hermann, I can see—" Elder One was obviously a bit flustered by Goldfinch referencing his prior name, one that had wilted alongside the bloc of other titles abandoned when the fence went up. Nevertheless, Goldfinch interrupted him.

"Do not repeat my illusory name. As long as I'm the head of this community, I'm *Goldfinch.*"

The elder began to settle down. Goldfinch said to him, "Ease your mind, friend. I fear you've begun to worry about this whole establishment. What is it that ails you? The location? The uncertainty? It is something inherent with the trip and the lifestyle." He stood, examined One, and moved about the hut. He walked toward the elder and patted the man's shoulder—almost brittle and stiff like his personality— and ushered him away.

"That is not so," One answered, soon standing outside. "It is the carelessness with which we move about, plan, and enact our whimsical decrees. Your abstinence clause, for example. It has no legs to stand on. It cannot work with both genders here."

"What other way is there to rule?" Goldfinch asked, his voice strengthening. "This is a novel experience. We've never once been left to determine our own destinies. Take me, for example. Structure has been my life. A soldier, a spy." He looked at One, who slowly sauntered back to his hut.

When One was twenty feet off, he froze, turned back to Goldfinch, and nearly shouted, "Just know that you best be careful with these crusades. Our written accounts might carry more weight than any loaded rifle. We can be a community of ideals, not necessarily rifles. And you send an antelope off to a lion's den, you best be ready to see blood. Solomon is no gunman."

As the man finished his thought, Goldfinch turned and went back into his hut. At last, he could rest. He made sure the fire would taper out, lay back down on the stiff mattress, and slipped right into a deep sleep.

Chapter Three

Beyond the Gate

A bland whiteness inundated his vision. Slowly, streaks of black revealed themselves. Goldfinch's eyes shifted from the white to a leafy, blotted darkness. It became clearer. It was Synod in the winter. The trees, brushed with powder, swayed in a light breeze. He looked off to the right and saw Reverend Richard Allen, the Minister Lyman Beecher, and 'God's Plowman,' the circuit rider, Peter Cartwright. They were all huddled together over a fire outside one of the small log houses. They pointed at the wooden fence, then at Goldfinch. Reverend Allen looked fatigued and grayed, but adamant and upright in posture. Beecher looked chronically angry. His droopy mouth slumped into a frown. Cartwright looked uncomfortable in his tight black suit. His hair strayed off in a few different directions. The Founders waved Goldfinch over. Time seemed to freeze—everything around him was pronounced, distorted, and echoed. They whispered the word "Synod" over and over, cultishly. They pointed up at the hackberry tree. Goldfinch turned to the cross nailed to the trunk. It was at least ten feet tall, eight feet wide. He saw blood trickle down one side of it. He looked back at the Founders, but they were gone.

He jolted awake.

It was already dawn and Goldfinch could see the sunrise, flecked with shades of purple. The sun poked over the colorful mountain. The Long Pond River curved intricately behind the Synod grounds. It hugged the many dips, ledges, and banks along the towering hill behind them, a Ramapough Mountain. Goldfinch rose from bed and fumbled with his things, in search of his tin coffee cup. He had a jug of cold river water in his hut and funneled it into a kettle. He mixed it with ground coffee beans and placed it on a thick metal ledge near the top of his hearth. He reignited the fire. Minutes later, he grabbed the kettle with two thick pieces of cloth and placed it on the brick ledge beside him. He enjoyed the tediousness of daily routines.

Outside, he heard a horse's hooves pressing against the hardening soil. *Solomon must be preparing his mount*, Goldfinch thought. He flung the door open and called to his friend. "Remember, Solomon, to Philadelphia and back again."

Solomon, nearby, smiled and tipped the brim of the black silken top hat he now sported. It was part of his Sunday dress, gifted to him by Goldfinch when the two lived in Philadelphia. Goldfinch smiled mildly at Solomon as the man strapped his rifle to his back, buttoned his saddlebag, and hopped on his quarter horse. The man tipped the hat again and nicked his heel into the horse's flank. It began to gallop, and Solomon called out, "So long, Synod. When I's return, this'll be a diff'rent place."

Goldfinch watched as he rode off toward the fence. Near that structure, Solomon dismounted, opening the village to the illusory world. Soon enough, he was gone. Goldfinch turned back to the interior and saw Harriet in front of her door. She was still in her sleeping garments, and Goldfinch could see the skin on her arms and legs, up to the knees. He couldn't help but feel some fluttering beneath his abdomen. He stood so far off, yet still blushed.

Harriet turned and went back inside. The others still slept. There were fifteen of them. Each Founder arrived with five people willing to see the world in a different light. And then there was Goldfinch, Reverend Allen's groundskeeper. He was invaluable to the aging Reverend—with maintenance, greeting the congregants, or being a sound, but surly voice of reason. There were no children. Each villager was at least twenty-five years old. There were ten men and six women. No couples yet. He enforced the abstinence decree somewhat doggedly, though he had no problem relenting, even indulging himself, when the buds cracked through the dollops of softened dirt in spring.

Goldfinch knew there was work to be done. He knew One would be stirring soon, along with Mulvane, Synod's ordained minister.

Thinking of the Minister, Goldfinch planned on visiting him. Minister Mulvane converted from Catholicism during Jefferson's administration and came to Synod with Reverend Allen. He was soon ordained at the behest of the Founders. It was a simple ceremony followed by midday meal. He served as a chaplain in the War of 1812. He assisted at Reverend Allen's church, and he was by all accounts, the only one of the villagers who knew more than a single Founder. He had met Peter Cartwright before. Cartwright was a peculiar fellow: circuit rider, ordained minister, and politician. He was a presiding Methodist elder in Illinois. Minister Mulvane served with him in the war. The Minister hardly ever spoke of the wartime atrocities—the sights, sounds, and tales. It was something Goldfinch knew all too well.

With Solomon gone, someone would have to pick up the pieces, and Goldfinch settled for doing the work himself.

Solomon regularly watched the community fires and housed and fed the horses. Goldfinch could complete the labor—he was not above such triviality. Still, he would have to visit Minister Mulvane. The Minister was a fierce man, rough around the edges in secular settings. Yet, he was gentle when it came to helping others with faith, and he endorsed a stern Protestant lifestyle. Goldfinch would visit his hut, adjacent to the church.

***

Goldfinch was about to knock a second time when the Minister swung his door open. "Morning, Goldfinch. Beautiful weather, eh?"

"Solomon's gone," Goldfinch remarked quickly. Minister Mulvane stood at his front door. He still had sleep in his eyes and his hair jettisoned off one way then the next. His long, nighttime robe had a hole near the right knee. But still, he smiled, stretched, and ran a finger down the bristly beginnings of a beard. He was a bit older than Goldfinch, fifty, if his memory served him right. He had a modest, tender face, dark brown eyes, and a slightly pointed nose. Yet somehow, his mouth belied all that—there was something austere about it.

Minister Mulvane ran his fingers through his hair, and he tried to pull it to one central mass behind his head. Letting go of it, it fell well past his ears. He took hold of a long black frock coat and sat down on the slate step at the entrance to his hut. Goldfinch watched him as he moved about confidently, and he knew he had a sturdy enforcer on his side. Minister Mulvane was a rough-and-tumble man when he had to be. There were many mornings he rose with the roosters to stalk mature bucks partnering with does on the ridge. He was no stranger to field stripping, either, and was sometimes left to haul the animal, rack in one hand, guts in the other, back to Synod. He was even left in charge of the gun trade. The cleric was said to have rather secretive sources down the Musconetcong River, at least a full day's ride south on horseback. Goldfinch only got morsels of details from Minister Mulvane, though. These cloaked men apparently traded the aging Long Rifles along some network due south of Synod.

It just so happened that Minister Mulvane was a man of God. "Shall we hear a sermon now, Mulvane?" Goldfinch joked.

"Brother, it is Wednesday. You can wait until Sunday. If not, I might suggest a prayer of confession."

Goldfinch ignored the sentiment, and the two briefly shook hands and patted backs. Goldfinch knew he had work to do, but he needed a favor from the Minister.

"Can you inspect our rifle inventory, Mulvane?" Goldfinch asked. "We haven't used them at all, save for the hunts, but I fear there will soon be a demand."

"We run low, I'll be in the paddock saddling up before you could even start molding some ammunition." Minister Mulvane paused, scratched his chest, and continued. "In the meantime, I'll round up a few men, clean the barrels, and fire them off, prevent jams."

"A lofty goal we've laid out, bringing back these runaway folk, eh?" Goldfinch pressed.

"We ousted ourselves from that destructive maelstrom of a civilization years ago, by practice at least. We're just putting our principles to the test now, is all," Minister Mulvane responded. Before returning to the solitude of his own home, perhaps to draft a sermon, he admonished Goldfinch. "With this excursion you've orchestrated, I feel compelled to say that if you get too big for your britches, don't be afraid to take a step back and reexamine yourself."

"Endeavor's larger than me," Goldfinch acknowledged. "We'd need a *national* reexamination, then." He tipped his hat and walked back toward his hut. He noticed that the village was beginning to come to life. Carts were rolling, Matilda and Sophie headed out to the creek, and Adam was walking out the rear exit. Goldfinch heard Matilda shout out, "Feels different here already, I'd say." Sophie seemed to nervously giggle. He saw Harriet gathering some tools at the shed. She would likely be taking a trip to her fields. Adam had beaten her up there today. What's more, he thought he saw Elizabeth hanging trousers, skirts, and coats onto clotheslines. He knew she would soon carry some bundles of clothing out the rear gate, off toward the Long Pond River for cleaning. It would be a busy day, with her ironworking to boot. One sat preparing food—shucking corn, grinding it, and pouring it into larger wooden barrels.

Goldfinch knew he would have to visit a few other prominent villagers at some point: Adam, the farmer, Shepherd, if he returned from his supply run, and the forge crew, William and Elizabeth, once she finished her hectic day. Goldfinch was not privy to the woman who patrolled and administered the forge at first. She was a vessel, just one piece of the larger Synod puzzle. She had the strength of any man and dressed liberally. She sketched the furnace before the first bricks were laid and cross-compared her design with the draft One had devised. She drew up measurements and commented on supplies they would need. She had blonde hair and rivaled the stature of any man in the community, even Solomon.

As for the forge, it was located off-site, about three-quarters of a mile from Synod, dug deep into the side of a precipice, allowing the rolling carts to approach with small loads of ore. There was also an alcove at its rear, with space enough to store goods or textiles, should the shed be too crowded. Minister Mulvane had ridden up there after a midnight run.

Elizabeth oversaw the heat-melt-mold process, filling thick, udder-like pig iron molds at the bottom. William, thirty-something with a frail but hardened body, spent his days digging into the hillside for the ore. It was no lucrative operation, but they'd build a few dishes, farming tools, and of course, ammunition.

Goldfinch moved about, sauntering over toward the center of Synod. He approached a community barrel, reached his hands in, and tossed a few kernels of once-fresh corn down his throat. He tasted nothing but needed the sustenance. Then he walked toward the huts. As he ambled forward, he heard a roaring gunshot circulate through the wilderness. It must have been Minister Mulvane following through with the gun chore.

***

A few hours later, when Goldfinch had made his rounds, he again paused to listen to the whispering winds and the distant chattering of the women beside the fire. It was Elizabeth, Harriet, Matilda, Sophie, and Jane, a petite and gentle woman. It was time for him to take up Solomon's tasks, including walking the horses. The paddock was large, comparatively — a half-acre perhaps. He paid special attention to Eder, his white Lipizzan. The animal seemed to recognize his owner and had a certain twinkle in his eye. He poked at the ground with a front hoof. Goldfinch stretched the reins over the horse's neck and walked around the perimeter. Soon Goldfinch's feet and Eder's hooves each progressed in neat syncopation across the paddock.

After guiding the last animal, he left feed down for the lot of them. He closed the gate and stretched his legs. He ran his fingers along the brim of his hat and tipped it toward Eder, a gesture he felt was reciprocated within the horse's careful gaze.

On his way back to his hut, he inspected the community pit, and a few villagers' home fires—stepping inside to do so. He was ready to head to the rack and grab kindling or burlier logs of recently felled trees from beyond the ridge. No blazes required the attention, though. He suddenly recalled a few of his sojourns beyond the ridge, accompanied by Minister Mulvane and Shepherd. They labored many hours in the rugged forests, blazing trails and hauling dry wood. He could practically still feel the strain of the ax on his shoulder. The post-hauling days were always trying. He would lie in bed until at least eight a.m., kneading the flesh along his right shoulder. It was one thing to be a man of forty, but it was another to be a veteran-turned-groundskeeper man of forty subsisting on New Jersey's version of the frontier. He re-entered his hut and lay down. On came the midday lull. He had a moment to breathe.

In this time away from his chores, he immediately thought of Harriet, the floral dress, the way her colors animated the village and contrasted with the bronze tint of the huts and the darker soil. Her boldness oddly aroused him, but he also had to corral it, curb it, and keep her harvesting and replanting. She'd just had her birthday in September, and was now on the far side of thirty. Goldfinch felt *they* could work, for their ages meshed well. Plus, surely stranger marriages had been forged. But how could he circumvent his own decree? How could he keep her happy?

He would start a conversation about the arable land, the layout of the fields, or the length of the growing seasons. From there, they could befriend one another further—she could confide in him.

Through one season, Harriet had grown corn, tomatoes, cucumbers, and green beans. There were enough crops to feed the village, and since Goldfinch planned to expand the population in 1830, the fieldwork would have to increase or multiply. The work would come the following spring, but he was not opposed to an *intimate* discussion on the matter.

***

After an hour-long rest, Goldfinch had returned to his chores around the fire and at the paddock. He made small talk with Adam and Sophie at one point. "Day's half-strength and still you move about, appearing so refreshed," he'd said to Adam. "Sophie, careful with those garments," he said to the female as she hauled a basket through the village center. Then, he watched One pickle some vegetables.

Sunset soon fell upon them. Goldfinch kicked his feet up in his hut and watched the sun move below the majestic mountain foliage. After a dinner of corn cakes and venison, he felt plump and satisfied. The food brought on another peculiar feeling, sentimentality. He wanted to discuss the success of the village to date—with Minister Mulvane, or the Reverend— and an idea emerged. He could share the story with the runaways once they entered the community with Solomon, should they be brave enough to follow a negro freeman. He would have to wait until Solomon returned.

When this interlude ran its course, Goldfinch rose, tightened his suspenders, and exited the small place. It was an instance of impeccable timing, for Shepherd was strolling back through Synod's gate. He was in the leadership echelon, too, a younger man of humble origins. He was in his late twenties, with raggedy clothing, no hat, and tattered leather boots. His parents, he liked to say, were from England, and the accent carried over. He had not shaved in a few days, and his angular jaw emphasized the stubble.

As he traipsed through the gate, he carried the leads to two haltered Black Angus cows. He smiled as Goldfinch approached him. He passed the leads to Goldfinch and said, "They're from Charlottesburg. Did you notice I'd left?"

Grabbing one of the leads, Goldfinch said, "Of course, watched your exit out the rear gate yesterday after sunrise. I have eyes, no?" Shepherd laughed, guided the one cow, and the two men helped see the animals over to the paddock where Solomon commonly cared for the horses. Goldfinch became eager to speak.

"Tomorrow's north, into New York. You privy to that?" Goldfinch asked. "After, we won't need to stock up for a time. That's if all stay on task, too."

"Of course, of course," Shepherd responded wryly. Then he continued, "Took two half dollars for these animals. Some farmer's homestead—he had plenty more. And it was those capped bust coins I've been sitting on since we arrived. If everything is this easy, I'll take to the road every day."

Goldfinch pondered this for a moment, deciding where he might want to send the villager, which geographic locale would be brimming with meats, herbs, and stews.

Before he could say a word, Shepherd interjected. "*Tucseto* then? Manageable trip, I'd say."

"If you feel it necessary. Check our corn levels. Look to barter, too," Goldfinch answered. "Remember, those parts were filled with Lenape. You come across one, you might try bartering, so save up those bust coins."

"All in the name of Protestantism," Shepherd said. As he did so, Goldfinch spotted Elizabeth—almost like an apparition—slipping through the village. Her face seemed charred, her visage fatigued. She did not bid them adieu, just lowered her head and trudged forward.

Soon, Shepherd ventured back to his hut. Goldfinch was left to himself and his thoughts. Looking out at the fence, as he had done with the hackberry, he recalled the labor, the long hours *there*. The sweat had poured in those late spring months when he sawed the wood and drove the nails into the pieces. He looked down at the scar on his forefinger from a splinter he had received hauling the posts to the meadow's edge.

For Goldfinch, the day had been satisfactory, as the temperatures were above freezing. The frosts would be blanketing these parts in no time. Heading back to his hut, Goldfinch crossed paths with Minister Mulvane. "Always a pleasure, Minister—" He was cut off in his greeting. A scream ripped through every grain and fiber of this cohesive village. It was no beast's, no gelding's. This was a female voice, and incessant.

Goldfinch ran toward the sound. It was the hut of one of Harriet's helpers, a woman who prepared the corn and assisted with the cooking. Hers was one of the voices Goldfinch listened to earlier, as the females conversed near the fireside. Her Synod name was Jane. Her illusory name was unknown to him. She was a Cartwright congregant.

Goldfinch lightly kicked in her door. Harriet was inside, on her knees, her head pressed against the chest of a woman lying idly on the hay mattress. She lay supine, her arms at her side.

"She's dead, Goldfinch," Harriet yelled frantically. "She had a fever only an hour after you made your rounds. She said she was going to rest for the evening. Of course, I let her go and then—"

Goldfinch cut in, looking to calm her. "Harriet, easy. She was a godsend. Beautiful, helpful, an asset," he said firmly, grasping for the right words. Really, he did not believe the woman was dead yet.

He was suddenly reminded of the violence he had seen in his forty years. Jane's apparent death made him think of the suffering deer of the Hudson Valley in the late 1790s, the agony of his brethren falling beside him in the war. He attempted to fight off the fervid memories. They cut across his mind's eye faster than Eder's gait. He relived his father's death after the war, his nomadic period in the Alleghenies, and his hermitic retreat in the twenties outside Johnstown, Pennsylvania. He exhaled and reopened his eyes. Harriet's sunken eyebrows studied him.

***

Goldfinch could hear Minister Mulvane trailing just behind him. The cleric nudged Goldfinch out of the way when he laid eyes on the scene. He pulled a small relic from his pocket and grabbed Jane's cold hand. He whispered a few prayers and thumbed his beaded necklace, which held a small, intricately carved cross. Goldfinch stood still, then inched his way to Harriet, pressing a hand against her side. She examined it, as she had done before, and spoke disapproval with her eyes. But tears welled up in them, and she sobbed.

Minister Mulvane remained calm, and Goldfinch retreated to the entryway, leaning against the doorframe. At this point, he was over his attempt to seek amity—an alliance with Harriet. "Next time something like this occurs, Harriet, you'll inform me earlier. That fever could've spread like wildfire."

Before she could respond, Goldfinch walked away, leaving the door wide open, receptive to the night. Soon, he was shrouded in darkness. He felt that in this instance, if she were looking at him, he was simply a silhouette to her, an apparition reflecting the moonlight.

Goldfinch walked to the center of the village. He called out to his people in a more pointed, demanding voice. "No one is to go near Jane's hut, on pain of justice I will personally administer." Goldfinch heard a few panicky voices. Looking closely, he found the source: Matilda and Sophie. Their words were largely indecipherable, though he thought he heard, "Fear of death in him!" Most of the ruckus, however, was the clamping sounds of closing doors and shutters.

Goldfinch walked to Shepherd's hut. He always seemed to be the most approachable person—to stick with a laborious task. He knocked several times before Shepherd answered. As the door then inched open, Goldfinch impatiently, but lightly, pushed it the remainder of the way in.

"We've lost someone, our first. I'd like the body removed," Goldfinch said. "Harriet says she was plagued by fever. We'll bring her plenty of paces past the field, up that incline toward the ridge. On the top, she will be buried. We'll mark the grave with a modest cross, etched with *Synod* and the name *Jane*. I'll prepare that now."

"It'll be handled," Shepherd said. He rummaged through his belongings, eventually coming out with an old coat from a trunk beneath his bed. Shepherd had sprung from his hut with zeal. The two hustled to Jane's home. Inside, they removed her things and readied the cross Goldfinch had been whittling as he waited. Goldfinch extended a woolen blanket over the lifeless body as Harriet watched. As he tucked it around the contours of the woman's corpse, he gazed at Harriet, an impassive look pasted to his face.

While Minister Mulvane, Shepherd, and Harriet stood back, Goldfinch left the hut and rushed to his toolshed. He clasped a shovel whose contents were forged in Synod, then the wooden cart. He placed the shovel on the cart then returned, walking coolly, slowly, to Jane's place. The wheel creaked as it rode over the unsteady terrain.

At Jane's, Minister Mulvane stood beside Goldfinch. "She's moved on to the next world, Goldfinch. I assured that," the Minister said. "Plus, her time here uncovers no dirt. No reason to believe she wouldn't be granted entry above." He smiled and pointed upward.

He swallowed hard, shut his eyes, and pressed on. "But it's time. Let's remove this body." He lifted his sleeves and prepared to slide Jane's body onto the cart.

"Mulvane, don't you bother with this, it's the drudge work. Let Shepherd and me dirty our hands. The village needs you. They can spare me."

"That is illogical, you were chosen to lead this place," Minister Mulvane said. "I am the nomadic preacher. That is a lifeless body, Goldfinch. Requires steady hands. Something I possess."

"Make sure Shepherd and I escort the lady properly, with dignity," Goldfinch countered. "There is something you can do. Lend me your kerchief. I'll need to clean these hands."

Minister Mulvane looked bemused. He seemed to recognize how hierarchical the conversation had become. He was being put in his place. He rolled his sleeves back down, reached into his pocket, grabbed the kerchief, and handed it to Goldfinch. Shepherd approached from afar.

Minister Mulvane stepped aside as Shepherd moved past him, toward the body. With weathered gloves, he lifted Jane's body onto the cart, her limbs flailing from the motion. Goldfinch stood beside Shepherd and added a hand here and there, but it took only seconds for everything to be in order. They were prepared to take Jane to her final resting place. Goldfinch asked Minister Mulvane to watch over the village in his stead. He wanted everyone holed up inside.

Harriet stood firmly entrenched in the corner of the small, wooden hut. "Wait until Mulvane's village-wide service for a proper farewell," Goldfinch said to her.

She stood, speechless, a hand raised to her lips. Her absent stare was obvious. Shepherd looked at her. "I heard tell you were close, you and Jane. Came together with Cartwright. Chances are you knew her in the illusory world some, eh?"

"For a time," Harriet responded reflexively, over a sob. Then she turned around and left the hut, nudging Minister Mulvane in the process.

Goldfinch began to watch Shepherd cart Jane's body off toward the rear gate and the dark veil of night. "Be vigilant, Mulvane, you hear?"

Minister Mulvane nodded in compliance. Goldfinch trailed Shepherd by a few steps, and the two traipsed into the chilly night. They walked and walked, hearing distant howls, fluttering wings, and crunching leaves. They pressed on. Goldfinch carried a small torch he had grabbed from a stand set against the last strip of fence before the shelterbelt. It had stood regally, a fortification lit in the night, its fire bisecting the thickening pockets of air. Goldfinch figured it would ward off just about anything—but only until the 'cargo' arrived. Then subtlety would rule the day—and night—not the wavy lengths of a torch.

They moved swiftly, like apparitions, hardly leaving a trace and gaining ground. Goldfinch watched as Shepherd rolled the cart forcefully, the bumps sending Jane's limp arm or leg a few inches into the air. Goldfinch wondered if Minister Mulvane could watch over their place.

Goldfinch also thought about the face Harriet had given him after they determined Jane had passed. She looked at him with cold, stony eyes, as though he was a monster, some brute who could not connect with his emotions. He looked back at Shepherd, then to the path ahead.

Shepherd struggled with the cart for a moment as the pair tried to climb a knoll that plateaued about fifty feet up. Goldfinch did not immediately come to his aid. Instead, he had simply fallen victim to the lure of the gloomy darkness. His mind traveled forward, then back, then deep into some memory—snowy horseback rides and his father's late-life madness and dementia. Goldfinch simply tapped his fingers together for a moment, listening to the cart's creaky wheel and looking up at the moonbeams sneaking their way through a thick cloud cover.

It took over an hour to get to the desired burial locale. It was a spot Goldfinch imagined Synod villagers would rest decades from now. He stepped around carefully, pressing his feet down into the earth and testing the give of the shaky soil. He did not want Jane in muck; he didn't want her in an unforgiving, root-filled section. There was an art to this. He found the perfect spot and stomped on it a few times. Shepherd wheeled himself over with the body.

As Goldfinch broke ground, drawing the first dirt with the Synod shovel, the moonbeams seemed to penetrate the soil, digging deeper, more fervently, than Goldfinch could with a measly hand tool. He hacked at the ground a few times, maintaining a steely composure throughout. Then, without saying a word, he handed the shovel to a winded Shepherd, who stood against a tree trunk, regaining his breath. Shepherd would have to continue the task. Goldfinch then stood statically, one arm resting on the other that held the torch. He decided Shepherd would be twenty-eight. In his head, he called him the twenty-eight-year-old, again and again. He watched as Shepherd dug deep into the earth, removing roots and pebbles in the process. The backfill pile grew larger and larger, and Goldfinch just played with his suspender clips. They really did not need much light. At this point, the moon was thick in the night. Soon, the crater glimmered from these white beams.

When the hole was deep enough, Goldfinch called Shepherd back up to the ground level. He proffered his hand and Shepherd took the help. As soon as the younger man's boots touched the ground, Goldfinch turned and reached into his pocket, retrieving a sheet of paper that had a few lines written on it. In this case, it would honor Jane's memory. It had been an insert, a bookmark, in his Bible. One had jotted it down some months ago and given it to Goldfinch. The elder pointed out the elegance of the language. Ever since, it had marked his page in the King James Bible.

"It's from Isaiah 35:10. 'Earth has no sorrow that heaven cannot heal. They shall obtain joy and gladness, and sorrow and sighing shall flee away.'" His delivery was abrupt and awkward, the whole gesture too ephemeral. But it was something. Goldfinch let out a restrained cough, tightened his hat, and took a few steps away from the grave. He could remember the men of New York Militia's sixteenth regiment jolting back, falling to the earth in explosive clouds of crimson. Something about the death, en masse, had set him off. He became unhinged, left to lead the drifter's life in the American east.

Goldfinch leaned in, placed the leaf of paper on Jane's covered body, and turned toward Shepherd. "Let's wrap this up and return."

Then, Goldfinch once again adjusted the suspenders, drawing attention to each twitch of his fingers. The seat of his coat dipped back below his thighs, and he made his way toward Synod. The return trip would take half the time.

"Don't you forget that shovel, Shep. Elizabeth will have your head, you know."

***

Inside the village, the community fire was out. Goldfinch passed through the center of Synod, watching the huts, looking for light, listening for chatter. He felt as though a few people watched him from afar with hawkish eyes, but he couldn't say for certain. He was still holding the weakening torch and walked to the horses' water basin to extinguish it. The torch grazed the water. He looked back behind him, as though someone was eager to press him for information about Jane. Still, there was no one.

Goldfinch walked the thirty or so yards back to his place. When he got to his front step, he reexamined Synod, assuring that order was maintained. He wondered if Minister Mulvane had fared well, or if he was barraged by Jane's companions.

He sat down and leaned his head back against the wall. It was cold and unforgiving, but the icy surface drove a chill down his spine, calming and grounding him. He took his hat off and flung it on its hook, removed his coat and the suspenders, but got no further. He was so fatigued, though he had not quite dug the grave. He passed out. It must have been two in the morning and the walking, at least, had taken its toll.

***

When he awoke, there was bright sunshine. He had slept far past eight a.m. He heard feet scurrying across the property, metal clanging against other metal, an ax grinding at wood behind the shed. Voices called out to one another. He thought he heard One discussing some passage he had read the night before.

He kept on yesterday's clothes, rinsed his mouth, tightened his suspenders and hatted himself. He grabbed some powdery corn. He mixed it with a cupful of the water, sloshed it around, and tossed it back. A sure substitute for a hot morning meal. Goldfinch opened the door and found Harriet staring over at him from her place. She stood with her own door ajar, her body half leaning against the threshold. Goldfinch left for Minister Mulvane's. He would ask about the village's response to Jane.

The Minister welcomed him. He seemed to be saying a prayer as Goldfinch inched by him. His head was lowered toward the ground, his eyes closed. Goldfinch looked at him, formulating something clever to say. "The service will be Saturday. Need time to prepare suppers and coordinate a trip to the burial site. Someone will have to be left behind to watch the place. Might suggest a supply run for you, Mulvane. What say you? We'll need to be armed better."

"If a village can part with its spiritual leader in such a—" He was interrupted.

"Day or two won't hurt a soul," Goldfinch barked, his face steely and poised. "I might suggest traveling with those rifles concealed. Bit too conspicuous—an armed minister. We have cloth sacks to spare, perhaps. Head out today."

If Minister Mulvane wanted to test Goldfinch and tell him to go himself, he didn't let on. He nodded at the Leader and continued to prepare his coffee and welcome the day.

One knocked at the door. He had been absent since the previous day, an old man inextricably bound to his mattress. He knocked lightly once more and leaned against the frame as if a lover were waiting inside. "My vote says Synod requires these extra armaments. I heard you talking amongst yourselves. Shame the eldest man here doesn't have a say." He chuckled. Goldfinch assumed it was an attempt to exude strength. One continued. "Myriad of other ways someone could perish here. You know we'll need these guns—Solomon's due soon."

"That's why I've made the decision," Goldfinch answered, hardly making eye contact with One, who wore polished brown boots, a similarly shaded brown frock coat and an unblemished black cravat. He held a few sheets of cotton paper—he had reams of it in his hut—and fiddled with a dip pen in his other hand. *He must have written, or embellished, the account of Jane's final hours*, Goldfinch thought.

Goldfinch gesticulated at Minister Mulvane, urging him to exit the place and take to the road. The Minister gathered up some belongings, inserted a clerical collar into his shirt, threw a coat over himself, and left.

Goldfinch remained, his gaze fixed on One. The elder spoke out, "Suppose I'll approve of your plan for Saturday's service."

"Glad to hear it. We'll make preparations for someone to stay behind," Goldfinch responded coldly.

"Easy choice, I'd say," One added. "Under thirty, your hand—

"Yes, Shepherd will do," Goldfinch confirmed.

He left One's company, turning toward the village center, watching as his people scurried about. Goldfinch cleared his throat and looked around. The ironworkers, Harriet, and the other ladies, at least, turned toward him, lowering pails to the ground. The others followed seconds later. "We've lost a villager," Goldfinch called aloud. "It was Jane, one of Cartwright's. You've all come to know her over these last months. She'll be sorely missed."

He tried to continue but saw his father's homestead, then the Brit who had limped to Goldfinch's bedside when he was a prisoner after Queenston Heights. The man had a bullet wound festering at his side. He had also secretly traversed the fort's halls to open Goldfinch's cell in the night. Goldfinch was thusly freed, able to crawl back to the American lines. The Leader tried to stumble ahead with the death announcement, his voice streaming from his mouth unevenly and awkwardly. "We will hold a remembrance for her on Saturday morning, at what's become the burial spot."

He looked out and saw Adam nod. Elizabeth gave her subtle show of acceptance, dipping her head at most an inch. The others found solace in their homes. Goldfinch heard shutters clip shut, door hinges rotating, corralling their loose subjects. "It's settled," he called out as if they were still listening. As had become his custom, he shuffled away. He felt a sense of fatigue. He was ashamed to admit—he'd been a military man—but he could no longer ignore the ball and chain beneath his eyes. This was the most trying moment since his inauguration.

He wanted to cordon the fatigue off in some secluded part of him. He would fight it until the last moment, though. Returning to his hut, he found himself daydreaming as he looked out the clouded window of his cabin. He imagined the pine needles shivering with the chill. He heard a pail swinging in someone's hand, pivoting on its handle, a liquid sloshing about.

Again, the image was fuzzy. It was dark, but a man with a wolf's head, the one who had howled earlier, stood motionless at Synod's gate, tilting its head, staring back at him. His eyes lit up red. It slowly unhinged the Synod gate and looked back toward the wooden cross at the hackberry. He took a step inside.

With the sense that someone was lurking nearby, Goldfinch shook himself out of the daze. He felt a chill forming at the back of his neck. He grabbed his rifle and left the hut to investigate the fence line. There, he stood idly, perceptive to all the sounds: pattering feet, twigs breaking, crows cawing. When there was really nothing of note, though, Goldfinch pressed onto the thickest portions of the forest.

For hours he walked through the woods. At times, he lifted his head to the sky. He found the moon perforating the rest of the daylight. It was subtle, but there it was. Soon the sun was losing its strength, setting over the ridge.

He stayed out through the night, guarding his fence, monitoring the fire, watching Harriet's body language, looking out for Solomon. It was now early Friday morning. His hat removed, he ran his fingers through his thinning hair. The act helped to awaken him. He grabbed the rifle and realized he would need a torch if he was serious about patrol. He walked to his hut and found one sitting in a wooden box built on the house. He would clear his conscience, patrol the entrance again, and deem it free of intruders—especially those with canine heads. Before making it to the gate, he dipped the torch in the cinders of the community pit.

***

He scanned the woods again. There were no noises—from people, animals, wind, nothing. Just a fragility that was bound to crack. Something was off-kilter. Goldfinch sighed, turning back toward the row of huts. As he did so, he heard leaves crackle off to the right, maybe twenty yards away. Then it reoccurred, louder. The noise intensified—the distinct sound of an approach, someone running toward the gate.

He held the torch out in front of him. The Long Rifle was strapped to his back. His heart raced, and he maneuvered the light source from side to side, trying to illuminate the area. The sounds intensified. Then, they stopped.

He stretched the torch out at an arm's length. There was nothing. He moved it to the right.

A young African boy, maybe twelve years old, stood staring at Goldfinch. He was wearing rags and was barefoot.

"Goldfinch?" the boy asked.

The Leader stood speechless for a moment. Then he managed a "Yes?"

Chapter Four

Psalms

"I'm Edwin Wright, mista," the boy said. He held his hands behind his back, and Goldfinch remained suspicious.

"Why don't you put your hands out front here? Is there anyone else with you? In those trees?" He used the torch to point to the forest.

"No, just me. Left Pa back in 'delphia. We'd already went few states up. But he done got tangled up with them slave catchers. Pa told me to hide. I saw 'em drag 'im off, right in front of my eyes."

"Son, what are you doing at our gate?"

"Yesterday, I run into a man in Paterson. Said he had him some AME contacts. He reckoned I'd 'scaped. Smart fella he is. Anyway, he took me 'side. Said he lived in a community for 'scaped slaves like me. Said it was up north in Jersey, near Long Pond, where the two states met. Said ask for Goldfinch.

"I wanted to go after Pa, but I knew they already had 'im in chains. Last thing he wanted was for me to go back to them cotton fields. I just up and run. I be askin' 'round, seein' where them mountains crossed toward Jersey. I tell ya I snuck on a coach for a few miles. Well, top a one."

Goldfinch used the torch to inspect Edwin's body. He appeared harmless. "Did the man say anything else? Was he bringing friends back? He near? Why's he in Paterson?"

"I din have time to ask them kinds a questions. I just up and run, like I said. But heard tell his source kept him up north, sent 'im your 'friends.'"

Goldfinch recalled the wolf dream. Surely this boy posed no threat, unless he was lying and had some infiltrators out in the brush. He listened closely for any racket but heard nothing, just the same whispering winds.

"Come inside, son. See if you like it here."

The boy approached Goldfinch with a hop in his step, stopping so that he was right beneath the Leader's face. Edwin smiled. Goldfinch turned away.

As the boy walked through the main gate, Goldfinch waited a moment, scanned the horizon, and fastened the hinge. He turned toward the boy, who was already making his way to the village center. There was no fire, but the smoke from the night's blaze still mushroomed a few feet overhead. It provided some heat for the young boy who had to be chilled to the bone, moving through the woods at this time of year, shoeless and with rags for clothing.

Goldfinch balked. What would he do next? He thought he could sleep it off—the whole ordeal was a figment of his bloated imagination. He pinched himself, closed his eyes firmly, and reopened. The boy was still there, standing near the pit. There was one solution: he would have to see if the Minister had returned. If so, he would wake him. Goldfinch wondered whether the Minister would answer the door with his customary swiftness in the throes of night.

He knocked. Before he tapped a third time, the door flung open. Minister Mulvane had returned, unsullied.

"Take a look outside, by the pit. See the boy watching us? He ran here, rode here rather, from at least Paterson. That's twenty some odd miles."

"What does that mean?" Minister Mulvane asked.

"For one, it means that Solomon made it down there—at least to Paterson. Two, we don't know how many people he told." Goldfinch paused but continued. "It's a trial run, though. We'll keep the boy with someone close. If the going gets rough, he stays in the runaway outpost."

"First a death and secret burial. Then an African shows up at our gate, and we take him in?" Minister Mulvane asked, apparently disregarding the Methodist tenet of protecting all God's children. Whether it was a latent sort of dogmatism, Goldfinch could not say yet. Minister Mulvane honed his patriarchal qualities again. "Right, right. Sure, we'll take the boy in. He must be a young lad—and to have connections with Reverend Allen, impressive."

"Great, he'll stay in your home tonight," Goldfinch responded. He whistled toward the boy, who rushed to his side. "This is Mulvane, he'll be your friend. You'll sleep here tonight."

"Sure, mista. Anythin' you want, I can do. I'm good wit' a saw. I can farm and—"

"Edwin, son, you do not have to impress," Goldfinch said, interrupting. "We will not put you in chains. This is a spiritual place."

Minister Mulvane proudly added, "Founded on equality and altruism."

The boy understood most of Goldfinch's response, but the Minister's seemed to fall on deaf ears. He smiled and scooted into Minister Mulvane's room. He went right beneath the Minister's outstretched arm that was leaning against the doorframe. Edwin collapsed onto the bed, his dirty feet dangling off the end.

"Make yourself at home, lad," the Mulvane said with a forced smile. "Enjoy the space. I'll rest at Jane's tonight."

"The woman just passed there," Goldfinch reminded him. "You can't sleep in there."

"I believe she died from a larger illness, one plaguing her back in the illusory world. See this place was a sort of ... infirmary for her." He paused, sucked his teeth. "She complained greatly about pains, and this and that. Didn't want you finding out. Figure she came here to settle the score with the Heavenly Father. God rest her soul."

"I thought I spotted you covering your nose with that kerchief when we moved her."

"Lord knows there could be all kinds of foul odors." Minister Mulvane snatched a bag of clothes off his floor and traipsed over to Jane's hut. As he walked, he called out to Goldfinch. "I've gotten you those guns. They're out near the toolshed. No ammunition, though."

Goldfinch thought about the execution of said mission— the Musconetcong was farther away than Paterson. But Minister Mulvane's people were ensconced in locales up and down the New Jersey farmland. Goldfinch asked no questions. He knew he would need the rifles sooner rather than later.

Minister Mulvane sauntered across the meadow, poking Jane's door open. He tipped his cap at Goldfinch through the window. The Leader walked off, ignoring the young boy who had already fallen asleep in Minister Mulvane's barebones room. As Goldfinch shut the door, the burn of additional eyes singed him. He could feel them and so instinctively turned to Harriet's, wondering whether she tracked him through all hours of the day. Nothing. Ultimately, he found his way back to his place and turned in.

As he approached the unique comfort of sleep, a state where he could seek some ablution, he thought about how Solomon had been gone for two days. Goldfinch did not know when to expect him, either. What he did know, however, was that an escaped slave was housed in the village now. Synod would be tested rather early.

***

Goldfinch awoke after dawn. He got up, dressed, shoehorned his heels into his leather boots and made his way to Minister Mulvane's. As he got near, he noticed the boy was gone. But then he caught sight of Edwin helping to start a fire at the community pit. He was surrounded by Adam, Shepherd, Elizabeth, and William. The latter two were apparently taking the morning off to catch a glimpse of the newcomer.

Harriet also stood near, but she was not huddled around the twelve-year-old. Goldfinch had an idea—maybe it occurred to him in his sleep. He approached Harriet. She looked wonderful, with another floral-patterned skirt, petticoats, and bodice. She did not wear a bonnet, and her hair looked silky and sensuous.

"You'll look after the boy, Harriet," he said firmly. At his periphery, he saw the cleft separating her breasts. His heart leaped in his chest again. Soon the giddiness sunk lower than his chest.

"I don't see a problem with that," she answered. "I've wanted to care for a child. Had a miscarriage back west."

Strange, but the statement had Goldfinch aroused, picturing her, the conception. He thought of her usual shamelessness. It seems there was, in another time, at least vulnerability. Perhaps the door was not completely shut on him. He smirked, looking at her and her liberal dress. He figured she was bold enough to simply throw caution to the wind and escape to some undefined village. Elopement, though, that was a different story.

"It's settled then. Do you have enough space to house him?"

"There'll have to be," she said.

"Can have him off past the state line by Sunday," Goldfinch added. But then he reconsidered this. "Although, the place has yet to sire a new age of … residents, bound by creed, of course. You see? He is this new age."

She let him bask in his newfound glory. "Very well. Of course, I'll make room for the boy."

Goldfinch the pragmatist returned. "You've heard his name?"

"Hope you don't think that back and forth with Minister Mulvane fell on deaf ears."

"Well, the boy is yours. See what you can learn from him about the stops he's passed through."

She bid him a slight curtsy. Goldfinch watched as she approached the boy, arms spread wide. She asked the others around her to step aside and grabbed hold of the boy's hand, whisking him off to her place. Goldfinch followed their progress for a moment then turned back to the fence's angular shape at the base of the pines. He looked at the peak that lingered ominously, a cautious reminder of nature's inherent beauty and its capriciousness.

Goldfinch would collect firewood, for the temperature settled around forty-five. At the tool shed, he grabbed a saw that had also been forged with Synod iron. He felt the splintered handle graze his equally splintered palms. He ran his finger lightly down the teeth of the blade. He threw a few more tools onto the wooden cart and ambled out into the less forgiving but more expansive forest.

Some hours later, when the cart was unpacked, the tools returned to their respective homes, Goldfinch wandered about the village, his fingers pressed firmly in his coat pockets. He plodded around the fire, each step a part of his larger contemplation surrounding Solomon's return. When he looked up, Harriet was staring back at him as Elizabeth gabbed on about something, perhaps the stress of her job, the impurity. Goldfinch caught Harriet's gaze at a perfect moment, as the flames painted her face with streaks of orange, enhancing and lighting her mousy countenance. It was a glaring juxtaposition—her petite frame and the fiery passion of a frontier woman.

As his boots crunched into the earth around the fire, he knew he had to prepare for Jane's service. He had nearly forgotten. Every few hours, he heard some chattering about it. Shepherd would need to be reminded of his role, too. They had enough food stockpiled, and his middleman could stay put and stand guard. He moseyed over to Shepherd's. As he got close, he saw Adam leave, a pickaxe slung over his shoulder.

Shepherd spotted Goldfinch from afar. "What can I do ya for?"

"Tomorrow morning, you'll be left to watch the village while we venture out to the burial site."

"Course. Couldn't forget something like that."

That was it. Goldfinch left Shepherd's company. Stumbling into Minister Mulvane, he found that the cleric had pieced some writings together for the service. Goldfinch also made his rounds, into most of the huts, inspecting the hearths. When he made it to Harriet's cramped place—after knocking a bit—he found that Edwin was sleeping comfortably on a pallet she had laid out for him. She had sewn two bedsheets together and filled them with rags. Just like that, he had an improvised mattress. She had also given Edwin some new clothing. He was no longer wearing the tattered rags, but instead, trousers and a collared shirt three sizes too big. She lent him a pair of shoes that had been lying around, perhaps from a man of the illusory world.

"The boy looks human again," Goldfinch asserted, staring down at the slumbering Edwin. "The shape they're in after their journey from those plantations. Deplorable."

"Ah, the clothes. Better on him than dry rotting on the floor," Harriet said. "And sure, the young boys are forced into the labor. Nowhere near enough nourishment. Separated from their parents. Cooped up in tight quarters."

"And here he has his own home," Goldfinch said, looking out the window toward the forest. "But he knows there are folks on his trail. I hope he has not doomed our Solomon." He watched as Edwin rolled over on the mattress, repositioned himself, and began to snore.

"Sneaky one, he is. You can't say for sure. The boy says he snuck atop a coach," Harriet said. "Chances are he's just a bundle of energy."

Goldfinch scratched his head, shrugged his shoulders, and left. Moments later, he wound up back at his hut, famished. He retrieved and unwrapped a cloth he had beneath his bed and pulled out a few small pieces of venison jerky. It was a serviceable supper, especially with the corn cakes that eased down the coarse meat. He undressed, threw on his night garments, and sank back into the mattress that had become a place of solace.

***

He was at the top of the hill where Jane was buried. The ground was trembling near the freshly dug grave. The sky was reddening, and there was a loud howl emanating from the forest. A gunshot shattered the silence. He saw the hackberry cross. He looked down at the ground, and half-decayed arms plunged from the unsettled earth. Sidestepping them, he noticed rain was falling, and horses were neighing. He turned toward their calls to examine the riders.

He awoke, trembling. Saturday morning. A light drizzle spilled from low-hanging clouds. *A perfect day to inter*, he thought. He rose from the bed and put on his customary attire. He made himself coffee, rinsed his mouth, and returned to Minister Mulvane's place.

"Round up the villagers!" Goldfinch called out to Mulvane before he entered. "I shall head to the site a bit early."

Minister Mulvane emerged from the front door. He nodded and Goldfinch continued. "Make sure those who need mounts have them. Exit out the rear gate. Follow the footpath until you meet the base of the hill. That hill gives way to the larger mountainside. Up that precipice some, upon the first plateau, is where you'll find her."

"And if I cannot locate your trusty burial ground," the Minister said, "we shall enjoy an outdoor service within the grasp of these whispering pines. In her name of course." He put his arms up in the air, in the shape of a V.

Taking long strides, Goldfinch climbed to the burial site. It was at least a mile walk, taking a half hour because of the rough terrain. He knew he had arrived when he saw the unsettled soil. He then spotted the marker with *Jane* and *Synod*. He somehow felt responsible for her death, though she had known about an illness. It connected to his larger place as soldier and superior, and one who had taken strides to liberate men, nations, sects, and now those confined by sickness. He recalled the day he buried his father. The man was seventy-four years old, nearly mad, but brilliant. The same unsettled soil had littered his father's gravesite. Goldfinch did the digging himself. The man was interred on that Hudson Valley homestead.

Again, he whispered a few words of remembrance for Jane, the sentiment slipping into the stream of wind. He turned back to his path and cleared the flatland area of sticks and debris that could clog the way for the other villagers.

He next thought of Edwin, the lad who would do anything to escape the clutches of the southerners. He would get anywhere if his father had willed him to do so. Goldfinch then remained calm for a few moments atop the hill, the wind pressing at his face like the sting of cold water. The air was crisp with the bite of autumn.

After another half hour, he finally heard the ruffling of leaves, which of course meant the Synod convoy. He heard the rhythmic plodding of horses' hooves and lighter movements. Half of the villagers came on horseback while the others walked. Elizabeth, Adam, and One were all aboard mounts. Harriet and Edwin were on foot. Minister Mulvane, walking, led the pack, nodding at Goldfinch as he ceremoniously traipsed by.

"Let us get to the service right away, for Jane," Minister Mulvane suggested.

"No longer than thirty minutes," Goldfinch said, a simple but probably cold request. Watching Harriet, he noticed that she was dressed in black, with an accompanying black bonnet. She lifted her head and glared at the Leader. Then she pressed her arm tightly around Edwin, whose wandering eyes finally found the ground level and Jane's grave.

"We bonded on the ride up here, Jane and I did," Goldfinch said, looking around toward anyone who would listen. "She mentioned wanting to be a part of a community, something she'd missed all her life."

Someone coughed and Goldfinch felt the silence it brought on. Minister Mulvane looked at Goldfinch, hoping to command the service. "Let us start by discussing Jane's role in the community," Minister Mulvane said aloud, the villagers listening carefully to the cleric's words. "She was a pivotal figure, helping Harriet prepare crops and tend the fields. She attended my sermons punctually, always offering her services to anyone in need within our fence."

Goldfinch stood uneasily, rocking back and forth, kicking up onto his toes. He used his periphery to watch Harriet, who held her arm around Edwin, but who also kept tabs on Goldfinch. Her glare seemed to have dissipated and morphed to a more amiable expression. He spotted a few rain droplets dripping from the side of her bonnet. A light fog crept up cautiously behind the bevy of idealists. He saw droplets fall from his hat and wiped the brim. He thought about the strange accuracy of his dreams, at least portions of it. They had foreshadowed the coming rain.

Minister Mulvane continued to speak. "We will press on with the service, with readings. It will be Psalm twenty-three." He bowed his head and spoke softly, effortlessly, without the aid of a book. "The Lord is my shepherd; I shall not want. He maketh me lie down in green pastures: he leadeth me beside the still waters ..."

Minister Mulvane continued on, but Goldfinch simply suppressed the sound—hearing but not listening. Instead, he discovered the muffled calls of the wild, the pitter-patter of rain droplets touching hats, and the whistle of a wind strengthened by their altitude and their exposure within the quasi-meadow. Goldfinch could hear a female sob from within the small gathering of people and animals, saddles, and dampened clothing. It seemed to be Matilda or Sophie. Minister Mulvane turned to this mourner and said, "God is with you, dear." His voice was steady but somber.

"We'll continue," the Minister added. "Psalm forty-six, King James. 'God is our refuge and strength, a very present help in trouble. Therefore will not we fear, though the earth be removed, and though the mountains be carried into the midst of the sea; Though the waters thereof roar and be troubled, though the mountains shake with the swelling thereof. There is a river, the streams whereof shall make glad the city of God, the holy place of the tabernacles of the most High. God is in the midst of her; she shall not be moved: God shall help her, and that right early. The heathen raged, the Kingdoms were moved: he uttered his voice, the earth melted. The—'" He was interrupted by a steady noise of an approaching party. Goldfinch turned to the forest, examining it like he had done when Edwin arrived, like he'd done on battlefields, and at the homestead. Minister Mulvane tried to press on with the service, stuttering on a few words. The village leader noticed that most folks turned their heads toward the drumming of hoof and boot. The noise pitched up and down, and hung out there for interpretation.

"The Lord of hosts is with us; the God of Jacob is our refuge ..." Minister Mulvane's voice trailed off as he looked toward the back of his congregation.

"They're here," the voice called out over the others. It was a quasi-English accent. "Our visitors."

Goldfinch identified the source: Shepherd. He had ridden all the way from Synod, through the thickets, and up the hill—he remembered where.

"Silence, everyone!" Goldfinch exclaimed.

"Solomon. He has returned," Shepherd said.

Chapter Five

Rainy Return

"He has three, there are three of them," Shepherd said, visibly winded.

"Then we've begun our runaway enterprise," Goldfinch confirmed. Adam, Elizabeth, and One stared at him—it was not distaste, but apprehension. Minister Mulvane flipped through the pages of his Bible, obviously nervous, questioning whether to continue with the service.

"We must prepare the hideaway, ready the Long Rifles," Goldfinch urged, rushing away from the scene, leaving the crowd that had gathered for Jane's service. Shepherd, still breathing heavily, held his eyes firmly on Goldfinch. The Leader returned the gesture but retreated down the hill.

He made progress on the descent. The rain now puddled where the villagers' feet dipped into the earth. He heard Minister Mulvane try to manage the situation, saying, "We must let the service continue. Synod is a refuge for those who want to escape the world of deism and skepticism. We are a welcoming place. We come to church every Sunday and help one another. Jane embodied all of these characteristics, and as such, she must be remembered fondly."

From that point on, Goldfinch could no longer make out the words of Mulvane preaching to those gathered at the graveside. As he descended, he felt the pressure on his knees. He heard the far-off and droning voice of the Minister attempting to salvage his service. Goldfinch no longer cared if the funeral had been torn asunder. He rushed back to Synod, slipping through low-hanging boughs, holding his footing on the rutted earth. His boots were muddied, and his face was damp from an angled rainfall. He rushed through the gate and saw a small party near the pit. He spotted Solomon, still aboard his quarter horse.

"Welcome back, friend," Goldfinch called out. Solomon swung from his saddle, landing on his feet. His rifle was still on his person. Goldfinch inspected him, looking for abrasions, gashes, bullet wounds. He found none.

"Mista Goldfinch!" Solomon answered, a smile fixed resolutely on his face. "These folks a few who been movin' 'long the system." He pointed at the three travelers standing behind his quarter horse. Goldfinch strained his neck to look over the large horse, finding three people each slumped in posture. One was a tough-looking male, unkempt, in dark rags. He had piercing eyes and an unmistakable scar above his right ear. The others, girls, were timid and small, slender and undefined.

"They the Sullivans. One, the pa, is in his thirties. Those his girls right next to him."

The girls faked a smile. Goldfinch took them in and wondered if Edwin had spotted them on the road, or had aided them somehow. "That's all of them, correct?"

"Yessuh," Solomon answered.

"Now, did you tell the Reverend to send the rest of the fugitives?"

"Well, see, I didn' make it down to 'delphia, no suh. Rode through Paterson, met Red Tail, the In-din fella that been workin' the system. He came on through Rev-rend Allen's, brought the girls. My guess, he was suppose to bring 'em here himself. Carried a message from the Rev'rend, too. Suppose it was for you." He reached into the pocket of his tattered frock coat then revealed a wrinkled sheet of paper.

Goldfinch clutched the note, looking back at Solomon. He ripped the seal and unwound the curled sheet.

October 27, 1829.

Dear Goldfinch,

With this letter, you will find the company of Red Tail. He is an associate of mine and has been for a time. Do not draw your weapons on him. That is my request. You'll also find a family who miraculously escaped together. They have already witnessed too much. They will fit swimmingly in our community. Do treat them with the kindness I know exists within you.

Your friend and confidant,

Richard Allen

He finished reading the letter and focused his attention on Solomon. "This Red Tail, he's returned?"

"Back to his runs, I s'pose," Solomon answered, shrugging his shoulders.

"He knows where we have broken ground, started anew?"

He shrugged again. "If the Rev'rend sent 'im, best not to worry. Plus, he done turn 'round in Paterson, rode off south.

"Ah, and Red Tail said Allen will only be sendin' a s'lect few," Solomon said. "Ones he knew could handle it. Rest will come through 'ventually, after this bunch."

Still holding eye contact with Solomon and staring at Synod's new visitors, Goldfinch said, "Very well then. We best show these fine people a hot meal."

Solomon smiled, then turned to the fugitive slaves and ushered them toward his own hut, which had been abandoned for a few days now. Goldfinch followed along at their heels. Inside, the group enjoyed some corn cakes, slivers of jerky, and green beans they had pickled in mason jars.

"Fine meal, *mmm-hmm*," Solomon exclaimed, chewing emphatically on the jerky. "Road'll make you miss somethin' like this."

Goldfinch looked at the Sullivan man, hoping he would mutter something. When he did not, Goldfinch glanced back at Solomon. "Was the Paterson-Hamburg route free of foes, Solomon?"

"Made fine time, Mista Goldfinch. Fine time."

Goldfinch turned his attention to the man again. "I have a small basket of apples I can retrieve." He left for his hut, found the small fruit stash, and returned to Solomon's.

He passed an apple to each visitor and then watched as they ate.

"Folks need some water?" Goldfinch asked. The Sullivans were huddled close to one another, completely taken by the quantity of food they had consumed.

The male slave shook his head and then took a healthy bite out of the apple. The girls had their faces buried in the food.

Goldfinch could feel the tension in the room. At first, it was palpable, but it slowly subsided as bellies filled up. The male took a deep breath and spoke. "They took my other girl in Virginia. We's on our way up north here, and they jus' took 'er when we was packing our things only a room away. We were leavin' a small town near the border, real empty like. But they track 'er down and took 'er away. They wanted us, too, but the girls' mama, my Celia, she said once, 'Get our girls to safety.' Chances are they jus' send my other girl right back to the plantation. Same masta already sent my Celia off. They's ruthless. All 'em."

The man looked at his two girls and smiled. "But they here, are the light of my life. They some tough young girls. They miss their sista."

"They'll get along wonderfully with our 'resident tough girl.' That's Harriet," Goldfinch said, cracking a smile.

The man continued. "My Celia, they sold her farther south last year. New plantation, new masta."

"My friend, what is your name?" Goldfinch asked, gently touching the man's shoulder.

"It's Reg, Reg Sullivan. Ma called me Reggie, but the masta kept callin' me Reg as I got olda."

"And the girls?"

"One's Regina, one's Amber."

"Pretty names. Now, Reg, why don't we show you where you'll stay for a few days. Monday you'll head on to the next stop. It'll be Saint James AME Church in Ithaca. You can make it there on foot, carefully, in about three weeks, faster if you can find mounts. And of course, there are other stops along the way."

"A trip soon? Can't we let 'em fatten up?" Solomon asked.

"You see, Solomon," Goldfinch replied, "New Jersey's a wonderful state and all, but slavery's just barely done rearing its ugly head here. They best keep moving."

Solomon shrugged his shoulders, perhaps examining his own life, his relative safety, and full-fledged freedom.

"We're real grateful, friend," Reg said. "We'll be happy to see our quarters."

"It's off-site, but I'm sure you understand. You can stay with us during the day for labor, meals, et cetera." Goldfinch hesitated. "Reg, you don't happen to have a son? A boy that beat you up here?"

"No, can't say I do."

Goldfinch thought about Edwin but continued on with his task. He led the visitors toward the small outpost past the fence. As they reached the premises, in the distance, he could see the Synod party moving through the forest back to the village. He wanted his people to meet the runaways, but told Reg to settle in and then come back down to Synod when he was comfortable.

The Leader then rushed off. A few women had tears in their eyes—perhaps from Minister Mulvane's poignant words—and most wore black, which hid them with the darkened tree trunks. Above them, colors enveloped the horizon. Goldfinch then walked closely behind the villagers back to Synod.

"A moving service, I presume?" Goldfinch called out to them. He thought he saw One's back. "The weather cooperated, no?"

The villagers failed to respond. But then, two people— Adam and William—stepped aside. In their place, Harriet stood idly as others around her walked ahead. She looked back at Goldfinch through the crowd. She studied him for a moment. "Went well *enough*. Shame I should be telling the Leader this. Why you'd leave, I cannot say. The visitors could've waited."

At that instant, Edwin's head also became visible. He still clung to Harriet but had turned back to look at Goldfinch, too. The group was now nearing the village, out ahead of the Leader.

Goldfinch did not want to embarrass himself in front of the others, but said, "And that's where you're wrong. These people come to us for assistance, which is what we will provide." He nodded at Edwin and picked up his pace again.

Once within the fence, the horses were placed in the paddock. The rifles were returned to the toolshed. Goldfinch was able to focus on his runaway plan. He wondered who would escort these people north across the New York border.

Goldfinch continued to move about and found himself back in the toolshed as Adam corralled his horse. The Leader peered into the matted grounds and saw the Black Angus cows that Shepherd had purchased. He felt his stomach growl—he was famished. The cows gnawed on some cud and returned Goldfinch's cold stare. There would be steak for supper.

He knew one of the cows was not long for this world. He wanted to warn Shepherd, let him know that his clothes would get bloodied. It was not even lunchtime yet, but he was already salivating, plus he thought it might be best to impress the Sullivans. Of course, though, the other Angus cow would be kept for milk.

At midday, Goldfinch headed over to Harriet's hut to check in on her and Edwin. He did not have to do Solomon's chores any longer—the fires and animal maintenance—and so the more removed process of oversight became his only task.

He knocked on Harriet's door. She answered, wearing a casual looking dress much more liberal in tone and vibrancy than her others. It was short, against the knees, and dipped low on the chest. It was light-yellow, and she wore a matching bonnet. He wondered where she was able to stash all of these dresses. Or better yet, how she could hide those curves—her sumptuous features.

"Where's the boy?" Goldfinch asked as the door swung open.

"Helping me mend my clothes. He's got a good sense like that. He can work with his hands."

"Mind if I step in?"

"Depends what your aim is," she answered.

He countered with a tip of his hat. He then let himself in.

"Just go right ahead," she said, chiding him. He watched Edwin stitch carefully while sitting on her bed. He held a sewing needle in one hand, dispersed thread in the other.

"Mr. Goldfinch, how fancy it is to see ya here," he said.

"Everybody been treating you all right?" Goldfinch asked, fiddling with the pockets of his trousers.

"Could say that!" the boy chirped, seeming content in Harriet's company. He turned back toward the materials on the bed.

"The boy needs a project to work on all the time. If not he's bouncing off my walls like a madman," Harriet said, smiling in Goldfinch's direction. He did not know if the smile was directed at him, but he was anxious nonetheless. It was probably more of a maternal smile, he decided.

"We'll slaughter a cow today," he said.

"How lovely," Harriet responded, her eyes rolling back. "Well, if I need anything, I know where to find you."

Have I overstayed my welcome? So fast? Goldfinch wondered. He tipped his hat and exited, looking for Shepherd. Goldfinch found the young man in his hut, writing something on a ledger.

"Shepherd, it's time we fed our guests a hearty meal," Goldfinch said, standing in the doorway.

"Mean you want to kill an animal?"

"There will be more, for milk and mating. But tonight, we must eat. It'd be fine to coat your belly with some salty beef, no?"

"The green beans are just fine, but I'm sure some folks are looking at my cows with ravenous eyes. They could use some red meat."

"When you're through, take its parts out to the dump, where we discarded the deer," Goldfinch said. Shepherd acquiesced, grabbing a long blade.

By the time Goldfinch got back to his hut, he saw Shepherd leading one of the plump cows through the village and outside the gate. Shepherd would return with hunks of red meat Goldfinch could cook for the Sullivans. Before supper, though, he thought he would go out to the outpost and check on them.

He pushed aside craggy branches standing in his way and withering weeds that had sprung up from the ground with fervor in the earlier months. As he got to the outpost, the Sullivans were poking their heads out—the girls from one hut, Reg from the other.

"Don't fret," Goldfinch called out. He raised his hands up as a gesture of innocence. "I'm just here to make sure you're settling in. I also had a question. You didn't come across a young negro boy of about twelve in your travels by chance?"

Reg looked puzzled, obviously connecting this to Goldfinch's earlier question about a son. "Ya mean that little boy that been living with that nice lady?"

"Sure do. He's a nice young man—considerate, well-spoken for his age. He arrived the other day, found our contact in Philadelphia who showed him the way up."

"That Red Tail?" Reg asked.

"No sir, this here's the Reverend himself, Richard Allen."

Reg pondered this for a moment. "We didn't come 'cross nobody like that in 'delphia."

"I'm just hoping he's been truthful. The wretched *truth* is that I had a nightmare a few minutes before he showed up in the dead of night. There was somebody at the gate in it."

"You know what they say 'bout dreams and things. They warnings from that man up there." Reg pointed skyward.

"Hard to believe he'd be lying to me, though. We gave him a place to stay, hot meals."

"Perhaps that boy's not hidin' somethin' as bad you think—just wants to cover his tracks enough to keep them meals comin'."

Goldfinch felt like he had pressed Reg enough. The man had already been through the wringer traveling north.

"You could be right. But anyhow, that's our dilemma. I'm just happy we were able to shelter you. Did you get a chance to meet the Reverend?"

"We didn't, but the Founding Mother greeted us kindly. We stayed at the church a few days 'fore hikin' up here. I like it here, but as you said, we gots to keep moving, or we'll lose our ground, maybe go to Canada so them slave catchers can't tan our hides."

"You're sure your master would keep sending some men after you?"

"They took my oldest, right front of my eyes. I can't hardly sleep at night. Best I just keep my head low, press on. But they sure send some boys after us. If they figure we's went to 'delphia, there a chance they trace us farther."

"Why don't you come to dinner? We're cooking beef and have some stocked vegetables. We will tell you about Synod."

"That's real kind of ya, we'll be down shortly." Reg looked nervous, but reached toward a splintery bench and grabbed a satchel that he strapped around his chest. It held all of his belongings. The life of an escaped slave was never easy—in constant motion, looking to stray farther from their masters.

Goldfinch examined the room, noticing that Reg hadn't unpacked anything. He said nothing, though, just tipped his hat at Reg's daughters and returned to Synod. Once back, he saw that Shepherd was cooking two large flanks over the fire. There were also tender sirloins sizzling on a large pan made from Synod metal. The smell was mesmerizing. Goldfinch inhaled deeply and his stomach growled. He wondered whether the Sullivans would actually follow him down.

The smell of beef wafted around Goldfinch. The villagers began to exit their huts, making their way to the fireside. There was some commotion, some idle chitchat.

"William, hurry on over here before these folks devour this," he heard Elizabeth say.

Harriet walked toward the crowd with Edwin. Goldfinch took his hat off and perched himself on a bench beside the fire. The smoke swirled around him, clouding his view of the others. Edwin's silhouette looked particularly warped from the spiraling clouds of smoke.

"You traversed these paths with ease, Edwin?" Goldfinch asked the boy as he stood around the fire.

Edwin looked up at Harriet, who nodded subtly. "Sure thing, Mista Goldfinch," he said. "Ya see, boy grows up like me, we know these things."

Minutes later the meat was done, and Shepherd began cutting it into small rations. There were plenty of vegetables circulating, too. Some passed bowls of them off to others. It was a true community supper.

Sure enough, the Sullivans followed close behind. Reg held eye contact with Goldfinch then timidly looked down toward the ground.

"No need to lower your heads, folks. Here, we raise them, no matter the situation," Goldfinch called out so that Reg and the others could hear. "If we did not practice that, we wouldn't be living this fringe lifestyle."

"The man is fatigued," the Minister countered. "He may sink his head if he'd like. But I reckon when he comes for Sunday service, that head will be lifted, proudly, far above the rest." He looked at Reg and smiled. The runaway tried to sink into himself, deflect the conversation, a habit of the old world, Goldfinch assumed.

The fire roared, and the villagers dug their attention into their plates. They sat on benches that bordered the rocky fire pit. Every few moments, Goldfinch watched Reg, noticing his head rising incrementally. There were nineteen people in attendance: fourteen villagers, Goldfinch, Edwin, and the Sullivans.

There were also smiles and a general playfulness prevailing. This was the first meal of red meat in over a month. While the vegetables were savory, it still never hurt to have a heartier supper. Goldfinch looked up at the other cow, which stood in the paddock with the horses. It simply jostled its mouth around, chewing and ingesting cud. He turned back toward the villagers, who gorged on Shepherd's meal. He felt his heart warm when he saw Edwin smiling beside Harriet. The boy chewed on the meat and held a twig in a free hand, carving intricate shapes into the loose dirt. Harriet glanced up too, shooting Goldfinch a hard but impressionable smile. Then she turned back to Edwin, presumably asking him about his earthly creations.

"The Sullivans will hear our tale now, abridged of course," Goldfinch called out, rising slowly, coddled and shunned by the strength of the fire. "They will pass on our generous ways as they progress north to the mountains of upstate New York or the icy cold of Canada." He glanced over at Reg, his vision of the runaway distorted by the fire.

"All right, mista. We'll hear your tale, right girls?" Regina and Amber nodded appropriately, finishing their plates of food.

"Do not scare them, Goldfinch. They've been through enough," Harriet warned, returning Goldfinch's austere look.

"It's just a tale to relay and for us to reminisce on," Goldfinch responded.

"Very well. Just don't scare the girls, and Edwin here." She patted the boy's shoulder, but he did not look up. He was still finishing every last morsel of food on his plate.

"I may pitch in on occasion," a voice called out from the back. It was moving closer. It was Minister Mulvane, clutching his plate of food. He donned his finest clothing.

"You're entitled," Goldfinch responded, hoping not to lose his train of thought.

"Ah, what a charming tale it is," Minister Mulvane said with an air of sarcasm.

"We are in the year 1829. It is a peculiar time in the outside world, the 'illusory world.'" Goldfinch narrowed his eyes, paying close attention to the runaways. He saw that Solomon was disregarding the tale. Goldfinch continued. "We longed for an escape, to find a narrow beacon of hope. Better yet, we hoped it would find us. And Lord, it did. Andrew Jackson takes office the fourth of March." He halted, carefully looking around the fire.

"The hero of 1812, a senator, military governor, and dueler. We saw him aiming to lead America down the path of destruction. We'd succumb to his brutality and militarism. I knew his type, his brand of governance." He again gauged the audience. Some were attentive, others still ate.

Goldfinch went on to discuss how the tenets of the Second Great Awakening guided them during their upheaval. There were already pastors—some of whom rejected slavery—

leading crusades across the states. He discussed the coalescence of the three clerics—of Methodist and Presbyterian denominations—Allen, Beecher, and Cartwright. As far as Goldfinch knew, they joined forces through pamphlets or some chance encounter.

The men had met in Philadelphia, in Allen's home. Goldfinch had worked for him for half a decade after the war and his time of isolation in the Alleghenies. Allen took Goldfinch in and gave him a job.

Cartwright came to Philadelphia from Illinois, Beecher from his ministry in New England, though rumors were he would take the presidency at Lane Theological Seminary in Ohio. It was a week after the Jackson inauguration. The men put aside any doctrinal differences to discuss the future. They spoke of ultimately 'winning the west for Protestantism.'"

Goldfinch relayed these facts as the villagers ate and spoke softly amongst themselves. Solomon seemed to listen only to the chewing sound of his teeth. Minister Mulvane, too, chewed loudly, but waited to interject. At one point, he tossed his plate down and spoke of the precautions the Founders took so that the villagers did not become secular ruffians. The Founders had met in the AME—an exclusive 'synod.' Goldfinch remembered this occasion—for he had been cultivating a garden out back. Goldfinch had been welcomed in, beside Minister Mulvane, to listen as they drafted their plans.

In between chews, Goldfinch next spoke of the Founders' creation, the village. By this point, only the Minister and Reg listened to Goldfinch, but he and Minister Mulvane persevered nonetheless. Goldfinch spoke of the Founders' intent to be live-ins at Synod. But they had their evangelical lives to consider: Cartwright the legislature, the rugged conversions, Beecher the Seminary, Allen his church. They had decided on at least migrating with the villagers. They would each bring five congregants and live in the village through spring.

At last, the tale came to an end, and Minister Mulvane sprung to life, continuing his conversation with the existing villagers. One of the folks the Minister chased down was Reg. From afar, it was evident that the runaway had an inherent distrust of the white man.

Goldfinch then exhaled an ablution, and thought about returning to his hut to read the Bible and continue a chess game he had orchestrated with himself. But before that could happen, Harriet and Edwin approached.

"Fine evening we have here," Goldfinch said. He looked past them, toward the tree line, shivering as if absorbing the cold that festered there. "You enjoy the story?"

"I reckon he does," another voice said. It crept up from behind. It was Solomon who had quietly approached. "Saw this little fella down in Paterson. He was mighty confused, wanted to get right out."

Edwin appeared to blush while sitting awkwardly in his borrowed clothing. "I thank ya, sir, for givin' me a place to stay," he said.

Solomon studied him, scrutinized each flutter of the boy's eyelids. "You made it all way up here by y'self?"

"I did, sir. Just kept followin' the mountains. Don't know the Appalachian or Ramapough, but they big enough. Saw where Long Pond seem stuck 'tween them mountains. Knew it must be 'round heres somewhere."

"I see," Goldfinch added. "Well, why don't we trudge on with the tale of this place?" Edwin shrugged his shoulders.

While only a few other people remained, Goldfinch was not deterred. Minister Mulvane, Solomon, Reg, his girls, Edwin, and Harriet, were present. The Sullivans sat down in the same position they had vacated. "Reg, you feeling up to it?" Goldfinch asked.

"Sure thing. We done heard much worse. Ain't that right, girls?" Regina and Amber nodded hastily, probably unaware of what their father had asked.

"March, the year of the Lord, 1829, this year," Goldfinch said, leaping into the story. He spoke in a low, storyteller's voice. "The Founders deliberated over their setup for days and days at the AME. They had their eyes set on northern New Jersey. There were portions of it so far removed from civilization. They wanted to work swiftly, but intended on purchasing no property. Beecher rose, saying he knew of a place where a pre-Revolutionary War village lay, which had coexisted with Lenape. It was near a meadow at the base of two Ramapough Mountains near the border of New York. He heard of a preacher who once went through there. Had been marked for some provocative pamphlets. He said the British were on his heels during the Revolution and that this preacher managed to escape their clutches out there. This was the spot Beecher sought; it was there they'd pitch their tents. They would find it, or a comparable place. The other two decided on a date to trek north, the 28th of March. Each Founder would round up five congregants, each one thick-skinned, seasoned."

The story continued on, cutting back between Goldfinch and Minister Mulvane. The Minister told of Goldfinch's acceptance into the group as head carpenter. Goldfinch spoke of the supply-gathering process, Minister Mulvane of his perennial sermons. Goldfinch clarified that the Minister was 'ordained' by Reverend Allen. It was not the proper course to the ministry, but it would work. Then came the anecdote of the trek itself. The convoy moved at night, pitched tents, and huddled close as the snow fell.

Then, out of the blue, a gunshot echoed through the landscape. There was a pause, a rowdy howl. It sounded like a human voice. There was another shot—it sounded thunderous but tinny, as if from a musket or old rifle. Goldfinch advised everyone to crouch down. He bent low and left the circle of people gathered for the story. He tried to get a look at the gate, but it was still cloaked in darkness. But the noises persisted. He heard bottles breaking against the boughs of trees, a raucous call from the woods.

He peered up toward the rattling trees. Time seemed to stand still. There was a sporadic wince or cry. Harriet took a protective stance over Edwin, who was trying to scoot away. After a few moments, there were no gunshots, so some stood, exposed, examining what had befallen them.

Goldfinch ran toward the toolshed. Minister Mulvane was right behind him, Shepherd at his back. Goldfinch whistled toward the Sullivans and waved them close. Elizabeth, William, Adam, One, and the other villagers were near their front doors, some dressed in nightclothes. A few others went inside to extinguish their fires. Narrow plumes of smoke spilled from the huts, and Goldfinch held his attention on the gate.

"What do you hear?" Minister Mulvane whispered.

"Quiet," Goldfinch advised. He took his hand and cupped the crown of his hat. He removed it and placed it on a bench. His somewhat narrow face was tense, and he scratched at his prickly cheek.

"They a-after us," Reg stuttered. "My girls, though, Mista Goldfinch."

Goldfinch ignored the plea, but only because he was mulling something over in his mind. "Shepherd, you'll take Reg and the girls to the outpost," he said. "You'll stay there with him. Take a rifle. There's powder and shot beneath my bed. The door's unlocked. Take as much as you need. Mulvane, you'll come with me. We'll approach the gate."

Minister Mulvane looked toward him. "Now where do you come off telling me to march into combat?"

"You'll do as I say, dammit, or these wolves could tear you up."

"Could've gone on my own accord, though, Goldfinch," Minister Mulvane answered. "Now, let us quell these intruders with God's fury." He walked a few paces, retrieved a rifle and cocked the hammer.

"Enough with your haranguing, for just a moment, Mulvane," Goldfinch said. "Let us now repel these intruders, whoever they may be."

Shepherd, nearby, ran off holding his own rifle. He ushered the Sullivans toward the gate and into the night's oblivion.

Goldfinch and Minister Mulvane inched their way toward the main gate, beneath the hackberry, whose orange leaves were almost visible in the blackness. The pair moved swiftly. Goldfinch gripped the rifle tightly. He carried a few iron bullets in his pocket. Another gunshot rang out beyond them. The bullet pierced the leaves of some far-off tree.

"*Aaawhooo!*" a voice called out some fifty yards away. Goldfinch spotted a single lantern, swaying as though someone was holding it precariously. Minister Mulvane stirred right behind Goldfinch's backside.

"We stay behind this cover until they creep nearer," Goldfinch said. "Then we confront whoever is trespass—"

A bullet whistled past Goldfinch and lodged itself in a tree beside them. Minister Mulvane breathed heavily, his hands on a set of beads he retrieved from his breast pocket. His gun was perched on the ground, propped against his left shoulder. The Minister looked to his left, toward the closest trunk, probably where the bullet landed. Suddenly, Goldfinch realized the gravity of the situation. He fell to his knees, then to the ground. Mulvane followed.

"Reckon ya'll enjoy all that," called out a tawdry voice from the thickets.

Goldfinch looked at Minister Mulvane as his breath shook a few leaves. The Leader listened for the trespassers and whispered to the cleric. "We mustn't lie here. There must be cover fire, and we'll move, tree to tree, closer to them."

The far-off voices tapered off, and Goldfinch took that as his cue. He kept his grip on the rifle and peered out into the forest. The Minister stood to move with him. They cleared about twenty yards without finding the culprits. They searched for the lantern but found nothing.

They rushed back through the gate, Goldfinch protecting their rear and fastening the hinge. Minister Mulvane stayed put, but Goldfinch rushed to the shed, retrieving a few animal traps. He grabbed hold of their chains, returned to the gate, hid them along the base of the fence, set them, and retreated. Holding his rifle, he scanned the woods. He saw nothing but heard a fluttering owl and the crackling of twigs beneath the hooves of deer. There were no shots or voices. He was about to turn toward his minister friend to tell him the party had exited.

Boom! Boom!

Two massive explosions rocked the entire property. It came from about fifty yards outside the gate. A brief fireball, rising from both explosions, lifted slowly into the expansive air. Goldfinch and Minister Mulvane took cover behind the closest tree, and someone gasped in shock.

Goldfinch raised his gun and slid toward the sound. He heard deep breathing and a metal gun barrel clanking against a rocky ground.

"Who's there?" Goldfinch questioned.

"Mista, M-Mista, I—" Solomon tried to get something out but just stared at the rising smoke cloud.

"You were out here, too, huh?" Goldfinch asked. He felt a bit safer with an additional gun on his side, regardless of the fact that Solomon had just been trained on the weapon.

They heard feet patter and dirt being kicked up. Goldfinch looked at Minister Mulvane, who was still. He watched the Minister trace the sound. Something then whisked by Goldfinch, bumping his leg and causing him to fall forward a few feet. From the ground, Goldfinch spotted the figure as it made for the gate, moving with haste.

It was Edwin. The explosions had signaled something to him, and he had responded. He watched the boy leap over a fallen tree. The gate had been shoved open, the traps carefully avoided. Goldfinch ran to the village threshold, then in the direction of the explosions.

Out of breath, he turned to find Minister Mulvane and Solomon trailing behind. He took a few steps, froze, and waited for the others to gather close.

Solomon stroked his beard. The men were baffled and idle. Goldfinch finally took the lead again and pushed forward. They all passed the cross. Goldfinch pointed his gun up at the structure, as though someone, or something, was hiding in the branches, or the labyrinth of offshoot oaks and other seedlings. The Leader continued a bit farther. There was a calm silence, no sounds or howls. Goldfinch kept his gun locked on his horizon.

At one point, Goldfinch paused and turned back to the Minister, who stood silhouetted. Then, when he looked ahead of him, he found the impact site, made from what now looked like gunpowder in wooden kegs. Next to the site lay a meticulously sprawled-out dress, the arms of which were outstretched. There seemed to be no wrinkles on the calico-patterned piece of fabric. It was dark and hard to discern, but the dress was purple. Someone had waited around after the blast, preferring to leave a particular message.

As Goldfinch reached down to pick it up, a rolled-up, weathered piece of paper fell from it. He unfurled it, noticing that on the top, two locks of hair were pinned to it. It was evident, too, that the hair was from a negro person.

"What in the name of the Lord?" Solomon exclaimed, his eyes widening, his voice fading.

Chapter Six

The Path

Goldfinch, his rifle strapped to his back, dropped the dress and its other contents on an oaken bench near the fire pit. Minister Mulvane and Solomon stood near their leader, eyeing the package intently.

"You reckon that there's a message?" Solomon asked, visibly nervous.

"We go to the community with this," Goldfinch asserted. "We'll let One have a say in our response."

Minister Mulvane turned around to the smoky remnants of the explosion, the smoke now narrow wisps fighting for a place in the sky. It was a drab gray color, beginning to mesh with the night. He turned back toward Goldfinch. "Doubt Harriet will roll over on this," he said. "Just like the poachers that came through the week the Founders departed. Reckon she gave you a scare then, and she's poised to do so again. She'll threaten you, your leadership. But it goes a step further. She was caring for that boy, the scamp."

"Those poachers never made it to the gate. They sniffed the Founders' trail, is all. They called us names on that thoroughfare." He pointed southward. "What they didn't do is instigate a bloodbath, with a coordinated explosion, mind you. Harriet may have qualms about the way I handle this, but she will acquiesce. I am the chosen leader. Mulvane, gather the villagers."

The Minister rushed off to the row of huts. Goldfinch found his hat and pressed it back atop his head. He thought about this demonstration—the approaching party, the explosions.

We've been spotted. The village is marked on some slaver's map, he thought. *By the looks of it, with Edwin fleeing, slave catchers are to blame.*

His mind continued to race. *Is Edwin running toward these folks? Is he off to find his father?*

Goldfinch fixed his eyes on the hair pinned to the paper. He thought about the flimsy fence with its simple gate. But he had no desire to fortify the place—it went against their very reason for absconding. He spotted Solomon breathing into the chilly air. It was cold enough to form a vapor that rose just like the bursting wooden kegs. Solomon's rifle sat at his back. He breathed heavily then looked at the tufts of hair on the paper.

Then Minister Mulvane, who had just returned, said, "The villagers have arrived."

Goldfinch sent him a painfully irritated and astringent look. "We've rounded you all up again, after that scare, to inform you about our brief investigation beyond the gate." He pointed to the hinged gate, and everyone looked.

"What was that madness?" Matilda called out from the back of the crowd.

Goldfinch ignored this query. He pointed at the pickets on the fence. They were menacing, to an extent, but could be breached with the proper zeal. The gate was feeble. But it was a challenge Goldfinch welcomed. If the British couldn't hold him down in 1812 and the woes of the city did not upend him since, he could manage what may have been an inbred gang of lawless southerners, far from their jurisdiction.

Briefly, he imagined marauders scaling the fence, scraping their flesh on the pickets. In this daydream, he saw Reg, One, and Shepherd charging toward the fence. Then he blinked and was grounded again.

He found the villagers' stares once more. Some observed the dress, others the paper beside it on a stacked rock pile. Shepherd, too, stood at the back of the pack with the Sullivans.

"Someone has delivered a message," Goldfinch said aloud. "I invite One to step up beside me here so we may discuss our response."

One obliged. He was carefully bundled, his frock coat buttoned to the top, only his cravat exposed above it. "Seldom do we encounter a group that can track us down like this," he said. "But I suppose it comes with the territory, the slave-running territory." His voice carried well.

He continued, "Our response should be calculated and deliberated. Let us not be hasty in this. We know not what these people are after, though I have an inkling."

He reached down and grabbed the dress off of its rocky perch. He held it up over his head. "As if this were to deter us from our every day—" He was interrupted by the sound of shoving. Someone was pushing villagers aside to approach One's position.

It was Reg. He unintentionally shoved Minister Mulvane aside while his head was lowered, likely pondering One's statement. Reg immediately grabbed the dress from the elder's hands. As he did so, the nearby paper and the pinned tufts detached from one another and fell to the ground.

"It's my girl. What they done? What they done?" He slowly collapsed. The dress folded over the crook of his elbow, its bottom absorbing the ashen ground. His girls, Regina and Amber, eyes widening, stood behind their father. One of them began to weep.

"I dunno what to do here, Mista Goldfinch," Reg cried. "It's from my girl, my girl they done snatched in Virginia. We best get movin', else I stay behind an' kill them folks. Then ain't none of my other girls gawn make it nowhere."

Goldfinch put the pieces together, and it made sense. The same bounty hunters that snatched Reg's other girl in Virginia had made their way up to northern New Jersey.

"Suppose we keep the rifles handy," Minister Mulvane said.

"Mr. Sullivan, I am terribly sorry to hear these folks are still after you. I'd hoped no one could breach these hills and make the trek," Goldfinch said. He reverted to a type of indifference, unsure of how to respond. Instead of fully embracing the Sullivans, he thought about the communal response.

"We must press on and continue as though nothing's happened. But no one goes outside the gate without a rifle," he said. He pointed at Reg and continued. "I am sorry that this wound cannot heal, but my people need to be safeguarded, and the best way to do that is to have you off the property, at least for a bit."

"This man's taunted by slave hunters and the best you can do is throw him off our property?" Harriet asked. "Shame on you, Goldfinch. I knew all along those Founders were mistaken, picking you for anything." She unfolded her arms and rushed off. Goldfinch gazed at Reg.

"Mista Goldfinch, sir, I dunno about that decision, all due respect," Reg said. "You wanted us here. I know, Solomon done told me so. You heard, he was talkin' to us 'bout his place when he was in the city."

"Something's been lost in the words here," Goldfinch responded. "I only mean for you to stay protected. That must come while you're monitored by someone at the outpost."

At this point, Harriet had slowly crept back up to the crowd. "Goldfinch, you do not speak to our guests like this. They are assets to this place. And you sought them out. You endorsed each one of the Founders' plans. This is a safe haven."

"I hardly need a lecture on the past, Harriet," Goldfinch said firmly. "While we stand here quarreling about rhetoric, these howling fellas could be stringing together attack number two." He looked at One for some sort of affirmation. It did not come. One knew how to feign indifference and play shrewd.

"You let folks prance right up to us last time," Harriet said. "Those damned poachers. And you think just because you're righteous and all, that killing isn't necessary sometimes?"

"You talk down to me again and I'll have you quarantined, cooped up in that toolshed for a week," Goldfinch replied. "And I'm a man of my word."

"You're just always thinking about who's going to do this and that and how we can maintain the innocence of this place. Well, sometimes you need to pull the trigger. Sometimes your eyes need to see the bloodletting. That time has come."

"Do not take out your anger over Edwin with me," Goldfinch answered. "It was an infantile act, taking the boy in so blindly. That's why you were passed up by the Founders when they sought a leader."

Harriet stepped to within inches of Goldfinch's face. Although he was taller than her, Harriet glared up fearlessly into his eyes, partially hidden by shadow from his hat. He maintained firm looks of his own, but she swung her arm back and slapped him across the face. His hat shifted to the side of his head, and the sound of belted skin reverberated off the nearby doors.

"For a man who cannot express the right emotion, you have an awful lot to say, to demand. You best keep your eyes open. You won't be the executive for life," she said.

Goldfinch scowled at Harriet as she concluded the diatribe. She quickly stormed off to her hut again. Goldfinch watched her strut angrily. The pallid tone of skin on the nape of her neck emerged and contrasted with the murky night.

Minister Mulvane watched the interaction closely. Goldfinch could feel his presence. The Leader turned toward Reg and told him to hustle to the huts. Shepherd would take him and his daughters out. "Now," he commanded the fugitive. They agreed and walked a few steps ahead of a now-flustered Shepherd.

"Something about that one you admire, huh, Goldfinch?" Minister Mulvane asked. "I see you looking her way every so often. You were on amicable terms for so long, you and her. I fear things have changed now that Edwin's run off. Some spark that was."

Goldfinch, irritated at hearing the obvious splayed out before him, stepped away. His former wartime self—apathetic and inscrutable—returned.

"Fugitive Act of '93," Shepherd added. "The government is legally required to track down runaway slaves. These men, they'll return."

Minister Mulvane countered this, saying, "Off topic, but important. We'll return to this conversation." He assured his rifle was loaded and moved away from the conversation, his gun pointed toward the front gate. He surveyed the fence— left, right—then followed Shepherd's trail to be sure he returned the Sullivans safely.

The only person remaining beside Goldfinch was Solomon, who had since been quiet through the altercation. By this time, the villagers had scattered. One had walked off toward the rear exit, obviously plotting out some sort of response, or writing one.

"Reckon I'll head back inside, Mista Goldfinch," Solomon said.

"Do stay, though. There are few other members of this village I'd want by my side. Your trek to the city was symbolic. We've entered a new stage. Let us disregard the foolhardy voices of some. She will not bring us down."

Solomon nodded. Goldfinch felt such animosity toward Harriet, but something deep within his belly welcomed it. He thought about her silky, pallid skin beneath the petticoats and various patterned skirts. He wondered how long she would continue the feud. He could not let her just poke and prod like this, though. He needed her on his side. Other than One and the proud Minister Mulvane, she was the only other person Goldfinch feared usurping him.

"Solomon, watch my rear as we find One, just a precaution. I have something in mind." Again, Solomon nodded.

They moved off to find the elder. The night was at about half-strength. There would be a few more hours of darkness. The pair approached the back fence, passing cottages now occupied by villagers. Plumes of smoke slipped out the top of a few chimneys. Some huts were vacant.

Goldfinch recalled what life was like just a few days earlier. He had made his rounds and gathered the horses. He revisited his life before Synod for a moment—repairing picket fences outside Reverend Allen's AME, listening in on the Reverend's or the Founding Mother's conversations.

Now, they did not have to search far and wide for One. He did not stray far, or for long. Goldfinch pushed his door in without knocking and found One building a fire in his hearth. The elder, instead of welcoming them, stood idly, waiting for someone to speak. Goldfinch tilted his head toward the door, in hopes of calling One outside. When One failed to respond, Goldfinch said, "Ignore the fire, step out with me." Eventually One rose to his feet. He was surprisingly agile for his age. When the three stepped out, limiting the noise they made, commencing a quasi-secretive meeting, they spotted Elizabeth and William huddled close near the fire.

When Goldfinch approached her, he found her slumped into William's shoulder, making no effort to greet the Leader. Something was amiss, but Goldfinch could not place it. Eventually, William looked at the three and nodded, a toothless smile forming. He went to speak, or to intimate something, but refrained. Goldfinch stepped even closer, and the flames cast light onto their faces. William was nervous, perspiring, the sweat building on his forehead although the chill was oppressive.

Goldfinch looked from one to the other, then toward his men. One shrugged his shoulders. The tension seemed to have no relation to the runaway mess or the powder keg.

Watching the fire's light dance across the ironworkers' foreheads, Goldfinch said, "What is the meaning of this conclave?"

William tapped his fingers together and looked past the men, into the blank night. "Out with it," Goldfinch barked. "We have these folks on our tail. Do you withhold something valuable?"

"Now that we've proven susceptible this evening, it is best to disclose this before anything worsens," William said.

"Disclose?" Goldfinch repeated.

"Elizabeth is with child," William uttered. The other two men sat on the benches beside the fire, their stares weighing on the Leader.

"You've broken the vow, I see?" Goldfinch responded, peering at Elizabeth. She was always a burly woman, but he never assumed she would be carrying.

She just nodded and leaned farther into the embrace of William's shoulder. She stared at the fire, which leaped back at her with fury, illuminating her face.

"I've anticipated this moment," Goldfinch said.

"As have I," One added.

"Since when?" Goldfinch pressed.

"Six weeks, I'd say," Elizabeth mumbled. She trembled slightly, out of nervousness or from the cold.

"A righteous man could give you lashes for something like this," Goldfinch said. "But on the threshold of civilization and chaos, it can be difficult to abstain." He held out for another moment. "Perhaps this is the beginning of a new chapter. There is so much new life in this place."

"News of this will spread," One said, admonishing Goldfinch. "What do you propose? Founders won't be so lenient."

Goldfinch pondered this for a moment, clearly afflicted. With his attention focused on William, he said, "It's not the proper moment—with marauders stalking the village—but it is best to maintain candor. William, you will be moved from your furnace post. You understand."

The ironworker failed to respond. Instead, he placed a hand on Elizabeth's belly. He then grazed her chin with his forefinger. He was one of the few villagers who did not sport a hat. He had said the forge's soot would tarnish it.

"You understand," Goldfinch repeated. "Should someone ask, you say you were not performing your duties adequately. And that is that."

Goldfinch felt distracted. It was as though Harriet had plotted out this revelation. She would rain down a deluge on him. Goldfinch decided: she was to blame. He breathed angrily, stomping his boot into the earth. A resulting cloud of ashen dust rose up past his ankles.

To William he said, "You're not to advertise this sexual expression. While it will be allowed, all you had to do was simply wait through the winter. Elizabeth's gestation is at risk from these temperatures and those men. You had to wait less than a year after arrival, make sure the infrastructure matched the will. There are still jobs to be done."

He was infuriated. Had Harriet truly orchestrated this? He removed his hat and squeezed the crown. One intervened, placing a hand on Goldfinch's chest. "Nothing more to say this evening, nothing more," he offered. Goldfinch looked him squarely in the eyes. One continued, "This is a separate issue. It's nothing to do with the men you spotted, nothing to concern yourself with."

Goldfinch pointed at William as One led the retreat. The couple watched their leader with wide eyes. "Only a few months. It's loyalty this place needs, not simply abstinence. Loyalty." He spared Elizabeth from much of his tantrum. At last, One calmed him by grabbing the hat from Goldfinch's hands and placing it atop his head again. He patted Goldfinch's chest, yet again. The Leader took the cue and left the scene.

The three men, led by a stirred Goldfinch, returned to the front gate, fearful of what could be lurking just yards away. Goldfinch then heard approaching footsteps. The noise drew nearer—it was Minister Mulvane, protruding from the shadows with his rifle in hand. Soon he stood at their side.

"Solomon, ready a few horses, we are going to escort these trespassers on their way. We'll slip past the explosion site," Goldfinch said. "When you pass those ironworkers, keep them privy to how the iron output will not fluctuate. She'll work, with child."

"Yessuh," Solomon answered, rushing off.

One turned toward Minister Mulvane, right in Goldfinch's view. "We must station ourselves near this gate, ward off anything coming close. I reckon with appalling looks such as ours, nothing will seek refuge in here," One said in jest.

Goldfinch shook his head. The elder continued. "Best we multiply, no? It is hopeless for me, but in a year's time we'll be needing these single-room cottages to be occupied by two."

"This is time to act, not to meddle," Goldfinch responded.

"A first birth," One called out. "It's remarkable."

Minister Mulvane spoke up. "It should wait until tomorrow, but then, we must gather the folks and discuss it. We cannot hide it. Her belly will grow."

"How much have you heard?" Goldfinch asked the Minister.

"As much as I needed to," he responded. "Well, pending whatever wisdom One wishes to impart, I assume we need to act now on this Sullivan affair."

"We wait for Solomon," Goldfinch said, dismissing whatever Minister Mulvane had urged.

"And wait for what?" One countered. His venerable white beard was now even longer. He scratched at it every few minutes.

"I'm acting on this runaway business," Goldfinch replied.

"Under what authority?" One asked stiffly. His cheeriness disappeared.

"I assume you can call it executive authority. But call it what you will," the Leader fired back. "If there's a problem, take it up with Reverend Allen." He headed off, abandoning this feckless conversation.

Using his forefinger and thumb, he whistled. "Mulvane!" he then called out. The Minister was already following him. "Over yonder, Solomon's gathered the horses. We'll ride."

Minister Mulvane kept pace with Goldfinch. He checked for a powder horn and propped his saddlebag over his shoulder. Goldfinch looked back at him as he fidgeted with his rifle, wondering what a spectacle 1812 must have been for the Minister. Chaplain or not, it was still a grisly affair. He acted unofficially for the church at the time, too. Goldfinch had a feeling that he saw combat.

The Minister fumbled with his weapon again. He checked his pockets for shot, the forty-five caliber bullets fired from the Long Rifles. *What a sight*, Goldfinch recognized, *that cleric touting a peacemaker.* The gun looked natural on him, juxtaposed with the pristine clerical collar.

Sporadically, moonlight peeked through the canopy, drawing odd shapes on their foreheads or against their leather boots. Minister Mulvane may have been righteous, but he was not afraid to exact vengeance.

Goldfinch was soon inundated with thoughts of Harriet. She was outspoken and strong-willed. But she had a purpose. Could he extol that? He neared his hut, hustled to the back and reclaimed his rifle. It was loaded but not primed. He grabbed more ammunition. Leaving, he heard the neighs of Synod horses.

Solomon sat on horseback some forty feet off, holding two horses behind him by their reins. When Solomon drew near, Goldfinch recognized his horse, Eder, and mounted. Minister Mulvane did the same. The Leader called Solomon over.

"Friend, ride over to greet our guests. Bring them outside the gate. Follow the footpath to the thoroughfare. Take them a few miles onwards—show them the way. Direct them toward upstate New York and toward Saint James AME Zion Church, Ithaca. They're comfortable with you."

"Mista, I will." He patted the side of his horse, slid his rifle over so he could get in riding position, fastened his saddlebag, and the horse stepped forward. Goldfinch followed his silhouette as Solomon trotted off. The ex-slave stopped at the paddock to round up two other mounts for the runaways—one for Reg, one for Regina and Amber.

Goldfinch turned back to Minister Mulvane and signaled toward the gate. Then he nicked his horse with the lace-ups. When he reached the gate, he dismounted, unhinged it, and pulled the weighty barrier to the side. He turned and saw the Minister trotting close behind. Back atop Eder, Goldfinch galloped from the place. Some feet later, mid-trot, he spotted the hackberry cross—the cross from his dreams.

The path in front of them began to narrow, and the brush scratched against his frock coat. He ducked beneath low-hanging boughs. The footpath wound through dense Ramapough flora. It was still miles to the closest thoroughfare. He would travel out that far and clear the way for Solomon. He would repel any trespassers in his way, too, should it come to that. He wanted his friend to travel subtly, by moonlight, off the main trails.

Eventually, they reached the intersection of the nearly hidden footpath and the more highly trafficked avenue. Minister Mulvane's horse neighed. Goldfinch gripped his rifle and studied the road.

"Path seems clear. Is this a similar route you've taken to obtain the rifles?"

"Man of God can't lie, Goldfinch," Mulvane said. "I have ridden these paths. Arms deals, they're peculiar transactions. Anonymity trumps all."

"I would simply like to know the optimal route, for our runaways," Goldfinch urged.

"I've taken this road plenty a time," Minister Mulvane confirmed. "We'd need to find our way to the Paterson-Hamburg route, which is, by most accounts, a smooth, inexpensive journey. Toll-free if you know how to ride it correctly." He nodded and looked toward Goldfinch.

A noise came from the same direction they had traveled from. Horses approached, and a raucous whistle preceded them. Like the sound of hooves, this whistle penetrated the brumal air.

The two quickly rode behind a few nearby pines. Goldfinch whistled back. Minister Mulvane appeared bewildered at the giveaway. Goldfinch shrugged, gave his reins to the Minister, and hopped from his animal. He aimed his rifle around. Minister Mulvane stayed on horseback.

Emerging from the dense brush, at the head of a single-file line of three horses, was Shepherd. Goldfinch recoiled a bit, hardly letting his confusion show. He thought it'd be Solomon. Shepherd pulled his horse off to the side, and Regina and Amber sat on horseback behind him. He shrugged his shoulders in Goldfinch's direction.

"What? Why?" Goldfinch called.

"There's no simple explanation. Basically, it's fatherly instinct. Wants to protect his young," Shepherd said.

"Reg? He stayed behind?"

"Has he snuck off?" Minister Mulvane asked from atop his horse.

"Easy, gentlemen. Allow me to explain," Shepherd said. "I showed them back to their huts, past the gate. It was a sort of frenzy, after the explosion and all, Reg seeing his girl's dress splayed out like that." He paused. "Solomon was prepared to head off with them. Reg just stopped in his tracks, before he got on his horse. He said, 'I can't continue like this, forsakin' my girl.' He planted his feet firmly on the ground beneath him. Said he would let his girls head on up to Ithaca. He wouldn't be shaken. So, I told him I could take them. Solomon agreed, knew I had a firmer grasp of the northern territory. I could tell Reg found me trustworthy."

"So far, no powder kegs to speak of. Should be a clear path," Goldfinch declared. "Haven't heard as much as an owl's hoot."

Shepherd pressed on undeterred. "He didn't hesitate for a moment, though on the inside I suppose he did. Solomon had arrived with the horses. He was just watching intently. He's a good man, you know. Reg insisted I take the girls to safety. He said Synod's great and all, but New Jersey's too close for comfort, even up here in the mountains. The part that moved me followed. He said, 'I have to find my girl. Won't sleep a wink until I do.' So, Solomon stayed behind with him. I took the girls out—down the same course I've taken dozens of times on your missions. And here we are." He spread his arms out wide.

"Well, we've flushed out this whole area. No foes to speak of," Minister Mulvane called down to them. "Reckon we ride back home tonight. No need to find a scuffle this evening, what with that explosion and all."

"Suppose it won't be a Bunker Hill standoff today," Goldfinch said, patting Eder's side. "Hard to believe Reg would proceed without his girls. I'm an abolitionist and all, but I still fail to see the reasoning. Why leave them in the care of mostly white men?"

"You can care for these girls, can you not?" Shepherd wondered. "If not, you're as hollow as a rotted stump. I suppose Reg's move was impulsive. Man saw the plucked hair of his child, along with her removed garments. Reckon any righteous man would exact revenge. And this righteous man, I suppose, would be forgiven in the eyes of the Lord. Plus, doesn't hurt none to have faith in the system."

Minister Mulvane's response to all this was not forthcoming. Goldfinch exhaled. "Suppose I'd agree. I can only hope our spooky tale did not instill much skepticism in the man. It would only eat at him, bit by bit."

Then he looked at Regina and Amber, and finally to Shepherd. "Best to be on your way, then. Keep them safe."

"I'd go about it no other way," Shepherd confirmed.

"We shall see you in a few weeks, then," Minister Mulvane called to Shepherd. "By the time you return, we'll have purchased the Synod land already and be hosting Reverend Allen for tea." The night seemed to hide most of the Minister's amiable features, but the white collar shone through his silhouette.

Shepherd whisked the reins and trotted off. As he did so, he whistled to the girls. Regina and Amber nicked their horses, and they followed along. The party moved past Goldfinch and Minister Mulvane. "Safe passage, girls," the Minister said evenly.

From afar, Shepherd shouted, "If you're purchasing the land that means other people are close—they've managed to shoehorn their way in. Now then, let's keep that from happening, shall we?"

The whistling pines spoke to them, swaying in a delicate breeze. Then, without saying a word, the two men rode back to Synod.

Chapter Seven

Sunday Service

Back near their territory, Goldfinch and Minister Mulvane spotted Solomon and Reg outside the gate. Almost directly above Solomon sat the wooden cross bound to the hackberry—a refined image with moonbeams and shadows. From afar, the shadows won the day. Goldfinch spotted Solomon's silken hat.

· The two men came to a halt. "We've seen them off," Minister Mulvane said to Reg. He placed a hand over his heart and modestly bowed to the girls' father.

"I, uh, reckon I'm stickin' with you gentlemen, least for the time bein'," Reg said.

"Teach this man his way around the Long Rifle, Solomon," Goldfinch demanded, his eyes on Reg. "It's our weapon of choice. Well, not so much choice, as availability." At his periphery, he noticed Minister Mulvane subtly nod.

"Mista Goldfinch, 'ready know my way 'round that there rifle," Reg responded. "Simple with the lock, the small bullets and all. It got some range, too."

Goldfinch thought about the prospects of Reg extending his stay. He then called for his people to gather around the fire.

"The mettle of this village has been tested," he called out. "But if there's one detail I've grasped during our time here, our trip north, it is that you have fortitude, a will to remove yourselves from that world. You will endure. You will succeed. We've been greeted by highwaymen, who sparked that fire. We will wage this as a battle against them, against the illusory world. Reg Sullivan has decided to allow us to guide his children northward. He's agreed to stay behind and combat those responsible for abducting his daughter. These people will be stopped."

Some villagers scurried off toward their homes. Matilda and Sophie were two of them. They had become used to battening the hatches. But Harriet *led* this exodus. As she fled, she bumped Goldfinch's side. The momentum of the contact turned him toward her. He studied her as she looked back with beady eyes. He watched as her threadbare frock coat slid side to side during her trek home. Somehow, he thought he spotted her smiling, flaunting her paralyzing charm. He felt as though she practically stopped, turned, and said, "You got eyes for me, huh?" He shook his head hurriedly, remembering just how ornery she had really become.

Among those who stayed were Elizabeth, One, Minister Mulvane, and Solomon. The Leader thought he heard the group speaking about conspiracies, outlandish theories about their attackers. Goldfinch approached Elizabeth. No one was within earshot. He peered at her, looking deeply into her eyes. The two acknowledged one another and then, to open conversation, walked toward the fence.

She must have understood that she was let off easy, without embarrassment in front of the village. Goldfinch was in an advantageous position, at least at that point, and could tell his flock when he felt it right. Her pregnancy was a pressing issue, though not as much as it should have been at the time.

"Is there a reason for withholding?" Goldfinch asked her. "Did you intend to flee before anyone spotted your birthing belly?"

"Not entirely," she answered. "What with the tension and all, and I had my job to do. Just didn't get around to it."

"If 'work' is what you claim to be doing at the furnace," Goldfinch fired.

"You've seen my molds. You've got bullets for your barrels, no?" she said firmly.

"I've seen the results, I've seen. But it was the vow—which was so integral," Goldfinch admonished.

"I—I did not intend to be with child. W-we fell in love and—"

"Do not pretend I am devoid of feelings, Elizabeth," Goldfinch interrupted. "I understand the urges. The rule was at the behest of the Founders, to provide stability. I too, have been in love. I'll seek it out again one day, you see?"

"He will be a ray of light for this place, the firstborn villager—"

"I understand," Goldfinch conceded. "Just be wary of the medical shortage and the biting winter months."

"I believe we are prepared," she confirmed. "But with William banished from the furnace and all, we cannot bond like we should."

Goldfinch ignored this. "Harriet, Harriet, she will care for you." He was lost in thought. He could tell that Elizabeth was becoming emboldened. "Could she? A midwife? Ah, yes, I will demand it," he confirmed to himself.

"Demands can be met by deaf ears, Mr. Goldfinch," Elizabeth warned.

"And 'exile' is not so preposterous a word," he retorted. "Just do not get tangled in the mire of lust."

"At forty, you haven't eloped before?"

"Off with you and your foul tongue now, miss. And don't you sulk about my having changed William's position. It is a destined-to-fail courtship."

Elizabeth laughed bitingly, turning her back to Goldfinch. He clenched his hands together and tried to clear his mind. But all he found in these depths was the powder keg. He tensed further. Although she could no longer hear, he said quietly, "Another jab and we'll bait those highwaymen in. Won't be wooden kegs they detonate next time." Lost in thought, he believed she had gone. But she returned and confronted the Leader.

"Who will you appoint as William's successor at the forge? Your love interest?"

"Pardon me?" he asked, taken aback. His brows angled toward a frown. She did not continue. "You'll work alone, up until maternity. Your output will be steady. I'll have eyes on you."

Her lips twitched slightly, rabbit-like, as though she was preparing some fiery retort. Instead, she kicked up some dirt which landed on Goldfinch's boots. This time, she left and did not return.

He walked back to the fire pit and found Minister Mulvane and Solomon. "I'm turning in, gentlemen," he told them. "I urge you to rest for tomorrow. We will go ahead with your sermon, Minister. Ten a.m. Tell the villagers to gather outside the nave. Solomon, take the night's watch. We need eyes on the woods, now more than ever."

"Yessuh, can count on me for that." Solomon stretched out his arms, yawned, and turned toward the gate.

"Eyes to our rear as well," Goldfinch added. Then he returned home. On his walk, he was so fatigued that his memory failed him. When his head hit the pillow, he was already seconds into a kaleidoscopic dream. He still wore his clothing. He had forgotten to remove his hat. In the night, the brim of it slowly folded down, shading his eyes. It was as though it concealed what he'd witnessed.

**

Darkness had fallen. He tried to recall a brighter time—light falling on Synod, green vegetation ingesting the sunrays. But he could not tack the image to the village. He was restless. He was outside holding a rifle toward the fire. He turned toward the rear gate and saw a collection of shovels leaning against the oaken fence. Back toward the fire, the wolf apparition, the same one that had haunted his earlier dream, was glaring at him through the flames. His red eye pierced these flames. The gaze felt hot, burning against his cheeks.

An entirely different scene soon lay before him. The ground was snowy, and the boughs were covered in powder. There was a late-winter air about it. He looked ahead and saw a row of horses, each animal hauling hundreds of pounds—people and supplies.

Goldfinch felt the uneven motions of a ride atop a horse, and as he looked down, he saw the legs and neck of his Lipizzan. There was a light snowfall stashed on his saddlebag. He looked off to the side and saw the Founders. He heard the words Unitarians, Trinitarians, consubstantiality. He thought he heard Lyman speaking about the grit and wherewithal of the congregants. The man seemed to say they were not bootless city folk. Lyman then trotted ahead.

Goldfinch rode beside Cartwright and Allen, who spoke of slavery, the intricate system of trails north, and sanctifying this new land. Goldfinch looked ahead to see One on his mount, which was flecked with white blotches. The stern man barked orders. Then, surprisingly, the Founders whispered and stared back at One. They repeated, amongst themselves, "No, another must rule." Goldfinch wondered how the regal One could be so unqualified.

***

By the look of the sun, it was about nine a.m. Goldfinch rose and dressed. He took a few moments to heat a new batch of coffee and gnaw at a hardened, leftover corn cake.

When he left the hut, he found the community gathering for the Sunday mass. It was normally a joyous time of the week, when everyone could set aside their labors to pray in their very own house of God. Harriet was in the crowd, and even when she spotted Goldfinch, she did not extend herself for a hello. Minister Mulvane was at the head of the crowd, clasping a Bible. His clothes were pristine and well-starched. Inside, the Minister rang a handheld bell to silence the crowd. Goldfinch filed in. He passed Solomon, who was patrolling the place, his rifle extended outward. Goldfinch placed an arm on the ex-slave's shoulder and whispered, "Lend yourself to this. Protect the gate."

He then slipped past Shepherd, who manned the church's door, rifle also at the ready. The Leader sat in the rearmost pew. Minister Mulvane called the service into session.

There were practitioners of two faiths present, Presbyterians, and Methodists. Minister Mulvane followed a loose liturgical format. The denominations differed on issues such as church governance, justification by faith, and social issues, but they were still wholly riding behind the Christian standard, believing that Jesus Christ is Lord and Savior.

Minister Mulvane called for those in the pews to stand in the call to worship. Then he spoke, and it gradually became more melodic. He was reading from "Love Divine, All Loves Excelling," a 1747 hymn written by Charles Wesley centering on John 4:16. Then he led the unison prayer: "You know each of us by name, O God, and in your sight we have found favor, yet our minds cannot comprehend the vision of your glory or the vastness of your love. Grant that as we glimpse your greatness, reflected in your many gifts, we may always return to you the praise that is yours alone. We ask this through Jesus Christ our Lord. Amen."

Goldfinch fiddled with his hat. Minister Mulvane led a smooth meeting. He asked his congregants to pass the peace. Goldfinch watched as Harriet patted Adam's hand. Reg, in his pew, looked restless but offered peace to William. Alone in his pew, Goldfinch had no one to offer the peace. He exhaled and continued to prod the hat.

"Next, I'd like to move on to lessons for this date," Minister Mulvane said. "Instead of preaching the firm stances of the church or reading from scripture, I would like to bring up someone who has, thus far, guided us both spiritually and politically, making this Utopia even better than anything we could find in literature."

Goldfinch knew Minister Mulvane was speaking about him. He felt he deserved recognition following the powder keg explosion. Leading the girls out to the AME. He cleared his throat, preparing to say a word to his people.

"This person has bridged the gap between denominations on these grounds. He's helped call us to one church every Sunday. Please welcome up to the pulpit, the community elder, One."

One rose hastily from his pew near the front. Even in his older age, he sported a youthful exuberance. He took his time making it to the pulpit. He looked around then spoke. "Minister Mulvane asked me up here today to share a lesson with you all. It is a lesson we all know but never hurts to repeat. It is the story of our genesis, here on these sacred grounds.

"Since our arrival here in early April, we have surprised one another. Yet most importantly, we have *not* surprised the Lord. He has known, since the outset, since He intervened, setting our Founders up with one another, that this place would prevail. We have proven His point thus far."

He paused for a moment to clear his throat. Goldfinch thought about the account One would write of this soliloquy of his. "We arrived here with little. We still have little. However, we have managed to build, extol God, and harbor runaway men and children who sought salvation. We are that salvation. We will continue to deliver ourselves, and our friends, from evil."

One lumbered on with his speech. Goldfinch dipped his head low and shut his eyes. He still remained conscious, though. He listened as One recalled parts of the congregants' journey. The horses had been rounded up, tied to a half-decayed hitching rail. They'd arrived somewhere near that forsaken Revolutionary-era village. Goldfinch remembered examining the meadow, the potential it stored beneath the heavy snow. And each traveler had some pertinent skill. His was woodworking. He remembered felling the trees, gathering the wood, and erecting the huts in a few short months.

He recalled hand-carving the fence pickets. The Founders had remained huddled up, pondering ways to distinguish themselves and the place. The Founders' subsequent suggestion was bold. Their consensus was helpful, though their hands were not, during construction. They had rested peacefully as Goldfinch toiled in the elements. But still, they had said, "We shall make arrangements for firearms to be imported from various contacts Mulvane has cultivated."

Eventually, spring had come, late as it was. Flowers were in bloom, and the boughs were at their early-season beauty. Cartwright and Minister Mulvane rode off on regular trips to some undisclosed locale. They had returned, each time, with weapons—the Pennsylvania Long Rifles. While these guns assimilated into communal life, some of the villagers questioned the endorsed violence. But the weapons were protectors of the faith.

Then, back in the church, Goldfinch reopened his eyes and watched the elder continue his speech. The man seemed poised at the front of the church, his finest clothing on display. "We do what we must. Solomon has shown that with his southward journey. We will continue our fervent pursuit of unity among God's children. So be it if we must pull back rifle hammers to do so." He smirked and looked at Minister Mulvane and Goldfinch. He was about to continue speaking when something disturbed the tranquility.

Solomon hustled inside, followed by Shepherd. They found Goldfinch's spot in the pew. Solomon said, "Best you rise up now, Mista Goldfinch. You'll want to see this."

Goldfinch left with these two guards before the others realized what had gone amiss. Out near the gate, Goldfinch heard what he assumed was the gate cracking and crumbling. There was a ping of metal against the oak wood.

Instinctively, Goldfinch slid to the church exit, warning his people to stay down. He placed his head a few inches outside the door and looked toward the gate. It was too blurry to make out, but he was sure of something, there were people by the fence. Goldfinch left this spot near the mouth of the church. Minister Mulvane was caught off guard still, holding his Bible. The Leader was out back behind the church in a few steps. He gripped the rifle he had deposited there. He checked his pockets for powder and shot. The rifle was loaded already.

The gunpowder horn was tethered to his belt. He also checked for the knife sheathed at his ankle.

He was then exposed—in the open. His guards had scattered a bit, making their way toward the noises. Goldfinch approached the gate, hugging his body against the fence. He jolted his rifle from side to side, watching his flanks, trying to identify the lurking figures. When he was about fifty yards from them, he heard a sound he knew he'd never forget. It was a god-awful screech, a shrieking sound that must have echoed up the mountain. A gunshot had burst out, a cloud of smoke spewed from the firing weapon. A horse then fell near the paddock, crying its last cries. Goldfinch strained his eyes to make it clearer. The horse resisted its fate for a moment but then lay still. The other animals acted out their visceral response—jumping the paddock fence and fleeing the scene. Most took refuge near the back quadrant, by the rear gate. A few led a charge right through the fence, escaping off into the hills.

Goldfinch carried on, attempting to dismiss the fact that one of the horses had just been dropped—it couldn't have been the Lipizzan!

The Leader heard pattering feet behind him. He examined the sound quickly, even militaristically. It was Solomon, who would now rally behind his friend. He held his gun at the ready, though Goldfinch knew he was no shot. A few steps behind him was Reg, also carrying a weapon.

Goldfinch went on, the left side of his coat brushing up against the splintered fence. When he was within earshot of the folks who had arrived, he heard a rowdy voice call out, "Reckon ya'll betta run for the hills, while ya can." There was then an uproarious howl. It came out of human vocal cords. Squinting, Goldfinch focused on the gate. Men sat on horseback on the far side of it. One was off his horse, holding an ax. Two fence posts in front of him sat demolished on the ground. The man responsible quickly spotted Goldfinch along the fence. He took his rifle and fired up into the sky.

"There he is, boss," the trespasser yelled. "Over yonda."

Goldfinch froze, still comfortably shrouded by natural barriers.

Chapter Eight

Renly Picket

"To hell with you, heathens," Goldfinch shouted. It took only a moment for this approaching posse to fire their weapons. Goldfinch couldn't tell if it was just a scare tactic or if one of the men was truly hoping to annihilate him.

Goldfinch, Solomon, and Reg kept their heads low as the bullets passed overhead. The Leader looked back and found Solomon's hands trembling on his rifle. Goldfinch turned back toward the gate, where he found the intruders reloading.

Goldfinch scanned the village, his eyes pausing at the huts. The villagers, it seemed, had stayed inside the church. Goldfinch detected movement through the church window. He hoped they had fastened the lock on the wooden door, at least.

This discovery made Goldfinch's goal simple: protect those inside the church. Protect the fragility of his village. He motioned to Solomon and Reg, then began crawling—slithering—across the raw earth, which did not yet retain the bite of a mature winter. He had witnessed a late-season blizzard on the group's journey to Synod. He knew how the ground could become a tundra.

Goldfinch could tell that the intruders saw him moving in the broad daylight. He picked up speed and rose to a crouch behind a tree. By this time, the guns were reloaded, and that piercing howl once again ripped through the premises. Immediately, Goldfinch was left with gooseflesh, recalling his earlier dreams of the conflagrant wolf.

He turned back toward his men and urged them to stay put, but Solomon did not listen. It seemed he had built up the courage to shadow Goldfinch. The Leader shook his head but monitored the gate to see if Solomon could safely make it alone. When he realized it would be close, Goldfinch lunged for his rifle. He retrieved it, already loaded, and fired off a round toward the fence. The bullet hit an oaken post right in front of the first man to dismount, the fellow with the ax. The wood splintered up into the air, and the ax man yelped as he leaped for cover. Goldfinch turned back to see that Solomon had reached his destination behind the narrow tree burgeoning with autumnal color. It was the crabapple tree the villagers adored and ate beneath. Some, like One, even painted it. While the mayhem had Goldfinch's mind cluttered, he still knew that the tree was not wide enough to shield two grown men from gunfire. Still, they made the most of every inch of bark. The intruders' attention seemed to be focused elsewhere. They were moving in on the church.

"Boss, 'm thinkin' our boys—sorry, them gals, too—are held up in that there church," the ax-wielding marauder blurted out.

Goldfinch studied the men near the gate to see which of the scoundrels was the Leader of the pack. The ax man looked off to his left, to the center of Synod's gate. There, a man, fidgeting with his rifle after firing, seemed to hesitate and then looked back toward the other one. His white hair jettisoned out from the sides of a buff-colored Marlow top hat. The more Goldfinch peered, the more he was inclined to assume that this was the Leader. Then, Solomon tugged at Goldfinch's frock coat.

"That there's our man, prolly startin' up them fires in the woods, callin' Edwin out to do they dirty work," he said.

"Your words couldn't be truer, Solomon," Goldfinch said swiftly.

"Best we look back for Reg. Don't ya think they'd be comin' after 'im?"

"Why, Solomon, the man's right behind us. We sure aren't going to sit back and let these twisted folk destroy this place."

Then they saw the white-haired man point at the church.

"Take out windows first, then fire where them support beams ain't," he called out to his cronies.

The man with the ax and the strapped rifle took a few steps inside the village. The closer he got, the clearer Goldfinch could see him. He was the spitting image of a rat. His cheeks seemed to point inward toward his nose, his brow bones arched circularly over his eyes and his brows matched his blackened eye color. His clothes were ragged, like slivers of dark paint. His boots were squeaky, and he carried an old, probably stolen, Charleville musket. The rat man was fixated on Goldfinch's location and advanced a few steps forward.

Goldfinch watched Solomon press his body toward the ground. His chin stuck to a small pile of accumulating leaves. Reg was nestled behind a small earthwork at their rear.

"Stay put, friend," Goldfinch called to Reg.

"Reckon so," the runaway answered.

"There, in that winda over yonder. C'mon now boy, look close," the old man with the Marlow hat said to another one of his men. He forcefully pushed this other man ahead. Just like the rat man, the other crony stepped forward.

Goldfinch pressed powder and a cast bullet down the barrel and placed charge powder on the flintlock pan. He was ready to pull back the hammer when the old fella chirped loudly again, possibly to stall or distract Goldfinch and Solomon behind the tree.

"That there boy, little nigger boy, he came right in here and made fools of ya'll, now didn'e?" This seemed to be an announcement, but one Goldfinch couldn't ignore.

"If you're talkin' 'bout our boy Edwin, why yes, we sure were a bit taken aback by his fleeing and all. My sense is that he didn't have much choice. You folks probably snatched up his kin down south," Goldfinch yelled back from the crabapple tree. It was impulsive but felt right.

The old man immediately spotted Goldfinch's position. He pointed the final crony to head around the fence, halfway up the hill beside it, to reach Goldfinch and the others at their flank.

Goldfinch looked out toward the fence and in place of the old man's warped, wrinkly face, he saw the wolf's, sewn onto the intruder's. It mouthed a couple of words that Goldfinch could not comprehend. He then seemed to return to reality.

He frowned, his heart heavy. Right at his fingertips, there was much to balance—the fate of Solomon, and the fate of Reg, whom these people were after. He had to protect the church where his villagers were holed up. He had to guess whether Minister Mulvane was planning his way out of there.

The old man's posse was dead silent, making only crunching noises in the freshly dropped leaves as they advanced. The closest person was about thirty yards from Goldfinch, with little cover. Still, Goldfinch did not want to expose himself, and thus Solomon and even Reg behind him.

"Hey there, fella," the old man called out from his position along the gate. "That boy didn' need an ounce a coaxin' from me—we picked 'im up in Paterson. Said he found one your niggers down there, told 'im right where to go. We just upped and followed his trail. Paid him a silver coin or two. Right is right. Boy put in a hard day's work. Reckon I'm gettin' this all straight, hidden leader?"

"Only thing straight is the path on out of here, and you best take it now," Goldfinch responded, his bodyweight pushing against the tree trunk.

"Ah, you see, what us bounty hunters do is, we don't take *no* for an answer. We's up and take our property on back. Like we gawn take Mr. Reggie Sullivan and his nigger girls back to North Carolina."

"You won't find those ladies here."

"Let us find out for sure after we pry open that there church door," the old man bellowed.

At that instant, the old man hesitated no longer, and spun skillfully in his tight trousers, his frock coat twirling accordingly. He had a handgun at the ready and fired it toward the crabapple tree.

The bullet pierced a hole in the fringe of Goldfinch's frock coat and then moved out into the woods. Solomon rose to fire at the old man, but Goldfinch patted him back down into place. The old man took on a hopping gait toward the church. Goldfinch could hear leaves ruffling beyond the fence to his left, through the dense pine forest.

While it felt like the marauders were closing in on them, Goldfinch still held his composure or as much of it as he could muster. Again, there came a ruffling in the trees. It was the old fella's other foot soldier, out to flank Goldfinch and company.

A woman's scream came from the church house. Goldfinch could not determine whose it was. He stood up and slid out from behind the tree and turned his gun toward the rat man who was hiding some yards ahead. Goldfinch lowered himself to one knee, repositioned the rifle and fired it off. Goldfinch's bullet hit the man's upper leg.

Goldfinch heard the rat man call out from his new spot on the ground, blood trickling from the wound. Goldfinch approached him stealthily, made sure there was no barrel pointed at him, and kicked the gun away. Before finishing the man off, he ventured down the village's center path, on the old man's heels. He was off of him by about forty yards.

Goldfinch kept a careful eye on the other bounty hunter who was shoved into this newly christened battlefield. He had abandoned his spot at the opposite flank and was taking up near the old man. Goldfinch saw the frustrated old man nimbly reload his gun while walking the open path to the church. He had a bullet and some powder at the ready and pressed it into the barrel of an old, Queen Anne pocket pistol. He was doing this with both hands, under cover of his other soldier. When he was ready, he hardly even took the time to aim before firing at the church walls.

This must have been the stimulus Minister Mulvane needed. Before the old man, probably about seventy, had time to reload or draw another gun, the Mulvane stepped out from behind the church. Goldfinch watched in horror as the witless crony took aim at Minister Mulvane. The Minister countered with a hollow look of his own.

Once the standoff ensued, Goldfinch retreated some. He was still not too far off from the crabapple tree, hidden behind some brush. There, he heard the distinct sound of a hammer being cocked. But he did not need to do much of anything, because, like Goldfinch, Solomon had reacted. In one fluid motion, the ex-slave aimed his rifle at the crowded tree line and pulled the trigger. Goldfinch imagined him closing his eyes and puffing his cheeks out as he fired.

The sound of a bullet encasing itself in flesh came a second later, then a few seconds of groans. Next, the seemingly hefty man tumbled down the hill until he crashed face-first into the rooted fence posts, dead.

Solomon stood, apparently aware of the bleeding rat look-alike just ahead of him. He rushed to take his place beside Goldfinch. Reg, too, jumped from his spot at the mounded earthwork and hustled toward Synod's leader. In a tight procession, the three Synod villagers then marched onward, toward the church, where the old man was stopped.

Ahead of Goldfinch, Minister Mulvane held his rifle up sturdily, in the face of one pointed back at him. The old man stood behind the witless crony, his arms folded, gun in hand, smiling. Goldfinch quickly looked across the horizon and saw movement inside the church. The villagers, peeking through the shattered glass window, were frenzied by the approaching gunmen.

Goldfinch picked up his pace little by little. From plain view, it seemed that Adam had cornered everyone inside the church. Within a few seconds, he was the only one standing near the window and door. From afar, Goldfinch saw the farmer rear back. Nothing happened. He reappeared in the church window, holding what looked like one of Minister Mulvane's Bibles. He grasped it with two hands then turned away. It appeared that he was not aware of the standoff between Minister Mulvane and the others just outside. He kicked the church door open, startling the gunmen who were standing rigidly, at an impasse, just outside.

"Adam, return inside at once, we've got rifles on the men—" Goldfinch shouted.

Adam paid little attention to his leader's comment and took two steps out the door. "Please halt, men. Spare these people for—"

The witless gunman fired, his bullet hitting Adam in the head. His body folded and then he collapsed to the ground, smacking his face on the fall. The Bible fell beside him. From yards away, Goldfinch heard the piercing sound of the skull cracking against the ground. Screams echoed off the whitewashed walls of the little church.

Minister Mulvane immediately turned and fired his rifle at the gunman's chest. The man toppled over.

The old man did not drop his unloaded gun but begrudgingly raised his hands into the air. As he did so, another handgun became visible in a holster at his side.

Then, Goldfinch was at the scene. He walked up from behind the aged intruder and snatched both handguns from him, shoving him to the ground.

"You're a ways too old to be out here doing the devil's work," Goldfinch said with authority.

"Reckon somebody best get along doin' it," the old man answered as he recovered from the spill.

"What's your name?"

"Renly Picket, folks call me Ren—besides them niggers, they cain't dare speak to me."

"Slavery is dyin' my good friend," Goldfinch countered. "It's about time you backward, dim-witted fools understood that."

"You cain't tell me you *don't* believe the nigger's the dim-witted fool," Ren said. "I get paid mighty fine money to come up here to these shit states, take them niggers back to bondage. Where they belong, you ask me."

"You're just a man of your times, Ren. A man of your times. And a man of your geography. It sure is sad to see southern folks so tangled up in this mess. Some of us northern folk, too," Goldfinch replied. There were still three guns pointed at Ren—Minister Mulvane had since reloaded.

"You best release me now to my kin—plantation owner down in North Carolina. My baby brother, Mr. Steven Picket. This here'd be a crime, you do anything to me." He flared out his chest.

"Quiet now, Ren," Goldfinch ordered.

"I's just actin' on principle, the principle that harborin' slaves *is* a crime. It's a crime punishable by a *five*-hundred-dollar fine. Agent can take back his property in any of these United States or territories. I bet you understand some legislation there, mister. Act of Congress, 1793."

"The name's Goldfinch. But you won't have to remember that for too long, where you're headed."

As the conversation heightened, Goldfinch heard the church door creak. Someone approached. It was Harriet, still looking fine in her Sunday dress.

"Goldfinch, after all, why don't you introduce this fella to the man he was seeking?" she suggested. "Mr. Sullivan, come on down here."

Goldfinch nodded in Reg's direction, and so he inched his way forward, still holding his rifle. Reg was too afraid to look Ren directly in the eyes. The old man was supine, looking at the villagers.

As Reg made himself visible, Ren called out, "There's that dark-skinned monkey we was after. You belong to Steven. You *and* your girls."

"I's a member of this fine community now. They took me right in, even taught me how to be kind," Reg said evenly.

"You know what your place is you filthy—"

Reg stomped on his face with the heel of his boot. Then again. He looked over at Goldfinch, as though ashamed of what he had done. The leader could only *assume* that the two had a bloody past.

Ren tried to sit up. One of his teeth came loose, and he spit it, along with a mouthful of blood, onto the ground.

The old man continued to talk. "That's the whippin' you'll get when you're tied back up to that post in the Carolinas. Dirty ni—"

This time, Reg took the butt of his rifle and clubbed the man across the face with it. Goldfinch could hear the cheekbones shatter. Amazingly, the man stayed conscious.

"My girl. One you took in Virginia. Where's she?" Reg demanded.

"The dark whore? She's back in chains where she belongs," Ren blurted, then guffawed. It appeared painful to laugh, but he did it nonetheless. He slowly reached into his pocket and grabbed an item, then held it up so that he wouldn't be shot on the spot. "See this here coin? That's part of what I got from my baby brotha for huntin' her down. That hair we left here, that's just us toyin' with ya. Hell, you know, boy, that if I turn up missin', there'll be plenty other slave catchers after ya, to put you right back. And your girls, I know they're hidin' 'round here somewheres."

"Enough of this talk," Harriet shouted. "Reg, go up over to the gate and show these fellas why you stayed behind while your girls got to safety."

Reg nodded. He gathered himself for a moment then marched upwards, along the path in the middle of Synod. After about fifty yards, he came to within a few feet of the entrance, with its measly wooden gate. A few feet from there lay the rat man. Goldfinch followed.

Reg walked up to the man, on the brink of losing consciousness from blood loss in his leg, and stood right over him. Reg took a deep breath, and with little hesitation, fired into the rat man's head. Reg did not take the time to even look at his kill. Nor did he bask in it. He turned back and glared down at Ren, then stood alone.

***

By this time, Minister Mulvane had transported the old, injured bounty hunter up to the spot of the rat man's body. Elizabeth had run to Adam's lifeless body. She held him for a moment, specks of blood gathering on her white shirt.

Soon after, One made his way up the path, toward the gate. Goldfinch heard him bickering aloud, and so did not stop to pay him any mind. However, One stepped ahead and called for Goldfinch. Harriet seemed to watch the Leader closely—he felt her eyes on him. She watched as he tilted his rifle down and took a few steps toward the elder.

"You must've seen what's happened to Adam," Goldfinch exclaimed.

"Goldfinch, I've decided that this man's to be taken to the hackberry before he's released, if that's what you prefer," One said. "Whether you maim him, or chastise him, it is largely your call."

"The hackberry," Goldfinch said softly. "It's perfect."

Goldfinch knew that Harriet had overheard much of this brief discourse. She glared at Goldfinch, apparently trying to gauge what he was about to do. "You best be over that damn pacifist nonsense," she called out to him. "I know what's inside you, Goldfinch."

Ignoring her, Goldfinch grabbed Ren and shoved him toward the village gate. "Onward, bounty hunter."

Minister Mulvane, Solomon, and Harriet followed Goldfinch to the hackberry, where nestled visibly on the trunk was the ten-foot cross.

"Stay behind, Reg, this is *our* burden to bear, you see?" Goldfinch ordered. "You've done your share. And you've done it admirably, I'd say."

Reg started on toward the back end of the village, out the rear exit, to his escape shelter in the forest.

Goldfinch prodded Ren with his rifle, pushing the man to a few lengths beyond the Synod gate. The injured man had managed to go on foot. "That's about right, bounty hunter," Goldfinch said, eyeing him up with a hateful glare.

"You gawn have your nigger take care a bin'iss for ya?" Ren said, spitting blood onto the ground. "Or you gawn let me off, like that old man said?"

"You heard the damned conversation?" Minister Mulvane asked the bounty hunter, still gathering his breath from the walk over.

"Don't cha worry none, preacher," Ren replied. "We had our choice, you'da been dead with them niggers. Always them collared folks gettin' in too deep."

"How do you expect to make a fair living off such heinous bloodshed?" Minister Mulvane queried.

Ren snickered, his dogged eyes locked on the Minister.

"Enough," Goldfinch called out. "Now, take a few steps toward the tree right in front of you, Ren. Take a gander, up there." He pointed, to direct the old man.

Ren obliged, picking his head up to look at the hackberry. The motion was obviously painful. "Big ol' goddamn cross, there."

Before the aged bounty hunter had a second to gather himself again, Goldfinch pointed his rifle at him. He could hear Harriet gasp at this. Goldfinch assumed that she felt it was out of character. The Leader pressed the rifle to the man's cheek, the muzzle molding a circular indentation on his face.

This bounty hunter's a tough old buzzard, Goldfinch thought. He slowly cocked the hammer back. He inhaled sharply and closed his eyes, letting the moment of exhalation cleanse him. Then he sharply lifted the gun and fired up into the blue morning sky. He began to walk from the scene.

"One says we let the man live, maybe see him off south." He paused. "I leave that decision to you, Minister."

He heard Minister Mulvane breathe deeply, pulling something from the depths of his soul, possibly that darker side he thought he shed after the war. The Minister appeared to pause, his breathing labored.

"Powerful notion to leave a man's life in another's hands," the Minister said.

"You bastards are lookin' to let me go. I'm a keep huntin' down them runaways, though. You know that. Done it all m' life. Man my age, he don't change," Ren said, likely glaring at the exiting Goldfinch. The Leader finally sensed some worry in Ren's unwavering voice.

"I think you'll make the right decision, Mulvane," Goldfinch said to him. "I'd press him, too. Find out if he has more inbreds on the attack." He deliberately reached far into his pocket and pulled out a forty-caliber cast iron bullet. He fiddled with it for a moment and tossed it up in the air. As it came down into his palm, he looked back at Minister Mulvane and tipped his hat.

Goldfinch could sense, in that fleeting moment, that Harriet was uneasy, fidgety. He knew what was about to happen. It took only a few more steps before Harriet's commanding voice echoed out. "Tell us where they are," she ordered. Ren just laughed, and spit, then did it again.

"One more chance," she demanded.

"One more chance to come around, take them niggers back to chains," Ren said in a raspy voice.

A shot rang out. It echoed across the village, out past the pines and the rolling hills leading to the mountain. Goldfinch did not even look back.

While moving onward, Goldfinch called back to his group. "Solomon, check the pockets. I'll have Shepherd dispose—" He paused. "But wait just a moment. Shepherd isn't here now. Solomon, you examine the body. He won't be buried with the rest. Nope, not him. That son of a bitch."

"Mista, yes, yes. I will," Solomon muttered.

"Harriet, I hear you on my heels. Catch up already, will you?" Goldfinch continued. After a few steps, she was at his side. He said, "Adam will get a proper burial, with a service. The others will go out to the animals."

"For a moment I thought you'd impress me, Goldfinch," she said.

"To kill a man? I've done that plenty a time."

"I know, I can see it in you, groundskeeper. Not entirely sure what that war did to you, but I do know you've come a ways since we've arrived." She fixed a few ruffled fringes of her dress and subtly grazed the fingertips of her right hand against Goldfinch's frock coat. He felt the embrace as though it had seared his skin.

"There are bodies that need tending to," was all he could say. He started to walk ahead of the woman he had grown to adore. She eventually trailed off and went into one of the huts.

"They've taken down a horse from our stock," Goldfinch said aloud to the villagers.

He was near the fire pit, close to the horse paddock and the corn cribs when he heard someone approach. It seemed caught somewhere between a bounce and a sprint. As wads of dirt and leaves were kicked up, Goldfinch turned toward the sound.

It was Solomon rushing at him, something dangling in his hands. "Oh, Mista! Mista!"

"Solomon?"

"It's a letta'. He got a letta' in his pocket. See, he knew this here tussle might go down."

"Specifics, man! What are you saying? Have we been compromised?"

"Read it for yourself. I'm not all that quick, though you know I can sure read." He handed Goldfinch a leaf of paper with sloppy writing scrawled across it.

Goldfinch read it.

Case I ever do slip to you sons of whores, you best reckon I ain't brainless enough to take all my men here. A man at our camp's told the law.

— Renly

Goldfinch flung his hat. "There's another one of those godless wretches?" he clamored. "Assume I won't be sleeping most nights now."

Solomon stood nervously in front of Goldfinch. One poked his head out from the church door after the commotion.

"Stay put, you old fogey," Goldfinch said to One. He sighed and then tore the letter into pieces, letting the fragments fly into the stiffening breeze. "Could just be a scare. He wants us fearing, is all."

"There are others out there? That's what it said? You read it through?" Solomon asked.

"That's right, assumedly another one just like our friend Renly up there. Speaking of which, I say we let him rot."

"The stench of that, Mista Goldfinch, would be ..." Solomon paused and made a look of disgust.

"I didn't mean it literally. It's all just streaming around in my mind, is all."

"Where does this put us with our cargo, Mista Goldfinch?"

"This won't deter us, Solomon," Goldfinch said firmly. "If you want spiritual guidance after all this, you best go talk to the Minister."

"That's not it. Just want to keep movin' things 'long, is all."

"In due time. I foresee another trip in your future. Perhaps this time you'll make direct contact with the Reverend. Meantime, we best wait for Shepherd to return from Ithaca, those girls and all."

"Speakin' of them girls, where Reg go?"

"Back over to his place, I suppose," Goldfinch answered, knowing full well the anxiety that must have built in his friend that morning. His journey had taken him from the Carolinas on up to New Jersey, while being chased and chastised the entire way.

"Like to get me another good look at that there dead bounty man," Solomon chirped. "See what them folks look like, stuff they made outta."

"Go on then, I best watch over you."

The pair marched over to the scene beneath the relic. Some fear, or shame, kept Goldfinch from heading down to the church to stare into Adam's lifeless eyes. Outside the gate, they spotted Minister Mulvane toying with his gun, rhythmically poking at the lock plate. As he did so, he stared off into the pine-laden abyss. One of the henchmen lay propped up against a fence post, dead.

Minister Mulvane simply nodded at them. Goldfinch and Solomon continued moving. As they progressed, they both spotted Ren's lifeless body, his head mangled from Harriet's bullet.

The spray out the back of Ren's head traveled with such vigorous force that it webbed out onto the cross. The bottom of the wooden relic carried a shade of dark red. The Leader thought about what a sight it must have been for Minister Mulvane. He felt a lump in his throat that he couldn't shake. He forcefully closed his eyes to help rectify the odd feeling. When he reopened, his field of vision was blurred. He gazed down at Ren's body, which was now covered in bedsheets. He picked his head up. But instead of finding Solomon standing there grieving—for Adam's loss or Reg's hardships—there was a cloaked figure with grimy fur protruding from the sides of the dark article of clothing. Goldfinch felt an uneasy sensation. His feet were wobbly and uncontained. With reasonable force, he tumbled to the ground, unconscious.

Chapter Nine

Oaken Cross

The figure looked at him with beady red eyes. It sniffed the blood from Ren's wound. Goldfinch turned to the tree, where he had nailed the cross some months earlier. As he blinked and reopened, everything was black and white. He was still at the hackberry—there was no cross, no bloodied corpse. He heard a boot crunch on the earth, like the sound of corn stalks being trampled. There was snow on the ground. Three figures approached him, with another behind them. They flattened the snow as they walked.

It was the Founders. Reverend Allen stood in the middle, buttressed by Lyman Beecher and Peter Cartwright. They stepped apart, and Goldfinch looked down a narrow fissure of vision and saw himself. He held a pouch of tools and a small ladder. This dream version of himself was prepared to fasten the cross to the tree, as the Founders watched.

"If neither of you will help the poor man, step aside, so I can be of some use here," Cartwright said. "Let me help Mr. Hermann with the cross. I'll climb the tree if I must."

Goldfinch sized up the hackberry, placed the ladder, and climbed to the uppermost rung. Cartwright heaved the mass of wood upward.

Goldfinch listened closely as Reverend Allen spoke of arming the villagers. They would fill haversacks with some old weapons. Lyman countered by offering to send Minister Mulvane out to retrieve them.

"My rebuttal is this: we must wait until the snow clears," Cartwright bellowed from the base of Goldfinch's ladder.

Goldfinch hammered nails through the wood and into the trunk. He bore much of the cross's weight. Cartwright, too, propped the structure up with his cupped hands. "Lyman, that fleeing preacher," he said firmly, "was he able to feed himself out here?"

Lyman simply shrugged. Then, the cross was fastened. Goldfinch's field of vision began to blur again, and he heard a raging Aaawwhooo *howl from one of the bounty hunters that had breached the Synod property.*

He snapped out of it.

There was no dreamlike version of himself. He realized he had fallen close to the bounty hunter's body. As he came to, there were plenty of villagers around. It was hard to make out facial features, for it had gotten dark. For hours he lay in the vicinity of that vile hunter.

He glanced up and found the pregnant Elizabeth, her darling William, One, Solomon, Reg, and Shepherd—who had returned! Goldfinch wondered how that could be. It was so soon.

It took him another moment to get his bearings and become acclimated to the darkness, after seeing all that snow. He was just feet away from the bloodied corpse of Renly. He looked over at the old man whose face was grimacing. It retained a surprised look, as if he thought the villagers would ultimately refrain from pulling the trigger. His unkempt beard had accumulated the trickling blood from his wound. The Marlow top hat had freed itself from the grasp of the old man.

It sat on its side, a foot or so away from the body. The blood on Ren, coagulated, looked thick and opaque.

"Up with you now, Mr. Goldfinch," Shepherd said, proffering his hand downward.

"I expect I gave you all a scare now, didn't I?" Goldfinch said, a grin forming on his face. He accepted the proffered hand and rose slowly.

"You sure did. We finally left the church, to find our leader lying here beside the enemy," Elizabeth said. "Now it's been hours. Mulvane and Solomon, they said we shouldn't move you, case you hit your head, which is how it appeared."

"Nonsense, all this talk about me. I'm all right. Shouldn't you be at the works?" Goldfinch joked. "Or tending to something *else*?"

Elizabeth blushed and took a step back.

"It's best we get a move on the burial, Adam's that is. We'd like to get him in the ground before the ungodly process begins," One said. He carried a stern look on his face, as usual.

Goldfinch nodded slightly. "If this man had another out there, it is best we hunker down for a bit. We need a night watchman. We'll be straying from our typical chores, as if we haven't already."

He tried to talk calmly. "Best we don't wait, though. I'll be sending Solomon out tonight, to Philadelphia. He'll talk to the Reverend and update him on our troubles here. He'll bring back a new group."

Behind him, Goldfinch heard another villager approaching. It was Reg and he simply half-smiled, lowered his head, and turned his gaze. Goldfinch could tell this ordeal made Reg happy, as if his troubles up to that point were not just futile. However, Reg seemed anxious to learn more from Shepherd. Clearly, details had been disclosed while Goldfinch was unconscious, but he was just gaining enough strength to conduct the conversation.

Before this, Goldfinch could not stop thinking about that piercing howl—a shrill wail. He assumed it had been the rat man making all that fuss, but it repeated in his mind.

Ignoring it, he finally turned to Shepherd. "News about the girls?"

"They are in capable hands," Shepherd answered.

"Doubtful you've made it to Ithaca and back within the span of a single day!" Goldfinch barked.

"I was headed that way, north across the border, then due west, toward Binghamton, where those folks went north for the Sullivan Expedition during the Revolution," Shepherd said.

"I'm listening," Goldfinch interrupted.

"We moved all night, off the beaten paths. I ran into a man—a real unmistakable fellow. Maybe in his early forties. Called himself the 'Christian Statesman.' Talked to me about New Jersey in the years after the War for Independence, of what he remembered. That's beside the point. He spotted my cargo, Regina, and Amber."

Reg visibly tensed up, although he had heard the tale while Goldfinch was out.

"He admired me for what I was doing out there. He asked what sort of stop I'd be looking for with the girls. I said AME churches—said I knew Richard Allen because I was one of his disciples. The man laughed. He'd obviously heard of the good Reverend.

"He told me his name's Theodore Frelinghuysen. Said he was attorney general of the state. Liked to get out on our roads at night, hold firm to the anti-slave stance. See who he could talk to.

"Now, I told him, 'That's how a man gets himself killed.' But again, he just laughed. That's when he told me he was a U.S. Senator. So, I said, 'Why you all alone? Who's supposed to believe you?' The man was one for laughing, because he did some more of it. Said, 'I'm not alone, my detail's off in the woods, to your left, up a ways in the hill to the right.'

"I paused a minute, and before I could say anything, he said, 'Tarrytown. That's your best bet.'

"Now, I'm not one to blindly follow a man—though I did come up here—but I knew these lives were in my hands. I made the trip with him. Miles and miles, due east. Opposite of Ithaca. But quite swiftly. We went to the Foster Memorial AME Church over there, ferried over. Horses stayed behind at some hitching post on our side of the Hudson. We came in sight of the church. Even saw a whole bunch of other negroes going in and out of there in the dark.

"See, the Senator turned back, shuffled on home to Jersey. But not before tipping his cap some and wishing us well. I never did tell him where we are, but I wouldn't put it past this man to know every square inch of his state—and this place. He just had the personality for it."

"Glad to know my babies is safe, Shepherd. You done a good thing last night," Reg called out. "I'll meet my girls there. I will. I's make that trip. Just gots stay here to settle things."

"I don't doubt you, Reg," Goldfinch said. "Now, Shepherd. This is a reliable place for ... our future runaways?"

"Precisely," he said. "And a heck of a lot simpler than trekking across the great state of New York."

"We'll utilize this." Goldfinch walked back to his hut, still slightly disoriented. Shepherd, Solomon, and Minister Mulvane followed him inside. Reg returned to his respective shelter.

It felt crowded in his little shack with only its hearth, a single mattress, and that much company.

"Night's fallen. We'll get a move on Adam's burial," Goldfinch said. "Mulvane, you'll go and round everyone up. Shepherd, you'll help me carry the body. Solomon, go prepare some holes out by the dump, where we'll drop those filthy bounty men. I'll be out later to escort the bodies over."

The villagers scattered, wasting no time in beginning their tasks. Goldfinch could hear the hollow-sounding knocking against the huts from the knuckles of Minister Mulvane. Solomon moved out the exit carrying a shovel. He took a long stride over Renly's body. Shepherd was down near Adam, placing his body in a peaceful position. He folded the arms and walked a few paces over, toward the horse paddock and the small toolshed, to retrieve the wooden cart that he and Goldfinch had prepared some meals on.

Everyone moved hastily. Goldfinch wanted Solomon to complete the task in a hurry so he could then ready his horse to travel out into the night. *The burial*, Goldfinch thought, *must be quick.* He'd improvise if he was forced to.

By the time he walked over to Shepherd's side, the villager had Adam's body ready to transport. The bullet hole had stopped trickling blood some hours ago, and the viscous liquid had hardened.

"We're off to Jane's spot, then," Goldfinch said calmly. "Shepherd, if you do not mind, please begin the climb."

Shepherd, gathering himself, especially after such a long journey, breathed inwardly, stretched, and rolled the cart toward the village's small rear exit.

Goldfinch picked up his pace and knocked at Minister Mulvane's door. It immediately flung open.

"Villagers are gathering at the pit in a moment," the Minister said.

"Very well," Goldfinch replied. "We must move this along. I suppose you remember where to go."

Goldfinch turned from the scene and started on after Shepherd's cart, first picking up his rifle and a shovel from the toolshed.

Not only did he catch up with Shepherd, but he carried on ahead of the younger man, swiping pine branches and weakening sticker bushes away as he raced through the woods. At last, he made it to Synod's burial site.

He spared no time in breaking ground on the next grave. A short while later, Shepherd arrived. The hole was soon ready.

The Synod troupe brushed aside the branches leading to the burial site a few moments after that. Minister Mulvane led the way. He sported a tight frock coat with a black collared shirt, trousers, and boots. He was dressed appropriately for the occasion.

Holding his King James Bible, he asked the villagers to stand around the grave. Reg was in the crowd, too. Shepherd and Goldfinch had taken Adam's body and wrapped it gently in a blanket Shepherd had pulled from his hut. They lowered him into the ground. Goldfinch was about to toss the first mound of dirt on the grave but allowed Harriet to have the honor.

"You were able to work with this fine gentleman for a time. Tilling our field some paces from here, transplanting useful crops from this rugged wilderness," Goldfinch said. "If it wasn't for Adam, this community would have imploded some time ago."

Harriet refrained from saying anything, as a few tears dropped from her saddened face.

"Let us say a few words in memory of this man," Minister Mulvane pitched in. "And let us read from the King James, for our mass was interrupted earlier on this tragic Sunday." The

Minister seemed to have a handle on the situation, and so Goldfinch rushed off.

Before he whisked past the pine boughs which enveloped this circular looking burial site, he gestured a goodbye to Minister Mulvane and tapped Shepherd's side. The two lowered their hands, muttered a prayer, and fled.

The men were off, speeding through the forest again. By some miracle, Shepherd kept up, it was probably his youth. Goldfinch did not stop in the village. He kept moving, past the gate. He even stepped near Renly's fallen body as he rushed through.

Only a moment later, they were at the dump. "This is where our bounty hunters belong," Goldfinch admitted.

Solomon seemed happy to see his friends. "You folks gawn pick up them rats? Place 'em in this here grave?"

"You bet, Solomon." Goldfinch turned to Shepherd, who knew the gesture meant another trip.

Back in the village, Goldfinch and Shepherd tried something new. They pitched lengths of rope around the dead bounty men's ankles. Then they tied these leads to the cantle of their saddles on separate mounts. Goldfinch dragged two bounty hunters the short distance into the woods as Shepherd dragged another. Soon, they were near Solomon's impromptu cemetery.

"It's that easy," Goldfinch said, chuckling and dismounting. Then, sarcastically, he added, "This being a religious refuge and all, we would surely honor the dead, no?"

"Forget propriety," Shepherd urged.

The men untied the corpses and tossed them into three separate shallow graves. There was only one shovel, and Solomon had it. The other men began kicking dirt back into the holes with their boots. Some leaves and twigs found their way in too. Before long, they had completed the burial in the most minimal sense. This left one body unburied, susceptible to the elements—Renly's. Goldfinch had something in mind for the fallen leader.

Goldfinch motioned to Solomon and intentionally directed the man's attention over toward his own Lipizzan horse.

"You best hop on, Solomon. You're going to miss your ride out of here."

Solomon was confused.

"You're going to Philadelphia this evening. There's so much to tell the Reverend, the Founding Mother. Tell him about the bounty hunters and the Sullivans. Tell him about Tarrytown and the Senator.

"Solomon, do tell him about Adam and our loss on that front. We're going to need more men to sustain this place. And another ... shipment is in order. Now, I'll let you take my animal, but you best be careful with him."

Goldfinch patted his horse on its flank. "Eder here is real special. Name's Hebrew for 'a flock,' because he runs like a whole lot of them."

"Mista Goldfinch, I can't take your horse from ya," Solomon maintained.

"You can, and you will, Solomon. There's no time. This is the only way. Ride back and gather your belongings. This horse is already saddled. He's primed to ride. Faster than your animal, I assure you."

"If you say so, Mista Goldfinch. You be all right while I'm gone? Who'll do my chores and the sort in my stead?"

"Don't you go worrying about that. Appears none of us will be completing our chores just yet, the way things have been lately." Goldfinch gave Solomon one pleasant pat on the back and then ushered him toward the horse.

"Shepherd and I here, we'll finish this grave business," Goldfinch said to him. "And I have to mention something that Minister Mulvane isn't too privy of just yet. I hear he has a boy, in town there. He's an able-bodied one. They say he carries some of the same beliefs as his pa, just never been as pious. Why don't you poke around, ask for this gentleman? The name's Blithe. Blithe Mulvane. See if you can get him on up here for us. Now, off with you, friend."

Goldfinch gave the horse a gentle push, saying "Giddy-up!" with tightened lips.

Just like that, Solomon rode off on Eder. Goldfinch stood, horseless, as his friend fled the place. The Leader was still for a moment, watching Eder's whiteness move across the path like a streak of fresh, contrasting paint splashed onto a granular wall. The task ahead was heavy on Goldfinch's weathered face.

Chapter Ten

The Outlier

An hour later, with Solomon and Eder sent off, Goldfinch ventured back to that sequestered dump. The graves were filled. Goldfinch spat at them as if they were some spittoon. His eyes were full of contempt looking at the miserable mound that was to be their final home. He had nothing left to do at this site besides admire the remorseless burial.

So, he strayed back to his hut, his mind still as unstable as a drunkard on the trigger. He sat at the foot of his buckram mattress. His thoughts rushed to Harriet, her tender touch, even her remarkably austere voice.

The sight of blood had enflamed a dormant passion in him. He found his heart longing, for exactly what, he didn't quite know. What he knew, though, was what he felt right down at the base of his stomach. A deep, slow fire, smoldering. He knew he had to keep it down, especially in trying days like these. Yet, as quickly as he forced his mind to focus on the thorny situation at hand, he saw the bounty man who lay dead near the gate. Renly's blood had begun to pool, modifying his skin tone.

Where contingency was concerned, Goldfinch dreamed up three possible routes; let the corpse rot like a sickened dog;

prop the man up to the sturdy fence posts; or take Ren, at least parts of him, to the locale of the other interloper, where business ends of rifles could spew iron. Still riled from the confrontation, he discarded the first two options, thinking that only a godless man would let another rot, bit by bit, in front of a peace-loving community. The last option seemed right. It would kill two birds with one stone—remove the body and bring Synod closer to eliminating its next most formidable threat.

His thoughts were on Harriet again. This time, it was not her voice, but her sculpted body, the unique perfume of hers, and the fractious attitude that surely hinted at promiscuity atop the unforgiving Synod mattresses. Goldfinch knew it was time to approach her, in his hut or hers.

He calmed himself and stood to rise. He planned on going to Harriet's hut and planting a kiss on her, gauging her response. If she asked, he would glide his calloused hand beneath her petticoats, all the while staring above the bodice, into the gaze of her light-blue eyes. He breathed deeply, feeling the air circulate through his lungs, which seemed to open wider in the brisk weather.

He grabbed his hat and slipped out the door in one fluid motion. He leaped to a jog. Everything was moving fast, and he had to keep up. It was like 1812 all over again—the strategy and reconnaissance. These memories permeated his thoughts. His immediate aim became fending off a pesky flashback and guarding against the soothsaying wolf.

An hour later, he found himself at the entrance to Harriet's hut, his knuckles knocking on the coarse, wooden door. He took a few labored breaths and closed his eyes. When the door slid open, he saw Harriet studying him.

They stared at each other; time seemingly slowed, the air moved in leisurely drifts across the hut. Without even a nod,

Harriet turned away. Goldfinch shifted his weight and pressed the toe of his boot past the midpoint of the oak-framed entrance.

She remained still. Goldfinch leaned inside the hut, trying to determine the subject of her fixation. Goldfinch knew, though, that it was an attempt to evade him. It seemed that another fruitless day would pass in this ambiguous relationship. Before any words were spoken, Goldfinch lowered his hat and spun out of the small hut.

He failed to communicate what was burning so brightly inside him. Goldfinch walked with a purpose, slipping through leaves, their stems cracking, their blades tearing. He brought his dejected self to the border of the Synod property and sat staring at the posts, rails, and sharpened ends of his fence.

"I'll move out to Reg's if that vile woman will not accept the inevitable," he said aloud. He slipped out the rear gate and rushed into the forest, toward the huts designated for new arrivals.

Goldfinch paid careful attention to the winding path. He arrived at the outlying huts. He saw a light plume of smoke emanating from the top of the center one.

"Reg, the intruders are buried, except for that devilish beast at the hackberry."

A splintered wooden door eased open. "Goldfinch? I'm a killa now, you hear? I come up to your place, and I become a killa."

"It's an action you knew you'd have to carry out once those men drew near. Reg, your honor is intact, I assure you. Times in North Carolina must've been more trying. Focus on all the promise, Reg. This village, your girls." He let the words simmer for a moment.

"I know it's not yer fault, Mista Goldfinch. You a good man, a good man," Reg answered. "I just feel like I be spoiled now, eyes a the Lord." His head fell into his hands.

"Much as I'd like to reassure you now, friend, I must warn you. There are fluctuant times ahead. I'd like you to help me. The aim's to rid this place once and for all of that crude, savage Ren. We're going to stuff him in a sack, behind the back jockey of my saddle. We're going to find his other man, so long as there is one. Either way, we rid ourselves of this plague."

"Anythin' to help, Mista Goldfinch. Quicker them boys get outta here, quicker I can up and head to Tarr-town, see my girls."

"A day I sorely dread, Reg. You've become a valued member of this place."

"Time for warm feelin's and such later, if'n you say there a job to do."

Goldfinch couldn't help but smirk. "We best be off, then."

Reg reached into his hut, where propped against stiff wooden boarding that passed for a bed frame, he found a hunting knife given to him by Elizabeth at some point in the past few hours. "Reckon this might help me," he said, smiling.

"While we're on the subject of this next task, best I update you, too. See, Solomon, he's out in the fields, on the darkened streets, headed for Philadelphia. He's going to update the good Reverend about our predicament here. He'll surely send word up to Lyman in Boston, if he's still up there, that is, and not venturing out to the Seminary."

"That's 'sides the point. Long as word get to Allen, we goin' somewhere."

"Well, Solomon's also picking up someone else. We lost Adam, so I suppose we could use some more men around here. He's going to pick up a boy named Blithe. Shouldn't say 'boy,' he's somewhere near twenty. It's Minister Mulvane's son, a man of high ethical standards. He'll be a welcome addition, rest assured."

"More slavery-hatin' folks 'round here, the better," Reg joked.

"Point to remember, we'll be without Solomon for some days. The village is going to have to look after itself, with this madman running through the woods—if he's truly out there."

"You best put that nice girl in charge in your stead," Reg added.

"Well, I thought I might have Mulvane hold down the place with One." Goldfinch thought back on Harriet's eyes shifting away from his loving gaze.

"That old one been real quiet since I put the bounty man down."

"I learned early on not to lean too heavily on One," Goldfinch confided.

Reg shrugged and took a few steps ahead of Goldfinch, moving toward the village fence. His frayed pullover was taking on a yellowish tint from its repeated use. The spats over his boots reflected the sparse moonbeams that pierced the forestry.

Back in the village, Goldfinch told Reg to update One about the Ren story. Goldfinch wandered past Harriet's hut, toward Minister Mulvane's.

Knock, knock. Not a second elapsed before the Minister shoved his nose and the tip of his top hat in the opening.

"Mulvane, you'll be manning this garrison. Is that understood, chaplain?"

"Chaplain?" Minister Mulvane wondered. "Alluding to war days?"

"It's war, isn't it? You'll lead while I'm gone. We're going to bring Ren to them, or him. Say he gets to a crooked government official, constable, looking to cash in on the duller side of that fugitive law. We could be finished."

"May I suggest sleep, Goldfinch? You'll never make it on a scouting venture if you've got about as much energy, as much agility, as a tortoise."

"I prefer the Goldfinch bird—lively little specimens," Goldfinch retorted.

Minister Mulvane grinned and slid the door open. He adjusted his hat and stormed off to approach Reg, who was in mid-conversation with One.

Although the Minister was out of reach, Goldfinch said, "Ah, so I'll see to it the horses are saddled?"

At the paddock, Goldfinch thought it would be slim pickings, for no stallion could compare to Eder. And a few animals had escaped into the woods. The cow remained. Still, a remarkable Friesian horse—a Dutch breed of raven-black color—awaited him. Someone had corralled the animals while he had taken the fall. They had plugged the hole in the fence with some materials that had been lying around. Goldfinch then saddled the Friesian, grabbed a horse for Reg, and trotted off.

As he passed his own hut, he noticed Shepherd out front. "Saddle up," Goldfinch advised.

The Leader approached Reg and Minister Mulvane. He heard neighs trembling through the oaken huts. He looked back at the paddock. Shepherd's saddling was complete, on a horse hesitant to move in the chilly, blue-black night. He had also gathered supplies and armed the posse.

Near the conversation unfurling outside One's hut, Reg had retreated, and Minister Mulvane was showing resolve, pointing his finger at One.

"Regardless," One chimed in. "I will ride with you in this undertaking. I've been ignored before. I'm still of able body. I shall ride."

Minister Mulvane scratched his neck, removed his hat and slid backward, toward Reg. "Goldfinch," he said. "Oh, do respond."

"Let the man make an attempt," Goldfinch bellowed. "If he cannot keep pace, he'll fall behind and wind up friendless in the mountains."

The Minister complied and returned to his hut. The door shut loudly, but Goldfinch knew his commentary was helpful.

Reg made a dash toward the awaiting horse. Shepherd trotted in behind. One rummaged through his things, fastening a black button-down vest to his thin, long-sleeved shirt. He slipped into his boots and ventured toward the paddock, to join the equestrian convoy.

From atop the Friesian, Goldfinch peered right into Harriet's hut. She was sitting at her makeshift, single-dweller table. Her fingers were interlocked, resting on the wooden platform. She stared ahead at her wall, away from the expanse of the glass window. Goldfinch knew he was in her thoughts, and was just as certain that she would be in his.

"Gentlemen, we ride. Before we pick up speed, One will compress this Ren fellow into a few burlap sacks and strap him, sidelong, over his horse," Goldfinch announced. "Shepherd has gathered ample supplies and rifles."

One nicked his horse near its belly. Its haunch muscles tightened, and it sped off toward the gated entrance. The elder, in his sixties, was not afraid to dirty his hands. His white beard stood out with the moon in the night. He stopped for a moment near the toolshed, picking up burlap sacks used to house corn. He grabbed two large ones and spare roping from the bales of hay that had accumulated in the previous months. Before he got out too far ahead of the curious Goldfinch, the Leader and the others caught up.

"For a single cause—which has significant ramifications— we unite here this night, to ride into these forests," Goldfinch said. One was still working to prepare the right resources for his haul.

"Let us help set the nation on its rightful course *and* set an example for the nonconformist, the spiritually enlightened," he continued. "Lord knows the Founders have shown us the way. And to them, we say: onwards!"

He trotted up the narrow path toward the hackberry, passing a labor-wearied One, who was fastening the sacks over the stiffening corpse, tying the loose ends together with the lengthy, narrow bale roping.

With great effort, One stood Ren up in the fabric that would become his tomb. He propped his arm at the crease in Ren's back, his nose turned from the carrion.

"Ah, but a little help, gentlemen?" One called out, taking his other hand and tracing the outline of his tight, whitened beard. His vest appeared stiff in the cold.

"November air is getting the best of your light clothing, One," Shepherd called down to the elder.

"I have divinity on my side. God has an aim for me and this mission," he responded. "I believe even Reverend Allen knows I will not tremble in a light breeze."

"So be it," Shepherd answered, pulling the collar on his frock coat higher up on his neck. He continued to gawk at the mobile elder.

One sighed, probably recognizing the thankless work he was engaged in. He made a weak fist and hammered it into the side of the crop sack, hitting what appeared to be the bounty man's oblique area underneath. In doing so, the body tumbled back to the ground. As it landed, there came the sounds of rattled flesh and displaced leaves.

"Let's fasten the man down, One," Shepherd called, nearly laughing now. He hesitated for another moment, watching the braggart fumble with the body. Then, he lowered himself from the animal and helped One pick up Ren. They threw him over the horse, buttressed him between the loins and the croup of the animal. The saddle was then motionless with this stabilizing weight on the horse's rear.

While One put the finishing touches on his mount, Goldfinch strayed for a moment, leaving his horse in Shepherd's care. Goldfinch's boots crunched in the unforgiving ground, and he ran through the village. He rushed to Harriet's, not bothering to knock, and tossed the door open. She sat in the same spot as before as if guarding her kitchen and only table.

Goldfinch swallowed hard and walked the two full steps it took to cross the hut. He held the sides of Harriet's head in his hands and crouched down to her level. Still sitting, she kept her head still but angled her eyes toward Goldfinch.

Before she could shove him away or turn her gaze, he kissed her. He kissed her so tightly his nose scrunched up against her face. He closed his eyes and felt her silky skin brush against his whiskery face. She did not hold back either, lightly brushing her fingers through his hair. In an exhale as he let go, he smiled at her. Before she could register a complaint, he took his forefinger and lightly skimmed it over her lower lip. Her silence confirmed that his attraction was, in fact, requited.

Goldfinch touched her chest tenderly. He wanted to sink beneath her frock coat. But his quest was larger than his hankering for Harriet. He quickly removed his hand, where it sat idly at his side. Before words passed between them,

Goldfinch again fled the hut, this time with his spirits elevated. At his Friesian, he mounted in one impressive motion and clicked his heel against the horse's belly. The others followed—Shepherd and his resourcefulness, Reg, and One with the posse's questionable cargo.

Within seconds, they reached the gate, then the hackberry and the site of Renly's brazen murder. After another step, Goldfinch was at last set to embark out beyond the pines. This was his first big trip outside Synod since its foundation.

"*Tttt-ttthhh!*" he commanded his horse. The Friesian picked up speed. It was not Eder speed, but still impressive. He hugged the edge of the path and slipped between naked trees. Reg trailed closely behind. Shepherd was behind *him*, and One brought up the rear.

"Suppose this dolt could take the case to the State?" Shepherd asked, his voice carrying to Goldfinch.

"He does, we're in heaps of trouble, long as Jersey conforms to that 1793 law. Freedom folks will be up in arms over it, should it come to that. The Reverend would cross the border to bring down any court that crosses us," Goldfinch said.

"Suppose it's an idle threat, Ren's?" Shepherd countered.

"If it is, we're able to breathe this purified air some more." Goldfinch picked up the pace atop the Friesian.

"You aim to go any place particla?" Reg asked Goldfinch.

"I suppose he'll go to the explosion site," One said, tottering into the conversation. "Moving southeast would be the finest choice. You have to figure this other outsider would work his way back to civilization at some point. All signs point east to New York."

From then on, they were silent. In the quiet of the night, the convoy journeyed on. The road was dark, but their horses seemed to know the way. The wind was chilling, too, but the men braved it, zigzagging through the forest. The quiet engulfed them. They passed and dodged trees that were lined along the path. In far less than an hour's ride, they arrived.

Goldfinch dismounted and flung his reins on his saddle. "One grows on you," he said to Reg. "He's power hungry, but he's got a good, pious heart. I saw this man at Allen's church. He was a demure fella then. See what even the slightest morsel of power does to a man? He becomes infused with new blood. Then he's corrupted, like those proprietors down south. You see, they don't hear each heartbeat. Instead, it's the sound of coin brushin' coin. It's what keeps them spry, the backward beasts."

Reg, who had dismounted, said, "I seen these men at their homes like that. Reckon that there's a good way to say it."

They found themselves at the explosion site. Remnants still charred the immediate ground. It was clear to Goldfinch that Reg was now thinking about his girls, the way the dress was propped over the scene, and the hair carefully pinned to the leaf of paper.

Goldfinch revisited the scene to try and spot something that slipped between the cracks a few days earlier. There were plenty of tracks; Goldfinch's, Minister Mulvane's, Solomon's, and the gunmen's. Finding a discernible path leading beyond this trafficked acre was hopeless.

With a streak of luck, though, Reg caught wind of something. In a half-squat, he squeezed through the bushes, and past the oaks and cedars. Even in the middle of the night, Reg found a sufficient lead. The placer of these tracks seemed to move sluggishly, his boot prints more firmly situated in the terrain. Looking to stay close to a deer run, this suspect matted the more malleable earth. Hoof tracks riddled a nearby trail of larger scope, perhaps an indication that this third party was lagging behind, staying in the shadows to ensure the survival of at least one in Renly's group.

"This a bigger man than the rest we seen—yours, Solomon's, the Minister's, rest of them 'truders," Reg said, examining the tracks and turning his nose even closer toward the ground.

"He could be onto something here, Goldfinch," Shepherd admitted.

"And what would *you* suggest?" Goldfinch asked One, poking fun at his earlier boast.

"An incapable executive?" One returned, hardly making eye contact with Goldfinch.

"It was my decision to bring Reg along," Goldfinch said defensively. "If we had listened to you, we'd be caught in some trap by now."

"For all the times we've shared at Allen's AME, I must say, I never saw you as a particularly capable fellow. Thinking with only your hands and the tools that could shield you from your aches? Simply regrettable. It's the brain that rectifies all."

"I think most would agree I've had to make some meaningful decisions here. Regardless, I didn't see you propping up that hackberry cross while Cartwright and I struggled with it," Goldfinch barked.

"We were busy building the place up," One countered. "Something that could outlast the measly sheds you constructed."

"Do hold your tongue, Erskine," Goldfinch said, this time angrily. One was nonplussed at the usage of his name.

"You'll make no references to that," One demanded.

"Gentlemen, it's time we refocused," Shepherd told the arguers. "Reg has picked up a trail better than I've ever seen."

The runaway had slipped ahead some yards. The sight of his meager clothing was an eyesore, but his boots with spats forged a dignified look. Goldfinch looked at his fellow villager with pride, imagining him, with his spats, as an infantryman moving in on his target.

One approached the runaway. Goldfinch could hear the elder praising Reg's keen eyesight. The group then rested along the narrow deer run, consolidating resources and deciding to move in unison. Finally, they hopped back atop their mounts.

After more acreage of decaying ferns, spidery vines, oak and pine boughs, and offshoots, the group arrived at the base of an intimidating incline. This was a foothill marked with loose shale and a slick blanket of fallen leaves. The four men bound their horses to nearby trees and dug their boots in for the upward trek. Goldfinch led the way. Shepherd carried canteens, and One looked back at the body propped on his fatigued animal.

The elder hesitated. "We're going to need to shove my horse up this hill, even if it's the end of us. The body sits overburdening my horse. A bounty hunter rots on the animal's back. The aim was to bring the man along as proof, as bait."

"Duly noted," Goldfinch responded, exhaling. "I thought we'd scale the hill, scout it out. But I see that your idea carries merit—we muscle the animal to the top."

"It's the only way to keep the threat active," Shepherd admitted.

One nodded, staring at the ground, his scraggly, unkempt beard surely clouding his periphery.

The group moved back to the tree trunks where the animals were tied and released One's horse, a brown-skinned, black-haired criollo. The four of them guided the animal to the base of the hill and slapped at her hindquarters to keep her in motion.

The precipice stood at least one-hundred feet tall, the animal pathway fixed right at its center. At this point, they were miles from Synod and the night was aging. The early November air allowed for light vapor after a breath.

"*Yeeyaaa!*" One called to his filly. Its narrow legs rose knee-high, and her shoes clamped down on the unstable ground. Except for her slight hesitation, she made excellent progress.

Halfway up the hill, Reg began to pull her by the noseband as she slowed. "C'mon there, girl. Find it in ya," he urged.

At the animal's rear, Shepherd held Ren's body in place within the tied-off fabric. The men carried on their backs their saddlebags marked with protruding rifles. They rested in fitted holsters, making them look like disheveled militiamen from the Revolution.

One pushed the animal from behind, standing at a risky position, within striking distance of an indignant rear leg. Nevertheless, it was an arduous push to the top, but eventually, the horse's hoof reached the plateau, not a half second before Reg's boots did, spats and all.

Shoving the lingering mass of animal over the top, the men paused to look back down toward their mounts. They rested along the path clearly trodden by smaller game.

Reg adjusted the knife at his side, keeping it taut in its leather sheath. One reached back to fix the angle of his rifle barrel in the bag. Shepherd took his out, peering down its sight.

Goldfinch stepped out ahead of the pack, rushing forward on the trail. As it came to a fork after about fifty-yards, he strode left. As his body weight shifted, he felt the forty-caliber bullets jangle in his pocket. His gun was nearly loaded. He was not planning on underestimating the visitor, should there be one.

"The more I think on it, the more I come to realize that this fella should've went to the Governor's office already, he wants any results," Goldfinch admitted aloud when the others caught up. "No local constable's going to do a thing."

"Dumont Vroom doesn't know of our existence. Ren's man could just be spewing some more scatterbrained southern nonsense," Shepherd predicted.

The Leader did not respond to this. "Powder settled on your pans?" he asked. The men nodded. Goldfinch paused to act on his own command.

Then, with each passing step, the men entered thicker, rougher terrain. Goldfinch heard the offbeat clanks of horseshoes greeting nuggets of rock. He also noticed a peculiar change in Reg. He had closed his eyes. He was whispering something through his illiteracies and peering up every few steps. It was as if he could sense that the lingerer was near.

Not twenty steps later, from the darkness of what looked like a patch of young maples and hickories, a yelp broke the silence. Then, the crackling of a few spotty leaves. Goldfinch reached for his gun. Rising from the canopy of this infantile patch of forest came a plume of smoke. It was narrow and ashen-colored, blending heartily with nighttime. Still, Goldfinch's eye was hawkish. This plume went against the tide of the easterly moving, low-lying clouds.

"Check your one o'clock, men. We have company," Goldfinch whispered. He heard a hammer cock.

Each man spread apart by about fifteen feet and then penetrated the wall of young trees and saplings. One joined this progression, but kept the horse behind the pack and held his rifle out steadily. With stealth, the three men quickly came upon a small dip in the earth's curvature. It was here where a portly man, a bow and arrow strapped across his shoulder, sat warming his hands before a small fire. He was wearing all black and could hardly be seen in the night. But with experience, Reg could easily pick out a white man—right out of thin air and with his eyes closed. Heck, it even seemed to Goldfinch that some mysterious, white-skinned stench permeated Reg's air.

Goldfinch, Reg, and Shepherd spread out around him. Keeping their boots as silent as possible, they came to within a few feet of either side of the stranger. Goldfinch immediately contemplated a hundred different maneuvers to subdue this man. Holding the barrel of his gun vertically and tightly against his chest, he thought of the Synod sermons, the amicable Reverend Allen, and above all else, the scorching personality in petticoats who demanded his attention at the village. He knew Harriet would have handled this scenario with ease. His muscles tensed. Another hammer cocked. This time, though, the compressed leaves made an echoic sound.

"You best raise them hands," cried out an immature voice. The fellow was on the move. A few steps later, Goldfinch could hear the horse's hooves moving. He disregarded the plan and looked back.

A young negro boy pushed the barrel of a Harpers Ferry flintlock rifle into One's back. The old man grimaced but did not let go of the horse.

"I's take you over to see Burt," the boy continued.

Slowly, One then looked down, glaring at the short, narrow child. "It's you. You ungrateful, grimy, little wretch."

"State of the niggers ain't so bad when there's money to go 'round," the boy responded, pushing One onward. He created a foot or two of space and pelted the old man with the butt of his rifle. One let out a quick cry and lowered a hand to knead the spot of the wound.

As horse and man passed Goldfinch, he eased out from his cover and threw his gun on the boy. It was Edwin. "Put the gun down now, son," Goldfinch ordered. "We showed you refuge—food, shelter."

"Ya think I really wants that?" Edwin asked. "Pa got took back in 'delphia. Never anything here for me's anyway. Show me a coin, I'll jump either way."

"We're out to help the lot of you," Goldfinch said. "We've done nothing to harm you."

"When Burt says you boys are the devil-worshippin' traitors, I see you as that, changin' the way things oughta be."

"Son, that's the slanted version of freedom they want you to hear—in the Carolinas, in Mississippi, Alabama," One chimed in, barrel at his back.

"Just you keep on walkin', old man."

As Edwin, One, and his criollo passed, Goldfinch glanced at the darkened tree line, flickering with the display of the nearby fire. He saw Shepherd and Reg. He motioned leftward with his head at Reg. The runaway slipped deeper into the forest. Shepherd then stepped out from his cover, gun stuck on Edwin. He still looked over near the fire, though.

As the unconventional group pressed forward, Goldfinch began to hear humming. It was coming from the fire—an obnoxious, boisterous racket that hovered over them. It left the lips of the Burt character, beside the flames.

The men approached, and the call grew louder. As Goldfinch neared, gun still drawn, a plump man gone horseshoe bald and wearing a black cutaway coat—cravat spilling out the top—abruptly turned and surveyed his facial expressions.

The gaze sent shivers down Goldfinch's spine. As he got gooseflesh, he stammered and dropped his gun. This man's fixed stare at the fire pierced Goldfinch's soul. It became the customary red eye he saw in his dreams. As he refocused, the man was the wolf, snarling with dank jowls. Goldfinch could not decipher right from left, north from south. The man's gaze burned into him, as had Renly's when *that* man appeared in canine form.

Burt barked and drooled into his fire, chomping at the bit to rip a fleshy chunk from Goldfinch. *It's just momentary, it has to be,* Goldfinch thought. His body and subconscious would not fail him. He pressed his eyes shut and reopened. The wolf still glared, and the fire still blazed.

He jolted his head side to side—once, twice. As he reopened his eyes again, Burt was just a man. But the red eye still tormented him. For a third time, he shut his eyes, reached for his rifle, and walked over toward Shepherd, who at this point was just watching Goldfinch struggle.

"Looks like my nigger here's gone and scared ya'll silly," Burt said. "He a quick one on his toes, like the whole lot of them Africans. Now, who's bringing a horse into my camp? And after I already done shot a deer out in them woods for supper."

He pointed to the young forest where the group had heard the noise of something yelping and then falling earlier on. Then Burt continued to whistle. He paused. "Its 'Oft in the Stilly Night' by More and Shaw," he said. "Recognize it?" The group said nothing.

As the portly man looked closer at the new arrivals, he saw the oddly shaped cargo on the back of the horse, resting sidelong and nestled behind the saddle.

"Either that's the product of a big-game hunt, or this here grandpa's getting a mighty wide hole in his back." He pointed at Ren's concealed body.

Since recovered, Goldfinch said, "Have your boy lower the weapon. We're not just a band of hunters. We're here on business. It's business that, well, involves the obliterated skull of your boss here, Renly Picket."

At this the man hesitated, looking away from the pack. He stopped playing clueless and reached into his pocket. He took hold of a Toby pocket pistol, already loaded for an instance such as this.

Then with little to no apprehension, he stormed over to Goldfinch, placed the barrel on his forehead, and continued to gauge his enemy. Still calm, Goldfinch said, "It's not me you want to point that gun at. Shepherd, show him his boss."

Shepherd did not turn his attention away from the standoff but still managed to walk over to the criollo. He hurled the weight over the side of the trusty horse, stood up the corpse, and let it tumble to the ground. The sound of lifeless flesh falling was disconcerting. Shepherd unwound the fabric that held the sacks together, which covered the slave catcher.

In front of the horse, One still stood with a barrel most likely forming an indentation at the curve of his back. At the sight of the body, Burt lowered his pistol.

"The man never led a subdued life," Burt conceded, staring down at his fallen gang leader. "He's better off in this here spot, couldn't keep his convictions to his damned self."

Goldfinch tried to read the heavy, austere accomplice. Turning back toward Goldfinch, the perspiring man said, "Name's Castervaugh. Burt. Had my eye on you's, down in your little settlement. It's touchin' to know you dreamers think you can create some sorta inverse world, where the shackles are deemed unlawful. Where the niggers walk out and about wit' you and me." He extended his chin toward Goldfinch, including the Leader on his exclusive list.

Goldfinch hocked up some phlegm, leaned in toward the mangled corpse, and expelled it. He lifted his head, tipped his hat at Burt, and said, "It's a shame. For a minute, I had you pegged as a thinker. Looks can be deceiving. In your case, there's not much to deceive. I take it your relationship with women tends to be … tenuous?"

Burt intoned a manly grunt and tightened the lapel portions of his cutaway coat. "A village full of nigger-lovin' thinkers. That it?" Before he could answer his own question, he abruptly changed directions. "I seen you with our buck. He's just wandrin' 'round your commune, ain't he? You know, as well as I, that there nigger belong to Mr. Steven Picket, though I'm sure Ren's guns made you aware. Aye, boy, ain't that right?" He looked at Edwin.

"Yessuh," Edwin answered mechanically from behind his gun.

"That's called compliance. You know it when you see it, Mister, Mister?"

"Goldfinch," the Leader answered. "Bunch of folks fixed on repairing the world, curbing the power of despots like you, tagged me with that name. I suppose it makes for a pleasant sound to be uttered off the tongue of a slave catcher, such as yourself, before his brains are splashed out."

"Idle threats, Mr. Goldfinch, idle threats," Burt responded. "It's a matter of seein' the mindset, steppin' into our way of life. Slaves got 'bout as much freedom down there as they do in these parts, slavin' on low wages, at your furnaces, pickin' at your ice."

"We seem to be at an impasse," Goldfinch asserted.

"Reckon we are."

"What's to stop me, right now, from having Shepherd here fire upon your twisted head?" Goldfinch asked.

"Well, for one, your grandpa won't see sunrise," Burt responded. "Don't play amateur with me, I know you're military. Can see it in your step."

"And suppose the elder is an expendable piece," Goldfinch added, his face unbroken by the tension. Near the horse, One tensed up, exhaling sharply, the barrel of Edwin's gun sliding with the labored breath.

"We already downed your whole gang," Goldfinch proclaimed. "Why stop at the brains behind it all?"

"You said it y'self, Renly was the Leader. You saw 'im, spoke to 'im."

"And what I didn't know was that *you* were waiting out here."

Shepherd's finger seemed to tighten on the trigger. He followed the conversation, back and forth between the Leader and the prowler.

"I confess. Burt Castervaugh—agent and breaker on the Picket Plantation of Carolina—at your service, you righteous freeman." He bowed, slipping his arm across his large stomach.

"How do you suppose we settle this dispute?" Goldfinch asked.

"To begin, I'll take the nigger that's in your service, a one Reggie Sullivan. I know his daughters are gone. Second, you turn 'round and go back to your doomed little village. This boy'll tag along with me. Specie says so."

"When the next batch of godless Southerners comes along, will you be making company with them?" Goldfinch wondered.

"Reckon you's don't make it that far, so you don't have to worry. Reckon today you've peaked. So, man, the niggers?"

Goldfinch sighed bitterly and directed his attention to the illuminated, youthful trees. He lifted his barrel slightly, kinked it skyward, and brought it back down to its unyielding aim at Burt.

This subtle move was actually a signal for Reg, still hidden within the saplings and offshoots. It came at a perfect time, with all the epithets.

As if moving like a careful brushstroke across a saturated canvas, Reg slipped from tree to tree, leaving twigs and leaves alike unblemished.

To Goldfinch, Burt said, "Time's come for you to march on home. You don't want that man meetin' his maker today. And you don't wan' me shoving my handgun back in your face."

One blurted out, "Listen to the man, he has a point."

Burt must have thought the threat rattled Goldfinch, and he turned his back to the Leader, hoping his forceful demeanor would scare the group of freemen off.

Goldfinch lifted his clenched fore and middle fingers and hinted for Reg to swoop in. Burt was toying with his gun, likely anticipating that the men would move out. Unexpectedly though, he lifted his arm, unfurled his trigger hand, and fired his weapon into the sky. He then sharply turned back to the group, Reg still hidden.

"The 'thorities been notified. Constables, politicians, try and name another that ain't been spoken to. They'll unleash hell on this friv'lous pursuit. And I'll take what's mine."

"Have you approached the Governor? A senator? Militiamen? Whom?" Goldfinch fired.

As the man stood, aglow from the nearby flame, he took on his red eye, staring through thick blankets of air toward Goldfinch. "The Governor has acquiesced. Ours is a stalwart cause."

Again, Goldfinch maneuvered the barrel of his rifle. Storming out from behind the close tree, Reg planted his boots and fired. Gut shot.

Goldfinch immediately swung his body toward One, where Edwin had him under lock and key. Gun fixed, he called out, "It's over, boy. Over."

Edwin, seeing the smoke clear from Reg's rifle, shoved One forward, relented on the trigger, checked his ground off to the right, and left, and then fled. He ran with haste, musket in hand. Just like the time earlier in the week, he slipped through the forest like a weightless apparition, undetected.

Goldfinch felt it would be the last time they'd encounter him. He hoped the boy would move north and be persuaded the other way.

***

The bullet pierced Burt's tweed undershirt. His hands immediately fell to the wound, pressurizing it, urging it to simply dissolve away. The look on his face read startled. That became exponential as Reg revealed himself between the mix of flame and luminescence. The runaway propped the butt of his gun on the ground beside the fire, holding the barrel delicately. His would be the last face Burt would see.

Burt's airways clogged, and the blood leaked out the wound, trickling over the side of his body. His demise was imminent. He grimaced and tried to mouth a word. "Vr—Vr—Vroo-m." Then, he died.

Chapter Eleven

Revised Plan

Reg retreated back to the horse. With great effort, he grabbed hold of Ren's body. He rolled it on its side toward the flames. With a final, emphatic push, he kicked the man into the fire.

"The fat man might go up in flames, too," Shepherd said. "Fitting, no?" As a bystander, he'd witnessed the whole ordeal. He looked back at Goldfinch, who was ridding himself of the ghostly dream.

Eyeing his friends, Goldfinch said, "Seems a whole new problem has emerged, one of my fears. The man's last word, 'Vroom,' the Governor." He sank his head, and his shoulders slumped.

"We're braving the elements already, let us venture south. At least for Paterson, learn more about the slave traders on the prowl," Shepherd suggested.

"Supply-less and hardly equipped to handle the cold?" One countered.

"If we're to be scrutinized for harboring slaves, and have more catchers on our tail after the next group arrives, we might as well prepare ourselves," Goldfinch said.

"Mista Goldfinch, if'n it any help, my vote is a yay," Reg said.

"Smother the fire. We can't have this man wrecking our forest from the afterlife," Goldfinch said. "We'll retreat down the hill, free the mounts, and ride south as Shepherd has suggested."

"We're bound to pass a depot, if not more, on that runaway system. Never know who might offer assistance," Shepherd continued. "Paterson-Hamburg Turnpike, as I've said, is rife with potential. We lie low, plus, our cargo has been lessened some."

"As the man says." Goldfinch made the first move, bade farewell to the makeshift camp, and stormed off. "Let the coyotes tear what's left of the fat agent from cheek to cheek."

Looking out from atop the hill, the group paused to check their weapons and the stocks of powder in horns within their pockets or on their hips. They stuffed the rifle butts back in their strapped saddlebags. One crossed the threshold first, slipping down the loose terrain toward the horses. He left the criollo to the care of the other three. It appeared he could not muster up enough strength to see the animal back down.

"Easy, easy," Goldfinch said peacefully to the horse as the three of them escorted her down the hill.

Shepherd took the rear, Reg kept the flanks sturdy, and Goldfinch soothed the animal from the front. The descent was tricky, but the animal was deft and skilled. This time, at the base, she carried much less weight.

There, on Shepherd's mount, lay a helpful satchel of canteens and rations from his hut. It was simple food—some venison jerky and cornmeal made to mix with water for solid cakes. Gathering themselves, they brushed the dust off their trousers, re-tied their ankle boots and rested for a few moments.

"Voting to camp till dawn?" Goldfinch asked his friends.

"Confirmed," Shepherd said.

"Affirmative," One called.

"Yessuh," Reg responded.

They camped, and Goldfinch soon found the others asleep, snoring away. Alarm was gone from their minds and calmness reigned over their weary frames.

***

At dawn, Goldfinch awoke first. He rubbed the sleep from his eyes, gathered his surroundings, and lightly kicked his partner's boots, rousing them. "Forthwith, we move out," he said with some zeal. The group gathered their belongings and mounted their animals.

"A little sleep informed me that we ought to move onto Trenton after we check in with the heavier villages," Shepherd called out, obviously hoping someone would expand on the idea.

"Let us see what we encounter along the way. We venture down to Trenton, we might as well see the Reverend in Philadelphia," Goldfinch asserted.

"Could he stop the bounty men from compromising our solace, stumbling into Synod?" One asked.

"Would do us no harm to keep him informed," Goldfinch answered. "Though Solomon's on track to do that as we speak."

"I'd like to see me some more of the Rev'rend, the Foundin' Mother," Reg declared.

"Our focus now is getting to Paterson, seeing who we might find," Goldfinch repeated.

"We *could* refocus our efforts, turn northeast a ways … past the Hudson, move to Tarrytown and the AME stop," Shepherd called out, presumably reflecting on his journey with Reg's girls. "See if they have any resources to distribute, guns to dole out. Comes to a problem, we withdraw, head to Paterson."

"Now that there's an idea I cain't refuse," Reg announced. Goldfinch assumed that the runaway, too, was reminiscing— perhaps on his days with his innocent children, who could have been in Tarrytown, or already stationed somewhere along the path to freedom.

Then, from Goldfinch, "Let us vote."

"Wouldn't say I'm opposed to Tarrytown," One said.

"Second that," Shepherd said, who'd already made the trip.

"Then across the Hudson it is. Shepherd has already informed us that the area was brimming with folks arriving, departing. This means it's receptive to our cause," Goldfinch said.

"But let us retrace the steps of our runaways, to prepare for Solomon's next journey," One said. "And *then*, determine who has knowledge of this here wayfaring group of freedom fighters and dissidents."

With haste, the horsemen galloped from this hotbed. Regardless of yearning for home or not, the men pushed on, hoping to expedite the Tarrytown affair.

"We can request men to travel in from Tarrytown, to ensure that our next folks move on pleasantly," Shepherd suggested. "I'm sure of it, how these other dens function. I heard it through some whispers up near the Cape in Massachusetts, around the time I attended Lyman's sermons."

"Then let us make this a fruitful trip," Goldfinch advised, already knowing this tidbit.

"On second thought, why don't we ride east to the falls at Paterson, then turn tail and make for the far side of the Hudson," Shepherd said hurriedly. "Let's see what we might dig up here, then retrace my earlier steps, see how the AME up there is faring."

"Duly noted," Goldfinch concluded. "Suppose that's feasible." It was settled, they would cater to the two separate objectives in one expedition. They would have taken the roads north across the New York border and into Warwick Village, before turning east for the Hudson. Yet their revised plan dictated that they pass through New Jersey for as long as possible, to salvage some information from the minds of local politicians or a visiting senator.

So, they drifted southeast, past the Pompton territory. The farther south they went, the more densely populated the hamlets became—a far cry from Synod's tamed landscape. The bustling scenery was becoming familiar to all those who met almost a year earlier in Philadelphia for the trek north.

After two days of off-and-on travels, hoping for subtlety, and scouting, they settled on the outskirts of Paterson, off the turnpike. They tethered their horses near an old barn. The city was within viewing distance of the visiting party. When they arrived, it was dusk and the streetlamps cast light upon the somber night. With the Friesian tied up, Goldfinch was the first to inspect the rickety structure that seemed to have once been the center of a thriving farmstead. It was a cottage nestled close to the removed barn.

Grasping his rifle, Goldfinch walked to the front steps, the first one with a hole of rot plaguing it. He stepped on the top stair, his boots creaking on the loose support. He thrust his barrel at the unhinged door. The others stood watch at the pathway this house forked from. One's gaze appeared set on the radiance of the city.

Goldfinch did not find anyone home. He made a quick round through the dwelling, searching for supplies. There was a pouch of old beef jerky resting atop a dusty kitchen table.

Goldfinch did not touch it. He slipped through to the back, searching for a well.

"Shepherd, Reg, come on back here," he called out over the small cottage. "Bring canteens and such."

Moments later, the party, save for One, gathered around the primed well. It trickled and then poured out fresh spring water. Reg worked the handle while Shepherd settled the canteens beneath it.

Seconds later, they walked back to the path where the horses were tethered. They stood, in procession, on the dirt path as the sun sank in the sky. Goldfinch could hear carriages rolling from stop to stop in the city, hooves battering matted dirt on the roads. They were close to this industrial crossroads.

Remounting their animals, the group decided to navigate a few city streets before backtracking to the forsaken farmstead. One rode side by side, sturdily with Goldfinch as they entered the city. The elder, Goldfinch guessed, wanted to emit authority. One wore no hat, but his lengthening white hair rested against his ears. His clothes made him look like a dignitary—tight trousers, ankle boots, and a long frock coat, almost a duster, that rested just past his knees.

Reg, behind Goldfinch, got his attention with a clumsy whistle. "Goldfinch, ya think there's more Burts and Rens, starin' down at us?"

Goldfinch peered into the second-floor windows of the wooden frameworks, one of many making Paterson this burgeoning city. "If they are, they're not going to like the sight of you."

They followed a central thoroughfare, from end to end, exhausting all the novel sites in between. They approached the downtown portion of the city, a parcel of land that seemed to gradually descend toward the base of other small hills.

In their passage, they encountered people of all sorts; peddlers, hunters, blacksmiths, bakers, and servants. All wore the dullest shades of gray or black. The women sported opulent dresses and bonnets that kept the hair steady for their homemaking chores. Though daylight waned, the city was still somewhat bustling with life. But the darker it got, the fewer people there were.

On their outbound turn, the four horses slowed after a strenuous day of travel, their only real rest coming from the hitching rail outside the deserted farm. On this painstaking return, Goldfinch determined which city buildings and taverns he could stop in to get acclimated with the clientele. He would see if any slavers were boldly passing through and making their claims. Some, Goldfinch assumed, must not have known whether to approach the federal government or just track down the local mayors and constables to plead their cases. Predictably, many just took matters into their own hands.

The men now simply desired sleep. One looked weary in the saddle, but a life of propriety and moral righteousness kept him prim and proper. Reg slumped slightly but maintained the dignified, watchful eye that any man of his experience would embrace. As they snuck through a turn, buildings encroaching on both sides, Goldfinch had his guard down for a moment when a peculiar sound rang out. He wondered if it was the call of feral dogs. In the distance, it seemed a pack of wild dogs were anxious, ravaging scraps of some kind or fending off another unwelcomed critter. Each man turned toward the noise.

Before Goldfinch had time to slip into his wolfish dream state, a sizable, dapple-gray stallion cut across their path. Then another horse did the same at the rear. Goldfinch immediately gravitated to the rifle, throwing his hand to the side of the Friesian.

"They're not dogs, Mr. Goldfinch," said a voice emanating from a shadowy figure still in the darkness ahead of them. Gauging the precise position of the moon and its trail, the man twitched the reins, and the gray approached the party. "They're coyotes."

Goldfinch's stomach dropped at the thought of the ravenous wild dogs—wolves, coyotes, dogs, no matter—that had been marking his dreams. He stuttered, and then pulled the hat past his brow.

Shepherd, however, involuntarily slumped in the saddle, gawking at the subject making the grand but ghostly entrance. "It's … the Senator," he claimed.

It was Senator Frelinghuysen, the man who had helped Reg's daughters get to safety in Tarrytown.

"Step inside," he said, motioning toward a shack beside an empty lot.

Chapter Twelve

Alaba

Six men sat calmly at a carved wooden table filling the room. The shack stood only a few feet wider than the table, stifling Goldfinch. The walls encroached in toward him, their chipped paint and faded beige mask spoke destitution. The city was quiet, quieter than it had been while their horses moved swiftly through the night.

Senator Frelinghuysen, a proud man with light brown hair, grinned and settled his gaze on Goldfinch. "It's no statehouse or manor, but it works for subtle purposes. It is a trusty ... hermitage," he said, widening his arms as if to embrace the bulk of the meager wooden shack. Moonlight peeked through the beams slapped lazily to the ceiling.

"It smells of whitewash and piss," Goldfinch said, placing his hat on the table. "And there are some kinks on this table."

"We don't all share superb carpentry skills, Mr. Goldfinch," the Senator said.

"I take it you don't visit with constituents here," Shepherd added almost mockingly.

Ignoring the banter, Senator Frelinghuysen returned the pitiless look to the Leader. "Point is, you hear the dogs. Yes?"

Reg, Shepherd, and One stared blankly back at Goldfinch. No one spoke. Goldfinch stumbled for a moment. "I'll go one further. By the looks of it, you've been on our tail for some time now. That said, you know that we've put five men in the ground in the past week; four on our soil, and one in the forest outside camp. A deplorable task, I assure you."

The Senator did not flinch. His eyelids sank to about half width, but his sharp stare intensified. "If you're hearing the howls, the shrill night noises, the tainted, fiery vision, then my presence has been felt."

Goldfinch cleared his throat and glanced at his other three men in the room. He shrugged, sighed, and turned back to the Senator. "We're here, I assume, because you know something of our predicament," Goldfinch proclaimed. "Now that you've tempted us into this here shanty, I suppose you have useful information. Who were those men?"

Senator Frelinghuysen tilted his head, shifted in his creaky wooden chair, and adjusted the lapel of a once-black, now stained, and tattered jacket. The collar of his white undershirt showed forcefully through, dominating the frayed fabric of the coat. As to what this coat shored up, Goldfinch could only guess.

He angled his head slightly upward and looked across the table, toward the other man that arrived on horseback with the Senator. He was of average height, thin, and dangerous looking. He had since been sitting quietly.

A light rain picked up outside. The droplets sank gracefully to the floor, through the leaks in the roof. Each landing held Reg's attention.

"This here is Mr. Boatwright, an unorthodox sort of ... chief of staff," Senator Frelinghuysen said. He continued, "I told Shepherd here a few days back now about my nightlife.

I may be a newly elected senator, but that does not force me to end a tireless pursuit. One of justice."

"The runaway girls, you remember them?" Shepherd asked, clearing his throat.

"You saw them over to Tarrytown," the Senator said. "You arrived with no setbacks I take it? I was forced to return."

"Only setback was that jarring ride across the Hudson," Shepherd said, moving his hand up and down as though mimicking the ferry ride.

"They're in good hands, I assure you," Senator Frelinghuysen added. "Hear that, Mr. Sullivan?"

The mention of his name startled Reg, who lifted his head a few careful inches. "Know my name, do ya?"

"It's not only your name I know, Reg." The Senator grinned—that unmistakable grin. He looked back at Goldfinch. "The rain. You see it, Mr. Hermann?"

Goldfinch winced, the name piercing him like one of Ren's bullets. He was unsettled, his stomach nearly churning, beads of sweat building at his temples. He couldn't tell if it was perspiration or an errant raindrop off one of the rafters. "Don't use that name. Haven't used it in, well, since we left this illusory world."

"Dogs will not take kindly to the rain this night. Befouls their vision." The Senator revealed a small wad of tobacco tucked into his lower lip. He slid his tongue across the brown bitterness and laughed. "Any second now."

Mr. Boatwright reached down and re-strapped a buckle on one of his ankle-high boots. Then he stood, a long frock coat resting past his knees. He took careful strides across the creaky floors—each creak with a resounding *erkk*—and unhinged the lock, pulling the door open as wide as the floor would let him. Without looking into the city's darkness, Mr. Boatwright turned and sat back at the table.

The droplets of rain bounced and spread on the table, reflecting the moonlight and illuminating the Senator's face. "Whether you're here or there, strong or frail, lost or saved, they'll be there, too," Senator Frelinghuysen said in a low voice.

Goldfinch shifted nervously in his chair. He looked at the moonbeams, and he looked at the door which sat widely ajar. Then it came. *Aawwwhooo*—a howl from right outside.

"If they're watching, I'm watching," Senator Frelinghuysen said. Instead of focusing on just Goldfinch, his gaze converged on Shepherd, Reg, and One, with little motion, it seemed.

Goldfinch thought that at last, the men may have understood his predicament. He saw Reg's eyelids flitter; One's hand trembled slightly on the splintery table. Reg remained still, almost petrified, from Senator Frelinghuysen's spellbinding words. Mr. Boatwright stroked his tamed muttonchops and removed his blue-tinted pince-nez. He breathed on the lenses and wiped them down with his jacket sleeve. The suit looked newer, more pronounced, than Senator Frelinghuysen's. Still, he remained silent.

The Senator spoke up, "Mr. Goldfinch, it is true. You are not alone in this endeavor any longer. The night visions, the red eye, the remote, ghostly howls. They'll see it, too." He looked pointedly at the others.

Shepherd turned toward Goldfinch. "All this mayhem, this is what you've seen? Why have you taken us here?"

"It is not me you should direct that question to." Goldfinch pitched his neck toward Senator Frelinghuysen. "It is he who has lured us."

"This is true," the Senator said. "I knew it would be the four of you who'd arrive. I know your camp, I know your fears, your yearnings, and most importantly, I know who's trailing you."

One appeared to grow upset at the ambiguity, this notion that the camp was watched by a United States Senator. "I won't believe it till I see it—watching us and all. It's nonsense."

The Senator closed his eyes for a moment and breathed deeply.

"Man's a necromancer," One declared. He abruptly rose and buttoned a single piece of his jacket. The Senator, however, still did not open his eyes.

The water dripped melodically onto the table. Mr. Boatwright smiled and looked at his boss. The four traveling men turned their attention to the door. With a slight, almost weightless stride, the silhouette of a wild animal walked up the creaky steps and snuck beneath the table at Mr. Boatwright's feet. Goldfinch felt the animal moving, its wild gaze settling ahead, on Senator Frelinghuysen.

Goldfinch heard the haunches of the animal sit noisily on the floor. It winced, and the Senator opened his eyes and locked them on Goldfinch. He said, "It's a full moon, gentlemen. They're out snaking through the grass, slipping stealthily from tree to tree. Their snouts turn upwards—they yelp and cry and long for a full-clawed swipe at the moon."

One had since reclaimed his seat, his old face taken aback. Shepherd shifted his weight to the right, Goldfinch followed. They poked their heads beneath the table. The animal—a coyote it seemed—rested at the Senator's boots, staring blankly up toward him, toward the moon.

"It was wise for you gentlemen to take refuge here," the Senator said. "Reckon you came aboard just in time. They're close."

"By God, man, can we drop the redundancy and the veiled threats? Just speak!" One fired.

"There are men, more of them, at your heels. You must listen carefully." The coyote then rose, came out from beneath the table and leaped up onto it. Its two front legs settled on it. Its hind legs were still grounded, but its paws pressed weight onto the table. The coyote panted and then put its head down on the table.

"Off the furniture, animal," Senator Frelinghuysen said. The beast did what it was told. It walked a few steps toward Goldfinch. "Better now, Hermann?"

The coyote locked eyes with Goldfinch, looking through him, appraising him. The Senator cut in. "Better yet, let us await the last arrival."

"More beasts?" One asked. "They smell of shit. They're mangy creatures. How do you suppose that helps our current quandary? We slip into the city, and you keep eyes on us. But how does that stop the stalking men?"

"No, old timer. It is not a beast, but a creature godlier than any man who has traversed these lands."

"What of the women who've marched across?" Goldfinch said sneeringly.

"Ah, see, that I cannot answer for the woman carries such obvious beauty. Take, for instance, your Harriet."

Goldfinch tensed up on the sound of her name. "Watch us as you will, but leave her out of it."

"Goldfinch, Goldfinch, friend. You're misinformed. My aims are pure."

"Do, rationally, tell then."

"The man is good for his word," Shepherd chimed in, obviously recalling his experience at the Hudson. "He was on the road. He found us—Regina, Amber, and me. But he did not harm us. On the contrary, he pledged unwavering support."

"I've heard your tale, boy," One said indignantly. "But until I hear *reason*, I will not back down."

Senator Frelinghuysen ignored the provocation and turned toward Reg. "Your daughters, I tell you, Mr. Sullivan, are better off now than they ever were on that Picket plantation. Renly, Burt, those men were just thorns in your side. But they're out of the way. It's the contingency portion of this ordeal you best be worrying about."

"Mista, I just want to get to my daughters. These folk have been very nice to me, though. Hope you can find it in your heart to help 'em."

"The more I look, Mr. Sullivan, the more it appears you've become one of them. Maybe it's best to embrace this now? Your partner, your daughter, they've fallen out of view. Your other daughters are in safe hands. Follow your heart and keep your village running. In their honor."

"My village?" Reg asked himself aloud. "Reckon I thought 'bout that a little bit, too, mista," Reg added. "Maybe it best I listen to ya."

"We can sort out pleasantries later," One fired.

"Now, Erskine, if you were to just show a slight degree of patience, your angst would subside, I assure you," Senator Frelinghuysen said, finally starting to show some emotion.

"That illusory world name will not be tolerated and—" One said, but was cut short.

"I understand your petty rules, I do, *One*, but now is no time for curtsies or idealism. The fact remains, there are men on the road after your camp."

"Where do you suppose these men come from? Some abundant fountain of witless folk down there in the Carolinas?" Shepherd asked, obviously befuddled.

Senator Frelinghuysen knocked his fingers halfheartedly on the table. The coyote took this as a sign and made a break for the front door. Mr. Boatwright stood and watched it run off. In the distance, Goldfinch and the men could hear its somber howl. Mr. Boatwright nicked the door with his boot, closing it, but not sealing it at the hinge. He turned back toward the four men with a big-toothed grin.

"It's only a few seconds now," Senator Frelinghuysen said as Mr. Boatwright settled back in his seat. "Mr. Hermann, ah, *Goldfinch*, will adore this."

"Damn you, man," One called out. "That's enough of this. You dance around the subject as though we have time to admire you. Just speak."

"The Castervaugh man, as you know, has alerted the authorities. Well, I suppose you can call *them* authorities. It's a bit higher up than that, taking into effect that 1793 law. Let's just say it wasn't the first time that portly fella had to alert the bureaucrats."

"Aren't you one of the bureaucrats?" One asked.

The Senator ignored him. Reg spoke up. "There were plenty of men, women too, that fled from that hell down there. No way that Burt fella ain't settled some odd dispute or 'nother."

"As I've told your Founders, it's an admirable operation you've set up. But do not think, even for a moment, that the government—or at least parts of it—has not been kept abreast. This tidbit will save your souls, each and every one of you."

"Souls are redeemed. It's not death we fear," Goldfinch said. "It is being compromised by the likes of these southern traffickers." He stomped his foot on the floor, his face reddening.

"The Governor's office has been notified. I suppose it is in your best interest now to shore up your gates, hunker down, and wait for this to pass. I shall do all I can at my end. There are many avenues to be strolled upon, many ploys hidden within my sleeve."

***

As he said this, they heard a peculiar sound outside the front door. There was a shallow whimper and a scratch at the wood of the steps. Time seemed to stall for Goldfinch. He wondered who it could be. Or, what could it be.

Who is this senator? What is he capable of? His thoughts ran rampant.

Mr. Boatwright stood, stretched for a moment in his constricting suit, and headed back for the door. When he opened it this time, there was no hesitation.

It was a lone, sharply white-shaded and firmly contoured arctic wolf—a Melville Island wolf. Here it was in Paterson. The wolf's tongue hung from its mouth, and it retreated back across its razor-sharp canines. It did not even scan the room before sliding across the floor with ease toward Senator Frelinghuysen. Like the coyote, the wolf sat at his side, staring up only to read what the Senator was hinting with his subtle gestures.

The wolf was a prodigious animal. It could prance nimbly through the room or do whatever it wished. The only person fixed on getting rid of it seemed to be One, but Goldfinch knew he would not dare push his luck and unleash more of his sharp tongue. Not now. Everyone else was too afraid, too quickly and too implausibly afraid.

The wolf snarled, and its jowls accumulated a layer of saliva. It turned and looked at Goldfinch. He did not imagine the inconceivable. There *was* a wolf staring him in the face. The angled moonlight brushed across the animal's eyes and tinted its pupils—they became the red eye he had grown to know. Goldfinch did not cower away this time, he looked the animal right in the eyes. There was no other discourse, no other yearning, except for keeping this animal at bay and understanding its purpose. The Senator, however, seemed to recognize every ounce of effort that Goldfinch was exerting. The village leader tried to remain focused on the animal.

"Quite a spectacle, isn't she?" the Senator asked Goldfinch. The other men were slumped in their chairs, taken aback. "Something to rival your horse, Eder, yes?"

"She is," Goldfinch concluded. "What's the animal's purpose?"

"If she sees the brutality, I see it," Senator Frelinghuysen said. For the first time, Mr. Boatwright made a sound. He laughed a clearly defined affirmation. "She'll go with you, on your return journey—keep an eye on things. She won't eat your beef or stalk any livestock. She prefers to stay in the shadows like Mr. Boatwright and me."

"By God, you're a U.S. Senator. The shadows?" One asked.

"A facade, One, I assure you. It is the night that rules the day, and the silence that preys on the noise—the bustle of the city, the slice of the scythe on the wheat." He paused. "Keep the majestic wolf, and the community is under my careful watch. As for the predicament, I will jostle the legislature in the way I know how to keep the Governor from compromising your settlement. Is that enough disclosure?" He looked intently at One.

"Has the Governor been tipped off? The Governor himself?" Shepherd asked calmly. He was always able to stamp on an non-erasable and firm expression. His fading English accent slipped through.

"No," the Senator barked immediately. "But I have reason to believe that a man in his office, the Governor's own 'Mr. Boatwright,' an aide of sorts, is on the prowl. Chances are, if he knew what was good for him, he'd hold off on the disclosure, scope the place out, and then move forward."

"So, this is the man we should fear then, Frelinghuysen?" Shepherd responded.

Goldfinch felt his knees tremble. "Who is the man?"

"If the wolf is close, and the man too, I'll know in due time," Senator Frelinghuysen said. Mr. Boatwright grumbled faintly, unintelligibly. It was the second time a noise had fled his flat, dry lips.

Goldfinch paused, putting his elbows on the stiff table. Thoughts raced through his mind. *The Pickets have alerted the Governor*, he thought, *but the Governor does not know just yet?* He tried to put the puzzle together.

Goldfinch spoke up again. "This man you say is on the prowl. He will not travel haphazardly to a fledgling community in the coarse soil, the mountains. He's sure to bring a detail, a regiment, and militiamen, no? How can we be sure?"

The wolf was silent, hardly breathing, its chest barely constricting or expanding. It just held its look on Senator Frelinghuysen. If he shifted slightly, the wolf would lick its chops, and her paws would fidget. Goldfinch could tell One was paying close attention to it. He swung his eyes from Mr. Boatwright to the wolf at will.

To Goldfinch, the Senator said, "While I stand and fight in Congress, I recognize that it's a strength—an advantage many others do not have. As I circumnavigate my state, ensuring the safe passage of runaways, I recognize that, too, is a strength. It's a strength to which the animals contribute. Like our girl Alabaster here. Nonetheless, I cannot part the seas. I cannot move mountains, though I've tried."

He paused and licked his lips. Goldfinch spotted his momentary hesitation, his nose taking in the moldy smell that passed for urine. "I shall do my best to safeguard your Eden. Rest assured, the good Reverend will be brought up to speed—the others as well."

"You know of our foundation, but you've done little to keep the Pickets from ripping apart every last shingle of our roofs," Goldfinch said. "I expect to see something actualized, for all your rhetoric."

"Gentlemen, do let me see you back to the cottage I've cleared for you. It's a farmstead—you passed it coming into the city."

The moon shone a radiant white through the ceiling beams. The only real, discernible motion in the room was the flurrying of dust particles finding their way to the mud-caked floor. The rain had subsided some. Goldfinch took in this room, sensing a sort of mystical quality. He wondered if it was the portal into the city's underworld.

"Even our shelter has been chosen, you say?" he asked.

Senator Frelinghuysen gave a wink, a sly testament to some sort of saintly power. "Let us trot back to the house. There, you can stay, rest, and prepare your mounts for the journey home."

"Will ya be stayin' with us? Time bein'?" Reg asked.

"I'll go as far as I must," Senator Frelinghuysen answered. As he said this, he rose, and the animal rose, too. She began to pant and even jumped playfully off the ground. She took her snout and rubbed it against the side of the Senator's cotton trousers. He made a gesture, moving his chin onward toward the door. The wolf let out an excited cry, and then fled out the opened door to the darkened canvas. Mr. Boatwright followed right behind. He hopped down the two front steps and then removed his top hat and brushed the brim, ridding it of the few rain droplets. Then he walked down the narrow passageway to an unlatched front gate and walked to the street, in the direction the animal likely traipsed off.

"Will we be seeing this Mr. Boatwright again?" Shepherd asked Senator Frelinghuysen.

"He'll make sure the cottage is cleared, and watch after Alaba, of course. She is young, but fearless, headstrong even."

One sighed deeply and appeared to whisper a few indecencies. A certain remark proved loud enough to hear.

"Our destiny lies in the hands—the *paws*—of a dog."

Chapter Thirteen

The Farmstead

Goldfinch scrutinized Senator Frelinghuysen's rickety, sloped, little shanty. The exterior paint was chipping off the siding, matching the interior's forlorn state. Goldfinch turned again, and Senator Frelinghuysen was taking long strides back onto the road. He hopped on a horse that stood in the street, tethered to nothing.

Their animals, on the other hand, were tied to the nearby hitching post. The Friesian rubbed its right front hoof on a patch of malleable earth. Goldfinch looked into the windows of the nestled buildings for any sign of suspicion, spies, or sabotage. Nothing.

The men made their way toward their mounts, each mindfully shooting stares over their shoulders. The city was dark, and no lanterns or torches flared. It was the middle of the night, but the windows of homes and businesses in the distance seemed eternally motionless, as though just plastered onto the map of some fleeting paper town.

Mr. Boatwright had long since disappeared, but Senator Frelinghuysen stood at the threshold of light and uniform darkness. He was on the cusp of being eclipsed by the shadows of the tall edifice to his right.

"Move along now, if you plan to rise early," the Senator said in his now-familiar, hazy tone.

One was the first to mount his horse. The animal neighed assertively, the vapors from it trailed off softly. "We follow the man, the wolf follows us. The village is compromised. We get torn from ear to ear by the wolf," he said. "Does anyone like this circularity?"

Shepherd was the next to settle on his animal. "Beats the pace of lugging corpses strung to sacks uphill and at the ass of a horse."

Reg was next. He pulled the knots loose at the hitching post, climbed up and then slid his boots into the stirrups. The humble man he was, though, he kept his thoughts to himself. He was loyal to a fault, likely never to cross Goldfinch.

Still aground, Goldfinch spoke up, "If we want to hold our ground, our faith, we'll honor the plan of this gentleman, necromancer or not." He saw the Senator slip on a tall, black top hat and tip the brim delicately in his direction. When he turned back to his convoy, he adjusted a loose rein on the Friesian, inspected the other riders' gear and glanced back at the Senator. He was gone—he'd stepped into the shadowy night, which became his plaything.

"To the cottage," Goldfinch exclaimed, whisking the reins on the Friesian. He led the pack, Reg, One, and Shepherd trailed behind in single file.

Goldfinch practically sniffed out a trail since the street was so dark and bare. He could see the dusty footprints of Senator Frelinghuysen's animal. They were marked every few paces with a colorful leaf, a drifter from the nearby highlands.

When they had added a considerable distance, Goldfinch looked back through the narrow passageway, which during the day became an artery of the city. There were a few distant lantern lights. He wondered where this illumination was when the group had settled around the table. He said nothing, though. The Friesian continued to plod along. On they went, through the undulating terrain of Paterson.

The sound of alternating hooves against the dirt became melodic. They reshaped their single-file line after passing the city's center, walking congruently in a row like a band of Hessians during America's great rebellion. So far, it seemed that Paterson, a city established by Alexander Hamilton, was largely a ghost town unless Senator Frelinghuysen's trancelike power over them won out.

They trekked, turned, paused, and flicked the reins. Soon they were ascending back up the hills that dipped into the city. The climb was long and arduous. Goldfinch reached his hand down the side of the horse toward his protruding saddlebag. He felt his fingers run down the stock of the Long Rifle. As he looked up again, the chain of Synod villagers was still moving steadily. Every hundred feet or so, their surrounding pocket of earth dimmed. They were leaving the city at their backs. What lay ahead, Goldfinch knew not. What was behind, he wouldn't soon forget.

"Hey there, slow up now, girl," Shepherd called down to his agile, young horse. "*Ttt-tttt*, easy girl." He tightened the reins, and the horse stopped. The chain of riders each took a few more steps but then paused to watch Shepherd. "Up there, the farm is straight ahead," he said.

Goldfinch flicked dirt from his fingers. With no notice, he took off on the Friesian. "*Yaaa, yaaa.*"

Within thirty seconds, he arrived. He dismounted at the same hitching spot they had come to when they strolled into Paterson. He took the reins in his hands and bound them to the elevated log, while his eyes were fixed on the glass windows of the house and the incline behind the small, crippled silo. He stood staring as the others made up the ground and came to his side.

"I dozed a bit on horseback," Shepherd said, bobbing his head as if each word carried weight—as if he felt them betraying their source. "And it's the animal I see."

He paused. "Could it be our deliverance from evil, or our punishment for escaping the throes of this world?" He was uneasy, jittery.

"Either way, it is a feeling you do not exclusively inherit," Goldfinch said. They were not looking at one another.

Mr. Boatright emerged from the farm's darkened yard, an area Goldfinch thought was rough vegetation and fading thorn bushes. As he had done before, he studied the four men before him and said, "Her name, is Alaba."

Senator Frelinghuysen strolled into view as well.

"The wolf, you say?" Goldfinch asked Mr. Boatwright.

"He won't speak again until he knows it's in his best interest, that Mr. Boatwright. There's no guarantees Alaba brings salvation from your slave-catching dilemma, but she will be our eyes, our vessel."

One glared at him. "I'll try to recall that as hunters jump the gate and a wolf tears smiles into us."

"*We* make our moves within the government and carry out our surveillance," the Senator said. "*You* worry about keeping the walls of your sanctuary secured."

Goldfinch carefully scaled the few rickety, rotted steps out front. The familiar smell of insects and rotting wood welcomed him back. The door squeaked open. When he saw the rotting of the cabinets, the blemished wooden floorboard, he was relieved. "Gentlemen, it's free and clear. Do enter," he said.

"We know this," the Senator added. "But we admire the bravery."

"Just enter."

The group settled around a hearth with darkening but still-active coals. Goldfinch wondered if Senator Frelinghuysen had made it to the house already. Had he started his own fire, one he also swiftly let die? One blew air into his cupped hands, and Reg rubbed his palms against his stained slacks.

"I have a meeting of the Senate tomorrow, a meeting I cannot be absent for," the Senator said.

Mr. Boatwright turned his head side to side, then back toward the flimsily latched doorway. The Senator acknowledged the gesture.

"For now, Alaba is out of our hands," the Senator said. "She is doing her work, doing it unabashedly." He got up and moved his wooden chair closer to the hearth, along with another one for his feet. He grabbed a bundle of kindling that lay nearby and thrust it into the fireplace. He slowly put his boots on the chair and reclined.

Mr. Boatwright stood and walked to his boss's ear. There were whispers, then a handshake, and Mr. Boatwright walked from the house without so much as a tip of the hat. Goldfinch caught a glimpse of the tinted pince-nez as he departed.

"Mr. Boatwright will be off now. He has much to tend to. I have constituents to converse with, others to grapple with," the Senator admitted. "But what I hear is overwhelming. You'll want to return to Synod tomorrow." He hesitated. "There's been word from the Reverend in Philadelphia. Your runaway is on the move. You know what this means."

Goldfinch had an inkling that the Senator was not letting on to all he knew. He was dispassionate and secretive. One recognized this from the start. "You cannot share the news?" he wondered.

"I've disclosed as much as I'm at liberty to right now." With that, the Senator's boots were swiftly reeled in from the wooden bench before the budding flames. He stood, grabbed his hanging frock coat, and placed his hat on his head. "If you do not hear from us again, then all bodes well, Mr. Hermann. Remember, the illusory world listens, as do senators, despite the misconceptions."

Senator Frelinghuysen did not take the time for farewells. He did not so much as wish the group safe passage. He evasively walked around a hearty beam of moonlight that shone on the floor. At the doorway, he spun back to look at them and then avoided the steps altogether, half-leaping from the top.

***

There was no sign of Senator Frelinghuysen any longer. After his horse had been unhitched, the four men stood from their chairs and gazed confusedly at one another. It was as though they were marked as properties to survey, as if their stomachs were churning following a disagreeable batch of dairy.

"Well, it's agreed, then. We leave at first light," Goldfinch said.

Reg stared up at him. He turned his head toward the wall where the rifles were now stashed. Then back. "'Yer man is on the move,' what he said. Our fate's got su'thin to do with Sol'mon." The faint sound of trees waving and brushing their seasonal coats continued.

"Anyone else hear something?" Shepherd asked. "That cry out there, in the distance?"

Chapter Fourteen

Group Two

Outside Paterson, the lay of the land seemed to widen as the villages, and smaller hamlets became rarer sights. The men had gotten much-needed rest the previous night, camping on the floor of the forsaken farmhouse. The four of them each had bedrolls and laid them in the warmer back corner of the place.

Goldfinch had dipped deeply into his saddlebag to come up with his remaining rations. The quantity of food was low. The corn cakes and grains were fair, but they were nothing compared to a home-cooked Synod steak.

"Reckon at this point in time, that trip to Charlottesburg would look mighty fine," Goldfinch said to Shepherd, recalling the younger man's regular trips in and out of the nearby community.

Shepherd had just nodded and dozed off. Goldfinch had sat up through the night staring out the glass windows, into the perilous northward direction and back toward this mystical south.

While shifting side to side on the saddle, Goldfinch lost himself for a moment in the beauty of the abolitionist spirit. He thought back on the moving sermons from Richard Allen, and the comfort his wife Sarah provided. As a groundskeeper, he had looked on through the smudgy glass of Philadelphia's AME Church and felt like he was sitting in the front pew.

He could not stay affixed to these more colorful memories for long because as he did, he saw the AME dissolve to a dark image of the Senator standing half-shielded by the moonlight. He saw Alaba's intense, uninhibited stare at the Senator.

Every now and then, he slipped away from his boundless but vitreous subconscious. It seemed so easy to mold, to fall victim to Senator Frelinghuysen's guile. It was fragile, though, and he knew a bullet from another Picket man could really inflict damage.

He gazed up from his mount and spotted One at the front of the pack. He was always asserting his dominance, pulling out some bureaucratic stop to latch on to just a morsel of power. At this point, though, Goldfinch did not care. *Men will be men*, he thought. *Better to let them flounder*. Goldfinch had also come to like—or at least appreciate—One through their arduous journey.

Harriet's smile then appeared before his eyes. Her shapely form dancing in the twilight. He could smell the perfume emitting from her loosened hair. The kind that lingered, no matter where he journeyed. He argued that the farther their distance from one another, the nearer his heart clung to her.

***

The days were short, but the journey was still long. They followed the Paterson-Hamburg Turnpike up through all of its windy stages. There were creeks, meadows, farmland, more congested shacks, and pockets of stronger infrastructure every few miles.

The troupe kept pace, the horses pressing on like the saintly animals they were. Every now and then, the Friesian would try to stick its tongue through the bit, but Goldfinch tightened the reins and moved on. He soon stopped to fling water from his canteen to the horse's mouth, to which the others made no protest. He reached into his pocket and grabbed a handful of corn. The Friesian's curious tongue immediately felt it out and then ingested the small offering. The other men did the same with their animals.

The signs became clearer and clearer that they were approaching their Synod home because the hills began to pitch higher. These hills gave way to small but dense mountains whose colors managed to brighten the monotony of the gray clouds.

As gusts of wind picked up, Goldfinch could feel its fingers attempting to snatch his hat. He held the crown of it tightly. He looked up and saw One's grayed hair moving fumblingly through the air. Shepherd, too, wore no hat but for some reason did not have the same problem as One, though his hair was also on the longer side.

Rounding out the pack was Reg, whose frayed shirt, trousers, and spats over his boots appeared to fit right in. On sounds streaming through the woods, he would jerk his head. Goldfinch wondered if he had witnessed a slight change in character within the past twenty-four hours. *Could it be,* Goldfinch thought, *that Reg is no longer fixated on leaving this place, our place?*

The daydreams proved successful because within no time the horses were readying themselves for their approach to the pass that led to the obscure trail, which wound its way up to Synod. Though it appeared to be a swift ride, the truth was that it had taken almost two days. It was now the morning of Saturday, November 7, 1829.

While Goldfinch felt reacquainted with his deep subconscious, he felt equally ill-prepared for his arrival at the camp. The men with him, it seemed, could tell.

"What is your position on the others?" Shepherd asked.

"In what regard?" Goldfinch replied.

"To tell them what has unfolded. To warn them of a man most obviously on our tail. Or another who has sworn to destroy us."

"I see," Goldfinch responded. "Well, *hmm*, sometimes deceit is a necessary evil." He paused. "We'll get this place running once again. I'm speaking about iron output, furrowed fields, supply runs. Then we'll get as serious as need be."

Shepherd said, "Eh," and galloped ahead of Goldfinch. When it seemed like the pathway through the rocky terrain would not allow another single inch of man and horse to continue, the horses still kept going. They pushed through the thick weeds, grasses, and boughs. At last, the hooves remained motionless, sturdy, in front of a hardly noticeable footpath.

It was not quite wide enough for a wagon, but a horse could easily maneuver its way through. One look at the path left Goldfinch thinking about Alaba's prance down the Paterson road.

"Check for strange animal prints, I would say," One added sarcastically. "After this week I'm inclined to keep an eye open while I sleep."

Goldfinch did not know whether to laugh or imagine a dog attack. The result left a helpless look on his face.

"Well, shall we ride?" Shepherd urged. The troupe pushed through the path, flanked by the thinning forest. The trail was windy, and there was a slight ascent as well.

Tttt-kkkk, ttt-kkk. The horseshoes pressed on the brownish ground with ease. When it seemed like his aching back would not survive another step in the saddle, Goldfinch caught sight of the cleverly disguised village, hidden between pines and oaks that stretched like arms upward into the daylight.

It would only take a few more minutes—of spiraling upward and weaving between trunks—before they'd reach the village. Goldfinch decided to pick up the horse's gait to a nimble trot. He felt the toes of his boots graze the papery foliage. He *yaaahh'd* the horse, nicking its left flank. He turned behind him to see if the others had followed. While they, too, increased their pace, it was nowhere close to the trot.

Coming to the widening expanse at the meadow, where the rear jutted up to the hills comprising the Synod burial ground, Goldfinch took in the aroma of his home—the pines, the stiffening air, the gritty soil. He slowed the Friesian to a walk, and it lifted its hooves to knee height on each step. Goldfinch peeled back on the reins and looked left. There stood the riotous wooden cross resting easily on the hackberry tree.

Goldfinch recalled the challenging few moments it took to hang the cross, with the Founder, Cartwright, fumbling with the base, the others talking aimlessly. He even recalled the loss of life beneath the cross. He could not dwell for too long because the thought of the Picket clan sending another group of backwoods kinfolk was terrifying.

He approached the gate. He expected someone—Minister Mulvane, Harriet, Elizabeth—to open it for him, to greet the chivalrous knight returning from his crusade. But there was none of that. In the distance, Goldfinch could hear some commotion. He glanced back at his fellow travelers. They were closing in on him now. He waited a few moments for them to arrive. They stood in a column at the gate. Each man's horse was fatigued. The wills of the four men were tested, though their hearts seemed to grow from the infectious spell of Senator Frelinghuysen.

One turned toward Goldfinch. "True story, then? All that whimpering, gawking you were doing before the journey?"

Goldfinch gave no reply. Meanwhile, Shepherd examined his yellowed undershirt, tested by the grit of the roads. Reg stood quietly, fidgeting with his horse's mane.

"There's no glorious reception," Goldfinch declared. "But they'll be a warm crowd." He patted the side of the horse and stretched a rein. The Friesian set its legs in motion. Goldfinch thought about the smell of coagulated blood, the blood that stained the bottom half of the cross. He took a few paces back on the Friesian and asked One to open the gate. The elder promptly dismounted, showing off the agility he still retained well into his sixties. His beard was thickening, like the gradual but inevitable crusting of ice slipping downward in shallow waters.

Without thanking the old man, Goldfinch paraded through the gate at full gallop, aiming straight toward the hub of the community—the fire pit past the paddock, just before the erected church. As the horse's momentum slowed with the opposing pull of the rein, Goldfinch settled loosely in the saddle. He whistled and then hollered unintelligible noises, waiting for a response. The sounds he had heard at the gate had subsided, but he turned an ear toward the church. There. The voices were unmistakable. The villagers were gathered in the house of worship, presumably to prepare for the next day's church services.

With ease, he climbed down from his horse. He slipped across the yellowing grass to the church. He pulled off his hat and entered.

"I suppose it's about time I've returned," he said. "You cannot even post a guard outside? After *our* ordeal?"

No one responded, but by the looks of it, all of the Synod folks were gathered there, and then some. He tried to run a quick head count through his mind, but the numbers would just not add up. There were too many frenetic thoughts coursing about; the deaths, the Senator, the elusive 'man on the move.'

He lifted his hat so that everyone could see him more clearly. Picking his head up, he spotted Harriet in the crowd, practically front and center. By the looks of it, she had been bossing someone around on one count or another. He felt a tingling sensation drop within his stomach. Then it sank lower. He looked around. There were a few more heads in the building. By some miracle, they fit into the small nave of the church.

The Leader felt a hand grip his shoulder, squeeze it, and then release its tight grasp. It was Shepherd, who stood at his back, gazing around the room as Goldfinch had done a few seconds earlier. "Suppose they didn't want to see us up here again—see us return," Shepherd joked.

"When they're told what's at stake they'll come around, I assure you," Goldfinch responded. The door of the church creaked open even farther. It was Reg and One.

"Gentlemen, ladies, let us treat you to our tale," Goldfinch called out. As he said this, he spotted petticoats, a naval frock coat, and a high-waisted skirt. It was Harriet. She turned toward the men who had busted into the nave.

"We've been just fine here without you," Harriet said, keeping her focus on Goldfinch. As she extended herself to assure she was heard, a space opened in her stead. Goldfinch could see next to and behind her now. There, waiting patiently, placidly, was Solomon. He had a white shirt, frayed seams on the pants, and was holding a top hat.

The man had returned from his runaway-gathering journey. So, Goldfinch tried to place every person in the room.

"Who are these stragglers?" he asked, placing his weapon against the church wall. He removed his hat. His hair was frazzled from the road and ever-thinning. He somewhat nervously rubbed at one of his ears. To Goldfinch, they were a bit large even for his face.

Before she could speak, Harriet was pried out of the way by Minister Mulvane. "Welcome back, gentlemen," he said. He frowned at Harriet, likely for her hostility. What the cleric didn't know was that hostility had sparked life into Goldfinch's jaded soul. "Seems like you've returned just in time. We're consulting with our new arrivals."

Solomon stepped from the pew he had sat down in. He fastened his hat to his head and walked toward Goldfinch. He grabbed the Leader by the shoulder and ushered him from the small building. Harriet called from inside. "You tell him, Solomon. You tell him. Even more people at this fledgling place."

Outside the church, Solomon slowly released his arm from Goldfinch's frock coat. "Mista, I just pulled back to camp today. Didn' get to see Reverend Allen down there. Was stopped just past Paterson, by that Red Tail fella again. He done kept me privy to all sorts of happ'nings. Thing is, came back with a group of seven. Red Tail done dumped 'em on me. We gawn have to share huts or build a few more, but these are real ones, Mista Goldfinch. They have a purpose here—'parently Reverend done say so."

"Who are these folks?" Goldfinch asked.

"One of 'em is Catharine Beecher, Lyman's daughter. She's a teacha' from Connecticut, has some private school there. Obviously heard about the Synod exper'ment, Lyman had 'er sent down."

"And the others?"

"Well, you rec'nize that one over yonda?" He pointed at a man of about twenty-five who stood firmly in the middle of the church. Minister Mulvane walked to the young man's side. They were surrounded by the ironworkers, William and Elizabeth. The new man wore a frock coat that sat at his thighs. He was quite tall, had a narrow face, and a pointed nose. He was clean-shaven and carried a golden, chain-linked pocket watch in the palm of his right hand. When Goldfinch peered at him, he stuffed the timepiece into his pocket, and the chain arched around the coat's buttons. "That be Blithe Mulvane, the Minister's son," Solomon said.

Goldfinch watched him fiddle with the watch in his pocket. He wore a high-brimmed hat and polished black shoes. "Some muscle for this place. Thank you for following up on that, Solomon. Was it an arduous task, corralling him?"

"If it was, I wouldn't know. That there job went to Revrend Allen. Man did all that, sent 'im up with Red Tail."

"How could he have known that I was seeking him?" Goldfinch responded.

"P'haps the Minister sent a letter. Or, maybe the Founder just knew. Could be one of them strange, heavenly things. Either way, he was waitin' with the rest of the group. I dunno if they was livin' down there some weeks waitin', or what. All I know is that I grabbed 'em, got 'em on home."

"I was meaning to ask about the return journey," Goldfinch said. "How exactly was it?"

"Well Mista Goldfinch, I didn' see no problems. Traveled at night some, traveled carefully. It's so dark up here you cain't see right from left, or if someone's trailin' ya."

"And the others?"

"You finally done got to the most important question," Solomon said. "See, there's a woman, she's in the front of the church now, covered by the whole lot of us. Name's Carlita. She a runaway all way from N'Orleans. She's been squeezin' through the paths up north, help of the system and all. You'll see her, come to the front of this here church. I'll introduce ya. She real old but she got a fine ol' personality."

"And the others yet?" Goldfinch fired. "Who are they?"

"Seems to me, they just be some nice farmhands. I know one of them names—Nance. It's Pete Nance. Reason I know that is 'cause he was just askin' questions like he'd go off to the gallows, he didn't."

Goldfinch craned his neck to gaze back into the church, to put a face to the names. As he did this, Solomon spoke softly. "Harriet there, she don't want these folk. Wanted me to ship 'em back to Paterson, or P'delphia or wherever, the second I brung 'em through the gate. I figures we can give 'em a place to stay like we did Reg."

"These folks shall not go anywhere unless I deem it necessary," Goldfinch said. "And I'll catch you all up on my tales soon enough. But for now, I must talk to Harriet. You tell all of this to Shepherd. He'll lend you an ear. He'll keep an eye on these matters. We need more weight on this. Have him see the new folks to their quarters."

"Where that?" Solomon wondered.

Goldfinch heard the question but deflected it with a simple swipe of his hand. He was fixated on Harriet. It was his libido acting now, not his rational self. He felt his pulse throb, his face redden. He knew she was ornery, distasteful even. But the prospect of her naked body had him forgetting all of which had transpired. He took both hands to Solomon's shoulders, placed him aside, and forcefully walked back into the small building. He sidestepped, and ricocheted, the greetings of a few villagers, but went right for Harriet. He saw

Shepherd leaving to speak with Solomon. Reg and One stood together near the unoccupied space by the back walls.

Goldfinch saw Harriet at the head of the group, talking the ear off of Blithe Mulvane, who had an inscrutable grin plastered to his face. Mid-stride, Goldfinch measured up this new Blithe fellow and then shifted his focus back to Harriet. She continued to talk to Blithe. She brushed the tips of her fingers sensually down his coat pocket. They arched over and cut across it, but landed in the pocket where the watch rested. She flung her fingers at a few of the small chains it was connected to and looked up at the young traveler. It was not so much jealousy Goldfinch felt, but disorientation. He had come so far and done so much. He felt like the romance would click almost effortlessly, as though she would be waiting for him with an open heart.

He ignored any pleasantries fired at him like the gut shot that eradicated Burt Castervaugh. He bumped into backsides or petticoats. Goldfinch arrived beside her and looked at the new teacher. "Do you have the time, young man?"

Blithe looked at Goldfinch, studying him. "Quarter to eleven, still early," he said.

"You know, boy, in this place we disregard our prior names. What is it you'd like to be called?"

"With all due respect, sir, I'd like to keep Blithe. It's not all that heard of. We can assume it's a new identity." He shrugged his shoulders and laughed.

Goldfinch simply looked at him and said, "The likely response of an unseasoned boy. You know, when I asked for you here, I didn't think you'd create such friction upon arrival."

"Like father, like son," Blithe said, the giddy look on his face slowly evaporating.

Harriet quit biting her tongue and spoke up. "Blithe, this is the impossibly difficult leader of Synod, Mr. Goldfinch. If you do not wish to be chastised like this, *do* please go and find someone else more pleasant to speak with." She took her right hand and gently shoed him off, winking at him as he stared down at her.

Goldfinch noticed the mutual tenderness. "You've known this man?"

Harriet sighed and said, "No, but it's charming to finally see a real man, a man of substance, walk through that gate."

Goldfinch inched closer, shuffling his boots on the ground—a clapboard floor that retained a sparkle that no Paterson floor had. He practiced Harriet's own tactic on her. When no one had the two of them in plain sight, under obvious scrutiny, he rubbed his fingers down the side of her arms covered by the frock coat. She wore a maroon skirt that jetted out at her hips. His calloused fingers slid stiffly down the coat, the rough skin hitching any unsettled fabric. He lowered his gaze to her eye level. He insinuated, through obvious body language, that they should return to his cottage, to christen his arrival. He wondered if she would resist his prolonged touch. The most she did was shift her shoulder blades. But she brought her index fingers to the corners of her eyes, sighed, and acquiesced. She looked up at him with her lips pressed together, save for the charming little pocket of air in the middle that held her curiosity.

He turned toward the door, adjusting the lapel on his coat. His eyes unfocused, his long-pent-up sexuality dictating every move, he rushed from the church. As he looked back, Harriet was attempting to make a subtle exit. She bowed her head at a few villagers, smiled at a few others. He watched as she once again met eyes with Blithe from across the small church.

As he latched onto this wretched image, he extended his legs out for a lengthier stride and bumped into the shoulder of a man cutting recklessly across his path. Goldfinch felt his own head rattle slightly, and his momentum carry forward. As he came to an uneasy stop, he looked at the interfering man. It was someone he had never seen before. He was shorter than Goldfinch, wore medium-length hair and spectacles. He had a black cravat contrasting with a pure white undershirt and a coat that fit comfortably over it all. He had a long nose, beady eyes, and unkempt eyebrows. He looked fifty, though he could've been younger.

"On your way, I presume?" the man asked maliciously. He stared down at Goldfinch's boots and then worked his way up to the hat, an unpleasant look on his face. "Sorry for the disruption. Can't avoid it sometimes. Just clumsy is all. Carry on."

Goldfinch glared at him. The trip, his anxiety, and his yearning for a female meant that he would not be reticent. "And you are?"

"Mr. Nance, Mr. Peter Nance, sir," the man said, smiling and even bowing a few inches. "And I see I've met Mr. Goldfinch. I'll be off now."

In the distance, a howl broke through the more barren trees. Goldfinch imagined the red eye he had seen on men and beasts. He shook away the thought. He looked behind him, and Harriet was leaving the church, following him.

For a fleeting moment, Goldfinch felt proud—of himself, of the village. He had halted the advances of bounty hunters. He also had 'stargazed' in the presence of the Senator.

The world quietened at Harriet's footfall. He glanced about, seeing everything and nothing all at the same time, except her. Harriet. Nance was talking with another soul. The sky was high and hollow, the land empty.

She strode toward him, elegantly slipping through the church door. Goldfinch's heart pounded. She was alone in this exit, but Goldfinch still felt someone nearby with prowling eyes. He ventured a few steps toward her, to see her countenance and whatever wandering spirit might have been lurking.

Goldfinch glided his fingers down his strapped rifle, toward the muzzle, to afford him whatever security that provided. Where he stopped, he could see directly into the brimming church. He searched from person to person as he had done only a minute earlier. Harriet was approaching him, reaching out toward his chest. As she landed on her outstretched arm, Goldfinch spotted a conspicuous stare beaming across the church, through the pews. Peter Nance was standing, his arm and hip leaning against the pulpit, two fingers set against his bottom lip. As they met each other's gaze, it was not so much the red eye that Goldfinch saw on the man. Instead, it was an obvious attempt to busy himself and strike up a conversation with a nearby villager.

***

Inside, Goldfinch moved his arm around her waist and turned back toward the church. He gazed out of his open door, wondering if anyone had seen them. Still, it made no matter. He looked down at her face and smiled. He held the smile, hoping she would return it. She clearly spotted this assertion but remained unchanged. She took her right hand and slipped it beneath her skirt, beneath more layers of petticoats. Goldfinch abruptly reached around her, closing the door.

She turned up toward Goldfinch, her eyes meeting his. Then she took the same hand and reached it toward her frock coat. With ease, she unbuttoned the top and then moved her fingers to the compressing bodice beneath. She strummed one of the top strings, loosening its hold. She took a breath and Goldfinch peered down at her now-visible breasts. At last, Harriet looked up at him and smiled. He took her cue, looking ahead almost blankly.

For a seductive moment, they gazed at each other in the hut. Only their breathing filled the room.

"Does a time-hardened face sicken you?" Goldfinch asked. "I see the way you look through me and judge me plainly. It is true I am not the dapper boy back there with the gilded watch, whom you've quickly grown affectionate toward."

She sighed. "It is not the face, nor the mistakes. It is that you are but a shell, a shell of a man with such hope. You say you are to lead this place with certain sternness and the rule of law. Yet, it is the rule of law we've fled from. We are in the forests. We need someone who is not afraid to pull the trigger or challenge the intruders. For Christ's sake, I was tasked with ending Renly's life. If you want such order, then return and be one of Jackson's puppets. I'm sure he could use men like you."

Goldfinch closed his eyes, hoping the rant would end. Any pleasure derived from the walk over had now subsided. All he could say to Harriet was, "It is not the boy who finds you irresistible. He will have plenty of others. Younger women."

He gauged her response. Harriet exhaled resoundingly and took her fingers to the strings on her bodice. She played a few of them like strings on a harp. "Insulting, aren't we? Well, you've come a ways." She walked to the door, assuring it was locked. He was hopeful again.

He twiddled his fingers within his pockets for a moment to determine what it was Harriet actually sought. She only stood seductively in the doorway. He looked through his window, toward the church. No one stared back at him. Harriet cut across his path, drawing the shade.

She concluded her strumming and tiptoed over to him. Her moves were both sensual and deliberate—like that of a knowing prey, delighted in being watched. He wondered if that was how she might act with Blithe.

"Let us step outside for a moment," Harriet urged. "Just *one* moment." She gently poked at his chest.

Goldfinch acquiesced, unlocking the mechanism on his door. It was a lever tumbler lock. He walked onto his front step. As he did so, Harriet approached, but turned back and sauntered farther into the hut, disappearing into the sealed chest that was his dark living quarters.

She half-closed the door as she scooted off. He eased his way back in, cracking the door back open with the toe of his boot. At the last creak, daylight shone into the small cabin. Harriet sat seductively on the unforgiving mattress, with an arm folded over the top her head, the other perched lightly where her navel would be. She had undone the bodice ties and was already removing the garments below. "Come, darling," she called to Goldfinch.

He turned back, closed the door tightly and removed his hat.

"I won't lie to you, Goldfinch," Harriet said, folding one leg over another. "Oftentimes, the sight of you repulses me. Your demeanor, the way you appear like a scarecrow, punctured, standing tall. In your case, it's an ideal that does the puncturing. Once settled, that impaling rod is always at your back, keeping you high above the rest. You scare off crows. You've nearly scared me off."

He was unbuttoning the pieces to his frock. He looked back up at her. "On with it, will you, for it pains me to see a beggar, a common street rat, rise to such a status. But you've found so much here, I can't take that away from you," he said.

"If knowing's supposed to be some sort of leverage, I fail to see its usefulness," Harriet answered. Goldfinch looked puzzled. "My background—I was orphaned at three. Folks around here know that already. Why, Cartwright knew it right away."

"I fear you have much to say, but not enough to offer," Goldfinch said. "But no breathing man can say that you have *not* been assembled wondrously." He smirked.

"You speak to me as though I'm your rifle," Harriet said. "*Assembled*? It's no wonder you haven't been graced with a wife."

"And what of you?" Goldfinch fired. But he collected himself and continued. "Why did you come here?"

"To this establishment?" she said shyly, falsely. "After that election, I started going 'round a local church. Thought I'd try to understand all this expansion, our attitude toward the Indians—"

"As an orphan on the streets? A concern of yours was politics?" He couldn't fathom it.

"The more I saw, the more I suffered," she said. "Call it lunacy. Call it what you will. I seemed to have found a purpose, after the abandonment. I found Him."

Goldfinch was feeling warmer. He couldn't tell if it was due to her heavy words or her presence. He chuckled, sat beside Harriet, and began to remove his undershirt. He loosened the woven belt he had worn since his 1812 days. "Go on."

She stared at him, her eyes seeming to grow scorching hot in an attempt to measure Goldfinch. "I met Cartwright at a revival. Visited him frequently—"

"*Shh*," Goldfinch urged, slipping his hand up her lowermost petticoats, up her silken thigh.

"Nothing unseemly, of course. He was just helping me see things, and showed me most of what I need to know about folks. He told me about his war days in Kentucky, trying for emancipation. Their disobedience down there. He rode up to Illinois, went to the assembly. Man's a miracle."

"And you? What did you tell Cartwright?" Goldfinch asked, pressing for an answer as he slipped his hand between her legs. She continued to speak.

"Well, you want a straight answer from me, so I'll give it to you." She paused to exhale. "I asked him about redemption for the thoughts I've got—about my ma, seeing my father kill her like he did in a drunken rage. Jagged glass bottle."

Goldfinch paused, taken aback. She continued, "I told him that after the trauma, I've had my doubts about men." She reached down, took his hand, and urged him on.

He moved on top of Harriet, his other hand pulling up the petticoats. She slowly closed her eyes and playfully bit her bottom lip.

Goldfinch freed both hands, removed the tight bodice from her chest and pulled up the undershirt below, letting her breasts fall from their hold. He looked down at her, and she up at him. Then, Harriet paused to lower his trousers to his ankles and pull him toward her. Slowly, they set forth.

It was a fitting compliment to the howling noise Goldfinch heard in the far reaches of his subconscious. He dove into her infiniteness, submerging not just his physical being, but his soul into that honeyed depth, letting waves of pleasure bury him deeper and deeper. He quickened his pace, helplessly, as if racing to drink from that oasis of sweetness deprived of him for years and years, since he had last congressed with a woman. The more he hastened, the thirstier he grew. The harder he forced himself on her, the tighter her fingers gripped around him.

It was a long spell of maddening love. Only after a long lingering did their bodies reluctantly part.

Adoringly, he studied her as they dressed themselves. He wanted to see her impression, to know whether it satisfied her, for all her baggage. Lord knows, it satisfied him. He steadied the gaze.

She fastened her bodice and adjusted the petticoats beneath the thicker, floral skirt.

"Do you miss the boy?" Goldfinch asked. "Edwin was a troublesome little bundle. Never saw him working for the Pickets." He knew Harriet blamed him for the Edwin mishap.

"No need to pick at old wounds," Harriet said. "He was a friendly boy, turned by the likes of this place." He had no response.

Goldfinch finished dressing in silence, glad to have lain with Harriet and to have not tumbled into another fiery dream. He slipped his boots on and grabbed the hat. He looked toward the corner of the room where the rifle was propped, then back at Harriet.

"Might I suggest you spending the night with me here, Harriet?" he asked. He was taking a shot in the dark with that question, maybe the same darkness that Senator Frelinghuysen thrived in.

She wiggled her hips, getting the clothing set just right. She looked up at him, ran her fingers through her tied-back hair, and then laughed aloud. Harriet took a few labored steps across Goldfinch's floor, toward him. She took her time in angling her neck up toward the Leader. When she finally did, she didn't say anything, but she didn't have to. She moved her eyes to the door and finished fastening her shoes. She struggled with the left shoe, trying to keep her attention on the Leader.

Goldfinch, feeling her piercing eyes, looked toward a small nightstand beside his bed. Atop it lay a glossy wooden shoehorn. He focused on the tool and then back at Harriet as if to offer help. She recognized the display but only rushed further, fiddling with the shoe. Once it slipped in, the clunking noise absorbing into the thinly lined floor, she spared no time in dashing from his place. He saw her off, watching her hips sway back and forth, settling back into the clothes she had quickly ruffled or shed. Her hair was in a bit of disarray, just the way he liked it. He got no pleasant smile from her, no fingertips grazing his coat. But still, he watched, he savored. Soon, she had sped around the corner, off toward the church.

***

Goldfinch walked over and grabbed his rifle. He felt his pocket for the bullets. He checked the other for his small gunpowder horn. He took both and dropped them on his nightstand. He was still jittery. The butterflies were just starting to settle in his stomach. He had endured a plethora of empty daydreams of Harriet—bouts of obvious longing. As it turned out, the whole affair had proven just as pleasant as he had imagined. She'd moved so skillfully, so deliberately.

He took hold of the Long Rifle and began to poke near the muzzle then back toward the chamber. He exhaled, holding the rifle firmly. He backtracked over to the bed and sat. He took a cloth and a small jar of polish and began to work at the rifle.

Some fifteen minutes later, he left and took long strides down the matted pathway toward the church. Upon entering, he noticed that Reg, Carlita, and Harriet were nowhere to be found.

At the pulpit, Minister Mulvane was speaking to a few new villagers. Goldfinch did not care enough to mix into their conversation. Continuing to search, he found Solomon, One, Elizabeth, and William. He approached the couple, conversing loudly in the nave.

"So boldly lovers, I see?" Goldfinch said bitingly. "It must've been a chirpy little vacation you both enjoyed while I was away. And together, I gather."

William looked at Elizabeth, waiting for her to reply. She opened her mouth, but only faint pockets of air snuck out. Then again, "I suppose we've just been awaiting your return, Goldfinch."

He put his hand on her shoulder. "Don't worry, friend. I say this in jest." He turned toward William. "Take care of the two of them." Goldfinch lifted an eyebrow and motioned to Elizabeth's lower half. "We've come a ways. I believe we've reached the time where you do not need to hide your affections." The Leader cracked a smile—but it was not directed at the couple. He was searching for something deeper.

He pulled his hand from Elizabeth's shoulder with haste after a howl towered over the pines at the eastern fence. He immediately rose to gooseflesh. His head jolted toward the sound. William and Elizabeth seemed stirred by the deviation in character.

"Excuse me," Goldfinch said, looking toward the hills. He felt a familiar tug at the side of his frock coat. It was Solomon.

"Mista Goldfinch," he said, "glad I found ya, there 'lot I need to catch you up on. Figured you's was out watchin' the fence earlier."

Goldfinch suppressed the lump forming in his throat. He wished he had stayed with Harriet, her perfume still pungent in his memory. "My friend," he said, "there's much to tell you as well."

"First thing's first, this here's Catharine Beecher," Solomon said. Sneakily moving out from behind him was the teacher Goldfinch had briefly heard of earlier. She reached her hand out to the Leader. Her face was long, and she had the intense eyes of her father. She wore a thick, white collar on a tight, gray shirt, with a shawl covering—constricting—her chest.

"It's a pleasure. My father says he's very confident in your abilities here. I've come, as you see, to live the experiment—to feel the ecstasy."

"Madam, I'm honored, but I fear your expectations may be a bit too lofty," Goldfinch declared, gripping the fingertips of her proffered hand. "We are righteous servants of God, but we carry faults like all others." The thought of Harriet's naked form still resonated with him.

"Lyman does not make such blatant mistakes in character. That, Papa must be praised for," Catharine said. "If he is a stout believer in you, in your values, then so am I. I know Reverend Allen was a witness to your altruism through the years."

"You speak so kindly, ma'am, may I offer you a place to stay?"

Catharine blushed. "I don't suppose you mean in a cabin with you?"

"Heavens no, ma'am. There is a place I have in mind and—"

"Why, I don't mean to interrupt you, Mr. Goldfinch. But your dear friend Solomon here has already mentioned a place to stay." Goldfinch peered over toward Solomon, who grinned and shrugged his shoulders.

"It was just a suggestion, Mista Goldfinch," Solomon said. "It was with Harriet if you's approve."

Goldfinch nodded. "I thought you might care for our young Elizabeth, who is with child, but I see now that you may do us plenty more good in Harriet's dormitory. She is, as you'll see, a lioness."

"And, is she your lioness?" Catharine asked, looking up at Goldfinch.

"We are all God's children, as I'm sure you know. God sees us in our times of wealth and in times of despair. Your father must've shown you His way. If you'd like, I can show you our relic at the hackberry."

"That cross you have dangling over your gate? I saw it. It is quite heartwarming."

"That cross was pinned there by your father and the other Founders, madam." Although his tone was stern, his face was far from it, and so Catharine smiled up at him. He was lying to her, in a sense. He had borne much of the weight of that cross. Cartwright had provided an extra hand. The memory actually pricked at Goldfinch's skin like a knitting needle. It had been a while since he'd slipped into one of his episodes. He fought off the thoughts—the animal visages, the fire, all the darkness—and smirked back at Catharine.

Solomon, remaining patient, had taken to watching the back and forth with his hands folded behind him. When Goldfinch called upon him, he stood stoutly again and curtsied at Catharine with his top hat. "I s'pose I'll show Ms. Beecher to her room, then?"

"See to it that she is comfortable. Let her get accustomed to the place, that is, a trip to the paddock to see my beautiful Lippizan." He paused. "Eder is a magnificent specimen, to be sure."

"The animal is magnificent," Catharine said, beginning to walk away with Solomon. "A heavenly white, I have seen it."

Goldfinch watched as the pleasant young woman left the church. As she did, he called out to her, "Ms. Beecher, why are you alone? Why have you come?"

She playfully bit her lip. "I was engaged once. It ended in shipwreck."

"I believe you'll get along with Harriet, your new roommate," the Leader responded, taken by the glaring similarities. "I am truly sorry for your loss."

"It was years ago. I have come to accept it. Now, this is my life," she said thoughtfully. "I aim for equality through education, just as you aim for equality under God. And to your earlier question, I believe I'm here at the behest of Lyman."

"I'll see you on the other side of this day," Goldfinch said to her. He tipped his hat and watched her get escorted off by Solomon.

Moments later, Goldfinch turned to go back to his place but saw Solomon quickly returning, his feet shuffling. "Mista, see, I was thinkin' somethin' while I was over there. Reckon you should meet up with Carlita. She was here few minutes ago but Reg done took her off," he said. "My guess that he showin' her the post, the huts, case we have to run there, some soldiers barge in." Goldfinch thought Solomon would bid him adieu again, but he just stood there.

"Let me show you to the forest, then," Goldfinch said. "Come along with me, and we shall speak with these folks who give us a purpose."

"Yessuh."

The two moved out from the church, weaving through some villagers. Calm seemed to resume in the village following that initial attack, although chores were still being forsaken. No harvesting or foraging was being done.

They moved briskly through the November air. Their frock coats bottled in the warmth but with daylight waning, the chill formed a grip like a seaman to his mainsail in a fierce gale. They trod across the path through the brush and up the hill leading to the base of the Ramapough Mountain, toward the Synod burial ground. They pushed aside small boughs that seemed jagged with the cold.

They were soon on their way to the outlying huts. Goldfinch cleverly hid them so that no southern slaver could wind his way through, easily at least. Only he and the other villagers knew about the route. Ahead of them, though, at about one hundred yards, something, *someone* sat in the path, unmoving. It was not in pursuit, but it almost looked like a bloated carcass clogging the trail. But this assessment was still made from afar.

Goldfinch lifted his rifle to shoulder height and pointed it ahead. He nudged Solomon with his right elbow, and the man removed a hunting knife. The blade looked underweight and paper-thin. It was deceptive, though, for as Solomon stepped forward and the sunbeams lessened their hold over him, Goldfinch could tell that he was truly no longer the passive ex-slave. He was a freeman and, better yet, an abolitionist.

"That's some yards off, Mista Goldfinch," Solomon said, removing his hat. He took the back of his knife hand to wipe the sweat from his forehead.

"The brush is too thick to tell. I see autumn reds and oranges, and this black mass," Goldfinch said, leaning forward and squinting. "Best we don't sneak up on it in the light of day." He pointed to the dense thickets at his side. He flung the barrel toward the woods, to send Solomon ahead.

As they entered, the leaves seemed to crumple one at a time, like a column of dominoes. They were steadfast in their approach, though, and the quicker they glided through the woods, the softer the sound appeared. With still enough leaves on the trees to shield them, they advanced, in unison. They soon gained a clearer view of what lay before them. It was no carcass, no rabid animal feasting on another. There were people moving about.

Two dark figures and another stood about one hundred feet away from them. They seemed settled on an ensconced rock along the trail. The dark figures leaned up against it with most of their weight. The other stood a few feet away and right amid the footsteps of the path.

Goldfinch lifted his fore and middle fingers toward Solomon, who was now behind him, signaling a halt. He made sure a bullet was already jammed down the barrel and that the powder was not compromised from moisture. He moved ahead. When he had the group splayed across his line of vision, he tried to discern just who they were. It was then he remembered that Reg must have been out exploring the grounds, showing the newcomer Carlita where she would most likely stay.

With vigor, he emerged from the thickets, keeping his eyes fixed on the other figure standing away from the rock. Before he could squeeze a word in, the man turned hastily and plastered an infernal smile across his face. "Mr. Goldfinch, we've been awaiting your arrival." He tilted his head a few inches as if to take in every fiber of the Leader. It was Peter Nance.

Reg, sitting against the rock, bowed his head modestly at Goldfinch, and Carlita simply smiled. "Mist' Goldfinch, it sure a pleasure, all way out here." Reg looked up at Solomon, who stood behind the Leader. Solomon's knife was drawn but was retreating to the sheath at his side. "Mista Solomon, man of many journeys."

"You feelin' good today, Mista Sullivan, I can sure see that," Solomon responded.

"It's a mir'cle, you see. It's that, nature jus' reach up and talk to me now. I hear all sorts of things."

Goldfinch stared at his friend, knowing for one, that he felt similarly since the trip to Paterson. Secondly, he hoped Reg would not disclose *too* much in front of the new villagers. That is, not without adequate vetting and time's due diligence.

Solomon spoke up, immediately changing the subject, as though intuitively. "Ms. Carlita, why you done run off with Mr. Sullivan?" He laughed as the final words trailed off. "Must be findin' y'self some wicked trouble."

Carlita was noticeably older than Reg, probably in her late fifties or early sixties. She wore a thick, woolen shawl over a button-up shirt which was tucked into a pyramiding brown cotton skirt. Her face wore the badges of time, and the bags beneath her eyes told Goldfinch that her lengthy escape north had in fact been arduous.

"Mr. Goldfinch, is it?" Carlita asked the Leader. "I s'pose you can lower that there gun now. We're just talkin', and Reg showin' me his hut, and another where I s'pose I'll sleep." She smiled widely, showing a missing bottom tooth.

Lowering his gun, Goldfinch looked toward the straggling man who had accompanied Reg and Carlita. "Why've you drifted so far from home?"

"Home?" the man laughed. "Well, I encourage you not to take this the wrong way, but here's what I've begun to notice. You, Goldfinch, all prim and proper like, you're a hollowed-out cast of a man."

Goldfinch was floored by this. His gun was lowered, but he did not forsake his hold on the butt of it. "I see you wandering out here with friends, and it does not bode well with me. Only because I am not familiar with you, of course."

Solomon looked confused and lowered his hat onto his forehead about an inch. "Well, Mista Goldfinch, he wunt actin' like this earlier, in 'delphia. No sir."

Reg looked at them. "Man's been mighty nice to Carlita and me."

"If the Reverend trusts you, I trust you," Goldfinch said. "Welcome to Synod." He reached a hand out.

Nance accepted the offer, shaking Goldfinch's hand with considerable force. "You know, it pays to keep the loons away. That elder, he seems to fit the part. Might I suggest a fine coastal retirement?"

It had been merely a minute, yet Nance had degraded the village and its people twice. "You're so full of comments, friend. I may challenge you—pass leadership in this endeavor over to you." He paused. "Yet, I fear I cannot. You are but a lowly greenhorn, despite your snide remarks."

Nance laughed and stepped toward Goldfinch. "I'm afraid I come off as a bit abrasive. I assure you that is not my nature." He swallowed. "I carry a heavy heart for these folks." Nance then pointed fixedly at both Reg and Carlita. Goldfinch could read the signal, and Nance's eyes stared through the villagers, as though it repulsed him to keep his pupils set on their Dark Continent ways. He reached for something in his pocket.

With the exertion, Goldfinch immediately tensed and reached for the loaded rifle. "Woah, woah," Nance called. He completed the move from his pocket. He carried a rabbit's foot. "It's lucky, or so they say. Like a touch? Could prove helpful."

Goldfinch took the rifle and thrust it toward Nance's stomach. The weapon was only inches from his gut—covered by a hand-sewn vest, overalls, and an undershirt. He wore wide sideburns and newer spectacles. His hair was trimmed and formed tightly around his ears.

Solomon took a few steps inward, perhaps feeling anxious. He tried to press a hand both on Goldfinch's rifle and Nance's shoulder, prying them farther and farther apart. It begot next to nothing, besides the added distance of about three more inches.

"For a leader, you're quite impulsive," Nance said, fixing the cufflinks on his shirt. Beneath his overalls, Goldfinch spotted a breast pocket occupied by some object.

"When you live as precariously as we have, any righteous man would understand," Goldfinch answered.

"For a religious community, you do not seem righteous, as you say," Nance added.

Reg appeared to tense up as well. He cleared his throat. "Mista Goldfinch, 'fore you go on from here, jus' know that Mista Nance was askin' about the place and all—how we get 'long, what we eat, who be in charge."

"What do you say we all head back to the village now?" Nance suggested somewhat cheerfully. "Why, it must be nearing suppertime, if you all prepare anything that is." He reached into the breast pocket to retrieve the item stuffed inside. When he pulled it out, Goldfinch spotted a gleaming, golden pocket watch with a trailing chain. He had seen that before.

"Suppertime, you say? Would you mind reading off the hour?" Goldfinch asked him.

Nance obliged, pulling it farther into view. He placed it in his palm and flipped open the front cover. "I have about a quarter to five."

Goldfinch studied the watch—its shape, its make or markings, its color, any tarnishing. The Leader remembered; it was in the pocket of the Mulvane boy. "Let us return, and forgive one another for that confrontation we just endured."

Nance chuckled. "Where I come from, confrontation is as inevitable as your next shit."

"Where is it you come from?" Goldfinch asked.

"Place never too far out of reach," Nance said nonchalantly. "A place lacking this sort of spiritual energy. That wooden cross alone, on that oak tree. It's extraordinary."

"It's a hackberry," Goldfinch replied.

"Irrelevant. Point is, my stomach juices are churning, and I've heard a man can get a nice steak around here," Nance barked.

Goldfinch looked down at Nance's watch, then at Solomon. He said to him, "What have you eaten during the long, empty days since my departure?"

"Nothin' to write home 'bout, I'm sure," Solomon said, shrugging. "Corn cakes, vegetables, I 'sume."

"Rations sufficed for me," Goldfinch responded. "Let's be moving now." He turned back down the path and without hesitation, rushed around the first corner to the trail. When he looked back, Solomon was helping Carlita get her bearings after she had propped much of her weight against the immovable boulder. Nance stood about twenty feet from the others, stopped in the road, staring down at Goldfinch. He appeared to pat the rabbit's foot.

Goldfinch thrashed at branches that got into his way and kicked at twigs that had the unfortunate pleasure of lying on the path. He picked up fallen leaves and kicked up loose earth. It also began to rain. It was only a steady drizzle, but with each pounce from the raindrop on his hat, Goldfinch grew more irritable. The population was increasing, but Synod's lot had not yet changed.

He descended the tediously long hill far ahead of the others. He left Carlita and Reg in the care of Solomon. He hoped the enigmatic Nance figure would begin to settle in. He could use his muscle in the fields, along the fence.

***

Back in his territory, he moved across the hut-laden meadow, toward Harriet's. Her place was near Minister Mulvane's, but Goldfinch had no desire to pay him a visit. As he knocked on Harriet's door, the bustle inside halted.

"I'd thank you to open up," Goldfinch said, aggravated. "It's just me."

There was another delay but within a few seconds the door swung open. It was Catharine. She was settling into her new spot. Inside, she had taken up space once occupied by Edwin. But *that* was not too bothersome.

Blithe Mulvane, the pompous boy, was sitting on Harriet's bed. "Mr. Goldfinch," Blithe said, "you really are a busy man. Are there moments of freedom?"

"This place *is* freedom, boy," Goldfinch said. "And what is it you've traipsed over here for? I trust you're not competent enough to help with any field matters."

Harriet sat quietly on her bed. Goldfinch did not want to make any form of eye contact with her, though from the corner of his eye he sensed her chest expand and constrict almost nervously.

Blithe rose from the bed to greet Goldfinch with a handshake. The Leader wanted nothing to do with such a gesture. As the boy approached, Goldfinch turned away and stepped back, onto the front step. Still, Harriet was quiet.

Catharine, however, was taken aback by the Leader's behavior. "Sir, I gather the man is simply looking to prove himself here. I've journeyed with him; he has the right zeal for this place."

Goldfinch ignored every word, for all he saw was this new man sitting on Harriet's bed, the same bed he should have been resting on. It was the same day that he had made love to her and begged her to stay the night.

Blithe froze and backtracked toward the bed. As he sat down, he placed a hand on Harriet's knee. Goldfinch angrily licked his lips, then again, as though they held the solution to this now-triangular bind. Catharine still stood beside the doorway, nudged up against the wall. She reached out and tried to reel Goldfinch back in, but he took the liberty of swiftly closing the door. It bounced off its hinges and opened again.

The Leader left for his cabin. When he turned back, Catharine was there, speechless, nonplussed, standing in the doorway. Goldfinch knew his behavior was untoward, especially to display in front of a newcomer. That fire of man burned inside him, seeing his lover being fondled by the likes of a fool fifteen years his junior.

He was storming off to his hut when it occurred to him that he should, in fact, drop by Minister Mulvane's. His blood boiling, his face reddening, he stepped firmly and knocked on his friend's door. Mulvane practically greeted him the instant Goldfinch's knuckles finished their last knock.

"Goldfinch," Minister Mulvane said flatly. "Good day."

"If only it was, Mulvane." His eyes wandered for a moment as if to flee his head before the harshest statement flew from his lips. "Your boy, you see, he's entirely unfit to live in this place. Surely you've seen it—the watch, the polished shoes, the tailored suit—and I believe we must act."

"Dear Lord, man, he has been here for only a day."

"A day too long, if you ask me," Goldfinch confirmed. "He worries me. He was simply waiting for Solomon in Philadelphia when he arrived?"

Minister Mulvane stepped from the door and closed it behind him. "I wrote to him. Told him of our wayward status of late. This was a month ago. He has not been told about the explosions, the slave catchers, or your excursion. My guess is that he moved to Philadelphia from Wilkes-Barre. He made his home there these last few years—was studying for the bar."

"Our wayward status? Before the powder keg, we were making progress."

"Excuse me. I've been corrupted by these last few weeks. I mean to say our daring experiment and its repercussions, at mealtime for one."

Goldfinch was suspicious but more agitated. "You should have informed me he's never used his hands constructively. He is no use here. We have, we *had*, all the minds we need— three Founders who will go down in history. I assure you, we do not need such arrogance and pomp within these walls. You'll remove him at once."

Minister Mulvane was flustered. "My son is a good man. You've hardly gotten the chance to converse with him. He shares a passionate adoration for our Lord. He has come, sir, to assist those in bondage now navigating the northward path. If I know my son, I know he has guiltless intentions."

"He could be John Quincy Adams or he could be John Calhoun. I don't quite care. Point is, I want him out of this village."

Minister Mulvane scratched his chin and looked at his friend. "I'll concede I haven't seen him in some time—four years—and he has changed in that time. His etiquette, and that propriety, it is new. He's different from the boy who was as ordinary as a pair of slacks. My guess is that he *has* found God. I trust those nightly verse readings as a child had some say in that." He shrugged his shoulders almost boastfully.

"I'll not repeat myself again."

Grasping Goldfinch's severity, Minister Mulvane then said, "You need to run this by One before you do anything. Let us see how he feels about this."

"One does not need to be privy to every Synod happening."

"Why, Goldfinch? Why must he leave? Because his hands do not retain the callouses yours do? Or, because he has not made his beliefs clear to you?"

"He's made himself clear," Goldfinch responded. "See to it that the boy is gone by morning."

Minister Mulvane countered, "I will see to it that One is informed." Goldfinch shook his head and stepped away, no goodbye, no tip of the hat.

He rushed off to his hut—a hut surely still disheveled from his earlier intercourse. As soon as his mind resorted back to thinking about the other villagers, he lost the butterfly feeling hatching in his gut. He felt his heart thump, and he saw Blithe Mulvane brandishing the pocket watch in front of Harriet. He remembered how she had seductively strummed her fingers down the small, golden chain links.

Goldfinch sat at the edge of his bed, the faint fragrance from Harriet lurking like a moth to a flame. He peered to the right and saw a figure leaving Minister Mulvane's hut. It wore a top hat and had a trailing frock coat. The distance between Goldfinch and this figure was considerable, yet still, in the maturing light, the breath lifted over it, eventually dissipating.

It was the Minister himself. He was slipping over to speak with One, who was settled near his front step. Goldfinch knew the topic for discussion. He knew the whispers that would circulate—*Goldfinch has lost his wits!* It did not bother him. All he wanted was the departure of that sniveling little Mulvane boy. Where just hours earlier Goldfinch was one of the Minister's dearest friends, it seemed as though the kinship was trailing off like the funneling whispers of breath.

Goldfinch sighed and abandoned his post at the window. He collapsed onto his bed and began to doze.

He went in and out of consciousness, in and out of obsessing over his capricious lover. The Leader built up enough energy to rise again and change into his night garments. He tossed the hat on its hook, kicked his boots beneath his bed, and looked at the rifle sitting idly in the corner.

Goldfinch then sank into his pillow for the second time. It was an emphatic recline. The sleep hit him like the thick words of Minister Mulvane protecting his boy, or the overt romantic display of Blithe with Harriet. He pressed his eyes shut. He saw the rolling hills of Paterson, the mysterious Mr. Boatwright, and the dirt-caked pads of the coyote which rested upon the wooden table at what Senator Frelinghuysen had called the Hermitage.

Then the howls came. They seemed to come from more than one animal and from a distance. They were long, boisterous howls punctuated with a yip. Goldfinch thought he was dreaming and imagined the noises weaving between the trunks of trees and the boughs with and without leaves.

His mind's eye began to conceive a magical dreamscape.

Everything was airy, white, and marked by small bonfires. The flames were orange, reddening and smoky to the point of obscuring some of the dominant white. He looked down to find bundles of muddied leaves, but the search was to no avail. This ground, too, was blanketed by white.

Pchonnn, pchoonnn. Two gunshots rang out from afar. This jolted Goldfinch awake. He thought it was part of the bonfire dream, but the noises seemed to reverberate in the sky. They echoed over the very same boughs he'd glimpsed during his slumber.

He walked over to the window and looked out at the sky, but there were no signs of smoky gunpowder. No one else lit lanterns and searched outside. He wondered if he was becoming as mad as the Minister probably made him out to be.

Goldfinch also wondered if he should have done more to protect the village from the Picket onslaught. He wondered if someone was really reconnoitering outside their village. These thoughts drove him deep into another daydream. It was not a white canvas this time.

It was summer. The leaves were a sharp green. Goldfinch spun around, gathering himself. He was standing beneath the hackberry. Gathered around him with folded arms were the Founders. Lyman glared at him. Cartwright looked at him and then peeled a leaf off his shoulder. Reverend Allen stood stiffly, showing his age and his fully white hair. He spoke. Goldfinch recalled bits and pieces.

"Samuel, we do not want a churchman to scare the congregants away with his piety," he said. "You're a man who's been there, seen the way paths lead. You know how to fortify this bastion."

Then Lyman said, "I know you were captured by the British near Ontario during the war. Reverend Allen told me what it took to escape when the Brits abandoned Fort George. And then, to work in intelligence for Old Fuss and Feathers. It's a shame you haven't been named an ambassador. We know Winfield Scott's spoken wonders."

Cartwright, of course, added something. "We see the people respond to you. Be sure to crack down. Mulvane will be your spiritual counterbalance."

Then Lyman said, and the words were still so clear, "We've voted on an identity for you. 'Goldfinch,' the state bird of New Jersey, where we have chosen to entrench this community."

Allen added, "The bird is migratory. And majestically colored, as your life has been."

"How will Erskine take this?" Goldfinch had immediately asked.

"I imagine Erskine, now 'One,' will see it a bit too radical," Allen said. "But you'll sort it out, for we must depart."

Goldfinch looked at Allen, the freed slave, and husband who had overseen this resurrection of his life. "This night, we leave. I've gifted you the Lipizzan you've bonded with."

"Eder," Goldfinch said. "He'll be Eder."

"Well, Eder awaits you in the paddock," Lyman added.

Then the Founders walked back toward the paddock, where they'd talk once more and then dispense goodbyes. Lyman, some feet off, turned back to Goldfinch and said, "And Synod, a fitting name, no? For our conclave at this place."

Goldfinch nodded.

Chapter Fifteen

Tarriance

Lunch the next day, Sunday, was uneventful. Goldfinch slept through a Minister Mulvane sermon earlier in the morning. He sat at the communal fire pit and picked on some jerky he had lying around from Shepherd's last excursion.

It pained him to think of Blithe sitting next to Harriet in the pew, probably attempting to caress her thigh or hold her waist.

While he sat by his lonesome, he watched gray clouds move in, with their offering of a silvery blanket to engulf the sky. As he gnawed on the jerky, he heard footsteps just behind him.

"Goldfinch?" someone said, sounding young and vigorous. It must have been Shepherd. Goldfinch turned around and there he stood. "We've a thing or two to say." Behind him stood the other two who had journeyed beyond the gate with him, One and Reg. They acknowledged the Leader.

"Go on, then," Goldfinch said. They gawked at him, reading his body language and any slight movements. "What is it?"

"We're sure you heard the gunshots in the night," Shepherd said. "The howls, the shots—spiraling and earsplitting—we're not certain what that was."

One interjected, in the abrasive manner he was known for. "I'm talking plenty of sleepless nights ahead, at this rate."

"I don't deny hearing the noises," Goldfinch replied. "Has anyone seen the beast?"

"Alaba, her name be that," Reg added. "Them howls got me thinkin' 'bout Amber n' Regina. But not jus' my two. Whole lot of 'em. Why, Carlita's 'nother one. Said she done got crossed up wit a man sayin' he on a Picket payroll in 'delphia."

"Solomon snatched her up before she was taken?" Goldfinch asked.

"Cain't say, Mista Goldfinch. Thing is, she's a tough one. Bet she don't stay here for too long."

"I suppose someone like Edwin can pass word to a whole lot of slavers working the area," Goldfinch said.

"And who will see her off?" One asked.

"I could see it through," Shepherd suggested.

"That's not why we're standing here, though," One insisted. "It's the noises. I hear them constantly. It's time for action."

"What do you propose?" Goldfinch wondered, placing his jerky on the wooden stump beside him.

"We start by weeding the animal out, scoping out the hills, up to the gravesite," One demanded.

"To what end?" Goldfinch asked.

"Get to the beast, get to that senator," One said. "Could rid ourselves of it and the noises. Perhaps they'll subside."

"The man said it was here to help. We cannot kill it. We must just trace it," Goldfinch said, tapping his boots into the dirt around the fire. "If it leads us to its master, perhaps he has news of the Governor."

Goldfinch looked intently at the elder. "And what of Minister Mulvane? How did his sermon fare?"

One scratched his head, parting a few tufts of unkempt white hair. "Wasn't bad. The whole lot of us—" He paused. "Come to think of it, the sermon was a bit surly. Not so much the content, but the delivery."

"Let it be so. He will come around. That's just ambiance at this point. When do we take to the forest, gentlemen?"

The four of them agreed to meet by the rear gate after retrieving their rifles, and to make it a hunting affair. They would round up their mounts and pick up any rations they desired along the way.

***

When the men regrouped at the gate, there was another party waiting for them, already on horseback. "I hear there'll be a hunt?" he asked. Goldfinch stared across at Peter Nance. He was dressed elegantly and even wore spurs on his riding boots. He looked too lavish for a hunt. He could have passed for an English duke.

"Where's your weapon?" Goldfinch asked him. Nance poked at a large knife holstered to his side. The image didn't fit his cultured persona. "Do you even know how to draw that?"

"Let us ride," he said, smirking.

Goldfinch took a position between One and Shepherd. He heard their whispers.

"How in God's name does he know?"

"He could be responsible for the howls."

"We never got a good look at that Mr. Boatwright, in the daylight that is. It can't be him?"

"Gentlemen, will we ride? Or, is this some sort of incapable community?" Nance stood about twenty feet away.

The four men—the Paterson Four—approached Nance reluctantly. Normally, Goldfinch would have taken the lead, as the chieftain leading his men to battle. However, he signaled Nance ahead.

On the trail, they made good time, with a bright sun shining above them, and the wind at their backs.

One, riding beside Goldfinch, said to him, "Do you suppose those howls were warding off that elusive man—the one the Pickets tipped off?"

"Let's not speak so loudly," Goldfinch maintained.

"But dammit, that was the purpose of this trip, to sort this out," One grumbled. He aimed his frown at Nance, at the front of the pack.

"It will sort itself out," Goldfinch countered. He thought about the Founders and their faith in him. Could he maneuver his way through this ordeal? He imagined them watching his every move, determining whether their decision proved worthy. Then, he thought, *How much are they actually invested in Synod?* He remained hopeful in those fleeting moments of contemplation.

"Word spread at the sermon this morning that the forge is firing up again today. Hasn't been in service since, well, before Renly's explosion. Suppose we should swing by and keep an eye on it," Shepherd urged.

"Now there's an idea," Goldfinch responded, also looking ahead at the current pack leader, the mysterious Nance.

Every hundred feet or so, Goldfinch would shout a direction to Nance, who would not look back to acknowledge it. He did, however, oblige. They came to the base of a hill, the one that stretched upwards toward the burial site, and then further upward toward one of the Ramapough Mountains along Long Pond. They decided to turn right and crawl along the base of the hill. After about a furlong, Goldfinch and Shepherd stared fixedly at the hill that eased up and gradually climbed toward a wider, craggier ridge.

Light from an open meadow soon pierced their fields of vision, protruding through tree trunks like prisms of blinding light. The light held across their entire horizon. Only a thin grove of trees stood between them and this tract of land. The horses, with little direction from their riders, gravitated to this spot.

When they came within fifty-yards of the field, Nance stopped and let Reg and One ride ahead of him. He was about to let Goldfinch and Shepherd ahead, too, but they stopped, lightly tugging the reins and nicking their horses with their boot heels.

Nance looked perfectly content, with a roughly scwn smirk planted on his face. He reached over his horse and patted its side. "You gentlemen should lead the way." Nance seemed to notice Goldfinch's hesitation. "I insist."

"We'll let Reg and One ride on, but you'll go ahead of us," Goldfinch responded. Beside him, Shepherd nodded. Nance's horse then trotted into the party, ahead of Goldfinch. As Nance's animal picked up its pace and its finely manicured hooves, Goldfinch studied him. He examined the hat, his tight, gray coat, and the boots with the spurs.

"At the field, we stay right, on down the hillside, to Harriet's fields," Goldfinch called out to Reg.

The horses continued on, plodding against the hardened ground, picking up straggling leaves. In the field, they were greeted by long, stringy grasses. The field was permanently overrun, likely an old hunting ground of the Lenape.

Once the hooves stopped moving, and the men loosened their grips on the reins, the group stood before a small, rock-framed finery forge. It was probably fifteen feet tall, maybe ten feet wide. Goldfinch remembered plastering the rocks to the outer walls, watching Elizabeth, William, and Cartwright adding their final touches to the hollowed interior.

"There's everything in this village, isn't there?" Nance said as he admired the handiwork. "I imagine when this isn't burning, the niggers hide out in here?"

Shepherd looked at the man and said, "You were told, on your trip north with a former slave, a southern runaway, and the others, that this *is* an anti-slavery establishment, no? We were founded on those principles and—"

Nance cut in. "I was told it was an idealist religious community for Protestants. And I know some Protestants. They're not as you are. Lord only knows what I would've done if I'd figured all these folk were passing through."

Goldfinch recalled his conversation with Minister Mulvane the previous night, about expelling his son Blithe. *If only all that fuss could have been directed at this new pest*, he thought.

"Question is," Goldfinch then said, "where are the plumes of smoke? Where is Elizabeth? I am quite sure she can take on a newcomer as an apprentice."

"Was told this morning she'd be out here, staking her claim on this place again," Shepherd said. "It was said right in church."

There was silence, shortly broken up by, "Perhaps it is a complication of the pregnancy?" from Nance. The Paterson Four turned inward, looking at one another.

Of course, the conniving, spur-wearing man knows, he thought. Goldfinch still wasn't sure who exactly knew about Elizabeth's condition. The news didn't surprise, or startle, anyone, though.

"Is that meant to be a ruse?" Goldfinch asked. "I expect she'll be out here soon enough. I see she has enough wood to burn here for another outing—forging a weapon, some bullets, any paneling, or miscellaneous items."

Nance rode about, his horse stepping mildly in the long grass. "What of the hunt?" he said.

Goldfinch looked from weapon to weapon. Each Synod villager had a rifle strapped to his back. Goldfinch's sat sidelong, across Eder. Nance had no rifle, just that lengthy blade tethered to his side. "You expect to kill with that blade? And those jingling spurs?" He laughed.

"Something like that," Nance said. "Say what you will, you've never hunted with me before."

"Place could use some venison," One said. He, too, wore a suit, but it was dappled with wear, and the gray was phased down to forlorn beige.

Imagining Elizabeth would arrive shortly, Goldfinch called his horse away from the rock furnace. "These fields are prime hunting grounds," he said.

Shepherd paired with Goldfinch. One, Reg, and Nance set off on their own. Goldfinch rode north up the small hill, the others south. Shepherd's horse wasn't lame, but it was proving slower than Eder.

Goldfinch and Shepherd dismounted, tied the animals to the firm trunk of an oak and grabbed their weapons. "Let's stalk the grass," Goldfinch said. They crouched at the threshold of field and forest, waiting for animals to wander through.

"Conceal yourself," Shepherd said to Goldfinch, whose chest dangled out from an oak, the trunk fixed and burrowed, the knotty roots cropped up, drying in the midday sun.

"The grasses sway," Goldfinch said, pointing down the hillside, his frock coat stained by the ingot-shaped bar of light pinching through the trees. In the fields, the light appeared to congregate, building up along the tops of stems and turning leaves, glistening and forging a glare.

Within this luminous pocket of earth, Goldfinch noticed the grasses moving gently, but against the grain, against the slight breeze. "It lies in there," he said confidently.

Beside the Leader, Shepherd raised his rifle. He looked over the barrel with an eye sealed shut to focus his view on the thick pasture. Goldfinch held a hand out toward him, stopping him. "I'll venture close to this one and collect it myself."

"And take with you all the credit of the hunt," Shepherd said, shaking his head with a grin. He laughed quietly and pressed on. "Goldfinch, by all means."

Goldfinch tipped his hat. Then, when the Leader was some feet off, Shepherd said, "Rattle this calmness and Alaba may be at our heels, driblets of blood falling from her jowls, her mangy hair."

The Leader did not flinch, inching forward from a crouch through the wiry greenery. At last, he made out the form of an animal, a deer, grazing with its head down. It was a doe. She was young. Her head and coat seemed to twitch on every step of the Leader's boot, yet still, she remained, nibbling grass daintily from the sloping ground before her.

In his crouch, Goldfinch could tell that his rifle stood above the rest of the grasses, like a steeple amongst modest brick homes. He stopped in his tracks and slowly removed the bag he had carried from his shoulder, before placing it on the ground, his eyes still on the youngling.

He cocked the hammer back and took aim, squinting like Shepherd had done. But when he saw, through the columns of slender grasses, the doe lift her head high and stare into him, he froze. He lifted the barrel of the gun and backtracked a few steps loudly, stirring leaves.

As he turned back to Shepherd, he whispered, "Shepherd, I must say, after Paterson, I fear I don't have the stomach for that sort of—"

He was cut off, but not from the curious Shepherd. Something stole his attention on the top of the hill. It stood in silhouette, its long coat swaying with the wind, its one ear twitching as though pestered by a fly.

When he turned toward the downward slope then over toward Shepherd, his lips moved, in hopes of relaying the wolf's name. Yet a fierce surge of pain stung at his upper thigh on his right leg. The pain waved through like the bite of a freeze on leathery skin, as if he had slipped a knife into the fire pit and dug it into his own flesh. Then, the pain radiated, and with each pulse Goldfinch's mind's eye saw fiery shades of red, like another illusion.

He tried to gain enough strength to open his eyes and find the source. The exterior world was blocked out. Shepherd *could* have shot a ball into his leg. He could have prepared to drive a dagger through his back, too. Goldfinch would be helpless. The wolf could have torn a lump of meat from his leg and been in the process of running it back to Paterson for the Senator to examine or curse.

The red grew brighter, and his brain felt like it was pressing against the side of his skull. The pain in his leg now paled in comparison to the pressure in his head. He felt his body tumble down.

When an eye cracked open, it was red he saw; red staining the thick fabric of his trousers. There was a knife skewering his leg, the blade an inch deep, maybe bone deep. *What force,* he thought, collecting his disparate thoughts.

He felt an impending darkness falling over him as if it emerged in the back confines of his mind and slowly dulled the parts that still functioned. As the darkness slipped over him, he did not so much fear what was next. He tried to look beside him, to gauge the blood spill. It did not appear like a mortal wound. The rationalizing brought the coat of darkness over him faster.

His breathing was labored, but he was able to open both eyes, though his vision was clouded, the product of a failing consciousness. He saw Shepherd standing over him, his eyes widened. Shepherd's rifle was in his hand but pointed off in some direction even he probably could not pinpoint.

Behind Shepherd, standing atop the hill, was the animal. It stood in front of the sun, seemingly deflecting the rays off to the sides, protecting the Leader from more blinding light.

"Alaba," Goldfinch managed to say, his eyelids fluttering as he slipped closer to the darkness. Shepherd yelled and motioned with his hands, but Goldfinch could not read his lips.

As his vision became eclipsed by this pain, this plague, he spotted other figures moving in. It wasn't the Senator. One was a runaway, another pale and brittle, and another steely and beaming. The other hunters—One, Reg, and Nance—had closed in on him.

The Paterson Four hovered over top of him, acting as barricades between the penetrating sun and Goldfinch's declining state. The Leader breathed heavily and looked down at his leg, the knife fixed perfectly into the flesh, hardly moving when his leg twitched.

Peter Nance stood behind the others, his face appearing more colorful than it had been earlier, brighter and satiny. He unfolded his arms and reached a hand into his pocket. He pulled out the rabbit's foot he had told Goldfinch was so lucky.

Goldfinch had a few more blinks left in him before his eyes, and his mind gave way, hopefully only momentarily. As he fell unconscious, the last motion he saw was Nance clasping the rabbit's foot between his fingers, smiling widely, and showing off his mostly white teeth. Goldfinch thought he heard a spur click, and Alaba howl as if voicing something through these men, toward something, someone else. *Mr. Boatwright?* Before losing consciousness, Goldfinch wondered if Mr. Boatwright could swivel the knife from his leg …

Chapter Sixteen

Convalescence

Goldfinch had been out for a time. He felt his own helplessness lingering like a bad scent in the room. Now though, Harriet did not know he was semi-conscious.

She looked down at his helpless frame which lay on her bed. She ran a finger down the buttons of his shirt, making a soft *tt-tt-tt* sound. He pretended to sleep as she peered down at him.

She took a step away, and Goldfinch crept an eye open. Harriet dipped a cloth into a bucket of warm water. She squeezed it out as though she thought he would thank her for it. She ran the cloth down Goldfinch's arms, leaving a trail of moisture on the hair.

Goldfinch learned, through passing conversation, that it had been two days since he was delivered to Harriet's by way of Shepherd. Apparently, he came storming through the gate, sweat falling from his brows, carrying Goldfinch.

A few hours earlier, as Goldfinch feigned unconsciousness, she had recalled those stressful initial moments. She spoke the words aloud as she checked his wound. "Bring him into the hut," she had called to Shepherd. "Place him on the mattress.

We must extract the blade, and quickly before he loses more blood."

Then she snapped back, looking inwardly, holding the expansion her lungs provided. When she exhaled, she ran a finger across the Leader's tough hands, through each finger, and across the palm lines. It took a lot for Goldfinch to remain 'incapacitated.'

Harriet then ran her fingers through the hair pressed behind her ears. She wanted to wake Goldfinch up with a magical command, a trigger word.

He was wearing suspenders, which held up his trousers, and a snug button-up beneath them. Harriet pulled the ends of Goldfinch's shirt from his trousers, exposing a few inches of the skin on his stomach. She ran her finger sensually across his stomach and onto his shirted chest, the way she had done to Blithe when he made his presence known. For Goldfinch, it took even more not to be seduced.

She ran her fingers back down the length of his chest and toward his wound, wrapped tightly with bandage cloth, a reddened stain at the middle of it. The culpable knife sat beside him on a bench. When Harriet was not looking, Goldfinch gazed at it—the sin it had committed. He had once felt so impenetrable.

Knocks then came at the door. Harriet twitched, for it seemed to resound in her eardrums. The knocks played off the constricting walls of her hut. "Yes?" she said as she opened the door. It was One, paying his leader a visit. Behind him was Solomon. The others had come earlier, had talked with Harriet, and had stared helplessly at Goldfinch. He had rested infirmly now for two days. They did not know he comprehended most of what was said.

"We'd like to pay him a visit is all, ma'am," One said kindly. He had come a long way since the day he lugged a dead corpse across the hilly backwoods. Harriet waved them in.

"I saw 'im not long 'fore this happened," Solomon said to One. "Now, you said all this done by Nance?"

One placed his whitened hair behind his ears and fiddled with the lengths of his suspenders. "Thing is, I can't be quite sure. He was standing beside a deer, well, near a deer. The man moved off to his own corner, some earthwork, and tried to end the little bandit's life." He paused momentarily. "The deer's life that is, though Shepherd said it was but just a yearling."

"I know yous come back with a deer. How'd 'at happen?" Solomon asked.

"Figure while we took Goldfinch down the hill and on back, Pete Nance just off and disappeared," One said. "Suppose he did take down that deer. We found it lying limp beside the fire pit when the mayhem settled that day."

"And what of that Nance?" Solomon asked. Still feigning unconsciousness, Goldfinch noticed Solomon's voice quaver, presumably a degree of guilt from guiding Nance through the channels of the slave system.

"Suppose he's around here somewhere. Chances are, hawking over Reg's hut, or Carlita's," One said. "Turns out, the man is as bigoted as the day is long. Sure as the Lord's Day, if Goldfinch was awake, he'd of had that man over the fire right now."

Goldfinch, motionless, wanted to nod his approval. Harriet then spoke up. "Gentlemen, if you don't mind, I'd like to dress his wound now," she said, raising her eyebrows and motioning to the bloody cloth wrapped around Goldfinch's leg. His pants were ripped at the site.

Both One and Solomon bowed their heads and moved out of the hut. As they ventured off the short step out front,

Catharine Beecher walked up. It was her hut now, too, and Harriet seemed to greet her warmly.

"I suppose the man is faring better?" Catharine asked.

"His breathing has calmed some," Harriet responded.

"I reckon he knows who's caring for him at all hours," Catharine said, smiling.

"I know I've taxed you over these past few days, but I must dress his wound, and so his pants as well. Bloody sight, not one for womanly eyes, I'd say." She smiled back at Catharine.

"Say no more, I'm on my way. Just wanted to retrieve a few items. I've been staying at Carlita's these few nights. She's a saint."

"She is an impeccable spirit," Harriet answered, smiling stiffly. Goldfinch, in his quasi-slumber, thought she did not want to appear impatient. "I very much appreciate your labors, in helping to keep Carlita safe. I know she is fearful of this intruder."

"I will watch over her. She'll relay tales of her days on the plantation, near the Mississippi, with her daughter." Catharine held her skirts at ankle length, turned, and left the hut. Goldfinch pressed his eyes closed again.

Harriet walked back over to him, hesitating, ruminating. Goldfinch felt her eyes upon him. For another moment, she stood still. Goldfinch remembered the passion, the way he had caressed her. He heard her take a step back.

She leaned in close, so close she could probably feel his breath on her. Goldfinch knew that she might spew out a revelation or two. He would not have been disappointed if he'd become her confidant in that vulnerable moment.

"I try, I try to see your face," she called down to him, her hands pressed gently against his chest. She took a seat beside him. "But I see Blithe's, his dapper suit, that pendulous timepiece."

Goldfinch's stomach dropped, and it took all he had not to squirm out of that tight confine.

She continued to confide in the man she believed was unconscious. "We've already made love, the boy and I." Her voice quavered. "I suppose this can be useful, your condition as it is. It can be like a Catholic confession. Minister Mulvane, in his older days, would've understood."

Then, the words flooded from Harriet, as if she wanted to expel them in the quickest amount of time. She no doubt wanted them off her chest. "But we are not in a confessional, and I'm far from the pious girl I was before my days on the frontier. Goldfinch, you see, Cartwright really saved me. I was the plaything of those men, those husbands losing their minds on the edge of civilization. I was the rare china you only ate delicacies from. Sure, I made my way, but Pa didn't like that much. I was estranged, I ran away. These men paid me better than a thespian, mostly they were rich folks turned frontiersmen, numbed by city life, out looking to have something pump their blood. I was nice to look at, but also nice to knock around a bit. Once there's been word that the china has a chink in it, you sure as hell don't use it again. And so, it's been told before, and will be told again." She appeared to sob, then sniffled, regaining her composure.

"But here I am, Goldfinch," she continued. "I've made peace with myself. Cartwright saw something in me—I was building material for this place." Goldfinch felt as though she paused to look around. "I don't feel cramped here. I could be the Queen of England. Yet, that adulteress, Caroline of Brunswick, is more like the queen I'd be."

Then he felt her searing eyes on him again. "I simply cannot be kind to you," she said. "It's a history of violence, around gruff men like you. They've maimed me. I can only see the boy, now. I fear he's stolen my heart."

Goldfinch, behind closed eyes, soon felt like he had received much more than a Catholic priest would endure during confession. Harriet proceeded to sob, softly, delicately. "He is the man I need. You are my vice."

Goldfinch briefly fell back into a cloud of memory—of their bare bodies, the trickling sweat. He suddenly felt the pain at his wound.

"Have I been swayed from you?" she asked aloud. "Toward the delicate, young preacher's son? I think of you, and I recall the cold nights in the lean-tos, pressed against a thin, frigid wall, a different man every night."

Goldfinch felt blinded and truly unresponsive. She sank her head into his chest and began to cry.

***

Harriet lay on Goldfinch for over an hour, sobbing, and most likely slipping deeper into thought. Periodically, she lifted her head, but then it would crash back down on him— heavy from their dilemma, her past weighing her down.

She turned her head upward toward his. "How much blood did you lose, Goldfinch? You've been senseless, here, for so long."

Goldfinch began to wonder if she had caught on. But she said, "I fear you are weighed down by something, some ghastly presence. Your eyes, they look *through*, not *upon*."

He wanted to answer by saying, "Love!" but he maintained the comatose state. Still, he thought of them sharing the bed—the ceaseless love they would make if she allowed it.

Within her fixed stare, Goldfinch twitched and moved his head. *She's surely caught on*, he thought. He moved ever so slightly but managed to exude just a broken grunt.

At this point, as she still rested beside Goldfinch's listless body, he wondered if she too dreamed of the lovemaking, the passionate, steamy nights that could be. Did she long for his cold seduction?

She proceeded to prod at Goldfinch's leg wound, examining it. It was now in dire need of changing. But he felt her move away abruptly, turning toward the door. She did not move but stared into the abyss just outside. Goldfinch slowly opened an eye.

Harriet began to whisper, but Goldfinch's hearing was still impressive. "I see a frock coat, a male's. Unbuttoning. But it is glossier than yours, Goldfinch. There's a chain jutting out the side. His chest, his pock-less chin. The blond hair is long but cast aside, behind the ears. Polished boots."

He could stand it no longer, he coughed and made a few grumbling noises. She ran to his side, assumedly more nervous about her disclosures than his health.

***

For a time, Harriet hovered close by, watching Goldfinch, seeing if he would come to life. But he did not. He refrained and slunk back to the inner darkness he had been resorting to since he awoke. Eventually, Harriet fled the hut. When she was a safe distance away, Goldfinch stood from the bed, applying the most pressure on his other leg. He grimaced but tried to move the troublesome limb. No one was around to stop him. Now that it was dark, he would limp over to the fire pit, or some corner of the village. He felt he needed to hear more of Harriet's gentle whining.

Goldfinch, with no cane to aid him, snuck along the fence to a point where he could see the fire pit. Sure enough, his lover was there. He used the cover of darkness to amble over to the nearest hut. Here, he could listen to Harriet and the others.

The fire burned bright in the center of the village. Harriet rested beside it, her palms faced outward for warmth. Next to her was Catharine, and next to Ms. Beecher was Carlita. Both women also extended hands toward the fire.

"We ain't get nights like dis down in N'Orleans," Carlita said, shivering ever so slightly.

"Hard to think about the cold with such a fiend untamed, running around these fences," Catharine said. She looked off toward the trees, almost in Goldfinch's direction.

"Better to have something to occupy our time," Harriet cut in. "Our Mr. Goldfinch can't say the same right now—a prevailing darkness occupying much of his, washing over him and that leg."

Catharine shook her head. "I fear there is more to this injury. Could it be an infection? He's been out for ... going on three days, from a leg wound."

"Something tells me it was the culminating affair to much more," Harriet said, transfixed by the flames.

Carlita spoke. "This Nance, could he be a N'Orleans slaver?" She twiddled her thumbs and breathed heavily, sending air, with gusto, into the fire. "I been dreadin' what that fella gawn do. That holdup 'fore the hunt them boys had, now that was nothin' to turn a deaf ear to."

Harriet's mood seemed to intensify. "The holdup?" From what Goldfinch could tell, she looked coldly at Carlita.

Carlita did not move a muscle, though her eyes slipped over to Harriet, probably with the weight of the world on them. "With Lizbeth, that fine pregnant girl."

"I truly fear your next words," Catharine said, holding her head up with her palm, an elbow resting on her knee.

Carlita continued, "Well, I seen her gatherin' some materials up, she don't seem like one to wait till after th' baby born to contribute. Anyway, she was over by that paddock." She pointed. "She was 'bout to mount the animal when that Nance fella came outta some hut, all prim proper like, but on a mission. No mission a God, that is."

"He laid his hands on her? Her baby?" Harriet asked.

"He wunt quiet 'bout any of it. Ya see, he took a hand to her throat. Grip looked strong, a healthy man that Nance is."

"Go on, Carlita, a life might depend on it," Harriet urged.

"Why, he pinned her up against one of them fence posts. Not for too long, but who knows what he was sayin' to her; 'I gawn cut chur throat, you go out there.' Somethin' long those lines, I imagine. But ya see, I didn' have no time to react. He was already mountin' up before the girl could tap her horse back into that pen. He was going to ride with them Synod boys, all right." She rubbed her palms together, the friction sounding off a *tss-tss-tss*. Goldfinch could hear it from his post.

"Shepherd had said she wanted to heat the flames at the forge again," Harriet reminded them. "So, Nance was free to roam, free to suggest a hunt?" She spun around and looked across the few yards between the pit and her house. She, too, nearly spotted the motionless Goldfinch.

"The man attempted murder, has assaulted a pregnant woman, and loathes our harboring of slaves," Catharine said. "And how was he selected?"

"Your father had no part in the selection of new villagers," Harriet said, speaking of Lyman. "Chances are Nance showed up at the AME in Philadelphia, feigned hunger or piety, earned the Reverend, or the Founding Mother's good graces. Simple as that."

Catharine nodded the smoke from the flames bordering her movements. "I wonder if he'll make for two goes at his luck." Like Goldfinch and the Paterson Four, she stared blankly into the forests. This time it was in the opposite direction of Goldfinch. He tried to alleviate the pressure on his leg by leaning on the hut.

Amid the throes of a distant howl, leaves began to shuffle beyond the fence. Goldfinch feared just a minor infraction, the intrusion of a critter on its traditional pilgrimage.

"Harriet," Catharine urged, "are you near a rifle?"

"At present, no. But I do have a Long Rifle under my bed, collecting dust."

Goldfinch also did not have a weapon.

"Let us not fret just yet. It could be a harmless creature. In any sense, he might want to get near the warmth of this here fire," Catharine said, quickening her breaths, pumping air into the fire. Goldfinch wanted to look toward the fence, but the women were all so captivating.

Leaves ruffled, boughs shook, and another party approached the ladies. Harriet immediately clenched her fists, ready to sock the Nance fella who was terrorizing the villagers without any actions or words. But the approaching person soon became visible. It was Blithe Mulvane. Goldfinch then wanted to clench *his* fists.

"Rumor has it," he said, nodding to the other women, "that Goldfinch wanted me removed from this place *yesterday*." He laughed, shaking his head.

"It's a pity, for if he knew the bond we've shared, I am sure he would accede to my presence." From afar, Goldfinch was glad Blithe made no obvious overtures.

Goldfinch knew that the day prior, she had obviously lain with Blithe, probably in his own cabin. It was so soon after she and Goldfinch had shared a moment—just three days had elapsed. The Leader wondered how Blithe treated Harriet. *Was it gentle? Could he have possibly been a better lover?*

"If there's a bond," Harriet said to Blithe, "then you'll go check the border for the prowler."

At the mention, Goldfinch thought he saw Blithe's face tighten, his mind churning over, spitting out vivid images of something.

"I will inform my father," Blithe answered. "For with your Goldfinch friend incapacitated, he is in charge."

"So be it, but someone must examine over there." She pointed to the wooded culprit. "We must protect Carlita, here. And Reg, you met Reg. Even Solomon, though he's been turned for quite some time now."

Blithe sat for a moment, resting on the log bench beside the fire. After a moment, he rose from his position, tipped his hat to the ladies and walked off, the black of his attire quickly blending with the night. Goldfinch strained, somewhat exposed along the hut, to watch him flee. Blithe did not walk near the Leader. Goldfinch turned back to watch Harriet gawk at her lover, or lament his departure.

Goldfinch noticed that Blithe did not make for the gate and thus the source of the noise. He then spotted Catharine rising, placing her hand on Carlita's shoulder. She escorted the runaway off to the hut at the outpost.

"Think one of us should fetch Reg," Catharine suggested, probably frightened by Nance.

"Reg can handle things his own damn way," Harriet exclaimed, focused on whatever blight lay in the forest.

"It's him they're after, is what you said, no?" Catharine asked, now about twenty feet away. They were getting nearer to Goldfinch.

"He's not a slave, he's a free man. A member of this village. This here shadow can come try and wrestle him away." She left her departing friends, on an investigatory plunge into the clear November air.

She carried neither torch nor rifle. But her austerity could scare off the most formidable opponent. When she had added some distance between herself and Goldfinch, the Leader snuck out from behind the hut. He had since been quiet, especially as the two other women sauntered away. Goldfinch, with as much stealth as he could wheedle from himself, attempted to follow Harriet's trail.

When he had traveled about fifty-feet, he hid behind another hut. Harriet stood looking off into a darker plain. He tried to glimpse what she had. He spotted Blithe, still at the fence, his head tilted upward with the contours of the hills beyond.

Harriet made no attempt to counsel the boy. Goldfinch wondered what the source of that earlier clamoring had been.

Harriet got ever closer to Blithe. Goldfinch wondered if he should make himself known. Then, however, the loudest, most confounding noises yet struck. For a moment, Goldfinch could not tell what Blithe Mulvane did or did not do. He was simply made victim to the chaos unfurling near the fence. A small tree tumbled down toward Synod, following gravity and the lay of the land. In the dark, it was just like a blotted shadow snowballing, engulfing the air, spreading its wings.

The tree was some feet away from Harriet and Blithe. Goldfinch was no longer shielded by the hut, but still, the other two did not look back. And no others rushed forward. He wondered why Blithe was so firmly entrenched in that spot along the fence. He was just close enough to them to hear them speak. They were slightly illuminated by two torches atop nearby fence posts.

"Blithe, you were worrying me—"

"He's gone and run off. That way," Blithe said, pointing at a hill nestled against the sides of the village.

"You didn't stop him?" Harriet said, about to pick up her gait toward the entrance. Blithe reached his hand across her chest, securely. Goldfinch wanted to emerge right then and there—if only he had his rifle.

"The tree, it's a message, obviously. You may be able to decipher it better than I."

Harriet fumbled with the thought for a moment. "Just that our cross lies in a tree, our village is built of the earth. To cut is to kill." She shook her head.

"The tree is either defacing this fence or was impaled by its pickets," he said.

On that word, 'pickets,' Harriet froze, swallowed hard, and sucked her teeth. She poked Blithe on the chest as if to boast of an epiphany.

"Picket," she said. "Picket—look at the downed tree, now."

Blithe scurried over to the tree, half protruding through the fence, half punctured by it. Goldfinch slipped even closer. Harriet followed Blithe. When she discovered something nestled in the tight, forking crevice on one of the tree's branches—an infantile cedar—she nudged Blithe out of the way and stepped toward it.

Goldfinch tried to mask his approach, but he was limping, and it was obvious. He carried along a layer of leaves with his injured leg. The two quickly turned around to see their leader approaching. Harriet looked at him, taken aback, then at Blithe. But her attention was soon focused elsewhere. She extracted a sheet of tightly rolled paper, its wax pressed by the

Governor's seal. Even in the dark, Goldfinch knew precisely what it was; a stamp of a horse's head, a knight's helmet, a shield with three plows distinguishing agricultural prowess, and Liberty with Ceres, who held a cornucopia.

In the dark, Harriet unfurled the sheet of paper. She walked to the closest torch—twenty feet off—and held the paper to the light. She read the note aloud.

"Pickets remember," she read. "Signed: P.N."

Chapter Seventeen

Charlottesburg

When Goldfinch returned to his own hut that evening, he was whisked off to a comfortable sleep, one that had eluded him since he awoke at Harriet's. Amid this slumber, he entered that hazy dream state yet again.

The darkness tampered with his bearings. He was finally able to perceive images, his life, his standing. He saw Harriet—her stare, the gooseflesh that formed when she stood in the cold. She said something to him. "Look away." She repeated it.

When he refused to heed her advice, he saw the waves of Lake Ontario crashing onto the rocky sands. He was airborne, suspended a few feet above this grainy shore.

He looked around at the barracks, the sturdy walls of the fort. Right on the water, he could feel a misty breeze. He still felt confined, unkempt. It was probably May 1813. He could wait and try his luck with the American expeditionary force or escape. He wanted to be a part of the swarming brigade, the Americans that would take the fort from the British.

For days he had been held without shackles, a product of reticence and submission. With the storm brewing—a storm, a probability, of American wit—he was surprised that he was not bound to a rusted beam.

The image was faint, but he remembered slipping past a British guard after midnight, the key to his cell slipped through the cracks by a sympathizer, a man he'd come to know in the cellblock for over two months. There were others, other Americans, but he knew his objective was strictly reconnaissance. The others would be saved when Fuss and Feathers stormed the gate.

With nothing but wool socks and the tattered undershirt he once wore beneath his uniform, he ran into the hideaway spot—the trees beyond the confines of the fort.

When he put distance between himself and the fort, it began to rain, slopping over his muddied feet. He looked back at the place that imprisoned him since March when he was gathering intelligence for Winfield Scott in preparation for something much larger to come along the banks of the Niagara River.

At the horizon, it wasn't the American lines he saw. It wasn't the American counterbalance, Fort Niagara, seized by the Americans in the Jay's Treaty of 1796. It was a snow-covered meadow, overrun by towering weeds—the spot of refuge for a 'malicious' rebel preacher during the Revolution.

There were hoof tracks in the snow, which sunk over a foot deep. Above, the thick powder fatigued the trees like the burden of a ball and chain. It was Synod. Goldfinch looked around, from his exposed lower legs at the knees, to the cross, pinned tightly to the hackberry. It felt foreign to him, as though a childhood home he had not returned to in years; but it still felt like a home. He was bruised by wartime, shaped into a rough laborer as a veteran, but here, he felt at home.

Goldfinch awoke. No misty images of the Great Lake, no illusions, no Harriet. He was alone, in his hut. He found a lengthy blade a few feet from his bed. He had grabbed it from Harriet's when he snuck out the night before. He had a bloodied bandage wrapped around his leg. He immediately felt disdain toward Blithe Mulvane. He knew the boy was still in Synod, against his wishes.

Goldfinch tried to stretch his cramped legs and wondered if the sojourn to the felled tree the night before had worsened his condition. He tried to stretch his ailing leg, and a shooting pain ran up his side, toward the heart afflicted by Harriet.

He flung his legs over the side of the bed. Flaring pain aside, he felt able-bodied and prepared to find Nance, who had been a menace during the entire hunting trip. He recalled the image that plundered his final thoughts—the dog on the hillside, the knife lodged in his thigh.

The Senator, he thought. But the man seemed reasonably upstanding. *The boy and that Nance, then!*

He was unsure of his own strength. Nonetheless, he sauntered over to the window, where he looked out upon the community. There were a few meandering people—Matilda, Sophie, and William—doing chores.

Then Goldfinch heard a tattering at the front step and against the door. Carlita pushed through without knocking. When she saw the conscious and sprawled Goldfinch, she was taken aback. "I'm a sorry, sir. Didn' mean to barge in on ya like such. Just that, you was under the weather and all. Harriet wanted me to check—"

"Nonsense," Goldfinch said, a smile on his face. "What is my home will forever be yours, for what you've endured."

Carlita looked down at Goldfinch's leg. "Seems to me, I done gone through 'bout half as much as you."

"The wound, as you see, is quite colorful."

She nodded. "And so ya done heard about the tree that went an' damaged yer fence?" She pointed off to the distance, beyond the thinly buffered wall that separated autumn and stab wound.

Goldfinch failed to acknowledge Carlita's outstretched hand pointing to the rangy pines. He hobbled back over to the window, where he spotted an infant cedar stretched ineptly over the fence he had hammered together.

Carlita lowered her hand and studied Goldfinch. He held his gaze on her, then peered elsewhere. He was searching for a cane, a crutch he could use to hobble longer distances. Against the hut, he discovered a splintered grading rake Harriet probably used on her fields. Perhaps she had left it for him. After pulling the bloodstained bandage on his leg tight, he opened the door, sidestepped down the stair, and grabbed hold of the rake. He used the tool as a makeshift cane, holding the handled tip, the tines pressed against the ground.

"Trouble with this place is," Goldfinch said to Carlita, who was still inside, "if I'm not astir, One, Harriet, Mulvane, they get backed up, stymied. They keep sounding off on the way things ought to be, but there's not a single one amongst them that can effect change." He guided the rake along the ground, moving toward the felled tree.

***

He reached the tool out to poke at the tree, only half the leaves clinging to the ridged folds of bough and bark. "He sliced into this one with a handsaw," he said aloud, and to himself. "Stole it from the shed, seems."

Soon, he was no longer alone, for Harriet approached. She sported a bright-yellow skirt and bodice, her frock coat draping over them.

Harriet paused, remaining silent. She sucked her bottom lip and pulled the bound paper from behind her back. "Do you believe it was just wrapped in one of those twigs?"

Goldfinch studied the document, with its cracked sealing wax. He looked back up at Harriet. "Sure is attaching himself to that Picket nightmare," he said. "Nance was in cahoots with those backward traffickers. He was the 'man on the move.'" Harriet failed to respond.

"Trouble is," he continued, "what do you have to say about the *boy*?"

"After all this, you're resorting back to Blithe?" Harriet replied. "He's a man of his word, and he almost nabbed Nance before he fled out that footpath."

"He's a child, and you might want to figure out why he was sharing a pocket watch with our *friendly* foe."

Flustered, Harriet turned a shoulder from Goldfinch and crossed her arms. "Say what you will about him—incriminate him. I know none of what you speak." She looked around to see if anyone else was near. "I sense the jealousy already. It was the hand on the knee, that day in my hut, was it not?"

He ignored the question, "Up in the woods. Saw Nance with Blithe's timepiece. The same one. They both came on from Philadelphia. Suppose Mulvane was tampered with before he got to the Reverend's place." He shook his head swiftly as if second guessing each word that slipped from his mouth.

Hesitantly, Harriet said, "Your mind is jumpy, after the trauma. Not every day a man becomes victim to a blood-letting."

"Don't presume to know my predicament, Harriet. Thing is, I saw a lot under the spell of that knife. That Nance, your boy Blithe, they're involved with the Pickets. Expect the Governor next. Should it come to it, we can't survive something like that—that scale. Just can't."

He turned from her, tightened his grip on the rake, and made his way back to his hut.

There, he unwound, remembering Harriet's whispers the day before. And some days before that, the lovemaking, the hunt. He knew he needed to speak with Minister Mulvane again.

***

The knock on the door was rapid, just a flick of the wrist and an effortless tap. Minister Mulvane swung the door open with ease and stood with an austere look on his face, appraising Goldfinch. No smile, no well-wishes.

"Mulvane, in the interest of brevity," Goldfinch said, "I'll apologize for my being rattled the other day. I consider you a close friend. You are second in command here, despite One's sentiments."

"Why are you standing here, your being clasped to that rake and all? God's wounds!"

"I do not take back what I said. But, the boy can stay, for now. While I probe him and his cultured ways." He tipped his hat. "The boy is reckless, luring Synod's women."

"You mean *woman*," Mulvane replied. "Do not lose sight of our aims, Goldfinch. It is Nance we seek—the man acquainted with the Steven Picket fellow in Carolina. What do we know of *his* background?"

"I was hoping you could tell me. You know, a preacher's privilege. Maybe the man had a few skeletons to sweep from his closet."

"Goldfinch, you know there are no closets in which to hide here."

Flustered, Goldfinch returned the cold glare. "In any case, be aware of your son."

"You come here to lecture me about propriety—he is the epitome of etiquette—and you stand here accusing him of luring. Harriet and Blithe? They are already coupled. And it is about time, if I do say so myself."

"Coupled?" Goldfinch said, struggling to remain poised.

"Attached, embracing, and toiling about as though they've already married. You ask me, it's jealousy wants Blithe out of here." He slammed the door shut.

The Leader stood, staring idly at the door for a few moments before making way, moving out to gather folks for a necessary trip. There were only a few people on his mind, those who understood this quagmire, the Paterson Four.

He limped over to the horse paddock where he found Eder resting proudly near an area of tough grasses and an inch of slop—mud and food dropped from the trough. "Here, boy." The horse failed to move, but he did appear to eye up his caregiver.

Moments later, with the horse saddled, bridle on, Goldfinch left the paddock to recruit his friends. It took only a few knocks, a couple of explanations, and the men were ready to ride.

Shepherd rode the Friesian while the others took their own mounts. They had gathered rifles and modest rations. By the time the men took to the path, the darkness had fallen. The remnants of a hued sunset rose off—back to God's grasp.

"There is no rotting corpse tied to my horse. I'd say it's the outset of a lucrative trip," One announced, his hair catching the amber light, the rest of his black attire slithering off into the night.

Shepherd nicked the horse's side, feeling it out, testing its response, its malleability. "Beautiful horse, and it's just been sitting in that there paddock. Liberating to let him run."

Goldfinch had his leg tied tightly under his trousers. He carried a cane, which sat sidelong against Eder's back.

Solomon had gifted him the supportive, evenly edged cane just an hour earlier while he rounded up the animals and the villagers. "For moving quickly through them bushes, dodgin' them bullets, which I know you's b'come good at," he had said.

Reg was the hardest one to corral. He had been living bravely in the huts at the outpost, even when Nance was on the loose. The "Governor's Man," as Nance had become known, could have hindered Reg's escape, shackled him on the spot, and made his way back to Carolina. "Call to action like this, always keeps a man loose, his blood pumpin'. Then he comes back, lay with his girl, have the right energy to keep her rememberin' that name." He laughed, obviously thinking back on experiences with his Celia.

Goldfinch did not lead the procession. He sat in the middle of the pack, letting Shepherd lead the way. Every few trots he winced at the pain shooting up his leg. As they passed the hackberry, Goldfinch tried to clear his mind and let nature overpower his doubts, his worries. Gazing at the cross, all Goldfinch could think about was snow—the weather could have easily summoned it.

Temperatures had fallen below freezing in the dark and through the pockets of aggressive wind dancing between the trees. Goldfinch remembered the stifled face Cartwright had made as he held much of the weight of the cross, the spiritual compass that was supposed to guide them. He shook his head, elevating himself out of the trance. Yet all he could dream about was Harriet and her recent betrayal. He imagined young Mulvane and his Harriet with interlocked hands. It nearly made him vomit. He wanted it to snow. *If I froze, who would feel the loss? Mother died in childbirth. Father had slipped into madness. My destiny is bleak*, he thought.

Goldfinch was a runaway of sorts—a valuable wartime conscript but a pariah afterward, slaving for work.

He was slightly comforted by the story Harriet had relayed about her earlier years and her numbness to men, who were naturally vain. In many ways, they were similar, cynical and terse. By the time he veered from these entrapments, he looked up, and the procession was moving along, breaths twisting into the dark labyrinth of night. The hooves, which minced small morsels of earth, emitted melodic sounds.

Their trip to Charlottesburg seemed lofty—to inquire about the mysterious Nance—but their wills had already been tested thrice. Each throb of pain reminded him of the objective, though. He could not see any frost just yet, but he could feel the ground crystallize, the air stiffen and become heavier.

He let out a long breath, his lips pressed outward, to watch the vapors creep up on the rider in front of him. Then he looked at his rifle. But within, he saw the rabbit's foot, the pocket watch, and Blithe's knee touch.

As they moved along through the pastoral backdrop of the Ramapough Mountains, valleys, and coiling lakes, the trip felt compartmentalized. Half was the climb, half the descent down the Apshawa hills. Goldfinch even spotted a stagecoach moving through the town with a burly team of horses. Initially, he feared there could be a relation to the Pickets or the Governor. But it moved off into some unknown trail.

***

At first light, the men trotted into the village. It was modest—a few buildings, ridge and furrow carved into the knolls, and an all-purpose store. Goldfinch decided he would make his legal inquiry in the post office. That, of course, was inside the general store.

"Gentlemen, let's post the horses up by that hitching rail." Goldfinch pointed to the trafficked path left by buggies.

Eder seemed cold, his haunches having absorbed much of the night's punishment. Still, he was not lame, and he had countered the dismal appearance of night with the stately white.

Goldfinch was not the first one to post up, but he led the group up the two wooden steps into the post office. The building was small, twenty feet by twenty feet at best. The ceilings were thick, unpainted beams. There was a small room, mainly out of sight, in the back.

Goldfinch approached a man behind the counter. He was wearing a carefully ironed suit, a cravat emerging from the collar. He had a stack of packages on his desk. His hands were folded neatly and propped on the polished wooden surface.

"I presume you might be able to help us, mister," Goldfinch said. "My name is Herm. These are agents of the state Department of Community Affairs. We're here on a lead, a man, a rogue agent, he was said to have passed through these parts. Witnesses say not too long ago, either." Goldfinch was being presumptuous with his query, hoping he could fish for something useful. "Reason to believe he's stealing from the treasury, some of the Governor's own money."

"A name would help," the man said. He looked Italian, and his English was broken. Still, he understood.

"Nance. Mr. Peter Nance. Sources tell us he's in close relations with our governor, Mr. Dumont Vroom."

The man looked at the others, stopping on Reg. "The negro is an agent of the state?" he asked.

Goldfinch did not falter. "Assumptions always fail us. Leave it to this man to find his way. The agent's qualified, I assure you."

The man narrowed his eyes as if to show skepticism. "You're agents of whom?"

"Community Affairs. Our department focuses on municipal fulfillment. We keep finances in check." The Leader folded his arms and placed them atop his stomach.

The postman paused to second guess but trudged on. "Man by that name came through here, maybe two weeks ago. Looked like he was out on the road for a while. All prim and proper like?"

"That's him," Goldfinch answered.

"Now, he didn't try to conceal much. He said he was a special counsel to the Governor. He wanted free food, lodging, and a horse to ride for a few days when he checked out and ran off into our woods up near Germantown, probably higher into the hills." He paused a moment. "I run the inn here, too. Well, my father does. His name's Niccolo."

Goldfinch looked back at Shepherd, hiding the enthusiasm, then back to the postman. "Special counsel," he said. "He is a deceitful man."

"Don't know what he was doing here, ultimately. Said something about an appraisal—here, there, up in British Canada—but it beats me. Stayed three days. Checked out without paying a dime. See, we assumed he'd bring down the wrath of the state on us for some inspection nonsense. We didn't know. I must say, it was rather strange."

"A shame for him," Goldfinch said. "He used his real name, no faulty alias. Incriminating is what it is." He pressed his fist down on the postman's counter. "He has eluded us for some time since leaving the capital. Now, did he declare himself to be close to the Governor?"

"Dumont Vroom?" the man asked, scratching his head. "No, can't say he mentioned anything like that. Just said he was special counsel to him. Don't know what that implies."

"Thank you for your time, Mister—?"

"Costa," the man replied. "Dantae Costa. Glad I could be of some assistance." He looked from person to person, still skeptical of the men before him. *Chances are,* Goldfinch thought, *honesty was the best policy for this man.* For all Dantae knew, the four men could've been hunters, agents, evangelists, or Lord knows what.

Goldfinch tipped his hat at the postman, who went back to sorting and filing the pile of letters before him. The four men departed, single file, and made their way back to the hitching rail.

Goldfinch limped down the front step leaning on Solomon's cane. "That confirms what we already knew then, gentlemen."

"If there's one thing we learned," Shepherd said, "it's that the man is brash enough to use his real name—and skip out on his debts."

Goldfinch looked at Shepherd. "Senator Frelinghuysen was right, then. He's in the Governor's office. The seal, the privilege—it stinks of Trenton." He cringed as his stony leg bent up into the saddle. He turned to fasten the cane into the bag at the rear of the saddle. The others followed his lead.

The last one to unhitch his horse was Shepherd, who studied the figuration of the small, hilly hamlet. He seemed to admire the diminutive post office, still a much larger structure than any Synod building. He turned back toward the Leader. "Dantae is telling us the truth, Goldfinch." He appeared relieved, as though he had come to some sweeping conclusion.

Goldfinch, too, felt gratified. They were learning more and more. He petted Eder's gray and snow-white mane just above the withers. "Suppose it's back to the village unless you find that monster hiding around Niccolo's inn." Still, they knew the man was long gone.

Once they began moving, Goldfinch took the lead for the first time since before his injury. He held his head high, his coat hanging low, contrasting with the thoroughbred.

***

It took close to two hours of ascending into the Apshawa hills, at a stalling pace, before Goldfinch sought refuge. The tendons in his thigh felt ablaze, as though the knife still wreaked havoc in his leg—as if Nance was still prying it into his flesh from whatever spot he lingered in.

When they dismounted, holding reins, they looked around the footpath along the Macopin trail for a spot to regain their bearings. Goldfinch led Eder with his reins, and he wrapped them around the trunk of a small tree. He stabbed the cane into the ground as if it was therapeutic or cathartic. He was plotting, contemplating. The others recognized this.

"Mista Goldfinch, why doncha settle on down, take a rest on one of them rocks," Reg said. He had since been silent.

Goldfinch shrugged and paced, his frock coat gliding in circles on each of his unguided turns. Ignoring the appeal, Goldfinch spoke up, leaning against the tree trunk beside Eder. "Reg, you and your girls, you moved mountains to come to this place. Carlita, she crossed rivers, went up the Appalachians for it. It's our responsibility to safeguard this place. We fight wars, our wars fight us." Frustrated, he hurled his walking stick into the thickets then ran his fingers through his hair. It was a culmination of leg pain and the larger, pressing ordeal.

One offered to pick the stick up for him, saying he had better not bend more and open up the wound. Goldfinch refused. He shoved his boots into the wilted grass. A few steps later he spotted the item Solomon had carved for him. He thought nothing of picking the stick up. But when he grabbed a hold, a peculiar sound snuck out from the grass a few feet away. When Goldfinch carefully focused on the noise, he saw a bushy tail, motionless, pressing out above a weed. He wielded the stick as a weapon.

He stayed as still as he could, his leg throbbing. The Leader made a *ttt-ttt* noise, luring whatever waited for him, flushing it from their path.

The tail began to sway. Slowly emerging from this dense sanctuary, a coyote showed itself in full form. Being the middle of the day, it should have been an illusion, a figment of his kaleidoscopic imagination. But the coyote locked eyes with the Leader, failing to blink, twitch, bark, or growl.

Goldfinch tensed up but pivoted his hips back over toward the group. "Am I alone in this sighting?" He went back to locking eyes with the animal.

From behind, Reg said, "Afraid not, Mista Goldfinch." The men spread out as if to flank the animal and simply scare it off.

As they moved, the coyote began to show its teeth. It still did not growl—it seemed like a friendly reminder of animal dominance. Goldfinch tried to slip away, but he was right in the animal's path, a part of the careful plan it must have conjured up in the grass.

Goldfinch shut his eyes and imagined his escape. He kept his lids pressed shut and began to inch his way backward. He could feel the cane in front of him, pointed ahead. When his ankles no longer brushed against the bristly grasses, he reopened his eyes. The world was grayer as he readjusted. The men and their frock coats, nearly disguised as bare trees, were spread around the animal, ensuring the Leader's safety.

Goldfinch swung the cane, a light, half-hearted swing. "Get, get, beast." As the words left his lips, he recalled how he had heard the bounty hunters say that time and again; "Nigger this, nigger that," they would say. He felt remorse, for Carlita, for the Sullivans. He lowered the cane, pressing his weight back down on it. He took his hat and waved it off to the right, as though directing the animal. With each hand motion, the coyote stayed affixed to the Leader.

The gusts picked up, sweeping down through the trees, tickling the manes of the still horses. With no forewarning, Mr. Boatwright emerged from the thickets. There was no path, no true sounds of his approach. Goldfinch could spot the muttonchops from afar. He still sported a satiny suit and blue spectacles. With his attire, he should not have been found within miles of a forest. He carried the air of a city man who had obviously gone awry or found his calling.

He remained silent, just as he had in Paterson. The man, like the animal, stared Goldfinch down. He arched his back to a half bow to show some sort of acknowledgment. Goldfinch took this as a cue.

"Mr. Boatwright it is, no?" he asked. "The dog was eyeing us, as though we'd be a midday meal."

"What are you doing over here?" Mr. Boatwright said, his head now lowered.

"Turns out your boss was right, there was a 'Governor's Man' following us. He infiltrated our ranks. The thing is, the last image I saw before giving in to my stab wound, was the damn beast. How can I be sure it wasn't you abetting the madman?"

Mr. Boatwright laughed and then looked up. "If Alaba saw the exchange, then the Senator did as well. This is good."

"Since the trip, we've, well we've—" Goldfinch stammered. "The images, the visions, and the red eye. It was all from you and your boss, was it not?"

"You speak in past tense, as though the ordeal is through. You've only scratched the surface."

From a few feet away, One butted in, saying, "Do us a favor, Mr. Boatwright. Tell us, is it the correct surface we've scratched?"

The man provided no answer. Instead, he clicked his tongue against his palate a few times, calling the animal. He turned from the group and retreated back into the brush. When he was twenty-yards away, he looked back at the Leader, his eyes red. They were aflame and impassioned like the visions Goldfinch had seen all along.

At last, Goldfinch knew what the red was. It was no scare tactic or superfluous intervention. In fact, there was nothing superfluous about it. The red was the eye of slavery, the blood spilled—the atrocities since the days of the slave ships. There was so much weight in the eyes, in the red. It was the weight of the Africans and their plight, the burden of inaction.

It was here, in the woods above Charlottesburg, at the plateau atop the hills near Apshawa, where Goldfinch became completely, doggedly determined to uphold his promise to Reverend Allen and the others. He pledged to preserve the sanctity of Synod, to help eradicate the rotten institution of slavery.

Here, he also knew that the Senator's intervention was by no means coincidental. He was the silent founder.

As Mr. Boatwright disappeared, Goldfinch remembered the July evening when the Founders departed. He remembered the ardent look that Lyman returned to him, similar to Mr. Boatwright's glare.

They had left in the night, to avoid exposure, and when they'd slipped past the hackberry, Lyman tipped his hat and spoke to Goldfinch with his eyes. It was a talent he was passing off to the new leader, for eyes are "windows into men's souls."

Chapter Eighteen

The Hillside

Monday, December 7, 1829

Monday morning's wrath was hard on Goldfinch's leg, which seemed to harden with the cold. Wiping the sleep from his eyes and grabbing his hat, he stretched near the doorframe of his dwelling. As he looked out at the village, the landscape had been altered and turned so homogenous. There was no palpable difference between the hills at the fringes and the paths connecting Synod's inhabitants. It was a fresh blanket of snow. Goldfinch came face to face with the new climate as he opened the door, the frosty air grabbing hold of him from the ankles up. As he began to focus, he saw a rifle propped on Shepherd's shoulder, but the sight was fleeting. Shepherd whisked himself inside his hut, presumably to start a fire. That was Goldfinch's cue.

Shivering, he stepped back inside. He had much to ponder; Minister Mulvane's disjointed sermon from the day before and the recurring dreams he just could not shake. At that point, it seemed as though the Governor's Man would never return. It had been weeks since they stalked his path.

As he turned from the doorway toward the village's center, he grabbed his frock coat and the cane Solomon had carved for him. Things had not been too cordial between Goldfinch and Harriet in the preceding weeks, though his mind never left the subject of their romance. She had betrayed him and was now courting the younger Mulvane.

With all that had unfolded, it was difficult to carry on with Minister Mulvane. It was worse with Harriet, who had hardly spoken a single word with the Leader since his convalescence. She spent her nights at Blithe's hut, turning in early and sleeping in late. To cope, Goldfinch would exert double the energy into his chores and take up secret meetings with the Paterson Four beyond the gate.

On one occasion, around Thanksgiving, the group had met to discuss perimeter security. Since the Charlottesburg trip, Nance had not left behind a single clue. He had turned the village upside down in his brief tenure there but exited with an equal amount of stealth. Their meeting was encumbered by an approaching cold front, the temperatures sinking as the sun did over the Ramapough Mountains. Each man— Goldfinch, Shepherd, One, and Reg—shared a tale on their nighttime burdens. The wolves, the Senator, Mr. Boatwright— they were all frequenters in the men's dreams and empty stares. "If it proves anything, it's that that man hasn't gone too far," One had said, adamant that Nance would return to further exact his hateful wrath.

The men were bundled carefully, sure to prevent fever. They would move from person to person, expressing opinions and sharing plans. The consensus was that no one would be released from the Senator's hold until the problem was handled. They usually rotated shifts near the front gate, protecting against the Governor's Man, hoping that the state was not involved in a grander scheme. This watch tended to be around the clock, and it was a revolving door. One man would watch for six hours, then the next. The Long Rifles would be at the ready, powder on the flintlock pans.

On this Monday, it was Goldfinch's turn, though his leg was still ailing from long hours at the fence. In the cold, a burning sensation would travel like wildfire down his leg.

The Leader had devised a fiery contingency plan, though, and he was ready to put it to the test. "All else fails, and the place is compromised, burn it up, look to that mysterious bureaucrat," One had suggested. The rest of the Four seemed to agree. The contingency; clouding Nance's entry. At every post, large wicker baskets held kindling, and one post connected to the next with pliable pine branches, and Arborvitae leaves, wrapping a larger, firmer network of boughs. At the weak points between posts, a support was driven into the ground to prop up the carefully weaved roping.

"Christmas is near," Shepherd had said in one of the earlier meetings. "A wreathing would look swell." And so it did. Their web of boughs, twigs, and wicker could create a fiery perimeter that the marauders would have difficulty passing through. They would be left with ample time to at least react, or flee toward the outposts, or the burial ground. The trouble was the time it would take to ignite.

Limping out near the fire pit, Goldfinch turned his gaze from the 'wreath' to the huts. He glowered at the changes that had ripped Synod apart in such little time. He looked around him, searching for any glaring carpentry needs. Nothing, just plumes of smoke from the villagers' fires spiraling upward. He slipped back to his hut, grabbed his rifle, buttoned his coat, and ventured toward the gate.

With a drum of hooves closing in, Goldfinch turned to the sound and spotted Solomon brandishing a wide smile. He was aboard the Friesian and wrapped tightly in an off-white frock coat that was probably gifted to him by another villager. "Reckon Christmas ain't too far off, now, Mista Goldfinch," he said. He awaited a response from Goldfinch.

"Let us hope we won't need to illuminate the fence for the holiday," Goldfinch offered quite coldly.

"That fella comes back, I don't think it'll be alone, Mista Goldfinch," Solomon said.

"Suppose not, but I hardly believe the Governor's behind that madness."

"Could it be, he a impostor?" Solomon asked.

Goldfinch looked up into the snowy hills, the naked trees, seeking movement, something strange. There was nothing. He continued to hobble along, his now-arthritic knees cautioning him farther. Solomon followed close behind on the Friesian. "Then how can we account for the statements from Renly?" Goldfinch said, mainly thinking aloud. "And from that Burt fella? The Senator, he knew so much, those dogs alerting him to something."

"S'pose you right, Mista Goldfinch. Senator woulda taken care a things if it were any other way. Ya know, I seen the way Shepherd worked with that man, bringin' Reg's kids over the river. He's a true one, he is."

"Pain in this leg doesn't give me any leeway for discussion, Solomon. Apologize for that. Right now, I'm just focused on getting to our post near that revered tree of ours."

"Ya know, Mista Goldfinch, I can help on any them watches you all do out there. You seen me with the 'truders, I'm capable."

Goldfinch took a moment to respond, remembering his various nights of patrol, the darkness lurking over him like it had as he succumbed to the stab wound. In chilling conditions, the thoughts only simmered more ferociously, seeming to sustain what little body heat he retained. He remembered the meetings of the Paterson Four, their tales on the omnipresent visions, the red eye. "There's something that makes us hold a keener eye out near the hackberry, Solomon. It's no slight against you."

"Wish I could've been on that there trip. Ya know, I've traversed that Paterson Turnpike so frequently, slipped through the tolling stations at night. There ain't much I's not akin to."

"Take that keen eye you've got and hold down this place, from the inside. My duty's to the rest."

"Yessuh, I'll see ya in a few hours, when er'body awake."

***

Goldfinch sat, blowing air into his cupped hands, at the post near the hackberry. The small shack was modest, and not roofed. The floor was a matted layer of earth, and the walls were composed of small, cylindrical boughs, a lookout hole carved through the middle. Goldfinch wrapped himself tightly in his frock coat and breathed heavily, watching the swirling vapors turn skyward.

With every snap of a twig, every sway of a heavy branch or whistle from a creaky tree trunk, Goldfinch held the rifle out the window, poised to release the trigger. He felt increasingly numbed against the frosty air. As he concentrated on the path leading toward the distant roads, he felt his senses converging, creating an impervious watchman.

Even still, someone approached. It was not from the patchy wood ahead but from behind. This interloper seemed to move with care, brushing only a few wiry branches that reached up from the fresh snow. These twigs would rarely stir in the winter months, and here they were being jostled, and right nearby. Goldfinch held his breath and turned his attention to his rear, where he saw a ball of cloth approach. As it got closer, he could make out a bonnet and several layers of petticoats. This woman also held a woolen blanket around her shoulders, and it crossed over her jawline.

"Only me," the voice said, and he knew exactly who it was.

"Come close," Goldfinch said despondently. "You couldn't be an easier target."

"Of what, exactly?" Harriet responded.

"The Governor's Man, of course, I've said it time and again."

"That Nance fella, you really think he'll return? Could he have been a passerby, the real perpetrator yet to show his face?"

"Doubtful," Goldfinch fired, his eyes peeled on the underbrush that was now buttressed by mounds of blown snow.

"Quite cold in here, Goldfinch," she said, shivering as she huddled beside him in the small post.

"If you'd like to warm yourself, go back to your hut. Blithe will gladly oblige."

"He is an ambitious man," she answered. "Wouldn't be surprised if he were to rise through these ranks, be your *fidus Achates*, in time, of course."

"You've brushed up on your Latin, I see. You do not impress," Goldfinch responded.

"Little else to do in these winter months, amongst so many unnerved people. We're in such close quarters with one another. And I have some old texts lying around. You understand."

"What I understand is the landscape before me, and that doesn't need to change. Now, who wrote that?"

"Virgil, *The Aeneid*."

"Well, Virgil doesn't need to interject, at *any* point, thank you." Goldfinch so badly wanted to speak easily, to caress her, to run his fingers through her hair. But that hair had become matted down by sweat during her intercourse with Blithe, surely. He felt his heart blare in his chest, as though it could tear through.

"I've just come to check on you, Goldfinch. You are not the same man you were, not even some months ago. There was a sparkle in your eye—the day those Founders left, and you had finally made something of your postwar life. Dare I say, it is diminishing?"

"If so, it is your doing." It was about to happen. He would spill his heart out. "To lie with that boy, so many years your junior. You hardly know him. I was under the impression we had found something between—" He paused and left the topic. "I have much to tend to out here."

"Goldfinch, there are parts of my past you do not know about. You know nothing of my experiences, of my taste in men. That moment, in the hut, the moment we shared, it was a release. Pent-up angst that needed to be released somewhere. You'd come through, had whisked me off." He could tell these comments troubled her, possibly belied her true thoughts. But he would not quarrel with her, not then.

"As I said, I have much to tend to."

"Ah, yes. That twig, some feet away, has danced with the latest breeze. You see?" She was scolding him.

"Off with you, now, Harriet. Blithe will worry."

"More than can be said of you, Goldfinch. More than can be *said*, of you."

They both now seemed content lingering in this middle ground. Neither one wanted to press the other. Their romance seemed to be a whimsical memory.

Goldfinch turned his attention back to the watch. Harriet brushed off the rear of her frock coat and took her leave. She lifted her petticoats as her boots sunk into nearly six-inches of snow.

He waited for her to be off before he stood. He examined the prints she left behind in the snow. With nothing—to that point—holding his attention at the post, he followed the prints. He suddenly felt warm, though the temperature was frigid in the hours after dawn. He was not sure whether the butterflies in his stomach were for Harriet. But they were there. He still wanted to return to that moment of carelessness, of ecstasy, when they had hustled off to his hut. Plus, with Nance sure to return, the time they could have shared seemed limited.

He tried to suppress the urges, and he carried on, his hands waving away thick, bristling little twigs. His boots crunched in the snow as his heart rate increased, the two almost syncing with one another. Goldfinch had the Synod fence in view, and he turned back toward the post. *Could something be astir?* He followed every step Harriet had left behind. Her path was straight, her strides short, a product of the petticoats.

Goldfinch began to dream of the warm fire pit that had swaddled him. He stood motionless, turning from the post to the fence, then to the other directions, powdery snow seemingly skewing his depth perception. What was far looked near, what was near seemed so far beneath the ankle-deep snowfall. He persevered, deciding against returning to the confines of his hut. He imagined Blithe waiting for Harriet in hers. Perhaps the answer to all of this lingered in spots the villagers rarely visited. Maybe nature would reveal a hint in every wind gust, or rapid in the river, or whitecap on the larger Long Pond. He rubbed his palms together for a jolt of energy and turned toward the untraveled portions of the Synod perimeter.

It was simply impulse that tugged Goldfinch out past the fence, through the snowy labyrinth that made up this Ramapough woodland. He placed one hand out in front for guidance while the other held the cane. As he carried on, he turned back periodically to get his bearings, his visible trail in the snow sneaking up behind him. The hollowed-out footsteps made him feel insignificant, just another presence coming and going, alone in these opaque forests.

Thirty or so paces later, Goldfinch still did not veer from this course. His hands were lowered, his frock coat greeting and bending each encroaching branch. He came to what looked like a crossroads between a thin deer path and an old stagecoach trail. Following the slender trail, he looked at the winding horizon, the lay of the land heightening slightly over the next fifty yards. He paused for a moment, sticking to the thicker, more troublesome terrain beside the trail. Then, he halted his gait mid-stride as a horse neighed in the distance, and someone coughed. He flung himself—as best he could— toward the closest tree and tried to silence his breathing so he could make out any words.

Slipping his head from the cover of the tree, he looked up the neglected coach trail. At the next open spot of terrain, a perpendicular crossing, a brown horse was tied to the trunk of a small, bare oak. There was a faint plume of smoke rising over the horse's back. It was not the animal's breath or sweat, and Goldfinch could make out shin-high lace-up boots planted in the powder. Almost at once, the feet shuffled to the right, toward the horse's saddlebag. From around the corner of a flicking tail, Blithe moved about, standing in a smoothed-out portion of earth near the horse. Around the other side of the animal, Blithe leaned against the horse's flank, a lit pipe hanging from the corner of his mouth.

Goldfinch squinted toward Harriet's lover, focusing on the trees surrounding him. Blithe rested against the horse. For a moment, Goldfinch thought he was spotted, but the longer he waited, the stiller Blithe remained. He wore a tall, black silken hat that contrasted with the fallen snow. For a moment he removed the hat, passed his fingers through his hair and put the bulky covering back atop his head. Suddenly, he moved to his right, widening his arms. As he did this, Goldfinch stood still, breathless, against the tree. He peeked around it and saw another man greeting Blithe.

He could not tell who had approached Blithe. But their discourse was warm. Goldfinch stood chilled to his core, propped against the frigid trunk. He pulled his frock coat close to his face, to cloak much of his waist, and leaned a bit farther out from the tree.

Blithe was now shaking the hand of the man who had wreaked havoc on the village, Mr. Peter Nance! His heart sank, and he watched as the conceited Governor's Man propped his arm around Blithe's shoulder. Nance looked behind him, then in Goldfinch's direction, before showing Blithe a sheet of paper. After a moment, he folded it back up and placed it within his suitcoat. Goldfinch could hear the conversation continue, then Blithe laughing, and Nance guffawing. Their collective bitterness penetrated the lifeless wood of the trees.

The two continued their brief meeting for another minute or so, talking indecipherably back and forth. Blithe then lifted his hat and hopped aboard his horse. The pipe still leaked out the corner of his mouth. Nance reached up and shook the young man's hand, and then snuck off. He followed the same tracks he had left when he came to greet Blithe. Then the younger Mulvane shook his reins and plodded off, away from Synod but also from Nance.

Goldfinch gripped the cane and leaned back behind the tree, absorbing the strange rendezvous he had just witnessed. He let his frock coat rest easier around his shoulders and rushed back toward the post. His aim was to try and follow Nance's departure. He remained surprisingly stealthy as he slipped past the trees and hedges alike. The persistent leg wound was not a factor.

***

As the sun rose higher in the sky, Goldfinch became hyper-aware of his surroundings, the sparse movement of a branch or a small paw packing the powder. Resting his rifle out the small opening, he had much of the perimeter within his watchful eye. There was no sign of Nance. He did not have the stamina to shadow the Governor's Man and trace his every footstep. But he could hold down the place and assure that no other gathering commenced nearby.

Again, he heard the distinct sounds of a person navigating the wood. It appeared to be behind him. It was certainly a person, not Alaba. *But Mr. Boatwright?*

He tightened his grip on the rifle, and although there was little room to maneuver in the post, he turned around. Out the rear opening, he spotted the bundle of fabric approaching yet again. He was relieved and loosened the grip.

"Thought I told you not to bog me down with more ancient nonsense?"

Harriet, devoid of her earlier playfulness, glared right through Goldfinch, her countenance brittle, her face red from the cold. "Come on in," Goldfinch said, recognizing her momentary paralysis. "You may not believe it, but I've spotted something."

"You saw him? You saw the man?" Harriet fired.

"He was donning his usual, inflated attire," Goldfinch replied. "Not Blithe, though *he* was present. I speak of the intruder." He rose from his post, propping his rifle on his right shoulder. He decided it was time. "We must get back, warn the others. The three other men will know what to do."

"You've stood out here without telling anyone? He surely escaped by now," Harriet declared.

"I hoped to scope him out," Goldfinch said, flustered, grabbing his cane. "I should leave you to handle this Blithe traitor."

She changed the subject. "You're not about to burn the fence down with that 'wreath' of yours, are you?"

"Not if he's alone," Goldfinch said. "By God, we might strike now, while he least expects it. The four of us, on horseback—end this Picket nonsense. Why a man would attach himself to another's burden is beyond me. Anyway, please get out of my path." He lightly brushed into Harriet as he fled the post, looking earnestly off to the area Nance traversed. He did not hold back, letting his feet sink deeply into the ground. Harriet followed close behind.

"After this mess," she said to his back, "what happened between us will simply be the past. Something we may relish, but in the past nonetheless."

He wanted to ignore her, but he couldn't. "If I may opine, I believe your feelings will change." He continued to prod the cane into the snow. She let out a frustrated *humph*.

Goldfinch stopped for a moment. "But what ensues *here*, is a fight for humanity, not just this measly little place, or you and I."

***

As he hobbled toward the gate, he looked at the hackberry, the wooden cross now adopting the thick coat of snow that stacked along the corners. The Leader trekked back inside the village, waving his rifle in the air for the other Paterson men to see. He heard a whistle, a horse's hooves bearing down on the earth in the paddock. As he looked at it, Eder neighed and rose up on his hind legs. Goldfinch trudged onward, knocking against Shepherd's door.

"Rise up, fool! The man is near. He's dared to return."

Shepherd squinted as the light appeared to cloud his vision of Goldfinch. "I'll be prepared in a moment. Have you seen Reg yet?"

"Figured he has been staying in someone's hut ..."

"Was adamant about staying at the outposts, should someone rush the place."

"Well, he's exposed out there. Where is Carlita? If the man has a posse, the whole place is doomed."

Shepherd processed this for a moment. "Think she's with Elizabeth, at her place."

"I'll trust her to Solomon," Goldfinch replied, pensively.

"So you leave two of *them* together?"

Goldfinch scratched his chin. "Man's been to Philadelphia and back. Hasn't been caught by any bounty hunters yet."

"You better hope he holds on to her. I see the way you look at her when she talks about that daughter of hers. Mind's journeying with her, is it not?"

True, Goldfinch was enchanted by Carlita's fireside tales of her daughter, but this was no moment to think of that.

Shepherd jumped in. "Don't plan on smoking us out with that wreath of yours, do you? It'd catch the forest, maybe a hut or two before we could get it out after a scuffle."

"Simply a last resort," Goldfinch said. "Just gather the men, meet me near the gate." Shepherd nodded.

Goldfinch's wound seemed to flare with the cold as he moved, but he made it to the gate. He looked at the 'wreath' wrapped around it, a barricade against the deviants that wanted to pillage and lynch. His viny creation sat nestled atop the fence posts and would be sure to at least ward off intruders for a few moments—enough time to grab the powder horns.

To Goldfinch, an eternity passed before the band of his villagers approached, guns in hand. Goldfinch could see Shepherd motioning to curious villagers as he walked, telling Matilda and Sophie and a few newcomers to hunker down behind their thin walls. With him was Reg, One, and Harriet. Solomon and Carlita hustled off toward Solomon's hut, the former trying to shield the runaway with the waist of his coat. Then, trailing a few paces behind the group came Blithe, looking curious yet impassive.

Goldfinch scolded Harriet with his eyes, and eventually, she turned around. As she saw her lover creeping up close, she let out a quick gasp. "Blithe, you hound. What is it you're trying to do?"

"Didn't mean to give you a fright. I saw everyone heading for the gate. I'd like to know why."

"Where've you been, Blithe? This whole morning," Harriet asked.

"Why, I was with my father, we spoke about his sermon. Talked about all those runs he went on for the weapons, thanks to his connections from the war. You would know, right Goldfinch?" He shouted as he mentioned the Leader's name.

"Well, huddle in close, then," Harriet said quite unconvincingly. The young man smirked and tipped his hat at Goldfinch.

A few moments later the group was lined up along the entrance of the community, almost forming another portion of Goldfinch's intricate fence. The Leader stood at the center but slyly held his attention on Blithe.

"Man from the governor's office, you don't suppose it goes any higher than him, do you?" Blithe asked.

No one responded. Harriet stood nervously between Blithe and Goldfinch.

"Where is your father now?" Goldfinch wondered, refusing to look at Blithe.

"Around, probably sweeping beneath the pews."

"Swell."

Upon these last words, Blithe grabbed Harriet's hand and snuck his fingers between hers. Goldfinch thought he even felt her nerves stir, but she did not stop the advance.

***

Goldfinch recognized the winds changing, the cold— compact and permeating—squeezing through his frock coat. He tried to stay loose, fiddling with his leg and tapping his cane into the snow.

It was midmorning, and still, there was no sign of Nance. Most of the villagers were fatigued, standing in the snowy landscape for hours. Goldfinch monitored the path, the route often taken by Solomon on his "'delphia" journeys. Then came riotous laughter and the sound of crackling branches. Goldfinch held his ground and assured each man did not flinch. This was followed by a gunshot that Goldfinch believed soared straight up into the sky. An announcement.

At last, turning the bend toward the straightaway leading to the hackberry, Nance rode on his quarter horse. Behind him was a formation of other riders each carrying rifles, pitchforks, and ropes looped around their shoulders. One held a flaming branch that he lifted strenuously above his head and hurled toward the villagers. Their artillery fire. It landed about ten feet in front of Goldfinch's formation and soon began to melt some of the surrounding snow.

Goldfinch did not move. When Nance was close enough, he yelled out, "Scared? Bet your visions couldn't foretell this, huh, Mr. Goldfinch?" His laugh was menacing. "Here I am, introducing some new ... villagers." He spread his arms out wide.

"You'll not pass through this here line," Goldfinch called out in an attempt to stabilize his own people. He drew a line in the snow with his boot.

"I see your nigger out here just begging to be shackled. Look at that fine, African smile he's got. I should've taken him out on the path when we were alone," Nance called. "Anyway, you all better acclimate yourselves with the finest men this side of the Delaware." One of the men leaned over his horse and spit out viscid mucus. Then he smiled, showing his yellowed teeth. He fiddled with the rope that wrapped around his shoulder and sunk beneath his arm. Nance turned from this ogre of a man back to Goldfinch, all the while fixing his spotless frock coat and then leaning over to meticulously brush at a lace on his boot.

"I'd introduce them, by name, but you know, Goldfinch, as an ex-government man yourself, we don't have time for such niceties. But, dare I say, you already know Mr. Mulvane here."

Blithe seemed to freeze, his breathing slowed, as the Synod men inspected him thoroughly. "Mr. Picket would be proud of him. And he'll pay it forward, Blithe, when this Sullivan fella is returned to bondage. Steven Picket does not forsake his own."

Goldfinch was wary of Nance making a move. To that point, it seemed that the day's 'visit' was just a statement, a show of strength. He interjected. "What makes the boy Picket's? What makes you a sympathizer?"

"Let's just say a few commonalities. Renly Picket, man you murdered, had a way with words when he came to town." Nance let his smirk take control of his face. "Pickets have a point, law's the law."

Then the spitting man smiled wildly again, this time pointing over at Reg. "I say we lynch 'im," the man said, growling. "Then you can send 'im to Steven."

Nance turned his attention to his companion. "If it comes to that, I'll let you have the honor. Mr. Picket will pay for his corpse, too, if he must. But let's not talk of that just yet. Mr. Sullivan, how do you feel about joining us today? It'll be a smooth ride back down to Carolina."

Again, Goldfinch jumped in. "A government man such as yourself shouldn't have time for such niceties. Is that how it is? Would you not be abandoning your post here in Jersey?"

"Duty's to the cause, no single governor."

"Though I hate to see what Dumont Vroom thinks of such a claim."

"Bottom line is, we're here today to rile you folks up. Be prepared for when the conclusive battle comes. I'll take that nigger, burn this place to the ground before some homeless veteran sort gets the best of me."

One put his arm across Goldfinch's chest, shielding him, and took a step forward. "Let today rile *your* folks up. No ten extra bodies are going to help you snatch our *friend*. Now get out of here."

Nance laughed. "Ten? Is that what you think?" He shook his head. "*Tttt, tttt, ttt.* Mister, come on, now." He smiled, then tipped his perfectly maintained top hat and tugged at his reins. As his horse plodded into the snow and turned for the trail, he said, "Just see what the cover of darkness provides, gentlemen. Oh, and Mr. Mulvane, thanks for that timepiece of yours, that map inside, your map, did us wonders. I tried telling you I can't draw none. So it helped me sign these boys up. And earlier, to pry all that information from your father and initiate our trip from the city, for 'the cause,' it's wonderful." He smirked. Nance was pitting the young man who had helped him against the village that showed him mercy, Blithe's father's village.

Blithe stood nearly frozen, afraid to look at Goldfinch. Just then, the Leader knew what Minister Mulvane had done on some of those rifle runs—he had corresponded with Blithe, opened Synod up to a whole new breed of southern folk. He assumed the boy drew up maps and other papers for this Nance fellow, which they exchanged deep in the Synod forest.

Goldfinch recognized Nance's sanguine eyes as he trotted off. The Leader thought he witnessed a growl spewing from the intruder's rotten mouth.

The cronies followed, in a tight procession, behind Nance, exiting. Goldfinch rushed over to the smoldering branch and tapped at it with his boot, assuring it had been extinguished. He thought he could kill Nance right there, while his back was turned from Synod. Yet, even Goldfinch knew that was no proper way—nor feasible, even—for he had been a respectable soldier in his day. He watched as the posse followed Nance's lead, their heads still turned toward Goldfinch and company, studying the faces of the ones they hoped to kill.

When they were far enough away, Reg let out an emphatic sigh and turned to the Leader. "Came with ropes for t'day? Woulda hung me from that hackberry ya love so much. *Whewwee*, it's been a while since I done got nervous like that."

Goldfinch finally walked from the line of Synod folks who had guarded the fence. He approached Reg, placing his arm around the man's shoulders. He was hard-pressed for the right words, but his visage said it all. One came around the other side, placing his arm around Reg's other shoulder. "They take you, they're going to have to pry the pitchfork from my lifeless corpse, too."

As the morning turned snowy, with gusty winds driving flurries every which way, the gang regrouped near the fence and took a moment to reflect. Goldfinch abandoned this contemplation by rushing to Blithe. He took the man by the suitcoat, holding him firmly with two hands. Blithe had nothing to say in return. Goldfinch could have spit in his eye. He took the young man and hurled him to the ground. None of the other villagers protested, even Harriet, though she probably sought to rush to his side. With that, the Synod folks carried on back toward the village center, letting Blithe fend for himself from the ground.

Goldfinch was no farther than ten feet away when Blithe spit onto the ground and cleared his throat. He stood up slowly and began to speak. Goldfinch turned back to him. "I told them where the village is," Blithe said. "He said he'd kill my mother back in Philadelphia. My father would never know if they'd done it; he's so adamant about this frontier life. You see, each time this Nance fella came around, I'd have to give him something useful—information about the place and that Edwin boy. And Sullivan's been on the loose for a time. Renly Picket made his advances along these northern roads a ways back. He knows how that slave-freeing system works. So, he drew Nance right in."

Even Harriet seemed to question Blithe's intentions. She folded her arms. Goldfinch approached the younger Mulvane. "We all have a choice," he said. He reached the cane out and made for the fire pit. He thought he heard Blithe rise and kick snow around with his boot.

***

A few hours later, Goldfinch stood staring at a roaring fire in the middle of the village. There were a few folks around him—the Paterson Four, Harriet, Matilda, and Catharine—though none of them dared speak with the Leader, not while he sank deep into thought.

Every now and then, Goldfinch would mutter a statement or two, maybe "tonight!" or "the wolf!" As he came to, he reassessed some of the personalities surrounding him. Each time they spoke, Goldfinch's eyes sprang to life. He rubbed beneath his eyelids and then muttered something incomprehensible again, and then continued his stinging gaze at the fire.

With each piercing flame, Goldfinch clung to the hope that the Senator, or Mr. Boatwright, or Alaba, would appear and communicate a vision that would be of some use. On this night, however, the message never arrived through the towering flames. When he snapped out of his daydreaming, he would walk to a large pile of kindling and retrieve some fuel for the fire. His passage to the kindling was filled with thoughts of Nance. He could not stand the ambiguity. He wondered when the man would return with the lynch mob.

Limping back over to the fire, Goldfinch noticed that the Paterson Four members were all present, and absently staring at one another, as though the same affliction Goldfinch suffered from was contagious. "Dipping temperatures we've got tonight, gentlemen," Goldfinch offered.

One looked at him wearily, as though the elder was hoping for some rousing call to arms. It never came. Goldfinch looked back at him, then the others. "Problem is, take a look at Minister Mulvane over there," he said.

One obliged, staring across the fire toward the ex-Catholic, who was in a place of his own. He was deep in thought, as Goldfinch was, his eyes wandering toward the fence and his church. One studied him while the Minister remained in something of his own creation—thoughts, worries, visions. The elder scratched at his bristly beard, a worrisome look forming on his face.

"It is the eyes, no? The red eye? The sounds? The snarl?" he asked Goldfinch.

The Leader felt content and shrugged his shoulders. "It's not explainable. What I know is that it won't stop until this ordeal has ended." He continued, "Reg, Shepherd, look through these unfettered flames." The other men did so. After, they returned the same look—one of confusion and acceptance.

"S'pose a gift like this, somethin' that wants to strike a dagger through slave-ree, it isn't such a bad trait, no suh," Reg responded, shrugging his shoulders as Goldfinch had.

"We take this energy, this vigilance, and we apply it to that Nance fella. He won't get the best of us again," Shepherd responded.

"As you say, Shepherd. But this won't happen tonight," Goldfinch responded committedly. "We've already ignored our patrol. Who wishes to take this on?"

Before any of the men could respond, a trailing voice penetrated the fire and swarmed the Leader. "I'll go." It was a female voice. Harriet stood firmly, her arms pressed against her hips.

"I don't normally recommend anyone other than the Paterson men, but—" Goldfinch said, hesitating. "Perhaps tonight is your night, Harriet. Head to the post and keep us informed."

She did not respond. So, Goldfinch pitched in. "Do not let your love of that Mulvane boy cloud your judgment. We'll deal with him later." He wagged his finger at Harriet. "Be on your way. No trickery—Blithe best be here tomorrow morning."

Goldfinch could hear Harriet's feet plodding through the snow. After a few moments, she was near the gate and had already obtained a Long Rifle.

"The wreath," One said, looking over toward Harriet. "It is not just a defensive tool. We know this. The smoke, if thick enough, will show Alaba and her master. The Senator will show us the answer. For, he shows us just about everything else." He sighed, rubbed at his eyelids, and kneaded his temples.

"Precisely," Goldfinch responded. "The question remains. What shall we do this evening? Utilize our otherworldly gift? Reconnaissance?"

The others nodded, a couple of them staring through the fire at the elder Mulvane.

One took a step closer to the fire. "Minister Mulvane, you've heard the news today?"

"God has slighted me with a deceptive son. I admit I am stuck here," the Minister said. "Yet, you will not take him away from me, from this place. It's what I … he … has been searching for." He pointed his finger angrily but then slumped back down on the bench near the fire.

The Four recognized the Minister's faulty reasoning and obvious digression into madness. This 'frontier' was slowly corroding his soul. His sermon the day before was a prime example. He had invoked the commandments, spoke of Exodus, and sins of the father. It had seemed so arbitrary.

They looked at him for a moment, studying his body language, his air. They did not respond.

Goldfinch looked at Reg. "Be sure the boy doesn't flee tonight."

Reg nodded, abandoning his pointed stare at the Minister. "Might as well have somebody look at this here minsta, though."

"The three of us will venture to the woods, beyond Harriet's post. We shall search for our enemy, keep him close," Goldfinch responded. "Governor's Man will be near if he wants to strike soon."

***

Goldfinch led the group of men, his cane pounding through the snow with fervor. It was nearly a single file line, their feet moving in unison. The snow had melted a bit during the day, but it was still a menacing setback in the dead of night.

Their steps kept up an even pace, and within moments they were near the hackberry, by the post. Goldfinch could hear two people speaking cautiously inside, and he soon spotted Solomon's off-white frock coat contrasting with the snow. The Leader reached out his cane and poked Solomon between the shoulder blades.

Solomon responded quickly. "Heard everybody approachin', figured it was y'all, with that strange mission."

Harriet, blowing into cupped hands, said, "Something about that Paterson trip changed you, gentlemen."

"As Nance said, 'no time for such niceties,'" Goldfinch responded.

Shepherd continued the progression, and One followed close behind. "Eyes peeled on that horizon, and as you know Harriet, out to that flatland to the left." Goldfinch emphatically pointed out in that direction with his cane.

The Paterson Four, sans Reg, persisted, trudging through the early-season snowfall. Goldfinch was in the back of the pack now, monitoring the rear. Passing trees and winding fields, the group retained patchy shades of the distorted moonlight. First, it shone on One, adding to his pallid tone. Then it brushed across Goldfinch's face. As it did, he felt rejuvenated—more aware of his surroundings. It was as if he was retaining the senses of the canines that had once stalked them. Shepherd turned back to Goldfinch, and as he did, his face was blurred, though his eyes carried a sheen of blood red. The Leader pressed his eyes closed to lose the wolf's stare.

The field began to climb upward, toward a thicker, suffocating forest. The path they traveled on also followed this incline and Shepherd paused at the confluence of trail and hillside. One walked to a nearby tree trunk, cleared the snow off of it, and leaned his body against it. The other two stood debating their next move.

Then, riotous laughter and whistling seemed to course over the hillside. Goldfinch looked up and saw a few towering plumes of smoke, rotating and fading into the night. "Seems we've gone the right way," he said, pointing up.

"It is the *gift*," Shepherd said. "It must be. How could we have known to come this way and—"

"Let's not debate the root of this evil," Goldfinch said, interjecting. "Let's utilize it. Shall we climb?"

One nodded, but Shepherd spoke up. "Two of us should make the climb, the other holds down this spot we've carved out."

"Very well" the Leader responded. "Shepherd is with me."

***

The pair climbed the hillside, slightly slippery, slightly crystalline, and navigated between the low-hanging boughs.

At that point, the flurries had commenced again, though Goldfinch only felt the odd flake through the trees. He plunged his cane into the ground and then hauled his bad leg along behind it. At last, the hill plateaued.

Goldfinch held the cane close, taking short, choppy steps across the hillside to where the descent began. Here, they heard ominous noises—the howls, yips, and chattering—and saw the steadily climbing plumes.

"Tighten up," Goldfinch whispered, pointing the cane down the hillside. "They've made camp only a hundred feet down. You hear?"

Shepherd's eyes widened as he looked from the hillside to the Leader. "You don't plan to go down there?"

"Of course not. Not unless Alaba's near. I don't sense the monstrous wolf."

Goldfinch pressed his boots into the ground, turning up powder and decomposing leaves beneath. "Only a little ways," he said. Shepherd followed.

Using the tree cover, the men slipped closer and closer to Nance's camp. Eventually, they were only forty feet out. Here, the words were clear as day, the smoke even seemed to stick to the fabric of their coats.

"That boy, walking around as though he were immune to the law," a voice called from below. Goldfinch decided it was Nance's. "Rather string him on up to my horse and drag his black ass through the snow—let a little white onto him."

Then came the voice of Nance's companion. "We burn him like we burn that whole place. That's what I say. Pete, another drink?"

Goldfinch and Shepherd heard the clattering sounds of metal, of cups—presumably being passed around the fireside. Goldfinch whispered to Shepherd. "Hard to believe a man like this is in such a position for the state."

"Listen close, we need to hear when they will attack," Shepherd said, a finger at his lips.

"Very well." Goldfinch tried to block out the whispering pines and focus on the men below.

"You fuckers weren't so drunk we could've reclaimed that field hand already," Nance's voice cried thunderously. "What do you say, gentlemen? A swift ride tomorrow and we collect enough money for plenty more whiskey."

The companion spoke up. "Not about the money, Nance. You know that, working as a public servant and all, eh? It's the principle. The damn p-r-inciple. Down with that black bastard. All of 'em."

"I'll drink to that, boys," Nance boomed. "Now, keep consuming, for tomorrow night we ride." A pistol shot rang out through the entire hill and adjacent valley. Then another shot rang out, this time closer to Goldfinch and Shepherd.

"Best we flee now," Goldfinch said, unnerved. "One will be waiting." As he took a moment to plant his boot into the hardened earth, to make his way up, his foot slipped, and the cane rattled against the side of a tall maple. The two froze, looking back down toward the camp. There was too much commotion, drunkenness, for the men below to react.

"Press on," Shepherd whispered. "Let's be rid of this eerie place." As Shepherd led the way, an owl's hoot bellowed out.

Rushing back down the hill, Goldfinch spotted One. Before filling him in, he started the trek back to Synod. Shepherd walked only a few feet behind.

Once far enough away, Goldfinch stopped the progress, turned, and said, "Let's prepare our refuge for tomorrow evening."

Goldfinch's next words were drowned out by the booming call from another canine nestled somewhere in the wooded expanse. When able, he said, "God forbid it, but the wreath may light."

One nodded as though he had been waiting for this climactic moment since their trip to Paterson. He rubbed his palms together, a grin forming on his face. "These men, I see now, will not persevere. They will not be victorious. Not in the territory of the Lord. Synod is protected. This place, friends, is divine. Shielded by an outsider."

"The silent founder," Goldfinch whispered, unsure of who heard his response. The group of entranced men kept up a swift pace, the Leader's cane smacking against the snow in between footsteps.

At the hackberry, Goldfinch looked up and noticed the snow had melted off of the wood, which must have been exposed to the limited amount of sun during the day. About to turn away, he had a fleeting, grayed vision of something. It was Cartwright bearing the weight of the cross, waiting for Goldfinch to help pin it up. Then, in a darker vision, he saw Renly's body lying lifeless next to the hackberry. He blinked and saw another image; Nance toying with his lucky rabbit's foot. He glared at Goldfinch with jagged canines and wolfish facial hair, a snout almost. Still, he had the pristine clothing, but yipped instead of boasted.

Coming to, Goldfinch noticed he had veered a few steps away from the pack. "Goldfinch, do not lose your wits now," Shepherd warned. "You see what's happened to the Minister. He will not be … present for next week's sermon."

"If Nance has his way," Goldfinch responded, scratching at his face, "well then neither shall we."

Chapter Nineteen

Maude

Tuesday, December 8, 1829

Midday and there was no sign of the infiltration yet. Goldfinch was rejuvenated, though he hardly slept the previous night after gallivanting near Nance's campsite. Life in Synod was business as usual, though everyone seemed to be on edge.

When Goldfinch had awoken, he made his usual rounds, gun clutched closely, and stopped by Minister Mulvane's hut. There was no swift answer, no sarcasm or lecture. The Minister sat inside on his bed, arms propped neatly against his knees. He looked at Goldfinch impertinently. "If it's what you say, Synod will not stand. Where is my son? Why won't the Sullivan man let me see him?" His words came out almost achingly, with desperation.

Goldfinch was not going to answer Mulvane. He would let him sort out his own familial ordeal. But he decided against it. "Under my orders, Mulvane. Reg has a careful eye on him."

"And that Nance fellow has a careful eye on *him*," he answered.

"Very well. I didn't think you would understand," Goldfinch said, shaking his head.

"What is there to understand?" Minister Mulvane urged. "You give up the man they're after, even the New Orleans woman, and they'll slink back to the filthy dens they crawled out of."

"Mulvane, they're not even after Carlita. Not these men. They want Reg." He paused. "And that's another point—what you've done, those letters or what not, encouraging your son."

Minister Mulvane ignored the last part of the statement. "You think that if they got their eyes on that woman, they wouldn't chain her up, offer her to the Steven Picket fella? Let us be honest with ourselves, Goldfinch."

"Acquiescing, giving in to their demands—their backwoods clamoring—would spell the end of this place. It is why we came. The Founders, they set this village up for that very purpose."

"Maybe it is time to keep this place a religious community," Minister Mulvane continued. "A haven for Protestants disgruntled with the industrialization. Not a place for these fugitives."

"I have a hard time believing this is your stance now, *Minister*," Goldfinch responded. "Man of God? Man of God, you say?" He paused. "More like a man after his own ends, a man protecting his kin."

"Blithe has not wronged us. Gave up a bit of information, sure. But we were bound to be discovered. We are only fifty miles from New York. Perfect access for bounty hunters following the oft-traveled paths."

"Your traitorous son is not desired here. He can save the selfishness for the city. He must return to Philadelphia, to his mother that was threatened. Of that, you know?"

"He has told me, yes."

"And this doesn't rile you?"

"His mother abandoned him, and God knows, a long time ago."

"And what do you call leaving him behind in Philadelphia?" Goldfinch pressed.

"He is twenty-five years old," Minister Mulvane countered. "I did no such thing."

Goldfinch knew he had ventured into a gray area he could not easily crawl out of. "That is still no reason to put her into harm's way," he said. "You've seen harm, in the war. 1812 was a foul mess. The stench of death. You know this. Do you want to see a similar violence brought down upon your son, or the mother of your child? Perhaps it is time to come to their side."

Minister Mulvane closed his eyes and shook his head. He was dejected, morose, and so bounced to another topic. "I thought I had found a place here."

"How much of Blithe's betrayal were you privy to? He was making regular visits with the man? Perhaps he drew him up here with Solomon's caravan? Or it was orchestrated all along."

"There was no stopping him," Minister Mulvane said, his eyes drawing closed again. "I had my son back. Hadn't seen the boy in years."

"It's best you stay cooped up inside here. Recover your wits, Minister."

"You'll not send him away. You know that without me, there are no more rifles."

"I think those pseudo-clerics you meet downriver along the Musconetcong can be found. Don't need you."

"A letter will cut ties. You won't be able to bargain. They're not Illuminati of the Bavarian type, not freemasons, but it's *order* they seek."

"There are other avenues to pursue. Plus, we have the forge."

Minister Mulvane glared at the Leader. Before any other words were spoken, Goldfinch backed out of the hut, closing the door firmly.

***

Goldfinch sat at the fire pit, revisiting the encounter with Minister Mulvane. He saw no others, for the temperature was too harsh. The villagers seemed to have forfeited this land to nature's capricious touch. The snow had melted some, but was piled up and left untamed in spots.

Eventually, he saw Reg making his way out of Solomon's hut, followed by Carlita and Solomon. The trio approached Goldfinch, who sat rubbing his palms together for added warmth.

It was the group that had instituted it all—the chase with its roots in North Carolina, and other regions of that onerous South. The three of them, they were the epitome of Synod, the reason the pilgrims, Goldfinch included, journeyed north. The place had succeeded in functioning as a depot for runaways, at least in moving Reg's children along. The others had just stayed put. He almost felt convinced that the function of the slave-freeing system was to find refugees who would just assimilate. But he knew the key was *motion*. He would have to sever ties with all of his escapees.

Yet still, Goldfinch thought it might be too late for such motion. Reg was a part of the Paterson Four, Carlita a valued storyteller with her warm heart. And he had known Solomon for a time, from the AME days. He could not part with any of them.

The trio approached, and as they did, they remained silent, focused exclusively on the Leader. He had informed them earlier about his discovery of the campsite and the wicked men's intentions. Reg had watched Blithe overnight but now made his approach toward the pit, for William had also taken on guard duties.

"Come and sit," Goldfinch said to the three of them, motioning toward the stumps positioned around the pit. Each one listened to the leader.

"So tuh'day's the day?" Solomon asked as he got comfortable on a log.

"Sure is," Goldfinch responded. "Though whether they truly use the cover of darkness, I cannot be sure."

"We done seen they's have a group of 'cm, so ya think we can hold 'em off?" Reg asked. "What if the man calls us 'scaped convicts? The gov'na calls up the militia, wipes us right off the map."

"Well, Dumont Vroom must be made aware of the true nature of his deputy," Goldfinch answered.

Carlita nodded pleasantly, as though she was content with any harebrained plan. "I've made quite a far journey, Mista Goldfinch. That, you know already. I don't plan on going back to N'Orleans, unless I can get my daughter. Ya see, it was them kept her a house slave, their paws all over her. She couldn't come 'long, ordered me to go. And here I am." She spread her arms out wide, and they stopped at about the width of the petticoats whose bottoms were frayed from the terrain.

"We won't let you be swept away, Carlita," Goldfinch said. "You've made it thus far. No reason to believe otherwise."

While the three villagers held Goldfinch's attention, another party approached from the row of huts. It was Catharine, long since hidden, hunkered down in Harriet's home. She approached, stretching her arms out wide like Carlita had done; she was obviously watching the discourse.

"Harriet says she's had duty at the post beyond the gate. Says it's only a matter of time before the men approach again," she said. "I'd like to go out there and hold down the place myself. So be it if it's me they see on their approach. *Let it be a woman*. A shame it can't be Carlita, as a matter of fact." She turned to Carlita, giving her a warm look.

Goldfinch also looked over at Carlita. "She's going to stay right here with us." He paused. "All right, maybe it's best you get to experience the watch, Catharine. You can spell One, who's been out there since the wee morning hours."

Catharine gave Goldfinch a bit of a curtsy and turned from the gang, making her way out toward the gate. Seeing her empty-handed, Goldfinch called out, "If you need a rifle, there are some in the shed beside the paddock."

Catharine waved her hand as if to brush off the statement. "The guarding *I'm* doing doesn't require anything of the sort. I'll operate best with just myself. Well, I hope that God bestows on me a bit of speed to return, should the mongrels show their faces."

Goldfinch wanted to object. He stuttered a bit but let Catharine continue. With tensions so high, there was little he could influence with just a fair word or two. He turned back toward Carlita. "Now," he said, "can you tell me some more about this daughter of yours?"

"Ah, Maude? I shall, Mista Goldfinch."

***

After Goldfinch had enough time to digest the aureate story of Carlita's daughter, he set out to accomplish something. There was little rapport left between Goldfinch and Harriet. Still, he wanted to watch over her—and even dig deeper. He wondered what else she knew.

Stabbing his cane into the layered earth, he hobbled over near Harriet's hut, staying comfortably close to the fence, to cloak his lurking presence. Looking squarely at the rear side of her hut, he ambled over to the thick logs that bolstered the little bulwark. There was a slim trail from his footsteps and the cane left in the snow, but he was confident no one would be pursuing him. Inside, there was no 'soliloquy' seeping through these logs, but still, Goldfinch pressed his ear up to them.

He was standing idly, his breathing slowed when a knock came at the door. Goldfinch tensed up. The environment around him was muted. Even his heartbeat was a silent afterthought. After a curt "Hello," Goldfinch knew that Blithe was her concerned visitor.

This conversation was faint, and he missed the odd word or two, but most of what was said between the lovers came to Goldfinch's attention.

"The Reg fella, and William, they finally *let* me out of their sight."

"And what of it? Will you flee?" Harriet tested him. "And run back into the arms of those monsters who hunt us down?"

Goldfinch could hear Blithe's pronounced steps across the wooden floor, the heels of his boots pouncing down, leading him farther into the hut. "Don't you understand? I had no choice."

"You could've never ventured to this place. Left us be. And me, look what position you've put me in. These people once listened to me. Goldfinch once listened to me."

"They found *me* in Philadelphia. I was at the pub these men tend to frequent." He paused, his voice worrisome. "It was nothing short of kidnap, what they did to me. Was Renly and Burt, said they were on their way up north, lawfully searching for a runaway and his girls. They wanted the girls. Most of all, though, they wanted to flaunt themselves, their power, in front of the Sullivan man. Not often someone escapes, with his children, you see?"

"The more you speak, the more I question your integrity, Blithe," Harriet said, her delivery stern but restrained.

Blithe continued. "Held a gun up to me. Asked about my family and me. Said my father was a cleric, a man who's taken to the road. Must've piqued their interest. That point on, I was their adjutant, suppose you can say."

"What has happened here, with us? What of that?"

"You know how I feel about you. And you know how I feel about that brittle old man you had feelings for."

"How do you—" She did not finish the thought. "He is a truer man than you. Truer to himself."

"What will you do, Harriet? If you stand with me, we will need to flee this place."

"And your father?"

"He is a grown man. A stubborn man."

"Again, you place yourself above others?" Harriet challenged.

"And again, you throw caution to the wind? Staying here is suicide." He stopped, probably to collect himself. "There is something you don't know about Nance. He has shown me the papers. The men he was able to ... conscribe."

"You say his posse is larger than we know?"

"To say the least," Blithe admitted, fear probably welling in his eyes.

Goldfinch switched his position on the hut, moving a few feet over to the left, closer to the source. He heard more of the emphatic steps across the floor, the boot heels stomping onto the wood Goldfinch had sawed and labored over. Then there were lighter, hastier steps, almost a scuttle, about the place. He wondered if Harriet was trying to avoid Blithe.

"It is now or never, Harriet," he said. He stomped his foot. "It is now! Who is here to stop us? We must flee."

She raised her voice. "It is not in my nature to flee, Blithe. Maybe it is yours."

"Suit yourself, woman. But don't claim to say you were trapped here. Maybe you'll read an account of this place, this crooked place, in the newspapers."

"Be gone, will you!" she shouted back.

Then there was some racket, some footsteps. Harriet continued, saying, "That must be the timepiece you used to pass along the map of this place? What else have you gifted him?"

Goldfinch wondered if she was eyeing that golden, chain-linked pocket watch that always rested in Blithe's black suit, usually some eight or nine inches beneath his cravat.

Then came a lull. Both seemed to be still. *Is Blithe plotting something?*

The younger Mulvane then slipped from the hut. Just like that, the late arrival planned to slither back to the safety of Philadelphia or New York.

Again, it was too much for Goldfinch to grasp. He turned and took the same route back to his hut, following the snowy footsteps. There he could recline and forget, albeit momentarily, the savagery of this world. His cane pressed down into the earth with the same authority that Blithe's boots had when he staked his claim over Harriet's cabin.

So be it if he sneaks out. The damage is done, he thought. As he moved along the fence, shrouded by the voluminous arms of the eastern white pines, he saw Harriet flee from her cabin. She was finishing up dressing. Had she set out to inform him, the Leader, on what had just occurred?

***

Back at his hut, Goldfinch felt warmed by Carlita's earlier tale of Maude. The blood coursed pleasantly through his body, even on this December day.

Maude; a woman in her thirties, loyal, beautiful, and doggedly determined to escape the clutches of the Louisiana slavers. The way Carlita had painted her—the elegance, the civility—left Goldfinch coping with different, even tender emotions. He had never felt this way about a captive, a slave. Thoughts of Maude suffused him, though. He forgot what it was like to feel so attached to something. It was simply the *idea* of something.

But the euphoria would not last, for Goldfinch heard Harriet's knock at the door.

"Wake up, Goldfinch. Suppose you'll want to hear this!" she called out.

Once inside, Goldfinch pretended to be surprised by Harriet's account of Blithe's escape. She said she watched him stomp out of the village. He was not carrying anything—no bags, no saddle—but he just slipped through the gate.

While she spoke, Goldfinch tried to snap out of the hazy state he had entered. He grabbed hold of his now-invaluable cane, walked past Harriet, and made his way out of the hut. She followed close behind.

"I fear he doesn't have the strength to leave this place," she said, somewhat frantically. "That is, not if he'll wind up under their intolerance again." Goldfinch did not respond but continued to press onward.

When he reached the hackberry, he found Blithe leaning effortlessly against the tree, his eyes peeled upward, fixed on the cross. He let out a *humph*, and smirked at the relic.

Goldfinch, now feigning concern for the boy, or for at least shoring up his village, called out to Blithe. "Boy, be still!" he commanded. He waved his cane wildly. "Where is it you're going? Where is Reg? What have you done?" He pretended not to know that Reg had abandoned his watch—that William probably went back to his chores after receiving no strict orders.

Blithe spoke up. He said, "Well, Mr. Sullivan allowed me to speak with my belle. If anyone, he can understand the longing. And that other fella had no business keeping watch."

"Stand down now, Blithe," Goldfinch said. But the young man continued, the chain of his watch swaying lightly with each step. It seemed he had finally built up enough courage to roam the woods.

As Goldfinch followed Blithe, they were both taken aback by the oncoming approach of Catharine. She looked frantic.

Goldfinch knew why Catharine had abandoned her post. She came to a halt near Blithe and bent over to collect her breath. Before she could speak, she pointed behind her, then exhaled vigorously, followed by a few bursts of breath. Her petticoats arched over the leather shoes covering her feet. Recovering, she looked right past Blithe, to the Leader. "Oh, they're coming quick. And a few more than you say showed up yesterday. Seemed to stretch as far as the eye could see."

"It's Nance?" Goldfinch pressed. "You must be sure, we need to prepare the place."

"I say you have but a few moments to prepare."

Goldfinch looked out toward the folks that were outside going about their business. He saw Solomon and company near the fire, and thought he spotted Elizabeth near her hut, still not really showing. Then there was Harriet, looking toward him, about twenty feet away.

The villagers seemed like phantoms, moving swiftly about the place. It was the approaching party. Certainly a war-ready one prepared to recover Picket property. An additional slave to boot wouldn't hurt, either.

Goldfinch, his back turned to the gate, paid little attention to the younger Mulvane, who had truly made his escape. He had entered through the Synod gate just weeks before. Now, he was returning to that warring faction.

Goldfinch looked at Catharine, who had watched Blithe flee. "Let him be. He's worthless here, undoubtedly worthless *there*, too," she said before pausing. "Now, the intruders, they were in that direction." She pointed the way Goldfinch had expected.

Catharine continued. "What do you say of the villagers? Take who we can to the outposts?"

"No, take Carlita and Solomon to the outposts," Goldfinch said.

"We'll mount a respectable defense," she said, fleeing.

The Leader looked at the boot prints left behind by Blithe, the coward, the traitor. As he did, the edges of the impressions seemed to melt, to mesh into small pools. He began to tremble, his mind unsteady, his limbs heavy. A now-familiar sensation. He needed to have his people coalesce around him. He knew the attack was imminent, that Nance would return with a vengeance, prepared to lynch a slave or make a sport out of death. The boot prints again took on a strange appearance, warped and disintegrating, taunting his eyes.

As this transition occurred, the slender holes filled with liquid that bubbled and steamed. Time froze as the wind began to brush against the raw branches. The sticks collectively swayed with the breeze, but painstakingly, languidly. There seemed to be a whistle that accompanied the breeze, but it was muted by the equally strenuous and audible exhale that Goldfinch released.

Inspecting the boot prints again, Goldfinch noticed they had become larger and were brimming with crimson-red liquid. The rest of his surroundings were muted by a cloud of gray, as though the woods outside Synod had been compressed into a dull paint, which was then smeared with haste across Goldfinch's vision.

When the Leader followed these puddles around the trees—along the path that Blithe had taken—he lifted his head up at a tall oak. When he brought it back down, the murdered Renly Picket appeared before him, arms down at his sides, a smirk lifting half of his pale face. He showed some of his teeth and slowly lifted up his right hand to point at the Leader. As the finger landed directly at him, Renly smirked then laughed, the exertion echoing through the dark forest.

Goldfinch took a step toward him, his fists clenching. He went to return the gesture, but as he did, the slaver had disappeared, the footprints had returned to normal. They were simply the tracks left behind by a meek, cowardly young man.

Goldfinch snapped out of it. He was still overwhelmed by the approach and needed to stand tall with the Four. The larger battle was about to be waged. It would be the culmination of a crusade fueled by *color*. The blood was coursing through his veins, and his heart raced. The preparations for the defense of Synod were underway.

It almost felt as though it was Queenston Heights, 1812. Or his consulting work for York in 1813. He felt as though Fuss and Feathers was not far off, as though he was waiting on some sort of an extracted bit of intelligence that could help the American war effort.

With steps that pierced the slushy snow, Goldfinch hurried back into the village. He looked around, waving his cane. The others focused on him.

"All of you must hunker down and find shelter in your homes," he warned. "Lie low while the bullets fly."

He hesitated and then pressed on. "The Paterson Four will stand beside me. A few others have been moved to the posts. Everyone else, stand guard."

He did not finish the instruction before his other marked men approached, guns at the ready. One turned back to a few straggling villagers. "Return to your homes, people. Return!" he demanded.

A few of them did, and Goldfinch hustled to his own place to reclaim his rifle. Once he grabbed it, along with the powder horn and a few bullets, he walked back toward the pit.

Shepherd placed his rifle up and over his shoulder, his eyes peeled toward the gate. Reg had a loose grip on his gun, and was surely hesitant to use the weapon again. But nevertheless, he stood strong beside his fellow soldiers.

"The wreath?" Goldfinch asked, gauging whether the men felt ignition was necessary.

"Let's lay our eyes on the enemy first," One suggested, scratching his white beard.

Goldfinch retreated a few steps in order to inspect the place as One had just done. Now on her front step, Harriet was pressing a rounded bullet down the barrel of her rifle. The dress she wore was a shade of yellow, adding necessary life to the dampened, gray area that Synod had become.

Her eyes met Goldfinch's, and she tried to smile, but the effort seemed too contrived. While Goldfinch watched, her face hardened again, and she reapplied her grip on the rifle. It was as though she confirmed her reluctance to flee or hide.

Before she could help the cause, however, Goldfinch retreated back to her hut. "Prepare Elizabeth for a mission at the furnace," he ordered.

"Is it not too late?" she asked, itching to come closer to Goldfinch and his gang of vigilant men.

"I do not wish for this place to become a burial ground. I must warn you, there is a cache to obtain."

She looked at him.

"The forge hides a secret weapon brought to us early on, during Minister Mulvane's initial runs with Cartwright. Something hauled by beast, in the night."

"And what of it?" Harriet asked.

"A five-and-a-half pounder, Howitzer. On its rolling carriage. You'll need someone to assist you in setting it atop the hill. Near the furnace, Elizabeth knows, are a few iron balls. Claim them. The weapon lies in an alcove in the rocks."

She nodded, assuredly thinking about the weapon Goldfinch, Mulvane, and Elizabeth had hidden from the rest.

"And when you return, be sure the Minister is sound, in the church," Goldfinch said. "And make haste."

Harriet remained silent but wasted no time in seeing to her duties. Goldfinch watched as her dress billowed out around her during the departure. He walked back over toward Shepherd.

"With that woman near, this place is safe," Shepherd joked. "May we expect fiery arrows or something out of Camelot—medieval castle raiding?"

"If all goes well, we'll have something much better," Goldfinch answered. He drew the others in with a quick hand gesture and the group traveled to the hackberry.

A somewhat hobbling Goldfinch led the men on their stealthy approach. Outside the gate, in what was now untamed territory, the Four dispersed.

"Eyes peeled," Goldfinch urged, while crouched and inching toward the guard post.

While the snow stretched out before them, Goldfinch was greeted by a blitz of sounds—hooves and far-off voices—and called his men back to him, to his attention.

The Four, cloaked by long frock coats, stood almost intertwined near the post. While One inspected his weapon, Reg grabbed onto his more closely, and Shepherd peered through the tangle of forest.

"They make no effort to remain silent," One said.

Goldfinch could finally get a better view of the men, and there was a great deal more than the previous day.

"Us standing here, waiting, he's expecting this," Goldfinch admitted. "Will he call our bluff? Expect us to slink back to our place?"

"Does the Governor ride with them?" Shepherd asked, opening up a squinting eye. "Looks like uniforms."

The invading party ceased to move closer when they were but a few hundred feet away. Goldfinch could decipher some voices. He could also see that Reg held a death grip on his weapon. The runaway was distracted by the slight wisps of smoke that enveloped the clear air over them.

The Leader assumed it was from Nance's campfires. "Wind's taking it over this way," he said. "And we may counter fire with fire." Goldfinch began their retreat back to the village.

"You don't suppose you'll light the wreath?" Shepherd called to him.

"Not as of yet. We'll hope Harriet and Elizabeth see their tasks through."

The Paterson Four hurried through Synod, passing huts, the paddock, and the fire pit, and made their way toward the narrow rear gate, then toward the fields Harriet had cultivated, and Adam had tended to.

Though they were not on horseback, the group made a quick approach to the forge, the spot Goldfinch had been stabbed near.

Drawing close, the Paterson Four wasted little time in probing the place and the surrounding property. They lucked out, for Harriet rushed from the base of the structure.

"It's here," she said. "You left me little time to move the contraption."

"What is this talk, now?" One ordered.

Goldfinch ignored this. "I trust Elizabeth will sort out the rest," he said to Harriet. "We will be near the village center, awaiting their arrival. There is not much else we can do."

One approached the small forge, again admiring its durability. He poked his head around the premises for a moment before Goldfinch called him back over. He cooperated.

"That's what you've been hiding?" One asked Goldfinch. "It's a shame you've hidden it. Would've made me feel a bit better. It's a Howitzer, gentlemen."

Goldfinch watched the others react. It was not nearly as challenging as he thought it may have been. Reg nodded while Shepherd cracked a smile. "Minister Mulvane returned with it in the dead of night. Was planned as such. But we mustn't waste time with such talk," Goldfinch urged, looking at One. "We'll leave this endeavor—to keep it hidden—to the women. They're capable."

"Then let's guard our homes," One confirmed. They began their trek back to Synod.

***

Coming back to what had become a ghost town, the group collectively gazed out across the place, ensuring the innocents were holed up in their homes. This time, however, noises from the intruders could be heard more clearly as they walked ever closer to the location of their last stand. It would be near the hackberry. The Four set out for it.

"The party approaches. It's imminent," Goldfinch declared. He squinted his eyes against the wind tunnel that had formed beneath the canopy of trees in front of the village. The breeze picked up, and the clouds seemed to stack up upon one another.

"I am not afraid to off our dear Governor, should it come to that," One said.

"Our visitors," proclaimed Goldfinch, his cane out-stretched.

On horseback some sixty yards away appeared a wide row of mounted men, some in lower-crowned top hats, others in military caps. Others sported no hat, though their hair seemed to curl out the sides or fall down their backs.

It was an eclectic mix of men en route to Synod. Some young, some old. Many of them looked as though they could be twenty, others sixty. Their presence began to envelop the landscape.

The Paterson Four waited for the first muskets to fire, or for a cannonball to rip the supports off the Leader's carefully crafted fence. But this devastation never came, not immediately.

The group paused to focus on anything other than their demise. An occasional yip or screech would make its way to the gate, perhaps a call from a Frelinghuysen animal. But still, Nance and his men did not progress much farther. Then, a rifle shot ripped out, and then another. The sound traveled to

Goldfinch and his men quickly, deadening their eardrums for a moment.

Goldfinch took a few steps forward, into the same forest that had now become so highly trafficked. "They hesitate for something. The rounds did not whip by us, either. Shall we?"

The others followed behind the Leader, as he dug his cane into the earth but maintained a respectable speed. His other hand clutched his rifle.

"It's as though we're out discovering their site all over again," Shepherd whispered. "Although this time the bullets will fly."

After fifteen feet or so, the men paused and took cover behind the nearest trees, for Nance's company was blurting out directions to one another. And then came Nance's unmistakable, disturbing voice. "Mr. Goldfinch, or so you're called. Didn't think we'd come right near midday meal, did you?"

Goldfinch pressed his index finger up to his mouth, urging the others to remain silent. Nance spoke up again. "The Governor has been made aware of your whereabouts. As of now, you are fugitives of the state of New Jersey. You will spend time in the Penitentiary House. Lawmakers will love to parade you through the streets, proverbially that is. I, for one, don't think there'll be anyone left to *parade*."

Goldfinch was compelled to respond, though he held his tongue.

"I know you are in these woods, watching, waiting for the right moment to drop one of us off our mounts. But even so, this place will be taken over handily. Heck, we will use it as a means northward, toward the rest of the escaped slaves," Nance said.

"Now, I'm on strict orders here from the state. You see, according to the law of 1793, you're 'empowered to seize or arrest such fugitives from labor.'" Goldfinch, peeking through tight crevices in the trees where daylight squeezed through, found his enemy in the middle of the row of men. They spread out wide, perhaps fifteen or twenty of them.

It was true. There were militiamen with him, their sharp, constricting uniforms in full-form atop the horses. However, from what Goldfinch saw, there were only a few of them, and they were interspersed amongst the rest.

It was not a military initiative. They were not on orders to raze the place. Goldfinch felt a glimmer of hope. He motioned toward his men, cupped his fingers, and waved them back. They would retreat to the trees near the gate, which afforded them some cover.

The four of them rushed through what now seemed to be jagged vegetation left over from the winter and stayed low in hopes of avoiding incoming bullets. It took only half a minute for them to reemerge past the hackberry near Goldfinch's gate.

"We spread out again, we can take a few down, scare them off," One insisted.

"At this point, if one or two of those men fall, it will not deter them," Goldfinch countered. "You see, those military men, they are *volunteers*. They were not conscripted. Anything Nance extracted from them was purely voluntary. Don't you get it? They are against the cause, the cause that burns so brightly in our eyes."

The men rallied behind Goldfinch, as he dug into the earth before them.

Some feet off, the hooves slowly cracked upon snow and soil, and the party drew ever nearer.

Finally, the muzzle of Nance's quarter horse turned the corner, the last natural barrier before Synod began. He kept a steady pace, the way the Four had while going the other direction, and he tugged at the reins when he saw Goldfinch coldly staring back at him.

"Woah, woah," Nance called to his horse. "Ease up, ease up. Our company is greeting us with open arms."

Goldfinch and his men lifted their guns toward Nance and the men that now stood at the ready at his rear.

"Do lower those pitifully archaic weapons, gentlemen," Nance said mockingly. He laughed at his opponents. "We outnumber you six to one here. It's an exercise in futility."

"Turn back now, and all your men can live," One called out, his cheek pressed closely to the stock of his rifle.

Ignoring him, Nance pressed on. "You see, there is some business before I reclaim what is mine."

"What is yours? The man and his family were property of the Pickets. I don't see Pickets. They certainly weren't the property of a measly legislative aide in New Jersey," Goldfinch responded.

Again, Nance smirked, taking the comment in stride. Goldfinch knew, however, that the jabs were being felt somewhere on the polished *gentleman* before him.

"Here is the business I've spoken of. Mr. Kruger, please show the gentleman our *prize*." A few seconds later one of the men emerged from the thick wall of horseflesh that had formed in front of Goldfinch and his men. He shoved another man to the ground. The victim's hat rolled a few feet from where he had fallen. Desperately, he reached an arm out to reclaim it.

"Recognize the fella?" Nance inquired. Goldfinch studied the man for a second, his face bloodied and swollen. He wore the same attire Blithe had sported when he fled from the protection of Synod.

"The young man who spent time with us, yes," Goldfinch responded, keeping his eyes on Nance.

"He's been through it all since you released him to us," Nance confirmed. "Made evident by his bruising, as I'm sure you can tell. You see, this is what the Picket family thinks of men like you, Goldfinch, who resist the law. Who shelter these folks from their God-given cotton talents."

Nance reached to his ankle where he lifted up a pant leg and retrieved a pocket pistol, perhaps a modified Queen Anne version. Its sienna-brown stock was outfitted with gilded edges. He took a moment to place the powder on the pan, for the charge. The weapon, it seemed, was already loaded. "Forty-five caliber," he said playfully, jostling the weapon around in his hand.

As the young Mulvane boy writhed on the ground, Nance walked over to him and kicked him in the gut. "He's no longer useful, you see?" he said.

Although Goldfinch had his differences with the Minister's son, he knew this was not right.

Nance hauled off and kicked Blithe again, who made ungodly, desperate noises.

"Sure, his map was helpful with recruiting the posse. Blithe knew plenty about this frivolous little place. And he sent young Edwin to these parts. Even got the Minister to open up some. But what then?"

"You back up from him," One said, holding his gun out at Nance.

"You pull that trigger, you'll fall before you even know what hits you," Nance countered.

"Boy's got a father here," Goldfinch said. "I wouldn't be so careless as to kill him."

"I'm tired of being here, tired of your place," Nance said. "And Steven Picket is obviously impatient. He just wants his man back. You have any others, too, we'll gladly stake a claim."

Blithe moved closer toward his hat, mostly conscious, slithering across the ground.

Goldfinch pinched his rifle even tighter. He felt bound to it—every chamber, the smooth stock.

Nance pointed down at his heel. "A blow to the face with this here riding boot won't feel too good. Wouldn't you say?" He allowed Blithe no time to respond. As the young man was in mid-crawl, Nance kicked him in the face, between the eyes, effectively immobilizing him.

"That's enough of that," Nance said. "As I've said, I'm tired of this." Nance scratched at his face, looked toward his men, and fired one shot into Blithe's head. Just like that, his breathing ceased. A puddle of blood slowly accumulated in the snow beside him. Blithe's hands were outstretched and bowed, his legs in the process of trying to find solid ground. Goldfinch was rattled, his fingers trembling on the trigger, but he closed an eye and held Nance in his front sight. Even still, he felt powerless.

"That's a death sentence," One said fearlessly to Nance.

"Do you want to die here, right now, old man?" Nance fired, raising his voice. "One word and you'll be next to this fella." He pointed down at Blithe. The pool of blood was larger.

Nance took his weapon and slid it back into the holster at his ankle. "Gentlemen, what say you? Shall we take that buck back to bondage?"

Amid shouts of "Yea!" and rowdy cheers, the men began to move in closer toward Goldfinch. They were moving slowly, though, only inching their horses forward, as if it were a game. Utilizing this delay, Goldfinch spun with all the energy afforded to him, managed to tap One with his cane, and began to shuffle back inside the village. His other men followed along. Nance must have been amused.

As they retreated, Goldfinch was expecting a bullet to the back, but continued nevertheless, the bulky Long Rifle and the cane slowing him down. He swung back for a quick glimpse of the death scene and saw one of the slavers riding his horse over Blithe's dead body.

A few of Nance's men crossed the threshold into the village but still moved sluggishly, as if taking in all that was before them. Goldfinch had little time to wait for the men to move even closer and looked toward the paddock as though he would grab Eder and made a break for the trees. He was unsettled, his mind clouded. The other men began to take cover behind anything they could find. The Leader signaled One. The man reached out from the tree he was planted near and fired one shot, knocking one of the bounty hunters off his mount.

Then Goldfinch motioned to Shepherd, who did the same. After he also dropped a slaver, he began to reload, and so Goldfinch looked at Reg, who was some feet behind him, effectively hidden within the village. Knowing Reg was too far away to be accurate, Goldfinch decided to lean out and let off a round. He took aim toward the gate, dropping one of the men near Nance. As this happened, Nance ducked on his horse and then dismounted. He slapped the horse's rear, and it ran off. He then stood somewhat exposed, using a portion of another horse for cover.

Nance raised his arm, preventing his men from moving any farther. As he did so, Goldfinch could hear someone or something moving through the forest along the Synod fence. It was Harriet and Catharine, presumably, orchestrating an ambush. Suddenly, they were no longer in motion. Goldfinch tried to listen as closely as he could.

"It's in place, Goldfinch," a female voice shouted. Goldfinch thought it was Catharine's. She must've been drawn in to assist Harriet and Elizabeth with the Howitzer.

Goldfinch couldn't help but feel redeemed. "Fire it off, if you can," he yelled at the top of his lungs. He knew Harriet could be fluent in the language of the cannon. He imagined her lighting the fuse near the breech, waiting for it to catch the powder, and recoil back amid a monstrous explosion.

Goldfinch closed his eyes.

Kaboom! The wartime cannon still worked. He had Minister Mulvane to thank for that. He opened up and found a massive smoke cloud rising into the air, from a strategic locale just atop the hill, past the gate. He eyed down his foe, Nance. The ball had struck along Nance's flank, shoving a few men from their horses. Other mounts neighed and dropped the surviving riders. Nance had seemingly leaped to the ground, to a fetal position. But he was still alive. Amid screams from a few of his other men, he stood, his eyes fixed ahead, toward Goldfinch.

"Be sure they cannot fire off another round!" Nance shouted to his men. He pointed off toward the hill.

Goldfinch suddenly feared for Harriet and Catharine. *They may not have time to reload*, he thought.

He hoped that the women, who'd saved the day, could move unencumbered through the woods. They had made it out there, that far.

Goldfinch, cleverly hidden behind a tree, looked where he thought the Howitzer lay. He could not see Harriet or Lyman's daughter. *Has one of them fled?*

Then, at the same flank that had gone up in a ball of fire, Harriet emerged, her yellow dress sullied, her legs moving with ease near the riders. She had made a stealthy approach as the slavers' ears assuredly rang.

She took hold of what looked like a fire poker and drove it through a man she had snuck up on, impaling him. She then drew the rifle from around her shoulder and fired at someone else. Then she needed to reload, and so fled to a tree, taking cover. She began her retreat back up the snow-laden knoll.

At this point, a few of Nance's men had dismounted and were chasing her on foot. She was just far enough away when Goldfinch heard another massive explosion rip from the forest. This time the soil in front of Nance's other flank went up, propelling shards of earth toward the riders.

Did Catharine shoot the Howitzer? He again tried to find Harriet. He could not witness his ex-lover being slain in front of him. He began to rush toward the noises. She was out of sight, now, but Goldfinch gauged where it was she might reappear along the fence. As he ran, he fumbled with his weapon, shoving a ball into the barrel with the ramrod. He stopped for a moment, under the cover of a young oak. He primed his gun with the powder and then trudged forward, hugging the fence. He had abandoned his cane.

From this distance, Goldfinch felt he could still lift his voice, bellow a clear order. Knowing his men were in the process of firing and reloading, he called, "Wreath!"

He searched the hillside. Finally, he saw the glorious outline of the Howitzer, their salvation. No one manned it any longer, for Catharine had probably fled back toward the outposts after the second round.

Goldfinch looked toward One and Shepherd, and as he did, he saw One fire a shot and move carelessly through the village in retreat. Goldfinch turned back toward his rocky path and nearly bumped into Reg. The runaway was suddenly leaning his arms through the fence, grabbing hold of something. In front of his outstretched hands, Goldfinch spotted two pallid arms emerging from the vegetative cover, handling glowing embers haphazardly tossed into a thick, tin firewood pail. There were a few coals inside. He heard the weighty pail crash against the ground at Reg's feet and suddenly the nimble hands disappeared, and someone rushed off toward the rear gate. At Reg's feet was the ammunition the wreath would require to envelop the village, to shoot murky sheets of smoke upward for Alaba to interpret. It would also help the women fire off the remaining explosives.

"It's now or never," Goldfinch urged. "This will take a while to spread. Some of the men have retreated beyond our borders, though. It will be done."

Reg picked up the pail and dumped the charred but florid coals into one of the wicker baskets the villagers had pinned on the 'wreath' network. The thin, splintery material quickly went up after the hemp and tinder inside it. It ignited, crackled, and the flames began to branch off in both directions. With the flames came the smoke, and as it thickened, Goldfinch and Reg used it to conceal themselves.

Chapter Twenty

Fisticuffs

The pockets of smoke had a hypnotic effect on Goldfinch, plunging him deeper into the dream state that had plagued him for months now. While he tried to ward off its hold over him, it was still inevitable. He would succumb to the gray visions, unsure of their destination. He needed to stay alive long enough to see the other side of this mess, though.

He had heard that the aftermath of York was no silent one. While laconic, the Leader — then infantryman turned intelligence specialist — still had much to say about the destructive fire that had ensued. The memories returned to him. He was in a conference setting with officers present, around midday. He heard that the Upper Canada parliament had been ransacked, the mace claimed for exhibition in Washington. Suddenly, he sat staring at the soldiers moving through the Canadian streets.

He imagined what the rampant flames must have looked like in the spring air. The Americans had won, handing an outnumbered British force a decisive defeat. Roger Hale Sheaffe's redcoats were only a few hundred strong, but Ojibway natives took up arms against the Americans too. He pictured belligerent Americans setting fire to the city.

Then, he seemed to shift through time and place—and there was no tedious overland progression. Back at the Chippawa battle site. It was the outset, 1814; it would open the Niagara frontier. Goldfinch was hunkering down, with only his civilian clothing to protect him.

The fires burned in his mind. The day's events unfurled in less than a minute, and he survived this Chippawa tussle unscathed, again. But then, he landed elsewhere once more. It was mid-summer, probably July, 1814. The war had been ravaging for a couple of years. He was numb to its egregious effects. Here, he was in his mid-twenties, back in an army camp near the south shore of Lake Ontario. All the sights and sounds of Queenston Heights, Fort George, and Chippawa flooded him. The winds were calm, the night oppressive, a void. Goldfinch saw a row of uneven flames, the reds, and oranges eclipsing the usually placid darkness.

Goldfinch reemerged from the state. He was no longer stuck in the throes of that war, no longer counting down the days of 1814 with the hope that 1815 would bring peace. He was enveloped in a cloud of smoke, a cloud that scattered every which way and was kissed and shunned with each gale.

He checked his surroundings. There was only Reg, who was restless, waiting for an order. The noises Goldfinch could comprehend were echoed and deepened, as though he was about to see Renly again. Recognizing that this state must have been fleeting, he tried to mouth something, though the first words came off garbled.

"The Redcoats can't claim this fort, I say," he offered, letting his hands fall down the barrel of the rifle on his person.

Reg's next words looked foreign coming from his lips, but Goldfinch tried to comprehend. "Mista Goldfinch, I said Nance has dropped Shepherd. Ya see? Ov' yonda?"

Gradually, the Leader's senses came back to him, and he was able to see that Shepherd was lying on the ground, wounded or killed, and a few of Nance's men were infiltrating the place, venturing beyond the area they had conquered near the gate.

Yet the 'wreath' had taken pretty quickly, the dry air conducive to such an act. At this point, the smoke signals lingered past the treetops before dissipating and soaring east.

He shook off the coma that had overrun him and refocused on Reg. "Keep back near this cloak here," he said, pointing around at the smoke that engulfed them near the fence. He held his forearm over his mouth and suppressed a cough. When a dry wheeze could not be avoided, he let it out, concurrent with the exchange of gunfire, and bullets whizzing near the gate. For a moment, he wondered how the other villagers were making out in their huts—Carlita, Solomon, Catharine, Elizabeth, even Minister Mulvane. If the fire spread too quickly and aggressively, he would be forced to help evacuate. But he had one lone goal; expelling this creature who wanted Reg's soul.

The bullets continued to fly, piercing different slivers of Synod. Goldfinch watched the wildfire spread along the perimeter. "If the smoke—if the Senator—is saying anything to us, it is to end this," he said.

"Know what that means," Reg confirmed, holding his arm over his mouth. "He alone. Saw a few his men ditch they mounts, run on up through these pines, afta Harriet." He pointed through the pines that were barely visible. "She in there."

"Harriet is safe," Goldfinch claimed. "And the Howitzer's done its duty. It's run out of shell. Let's move."

Reg shrugged his shoulders, cloaking himself from the smoke. The two huddled closely against the fence and crept up the slight incline toward the gate. Goldfinch noticed the pit in the village center was doused, though there were plenty of flames near him still wandering about. The fledgling line of smoke did not so much become a strategic defense, but it did help conceal the Leader on his ambush attempt.

At last, Goldfinch had Nance perfectly centered down the barrel of his rifle. But amid the chaos and the grayness that suffused the place, the Leader lost track of the powder horn, his hands trembling slightly. He paused, fumbled through his pockets, and snatched the small item. He brushed a bit of it across the pan to prime the thing and ditched it before it found its way back to his pocket.

He pressed onward, using the barrel as his center of gravity. Reg trailed behind, his gun raised. When Goldfinch found Nance again amid the disarray, the man had spotted *him* as well. He turned, smiling like Renly had, and headed toward Goldfinch. He did not reach to his ankle for the pistol. He did not grab hold of some weapon which had tumbled to the earth. He simply walked closer, his body parting the smoke, the vapors mushrooming atop of him.

Goldfinch tightened his grip on the rifle and checked his flank. The other intruders were scattered, headed toward the huts. A few squeezed through the woods. One of them yelled from afar, "We'll need to douse this structure before the slave comes back with us."

None of that mattered now—the smoke was signaling the U.S. Senator or the nearest settlement.

Goldfinch fired the weapon, and the ball burst out of the muzzle, kicking him back a bit. Reg, recognizing the quick release, did the same. It took a moment for them to determine what Nance's fate would be. But emerging from the cloud of smoke came a dark frock coat, maintaining its swift advance. Nance's cold glare still pierced the smoke.

What Goldfinch did notice, though, was a hole beneath the clavicle, blackish liquid slowly oozing out. It did not deter the

Governor's Man, who then reached down, lifted a pant leg and grabbed the modified Queen Anne pistol.

Goldfinch fumbled with his weapon, searching for the powder horn, the ammunition in his pockets. An obscenely loud noise burst out, stinging his ears. *Did the Howitzer fire off some concoction of shrapnel?* The stinging noises were soon trumped by the bullet that found Goldfinch's right arm.

The ball drove through the flesh, escaping out the other side beneath Goldfinch's shoulder. The injury shook him, he fell, and his rifle crashed to the ground.

"Mista Goldfinch!" Reg yelled, stretching his arms out toward the Leader. "Reach up, sir. We need to sneak ya outta here. Reach!"

Goldfinch was disoriented but extended an arm upward toward the escapee, who was returning the favor. At that point, the noises slowly faded out. Goldfinch could only see the village, and One, who had been making his way closer.

His eyes began to roll back a little in an effort to suppress the pain. Some feet away, he saw One fidget with the rifle and prop it up before him, pulling the trigger. He saw one of Nance's men—who was closing in on Reg, bayonet drawn—drop from an apparent gunshot wound to the neck.

A few other men failed to shoot, retreating a few steps back to see what Nance would do.

"I've dropped the powder. I'll need some if I'm to shoot again," Goldfinch said to Reg, though he was consumed by One's stealth.

"You won't be able to hold that gun, mista," Reg said. "Govna's Man near, he right here."

Nance had approached, "You," he said, pointing at Goldfinch. "And you," he continued, looking at Reg. "I'll escort you out now before the rest of these men turn more of this place to ash."

Nance was now within striking distance, moving unflappably toward Goldfinch and the escapee. The Leader looked around him. Nance's men were still mainly passive, though a few of them crept uncomfortably close to the huts.

Goldfinch reached far into the depths of his frock coat, extracting a small, four-inch blade that was there, sheathed, for this very situation. His arm burned from the bullet wound, which swelled up his shoulder and shot pain down his forearm. He clutched the weapon as though it would determine life or death.

Reg was in the process of reloading when Nance stopped his approach. The sudden movement startled the two villagers, unsure of how to react. The intruder abandoned the flashy pistol rather than pressing metal into its small barrel. It clanked against the ground, though Nance did not pay it any mind. He reached toward his other ankle, where a sharp, glossy blade was sheathed and fastened around his leg. With one fluid motion, Nance extracted the blade and held it out before him, as though it was a torch helping to navigate the mouth of some blackened cave.

"Prepare for those chains, slave," Nance said, extending his arm out even farther. While his bullet wound was surely only worsening, the Governor's Man did not let it deter him.

Reg's rifle was finally loaded, poised to inflict some bodily harm. The arms that held it were just as charged as the weapon, the two blending to create a formidable freedom fighter. Yet before he could squeeze the trigger, an action he surely held no reservations about any longer, Goldfinch motioned to him with his functioning arm. "Lower the weapon," he said. "What needs to be done will be done."

Goldfinch took a step toward Nance, who was only eight feet away. As Goldfinch rushed ahead, Nance did not flinch, though he tapped the back of his boot heel against the snowy earth. As it met the harder mass beneath the snowfall, his spur clicked.

The Leader lunged at Nance, taking his anger out on the man who had been the single most ill-natured, calamitous figure associated with Synod since its founding.

Goldfinch tried to grab hold of the man's draping frock coat, to pull him close, to find some meaty pocket to land the blade. But Nance only avoided the tug, side-stepped Goldfinch a few times, and smirked at him. "You'll have to do better than that, slave lover," he said.

Reg stood waiting, clouded in smoke, watching. He then crouched as the odd bullet surged through the air. Goldfinch continued the struggle, trying for the life of him to drop the trespasser.

"My men admire your courage," Nance said. "If they didn't, you'd be buried near the rest of your idealists by now."

Goldfinch took the statement as another irritant and tried to thrash Nance. In an effort to avoid Goldfinch's claw-like hands, Nance stepped backward but stumbled for a moment on the clotting snow. This was all Goldfinch needed to latch on. As he did, he hesitated no longer and pounced on the man, driving the fist from his damaged arm into Nance's face.

But he only landed two powerful punches before Nance slipped from the Leader's grasp. He was bloodied, but he stood and swiped at Goldfinch, who attempted to match Nance's speed in rising. The gash tore through Goldfinch's frock coat and sliced him open at the ribs. He winced and threw his good arm to the site. As he did so, Nance took his riding boot and slammed it into Goldfinch's wound, nearly breaking the Leader's wrist as well.

He was on the verge of being killed. He writhed in pain, as Blithe had done before the Governor's Man. Nance laughed through his bloodied lip. He kicked again, Goldfinch clamoring. Nance had Goldfinch where he wanted him. He took a step away to retrieve his pistol.

Goldfinch still held the knife. As the aide turned from him, the Leader stabbed at Nance's right calf, immediately slowing him. Nance rushed his hand to the wound and turned back. "You ravenous fiend," he yelled. He ran back and dove on Goldfinch, but the Leader rolled away just in time.

Nance tried to recover, to get back to fisticuffs. He still gripped his own knife, and Goldfinch tried to kick it from his hands. He was not successful. Nance swiped at Goldfinch, missing, the sounds nearly making whistling noises.

A damaged Goldfinch then looked down at the man, who slithered across the ground, trying to land with his blade. The Leader timed it perfectly; as Nance swiped, Goldfinch kicked at his forearm as it was extended out. He freed the knife from Nance's hand, except Nance used his other one to upend Goldfinch from the ankles. The Leader tumbled down to the earth, crashing right beside the Governor's Man. Goldfinch landed a quick jab with his left hand and used the momentum to carry his body to his left, with force. As he did so, he gripped the knife and dug it into Nance's bullet wound. Gravity held Goldfinch atop of him.

At last, Nance cried out in pain. He managed to fuss and gripe at his inescapable plight and capitulation. Goldfinch could not bear to hear a plea dotted with slave hatred. He waited no longer. He simply lifted his fist and dropped it like the hammer he always used in construction, on Nance's face. Within four or five punches, Nance's exterior was ragged and badly beaten. At seven, he faded in and out of consciousness.

With bloodied knuckles, Goldfinch looked up at the other men that were seeing the exchange in bits and pieces from afar. As they finally understood what had befallen Nance, Goldfinch rose, his arms falling to his side. He gawked at the other slavers as though under some sorceress's spell. A few of the militiamen still appeared poised. They must have adopted looks of consternation.

Goldfinch then searched behind him for Reg. But what he saw was appalling—the runaway had fallen to the ground, at least one bullet lodged in his hip. While he thought Reg was dead, he was proven wrong when the man twitched slightly. His breathing was labored and only worsened. "Mista Goldfinch, ya see, I been hit. Jus' like you. Blood brothers, a sorts." He grimaced and placed his hand on the wound.

Goldfinch looked from Reg, who continued to whisper, to Nance, who was slowly regaining consciousness. The man was vulnerable, his bloodied face swelling exponentially each passing second. Then Goldfinch looked at the slavers who had their guns drawn, taking aim down the knoll to where the Leader lay. They were on the verge of firing, but Goldfinch was hard to spot within the curtain of smoke that had expanded.

It was a crossroads. *Kill Nance or rescue Reg?* Goldfinch opted for the latter, looping his good arm around Reg with a tight grip and tugging him along through the snow. With each inch of land they cleared, Goldfinch awaited another bullet greeting the flesh at his back. He hoped it would just be quick.

Goldfinch jolted his head left then right. The fence was aflame. The top half of his sight found thick, broadening blankets of smoke. Just seconds later, his burden was lightened when another figure grabbed hold of Reg's body. Goldfinch struggled to make him or her out, the smoke straining his eyes.

"You'll need to move quickly, Goldfinch," One called out quite evenly. The elder, to Goldfinch's surprise, was left standing. There were posse men close, but not within an arm's reach, the way Nance had been.

"There is a visitor," One continued. "Leave the slaver to rot on the hill here. Solomon has evacuated the place, do not fear."

The pair continued to half-drag, half-guide Reg across the snowy expanse. "They'll be on our tail in just a moment after they recognize the state of their commander," One said.

"Where?" Goldfinch ordered.

"Visitor is awaiting us—at the back of the place," One claimed, a cough interrupting his response.

A few feet later One dropped the left side of Reg's body, taking up the rifle that was strapped around his back. He turned around to the swarm of men closing in on the huts, a few of which were gathering around Nance. "To keep them on their toes," he said, as he primed the gun with careful haste. He fired into the congealing clouds. Goldfinch heard what sounded like a body tumble to the ground. Then, feet scrambled, making their way closer to the villagers amid their escape.

One clutched Reg's sagging side again and picked up the pace. "There'll be a shot fired any moment—"

He couldn't finish the thought before a gunshot echoed out through the place and fled the gates, perforating anything in its path. The sound of it clipping something—bony mass, tissue—was unmistakable.

Goldfinch took his open, wounded arm and inspected his body, touching up and down his chest, near the wounds from the scuffle, and the stab scar on his leg. He would live.

As they moved, One seemed to recognize Goldfinch's bodily assessment. Then Reg began to wail in pain.

"The hip?" One asked him.

"No suh, done got hit again. Feel it in my legs."

Goldfinch abandoned the hold he had on Reg's right side and began to inspect the runaway. He wondered if Reg had been struck in the back. To feel it in the legs, it could have been residual effects from the spine.

Goldfinch saw a small accumulation of blood beneath Reg's foot, and he determined that the runaway had gotten hit on the underside of his foot while in mid-stride.

"It's your foot, Reg, you'll make it out of this," Goldfinch said, restoring his good arm around Reg's shoulder.

"We will not make it back at this rate," One said, seemingly searching for an alternative. "We'll have to slip beneath the fence at some point. The gate's too far off."

Goldfinch knew it would have to be done. The two slid Reg across the snow, leaving behind a wide, flattened path. They heard boot heels sloshing in the melting snow behind them. The advance was slow, the soldiers unfamiliar with the grounds and navigating the thick plumes that emanated from the fence to their left.

Goldfinch halted in his tracks, and One stumbled momentarily to do the same. "It'll have to be here," the Leader said, pointing at the thick, splintery bottom rail of the fence. "We'll have to kick it off its perch against the post. It can be done."

The two men quickly placed Reg down onto the moist snowpack and hustled to this rail. With coinciding kicks, the rail fell off the post, freeing up about a foot and a half of space to slip under. This part of the fence was hidden just beneath the dense, smoldering fire. They knew they would have to risk the close encounter.

They ran back to Reg, who had tried to crawl closer. They crammed the bulk of his weight beneath the fence. As he slipped through to the other side, he rolled over, so that the next man could do the same.

"You're next," Goldfinch said to One, though his attention was held by something else—the first man emerging from the smoke, gun in hand.

Goldfinch kicked at One's boots as the elder crept beneath the fence. The new combatant did not see the swift exit. But Goldfinch now stood face to face with one of Nance's men. He sounded like the same one who had been present at Blithe's execution. *Mr. Kruger?* He was wearing a militia uniform, though he appeared unkempt and undignified. Goldfinch could not imagine this man being a soldier.

"I won't shoot ya just yet, sir," the man said, his gun firmly pointed at Goldfinch, who was now idle. "Want ya to see what you've done to the man that was about to free this place, free you people. He was snapping you out of the daze you got stuck in—harboring all those ni—well, you know."

He continued, "Nance, you see, he has a broken jaw now, thanks to you, slave hider."

In a fleeting moment, Goldfinch recalled his time pressing into Upper Canada, helping to free up maritime space on the Great Lakes for the American Navy. It was some feat. He wondered if there was another feat in store for *this* conflict. Goldfinch knew at least one thing; the Synod fires had morphed into his longstanding vision of York.

He had it planned. He would merely drop low, hoping the smoke would cloak him enough to kick the man's legs out. He breathed deeply, still examining the soldier and his loaded weapon.

Then, Goldfinch quickly dipped low. As he did, a gunshot just barely missed striking him in the chest or even the face. Yet, he had no time for the hand-to-hand combat portion of his plan, for another earsplitting noise broke from a rifle not too far off.

The soldier, hardly aware of his plight, plummeted to the ground, his eyes wide open, blood spewing out from a rounded hole above his right ear.

Goldfinch rose steadily, as if the natural reaction was to lift his own arms in surrender. He tried to pinpoint the source of the shot. He wondered if it had come from behind, or off to his right, amid the cover of the pines beside the fence. He could no longer see the small, rising cloud of smoke from a rifle, for the whole place was shrouded by it.

He did not want to speak louder for it could alert even more of Nance's foot soldiers. He knew they had scattered. Nonetheless, footsteps pattered nearby, but no one approached him.

"One?" Goldfinch inquired, snooping low and checking along the gate, though he had to stay back from the thicker smoke and flames.

There came no answer. In an impetuous move, he sank to the ground. He slipped beneath the gate, the flames above him almost searing him, catching hold of his face. He got to the other side, in what was now New Jersey, not Synod. He trembled, the fire blazing deeply into his subconscious. He did one complete roll in the now-handy accumulation of snow. There were no flames emitting from his trousers. He felt no scalding pain against his skin—at least from this fire.

He rose up and rushed to a nearby pine. From there, he poked his head out from the side, checking his flank. He heard something, but there was no sign of One or Reg. He knew they would venture to the rear gate, toward the 'visitor.' Goldfinch was also aware that in his absence, One could be a masterful leader. It was a job he was always cut out for, possibly more so than Goldfinch, the calloused carpenter from Philadelphia's AME.

As he explored this grove, he heard something stir behind him. Then, Goldfinch turned, and Harriet was no more than ten inches from his face, her rifle dropped at her side. Goldfinch stood, helpless for a moment, inspecting her. She was disheveled, her petticoats muddied, but she still looked beautiful.

"They've killed Blithe," Harriet said. "And trampled his body. Shame you couldn't finish the deed, with Nance, as you trounced him."

"They had no use for the boy any longer," Goldfinch declared. "After the map and their correspondence with the timepiece, their rendezvous, it was inevitable."

"Explains why he was making his flight when Nance reared his ugly face," she said. She did not let him respond. "You'll get to the gate at the rear, right up toward the path you'd take for Reg's hut. You'll find them there."

She rushed off, her dirtied body blending with all the discord—it was too poetic, even for her, an apparent student of classic literature. She slipped from tree to tree until she was out of sight.

Goldfinch, hatless and gunless, felt more susceptible than he had since the war. Like Harriet, he fled the scene—without the cane he had been using beforehand to steady himself. He hobbled through the grove of pines and followed the bend of the village from about twenty feet away. The 'wreath,' after about forty minutes of being lit, was too dense to pass through.

He felt himself breathing loudly, his heart racing to keep up with his gait and the whole ordeal. Then there were the signs of life—conversation, footprints—and so Goldfinch approached with caution, hoping it was not the rendezvous of Nance's men who had scattered.

Then, however, came a wince—obviously Reg's—from thirty to forty feet away. The runaway had wounds in two spots and had just barely escaped the clutches of Beelzebub himself.

Goldfinch followed tracks that had been placed in the snow, leading right up to the assemblage he was looking for. As he drew close, he noticed One holding him at a distance, with an outstretched arm, a warning.

"Approach with caution," One said lowly. "They're all around. They'll find us in a moment."

Goldfinch obliged, only creeping toward this group. Arriving, he parted the crowd, setting One, who was holding Reg up, aside. He found the Senator. His horse was bound to tree trunk some fifty feet away. Amid the fiery, heated exchange, he had just ridden up to the grounds, probably taking his time in securing the animal to the tree.

"Mr. Goldfinch," Senator Frelinghuysen said. "It has been a while, has it not?"

Goldfinch did not respond. He was busy checking the area close to Synod. The Senator continued, "Although I must say, we really have not been apart too long, as you know."

At last, Goldfinch spoke. "Did the wreath—the fires—alert you to us?"

"Mr. Boatwright and I have been en route for a time now, under strict orders. You see, Dumont Vroom and I, we've had a conference on this place, and about his subordinate."

"What of it?" Goldfinch asked. "Will he send aid?"

"I don't suppose so," Senator Frelinghuysen responded. "Although, I've come here with further news as well."

There was no time for additional discourse, for Mr. Boatwright, who stood beside the Senator and had since been quiet, spoke up. "The men who scattered have caught wind of us."

"Take Reg to the outpost," Goldfinch ordered. He appraised the Senator and his intentions. "Senator, will you accompany me?"

The level-headed, temperate senator offered the slightest nod. He pulled back the opening of his coat, showing a holstered Springfield Model pistol.

A few paces off, Mr. Boatwright picked up an M1819 Hall Rifle off the ground, where it precariously rested against an oak. From there, One and Reg hobbled off, Mr. Boatwright fled, and Goldfinch and his new affiliate approached the smoldering mess of a fence.

Chapter Twenty-One

Abolitionist

It was the Senator who led Goldfinch into the thickets once more. There they felt the wrath of the smoke and heard the noises of Nance's other men. A few were still riled, searching for answers, for villagers, for slaves.

"Keep close. There is plenty for you to see of Mr. Boatwright and his capabilities," the Senator hinted.

Goldfinch was in no position to protest. He followed closely behind Senator Frelinghuysen as the man weaved his way in between trees. Eventually, they came to a spot overlooking much of the village, specifically the horse paddock.

"Look closely, and you'll find your woman, and Mr. Boatwright, of course," the Senator said. He held his hand at his hip, on the Springfield Model, and pointed down the hill.

"Can't see through much of that smoke," Goldfinch said.

"Look closer. They're there," Senator Frelinghuysen urged.

Eventually, he found the two. "Where are they going?" Goldfinch asked.

"To free your horse," the Senator declared. "Pay attention, will you?"

He spotted Harriet's dirtied dress and her body moving swiftly amid the chaos. A serpent-like Mr. Boatwright crept along beside her. Goldfinch wondered if the tinted spectacles darkened his vision.

Harriet seemed to be stalking the men who congregated a hundred or so feet inside the village, near the paddock below Goldfinch.

The paddock was not yet aflame, though the horses stirred. Amid the chaos, Shepherd's cow had finally escaped. Inside was Eder, Goldfinch's prize possession, and Solomon's Friesian mount, an equally impressive animal. Both of them neighed and lifted up onto their hind legs.

One of them—Harriet, it seemed like—pulled the trigger. An intruder fell and the others near him dropped to the ground for cover. Still, two cronies made an advance toward the gunfire.

Harriet retreated twenty feet, impressively sliding back while her petticoats dragged against the snowy earth. To Goldfinch, she seemed about a hundred feet off. She regrouped near Mr. Boatwright in the forest. It was still within viewing distance for Goldfinch and his senator friend. Mr. Boatwright held his rifle high and pulled the trigger. Goldfinch checked the land beneath them near the paddock. Another one of Nance's men had fallen. And still, Goldfinch and the Senator were unscathed with a godlike view above the village.

There was one Nance follower left standing in the vicinity, but he fled, running off toward the main gate where assuredly others awaited him.

The Senator turned to Goldfinch. "Sorry for the imposition, Mr. Goldfinch. Felt you needed to see that. Man and woman, working in perfect harmony, protecting your place. You see, it hasn't been for naught. But there's more in store for you."

Below, Goldfinch spotted Mr. Boatwright beginning to venture down the hill toward the paddock. He breached that fiery hellstorm burgeoning in the village.

Harriet followed behind as Mr. Boatwright proceeded to kick the rails of the paddock fence. He kicked with strength and drew a couple of steps back as the smoke billowed.

"He's there to free the horses before the trees catch or embers shoot out toward them," the Senator told Goldfinch.

When it was passable, Mr. Boatwright walked to the tall fence that corralled the horses and freed the metal hinge. As he stepped back, the frantic horses plowed their way out of the paddock, first making their way toward the village, but then dashing for the open gate.

All but one of the horses fled. Mr. Boatwright seemed to stare at it carefully. It was Eder. Just seconds later, the horse trotted off toward the gate. Mr. Boatwright followed him, and Harriet trailed the wounded governor's aide.

"That animal won't venture off," the Senator said to Goldfinch. "That is your ride. He's not through with you."

***

Goldfinch and Senator Frelinghuysen soon ventured nearer, pausing at the threshold of Synod and wilderness, arms hovering near their mouths. Different thoughts infused Goldfinch, *how many of Nance's men still stood? How many bid him adieu, heading back to New York or wherever they crawled out of?*

There was some activity inside the village. Goldfinch could see through the erratic flames, especially as a breeze guided them one way or the other. There were two or three men pounding on the Synod doors, inspecting the huts.

"A futile act," Senator Frelinghuysen said, shaking his head. "Their time here is through."

The two waited, hidden amid the blaze, watching Nance's men scramble about, trying to fulfill their mission. "They come across any of your people, the trigger will get pulled," the Senator warned.

"I have sound information. Indicates my people are out of here. A former slave handled it."

Senator Frelinghuysen nodded, probing the place. "As for the rest of these men, dare I say, their fates appear bleak."

Goldfinch did not dare question him. "The visions, they're so … unrelenting. Why?"

"The mission, Mr. Goldfinch. What better way to remain vigilant than to have a fire lit beneath you?"

Then, emerging from the fog that seemed to suffocate the place came Mr. Boatwright, his boots pressing firmly into the ground, his gun pointed fixedly on his horizon.

"There's something Mr. Boatwright has for your troubles," the Senator said. "And it will arrive any second."

"Don't want to meddle, but last time you said there was a surprise, I—" He was promptly interrupted by the most boisterous natural sound he had ever heard. A howl reverberated from every which way. It was hard to tell where Alaba was.

"The beast returns," Goldfinch proclaimed.

"Returns?" Senator Frelinghuysen asked. "She was never absent."

"A bit late, wouldn't you say?"

The Senator shook his head. "A man needs to be in Washington, amongst his constituents in New Jersey, *and* watching over a religious retreat? Would you say that is an easy task?"

"You say she was never far off," Goldfinch replied.

"*Ah*, but she cannot act on distant orders."

At this point, Mr. Boatwright had rejoined them. The Senator waited for the optimal moment and slipped through the gate where a channel of pure, unfettered air still remained. Still, Goldfinch coughed as he sauntered through.

The Senator held his hand at his belt. He stopped moving. He was still looking ahead when he said, "The *coup de grâce*, Mr. Goldfinch. You see?"

The Leader paused, realizing the inevitability of all this— his gradual discovery of the red eye, the silent founder. It was all predestined.

"How much of this did the Founders know? How much did you tell them? You've known all along. Known that this showdown would occur, and right when it did," Goldfinch said, pressing the Senator.

"Sometimes the greatest action is inaction, Mr. Goldfinch."

Goldfinch practically coughed up puffs of that billowing smoke. When he was through with his fit, he glared at Senator Frelinghuysen again. As he did so, Alaba let out another raucous howl, the sounds of which reached, and seemed to vibrate, the depths of his being.

The three men ventured back through the village, the outskirts of which were smoldering. The fire was still weighing the place down. At sporadic areas, it clutched a dry bough or the remnants of foliage that crept through the widening holes amongst the snow. The paddock was about to light, the structure sending off the initial plumes of light smoke. Goldfinch checked for Eder—the horse had fled.

Still, they advanced across the place, marching through the matted snow. At last, they came to a half-conscious Nance who had since tried to crawl his way out of Synod, his face bloodied, his jaw broken. Disoriented, he tried to lift his body, but managed to get his head only a few inches off the ground before he stumbled back down. His men, it seemed, had forsaken him.

The Senator froze, hand at his holster, for a few prolonged moments. He stared at the governor's aide who was now helpless and frightened. "Mr. Nance, you've been a nuisance for these fine people."

Nance obviously could not respond, but there seemed to be a groan, with spittle, that found its way out of his mouth.

"You should let freewill take root here," the Senator continued. "Why meddle in other folks' business?"

Harriet emerged from the brush, muddied. She lifted her rifle up toward Nance. Goldfinch felt the angst as she held her breath. The Senator, however, lowered her weapon, his hand on the barrel.

"It is not your place, miss," he said. She quizzed him with her fearless eyes but decided to acquiesce.

"Any moment now," he added.

"How long must we wait on you, Frelinghuysen?" Goldfinch asked. "My people are growing impatient, out there past the tree line."

"Here, now," the Senator said, pointing toward the gate. What the group found was a dirtied and slightly bloodied Alaba. "A blackened coat once helped her blend here. But with the snow, she can be free of the burden."

The animal, its tongue hanging lazily out of its mouth, scampered over to the group. Once at the Senator's feet, she sat, panting, waiting for the cue.

"You see she is bloodied?" Senator Frelinghuysen asked. "It is not her blood, but that of the stragglers."

He desisted for a moment and then spoke again. "There was a time, at the hermitage, I spoke of the utility of speeches on the Senate floor. The birth of some healthy debate. You see, there is only so much a filibuster or a 'nay' vote can do. It is brought upon ourselves, squarely upon ourselves, to help eradicate this institution." Again he paused, his eyes locked on Goldfinch. "And your friend, Mr. Sullivan, he will live. There is no question. As will the elder."

Goldfinch was obviously at a loss for words, the gravity of Senator Frelinghuysen's speech practically paralyzed him. He was in awe of the man—and his pet. "Then let freedom ring on this day."

"And then let us flee this wasteland," Harriet said, gauging the strength of the fires.

"There was a purpose to Goldfinch's idea, madam," the Senator said. She simply turned and watched Mr. Boatwright with her arms folded.

Concentrating yet again on Goldfinch, the Senator said, "Then let it be done." He looked down at the animal, the eye contact obvious and remarkable. He snapped his finger, and the beast snarled, growled, and leaped toward the defenseless aide who had long dampened the mood of the village.

Neither Goldfinch nor Harriet could watch as Alaba tore him to bits. He gave up his muddled screams after the first or second puncture. As Goldfinch took leave of the Senator, Harriet dipped her fingers into Goldfinch's hand. Instead of looking back at the consumption, Goldfinch stared down at Harriet's overture.

He did not pull his hand back, but he refused to exert any pressure on hers. The two just walked toward her hut.

Once inside, they both sat against the bed. "The place goes up, I'm not sure I want to leave," she said, entranced and depleted from the day's events.

"There will be a time for that, but it is not now," Goldfinch responded. As he did so, he heard the jangling of boot spurs coming close to the hut. Senator Frelinghuysen climbed the lone stair, poked his head into the hut, and found the two villagers.

"The other news I bring," he said, "is that the Governor wishes to grant your people asylum here. Although, knowing the fate of his man and the others, he wishes for someone to answer for all the crimes that have ensued here."

Goldfinch stared at Harriet, who was clearly befuddled. "Speak, Senator," she urged.

"I am not innocent, either—I am a silent part of that indictment now," the Senator said. "I do not wish for you, or the place, to perish in the flames. That is why exile is the obvious choice."

"Of who?" she challenged.

The Senator hoisted his chin upwards, pointing over toward Goldfinch. "You see, the gift I've *bestowed*, it will not just dissipate. He will need to extend his influence. Plus, the northward paths are open for travel for a rising number of runaways."

Goldfinch held his breath for a moment then exhaled against the oppressively dry air of the place. "You cannot help silence these visions? You cannot make me whole again? I'll need to stay *canine*?"

"Why would I want anything else? Mr. Goldfinch, you've been chosen for this endeavor."

Goldfinch sighed as if to give in to the assessment. He looked toward Harriet, who, much to her chagrin, it seemed, felt helpless and ashamed of her earlier actions.

Reading this, Goldfinch said, "Someone will need to tell the Minister about Blithe."

The Senator interjected, saying, "You will want to round up the others, One and Reg. The Shepherd, you see, has fallen. You'll want the other runaway, too. There's a higher plan for you, Mr. Goldfinch."

"And what of this place?" Goldfinch asked. "It will be scorched to ash, devoid of its luster. The flames are drawing closer to these huts."

"As I've said, Mr. Goldfinch, that fence, that 'wreath,' as you've so eloquently named it, was not constructed on a whim. In fact, it was an order. From me. Discussed with your superiors."

To this, Goldfinch had no words, but as he closed his eyes, feeling the visions, memories, and fire course through him like an opiate, he knew there was no escaping this predestination.

As he reopened his eyes, everything had slipped into that gray, sideways world again, each movement of an extremity slowing more and more. The Senator nodded at him. Behind him, Mr. Boatwright peered over, too. Goldfinch rose up, patted Harriet on her knee and ran his finger across it for a moment. He walked toward the freedom fighters he knew would become his only company. Senator Frelinghuysen and Mr. Boatwright moved aside as Goldfinch stepped toward the door.

As Goldfinch rounded the corner, everything still drawn out, he blinked strangely slow. As he reopened, there came at first a drizzle on the land, then a steady rainfall, then a torrential downpour. The temperatures had dipped below freezing; the droplets would freeze on these makeshift homes. It was the Senator's answer to the conflagration. *He* was dousing the fire.

Soon, everything returned to its normal pace. Goldfinch looked behind him toward the Senator, who just extended his arms. "You're an abolitionist," he said. "Now, there's much work to do."

Chapter Twenty-Two

Return, Ye Children of Men

Wednesday, December 9, 1829

Across Synod, frozen sheets of ice strangled the ground and icicles gripped roofs and boughs. There were odd crackling sounds—the spikes crashing to the earth.

The villagers had returned late the previous night, the huts intact, the paddock scorched.

But it was soon midmorning on Wednesday and Goldfinch had hobbled over to the rear gate, then beyond.

He recalled the moment when his people had returned in the night. Harriet had taken Goldfinch aside, her fingers touching his coarse palms. Inside the hut, she sewed up his arm and side, applying bandages delicately and caressing the skin near the wound.

It had gone nowhere, though, for the two were fatigued, depleted from the day's events, the darkness they had witnessed. While he *did* spend the night, he was out before sunup.

Then, in the open, everything seemed so abstract and distant. He was watching the position of a cloud in the sky above as Minister Mulvane, frail and bedraggled, finished his brief service for those who had fallen.

When the Leader reentered the anguish and heartbreak that affected the village in the past day, he looked at two holes in the earth. He checked around, the ice making the horizon so silky, mystical even. The more he focused, the easier it was to make out the occupied coffins at the bottom. Pine boxes housed their remains, which were also lined with layers of bedsheets.

"Lord, thou hast been our dwelling place in all generations," Minister Mulvane managed to mutter, paying careful attention to the grave that held his son. Atop the pine box holding his body lay the timepiece that had been so instrumental to Blithe.

The elder Mulvane wore his finest clerical clothing. "Before the mountains were brought forth, or ever thou hadst formed the Earth and the world, even from everlasting to everlasting, thou art God. Thou turnest man to destruction; and sayest, 'Return, ye children of men.'"

Goldfinch shut his eyes, letting the words inundate him. He felt an arm slip beneath his elbow, locking onto it, squeezing it ever so slightly. It was not the first overture Harriet had made since Blithe had fallen. It did nothing for Goldfinch. For him, Harriet's charm had lessened the moment she became so perfidious a lover.

"For a thousand years in thy sight are but as yesterday when it is past, and as a watch in the night," Minister Mulvane continued.

Goldfinch looked down toward Harriet, who clung to him like a forlorn widow. Then he looked across the group, where

Carlita held eye contact with him and smiled. He returned the gesture while Harriet sobbed and hung her head.

Surrounding Carlita were a few other villagers; Reg, propped up by Goldfinch's cane, One, sporting a recently dusted top hat, Elizabeth, who stood in front of William, *his* arm gently placed around her belly, Solomon and his dirtied white shirt, and Catharine, the seasoned watchwoman. Behind this row of residents, Mr. Boatwright and Senator Frelinghuysen remained. Mr. Boatwright's head was lowered, though if it was in prayer, Goldfinch could not say. Then, the other Synod folks trailed behind, their voices silenced, their dress ragged.

"Thou carriest them away as with a flood; they are as a sleep; in the morning they are like grass which groweth up," Minister Mulvane continued, his voice blending with the light gusts of wind.

Inside the other grave was Shepherd, who had fought valiantly until he met his demise. It was with great sorrow that Goldfinch had to gape at Shepherd's corpse earlier that day. He had helped Solomon tighten the woolen blankets around his friend.

Beneath this woolen padding, Shepherd's arms were folded across his chest, covered by a thick frock coat. Goldfinch's heart was heavy. He remembered their trek to the hillside just days earlier.

"In the morning it flourisheth, and groweth up; in the evening it is cut down and withereth," Mulvane said. He continued on with the words, but Goldfinch could not quite take it any longer.

He turned from the improvised graveyard, a spot that only a few months earlier held burgeoning life, not death. Goldfinch stepped a few feet back, patting Harriet's side as she fumbled for a moment, looking for a place to rest her body. He pulled his hat down his forehead and took leave of the ceremony. Still, he did not venture far, waiting for his people at the edge of this plateauing land.

He sat, his body perched against the trunk of a hemlock, which was slippery from the precipitation Senator Frelinghuysen managed to bring forth. As the wind picked up, so did Minister Mulvane's voice. It was marked by grief and a bit of hysteria, but the man had to be praised for standing up with his community during this trying time. As the battle was waged, the Minister had found refuge in the church until Solomon escorted him out, his mind surely clouded by the Blithe business.

Goldfinch watched the Minister. After each sentence, his commitment to the Psalm strengthened. "And let the beauty of the Lord our God be upon us."

For a moment, there came only the sounds of whispering wind and the rattling of naked boughs. Then came the punch of a metal shovel tapping into the hardened earth. The ice cracked, the snow sank, and the dirt turned up.

A clatter of footsteps then shook this equilibrium, the Synod folks returning to their huts. As they began to file past, Goldfinch tipped his hat at a few of them, though the effort burned his shoulder.

Carlita approached, lifting her dark petticoats and taking short, choppy steps on the snow. As she came close to Goldfinch, she extended her arms, slipping. Goldfinch grabbed hold of her and pulled her in. As he did so, he looked toward Harriet who was now making a similar exit. From about ten feet away, she examined the Leader's face. The two locked eyes and then Goldfinch turned away.

"You have seen it all here, haven't you?" Goldfinch asked Carlita, who used the Leader's healthy arm as a way to prop herself up.

"Different winta's than down in N'Orleans," she responded, a smile forming on her face. She exhaled and watched the vapor trickle off.

"And Maude?" he asked. "She'd be warm right now, but licking the boots of those slavers."

She playfully slapped at his arm. "Mista Goldfinch, it isn't something ya need to remind me of."

"You may not have to worry about her being in bondage for much longer."

"Why ya say that?" she asked. "Not nice to get an old lady's hopes right up."

"Something has happened, solidifying this crusade. It is something I fear I cannot escape now."

"What ya sayin'?" Carlita urged, her grip strengthening on his arm.

"By sundown, we'll be leaving this place."

"We?"

Goldfinch lifted his head, focusing on the trail before him. While his sight seemed to be ever-graying, with visions of Alaba, the contours were still as clear as day. He took his painful arm and extended it wide as if to open the invitation to Carlita. She let go of his arm and continued her choppy approach through the woods back to Synod.

She was some feet away, but Goldfinch lifted his voice. "Tell me of her," he urged.

"Who? Maude? Ah, a right fine day for that."

As they made the descent toward the flatland the huts had been built upon, Carlita opened up some more about the beautiful house slave who would need emancipating, and who had yet to find love.

***

Once the descent had been made, Goldfinch paused to wait for Reg and One. He watched as William and Elizabeth completed their return, using each other as support while maneuvering on the ice. Behind them, Matilda and Sophie each took a side of the wooden cart and rolled it toward Synod.

Eventually One—who was guiding Reg—caught up with him. The two hobbled by and Goldfinch took up Reg's other side. The runaway's feet crashed down against the ice with each forceful, lopsided step.

"Mr. Sullivan, can we claim to have met victory?" Goldfinch asked.

"Girls is safe. Them bastards came huntin' for me is gone, for now. I'd say it's a *part* of a vic'tree."

"Must've taken a lot out of you, coming up here today," Goldfinch continued.

"Was worse gettin' shot up, Mista Goldfinch," Reg responded. One gave a quick laugh.

Together, the trio continued on. Ahead of them lay daylight and the warm embrace of like-minded individuals.

They moved aside the last branches which acted as a shawl, insulating and protecting the grove of pines near the charred fence. When the hobbling ended, and Reg rested on a stump near the fire pit, Goldfinch bid them adieu and headed for his hut.

Once there, though, he was alone with his memories and that fiery transition that was lurking just behind his lids. He sought the company of his friends and headed toward Solomon's.

Solomon took only seconds to open. "Mista Goldfinch," he answered.

The Leader looked around, finding Carlita, Harriet, and Catharine sitting on the mattress. Harriet met his gaze, her eyes curious. Immediately she spoke up. "Goldfinch, if I can have just a moment," she said, looking at him with vulnerable eyes.

Goldfinch decided against grabbing a piece of corn pudding resting on Solomon's nightstand. He noticed a small fire brewing, a pan smoking from the hunk of mashed corn, flour, and water that had been heated on it. He bowed to her slightly, took leave of the others, and left the hut.

She followed him out. Goldfinch could feel the tension lingering between them—it was palpable. Still, he fought it with every ounce of energy he had.

"Goldfinch, there have been rumors," she said, hinting at something. "Rumors that you'll *really* leave this place abandon all that you've buoyed for so long."

"You've heard the Senator, his demands, his sway," Goldfinch responded.

Her eyes took on a look he hadn't seen before, and she thrust herself at him, her arms falling around his shoulders.

For a moment he did not care about the blazing pain at his shoulder or the way his leg buckled. He embraced her, hugging her tightly, rubbing his hand up and down her back.

The hug was lengthy, and when he placed her back down, she said, "You cannot leave here—us. It was, well, the wrong decision I made."

"That is not why I must leave," he said. "The fact is that I will not be able to lead a normal life as long as the Senator keeps his eyes fixed on me."

"The trip you took, it changed everything," she said. "But that cannot be helped now. Nor do I want to know the details. You can, though, stay here until the Governor drives you out with torches and pitchforks." She leaned up on her tiptoes and pressed her lips against Goldfinch's. His stubble pressed into the skin above her lip. Her eyes closed, she did not let the embrace end.

At last, Goldfinch severed the tie, taking half a step back.

"There can be no relationship or euphoria," he said. "This new affair, it consumes me. You see what it has done." He took another step back and widened his arms as if to open himself up for inspection.

"My duty is to the nation now, and the backward institution that propped *this* place up," he continued.

Harriet welled up. "Everyone, my whole life, has left me. It is what you are about to do."

"I am leaving this place to you, Harriet," Goldfinch said firmly. "I'm bequeathing it."

She sniffed and sobbed. Pulling herself together, she said, "This expedition you embark on. Is it permanent? You'll abandon this place?"

As she inquired, the Senator approached their conference and immediately pitched in. "He will ebb and flow with the breeze, taking only to where he is called. Traveling this young country." As he thrust this verbal stake through Harriet's heart, the wolf's call resounded in the background, up the foothill out past the back of the village.

"You'll need to take time before you greet more runaways and recruits. You must rebuild this barrier," the Senator said to Harriet, pointing at the ashes and the half-charred fence posts.

Goldfinch turned toward Senator Frelinghuysen. "Senator, can we just have a moment?"

"As you wish," he answered. He and Mr. Boatwright withdrew.

The Leader then gazed at Harriet once more. "I fear that it'll be just after sundown when we depart," he told her.

A bit of spittle formed at the corners of Harriet's mouth. "And from there?"

"You will guide this place. You will be an appropriate leader here, not a divisive one as I was."

"Divisive only because of my promiscuity," she answered, shaking her head which she pressed onto to her right hand. "Which leads me to another point, Goldfinch."

"Yes?"

"I'm with child."

Goldfinch's stomach dropped. How could he respond to this? He was over her, her sharp tongue, her calamitous nature. He had planned to flee this place, to free Synod in the process.

"You are sure?" he asked.

"I've been sure for a time," Harriet declared.

"And who is the father?" Goldfinch asked.

At this, she began to cry. It was a loud, unpleasant wail—one that could not be easily tamed.

Goldfinch grazed her chin and lifted it with his forefinger. "You believe it to be mine?"

"I only wish it could be so," Harriet said in between sobs.

Goldfinch sucked his teeth and poked at his hat, speechless. Would this prevent his imminent departure, his exile?

"I am afraid I am not fathering material, not now," Goldfinch maintained. He had begun to sever the tie. "You and Elizabeth, you both carry new life, and will usher it into *this* world." He pointed around.

"But you could be a father here. There is a life here for you. Don't you see?"

"What life I had was drained the day I entered a building in Paterson. It's certainly gone now, as the Senator lingers with his prying eyes."

"Why don't you ignore the man, use the 'gift' to safeguard this place? We've been granted asylum."

"I wish it were that simple," Goldfinch replied. He wanted to touch her belly, to feel that new life.

"But it is," she said, trying not to raise her voice too much. She took off Goldfinch's hat and ran her fingers through his hair. But when she had made it halfway, he grabbed her arm and removed it.

"It cannot be so," Goldfinch said. "You will be a wonderful mother. But the Senator, he has shown me that all along, this has been my destiny. This child, this is your destiny, Harriet." With that, he walked away, unsure of how to feel. His chest tightened up, his breathing became labored. Still, he plodded on.

"The Minister, he'll need to stay and regain his wits," Goldfinch said to her as he was in motion. "And Solomon, well, he'll be your second in command. They *will* remain responsible for the runs—munitions or runaways."

She did not answer and just followed him. Goldfinch continued with his back to her. "Catharine will want to return to Connecticut to be beside her father. Jackson's provoked the ire of her. Something will come of that Indian Removal nonsense. And the others here, well, they will sustain this place, you see? Leave Nance's men for the vultures."

"Why is it you they've chosen?" she asked, reaching an arm out toward his shoulder.

"I cannot say. But it is *exile*, Harriet." Again, the statement could not be finished before Alaba howled.

Once more, Goldfinch took his leave of her, not even looking back to impress her image into his memory. As he sauntered off, he said, "I may write you."

4:45 p.m.

Sundown at Synod was beguiling. Goldfinch thought he would savor this last one. He could tell the Senator was becoming impatient, hovering near him as he conversed with the others.

The sunset was a spectacular sight—the light refracting off the crystalline ground, the colors of the sky taking on the ones that autumn once boasted.

He stood at his doorway, half inside the hut, half exposed to the harsh cold. It took only a few moments for the sun to dip. The daylight seemed so sparse at that time of year.

He grabbed hold of a small trunk and collected his things—a few starched, collared shirts, another pair of boots, robes, a single cravat, and a small toolkit he'd had with him since their April travels. Lugging it from his quarters, he exhaled with some authority and left the place he had called his home.

Goldfinch stepped out into the icy terrain. He could see Harriet watching him from her place. He still could not fathom it—a child! While he thought that she needed a proper farewell or a proper father, he knew he would not be adequate. Synod, too, including its citizens, deserved some pleasantries and heartfelt farewells. Again, he knew it just wouldn't do. It was not conducive to his personality, not with the red of slavery burning in his eyes. It was a calling. Synod was a stepping stone. He did, however, knock on Solomon's door, which opened slightly.

"You'll need to look after this place now, Solomon," Goldfinch warned. As he did, Carlita abandoned her perch inside the hut and snuck past Solomon. Goldfinch looked at her and said, "You'll be joining me, Carlita?"

She did not respond verbally but nodded and joined his side. She was willing to venture *back*, to return and free her daughter. Solomon looked at the two of them. "Been through a lot, you and I have, Mista Goldfinch."

"Who knows if this is farewell," Goldfinch reminded him.

"Best move on out, in the dead of night, mind ya. You have run'ways with ya," he urged. "Somethin' you done told me."

Goldfinch smiled and shook Solomon's hand tightly, grabbing the freeman's forearm with his other hand.

"And you take care of that shoulder of yours," Solomon said, smiling.

Goldfinch nodded, leaned inside, and found Catharine. "Please tell your father what resistance the slavers met at this place, Miss Beecher." Catharine, like Solomon, nodded sullenly back at the Leader.

With that, he departed. He heard Solomon's door close tightly. His mind was flooded during this hasty flight. Carlita stayed close but then veered off toward the gate.

Near this rear gate, the Senator and Mr. Boatwright stood waiting for Goldfinch. The Leader called to them. "There is one person I simply cannot ignore. Lord knows I've just tried."

He hustled back over to Harriet's hut, his gait improving. As he approached, Harriet was out waiting for him. Like before, she did not allow him to botch this exchange. She kissed him passionately, as though the affection was long cooped up. When their lips separated, Goldfinch stared deeply into her eyes, and through them, into her soul. "I know I am leaving this place in capable hands," he said.

"There will be a young one, fatherless, roaming about in time," she said.

"His father may've died in that clash," Goldfinch replied.

She took her forefinger and pressed it tightly over his mouth. "Time is now to depart before I lose all my wits and strangle the Senator, releasing you of that hold he has."

Goldfinch smiled, brushed his left hand through her hair, and gently pulled it back. "You must take special care of this place. The Pickets, you know, may one day return. And for such a return, make sure they are greeted with our woodwork. The hackberry must flourish."

There were no other words spoken. He left the hut, picked up his rifle near the shed beside the paddock, strapped it to his back, lugged the trunk over the ice, and made for the Senator. As he did, the memories overwhelmed him, on top of the haziness that had manifested itself within him for a time now.

He saw Lyman Beecher, the glowering, zealous look pinned to his face. Cartwright was on horseback. Reverend Allen stood near Goldfinch, using his hands enthusiastically in conversation. Goldfinch could not recall the exchange, but now, he knew the larger meaning of their gathering. The groundskeeper had just been named Leader of this fledgling place.

Lyman Beecher removed a small skeleton key from a sack he carried atop his colt and carefully handed it to Goldfinch. It was a key to his hut. But it was his house, a dwelling where he would oversee the fight of the century, for him, for Reg. The gift, the Founders' rite of passage, was something of a coronation for Goldfinch.

As he held the key, Beecher cracked a smile. This memory was pervasive, cutting to his core, revealing the man he had become. He was a patriot, far from the soldiers of fortune he had encountered in his day.

This image he had—or was seeing—of the Founders, vibrant and gleaming from the crepitating fire, was a lasting one. These leading clerics had faith in him, just as the men in bondage had faith in him. Yet to most of them, he was still faceless.

***

"There is a pleasant surprise," Senator Frelinghuysen said to Goldfinch as the Leader closed in.

"About time you've joined us," Mr. Boatwright said. "There's work to be done."

"As in slavery still persists? I am aware," Goldfinch added numbly.

"Ignore Mr. Boatwright," Senator Frelinghuysen said. "Check the trees where my mount was tied yesterday."

Goldfinch tipped his hat and walked the fifty or so feet toward the spot. He had to climb a small hill, but when it plateaued, he found One holding the reins of Eder. Carlita was close, too. Behind the elder, Reg also rested atop his animal, prepared to face a changing world, or at least one capable of questioning the norm. The surviving members of the Paterson Four were united.

He rushed toward the animal, taking the reins and petting its pure, white coat. Turning back, he found the Senator right behind him. "The animal would not forsake you at such a time. As Alaba cannot forsake me."

Goldfinch did not respond, but this collection of abolitionists propped themselves atop their mounts. Goldfinch did the same, a smile escaping his normally steely face, widening as he patted the horse's neck, then forelock.

They exited the place with the same resolve they'd had as they battled an early-spring snowstorm and broke ground on the village.

Walking beneath the moonlight, the group progressed as one, their horses—both black and white—so close they touched during the canter.

"We will ride to D.C.," Senator Frelinghuysen advised. "There, I must return to work. Mr. Boatwright will see to the rest."

Goldfinch, looking at Carlita, who was aboard the same horse as One, said, "I can't say a trip to N'Orleans would be frowned upon."

Carlita smiled. "That to say you'd like to hear about Maude, Mista Goldfinch?" she asked. "A right fine time for that."

***

To Goldfinch, the horizon was clouded, but not by darkness. It was the misty vision he had come to know since encountering Senator Frelinghuysen. Still, the road ahead was suddenly embraceable.

Epilogue

Saturday, December 3, 1831

Harriet watched from the fire pit as the Senator's aide, Mr. Boatwright, pulled out of the thick cover of the Ramapough Mountains, right up to the wooden cross at the hackberry. Synod, the pillar of faith, was still preserved and as fortified as ever. It had already collected the season's first snowfall. Harriet wondered whether a letter was arriving by way of the aide.

Mr. Boatwright nicked his horse with his spur, bringing it to a halt. He swung his other saddled foot over the animal and dismounted. Without saying a word, he entered the place, reaching over top the gate to unlatch the reconstructed access point.

Inside, Harriet received him. Mr. Boatwright challenged her stare and attire, then handed her a sealed letter. The hardened wax, with a United States Senate seal, had not been tampered with. As she reached out to grab the letter, she heard small feet pounding on the ground. She looked over and saw her one-and-a-half-year-old girl—brown hair, a serious face—scooting toward her. The girl wore a floral-patterned dress. Harriet looked up at Mr. Boatwright, who had noticed the child. "Don't mind Samantha now, Mr. Boatwright." She smiled.

Mr. Boatwright also smiled but did not say a word. When he knew she had received the letter, he turned from her and made for his black, burly mount.

She watched Mr. Boatwright slither back into the thickets he had emerged from. She gently patted Samantha's head as the child leaned against her leg. She finally concentrated on the letter, tearing it open, cracking the wax.

Samuel "Goldfinch" Hermann
Jerusalem, Virginia
November 15, 1831

Dear Harriet,

Not writing you until today has been much to my chagrin. I fear that I have lost all orientation to time. Moreover, the larger cause has been met with resistance in many places.

However, I can say that I have traversed these United States. From the fledgling state of Louisiana to the bowels of Virginia slaveland, I have seen it all. It is much to say for a Philadelphia carpenter.

In other news—just days ago, an uprising was officially squelched. It was one of violence, but nothing dissimilar to what we witnessed at Synod. Nevertheless, this resistance was gagged. The Leader, one Nat Turner, a slave, now a martyr, was executed— beheaded and flayed. I took no active part in the rebellion, but cannot deny an <u>indirect</u> connection. I stand in the village where he was slaughtered. As I drive the quill to the paper, I am alone. The Senator, though, has shown me the way on many an occasion.

Again, it is with a heavy heart that I write, for having to depart Synod, our creation, so hastily was quite difficult. While I am sure you have moved on, I admit that memories shared with you will remain affixed to my being, for all my days.

I have connected with One intermittently, manning the stops on this 'Underground Railroad.' Perhaps I should tell you of my— our—loss. Reg has fallen, a victim of mob violence during Turner's rebellion. He left this world with all the dignity a reasonable man can assume. For him, the Senator's fire went out. He was taking up a final crusade in these parts of Virginia with Nat. Planned on moving north, to his girls, after. He was an honorable man, this you know. I have made it my life's mission to pursue Steven Picket, the man who for so long tormented Mr. Sullivan. Picket's the faceless man of rumors whose destructive tendencies have reached the highest levels.

In the meantime, while I acquire resources, I also feel it is my duty to inform you that I have met someone. Her name is Maude. She is Carlita's daughter. One and I rescued her from bondage in New Orleans in January of '30. If you thought our ignited fence was a spectacle, you should have caught sight of the Great 1830 New Orleans fire that hastened our flight from that place.

We made our way back north, and at present, Carlita has ridden to New England, a place of refuge, a place to retire. Maude and I continue the perilous, but requisite fight for freedom.

Perhaps in time, I shall return to that great sanctuary up north, for I have missed my dwelling, those sunsets against Long Pond.

The same could be said of One. We may reunite and return when the time feels right. Yet, we may also stay rooted in these lands of enslavement.

The light still burns bright for me, the visions ones of guidance.

Please, remember the times—your fields, the night skies we unraveled star by star.

With love,
-G

Dan C. Gunderman

Dan C. Gunderman is an author of historical fiction and nonfiction who holds an MFA degree in Creative Writing from Fairfield University.

His forthcoming books include two biographies for an educational publisher in the Spring of 2018, and a six-part YA fiction series. He specializes in writing nineteenth-century historical fiction and screenplays.

Dan's particular research interests include Tudor and Victorian England, along with Gilded Age U.S. politics.

He is a former staff writer for the *New York Daily News*, where he also served as a film and television critic. He is currently the associate editor of a B2B media site, and a contributing film critic to different outlets.

Dan lives in West Milford, New Jersey with his three dogs.

1) Thematically, what does Goldfinch's obscured vision represent?

2) In what ways did revivalism contribute to a growing awareness and obvious distaste for slavery?

3) Senator Frelinghuysen's title as the Silent Founder is both symbolic and essential to the workings of the village. He is not charged with simply endorsing the clandestine outpost. Instead, his work digs much deeper. In what ways does he actually shoulder the narrative?

4) Renly Picket's stubbornness can come to embody both a geographic mindset and a timeworn institution. How does this mindset affect the outcome?

5) Is the novel's opening chapter, "Minus Ten"—about Goldfinch and Solomon's hunt—a glaring and somewhat unique juxtaposition? How does this imagery clash with traditional social positions of the time?

6) In what ways does Harriet fit into this turbulent century of change? Remember, the same span later saw the Women's Rights Convention in Seneca Falls, NY (1848).

7) Is Goldfinch a dynamic character and how does he change throughout the novel? Might this arc match the plight of a war veteran of the early nineteenth century?

8) The author keeps certain genre moments somewhat ambiguous. Are the Senator's powers indicative of an entire political, cultural and social movement?

9) Is the anthropomorphic wolf, Alaba, a manifestation of the day's violence? Or is she simply the 'brutal' agent of change?

10) Peter Nance is a composite character based on many northerners who were sympathetic to slavery. He rivals

people of the later Antebellum period and Civil War, like Fernando Wood, a 'Copperhead' New York Democrat who supported the Confederacy and opposed the Thirteenth Amendment. How significant are Nance's political leanings in the novel? Or does he simply advance the plot?

11) Communal living was indeed a facet of nineteenth-century life, as evidenced by Nathaniel Hawthorne's experiences at Brook Farm in Massachusetts in 1841 — something he later transformed into the romantic novel *The Blithedale Romance*. In what ways does *Synod* remain faithful to that romantic literary spirit?

12) Although Goldfinch's arc is the lifeblood of the narrative, other secondary characters undergo vast personal transformations as well. The elder, One, is a prime example. Do you feel these transformations were natural?

A Note from the Publisher

Dear Reader,

Thank you for reading Dan C. Gunderman's historical novel, *Synod*.

We feel the best way to show appreciation for an author is by leaving a review. You may do so on any of the following sites:

www.ZimbellHousePublishing.com
Goodreads.com
Amazon.com
or Kindle.com

Join our mailing list to receive updates on new releases, discounts, bonus content, and other great books from

Or visit us online to sign up at:

http://www.ZimbellHousePublishing.com